The Beautiful Hammond Girls

Sue Sully

Riverside Books
Fairview Farm
Littley Green
Essex CM3 1BU

ISBN 1 904571 07 7

Printed and bound in the United Kingdom

CONTENTS

Once, when Sasha was a child, an indulgent family friend gave her a tin of barley sugar to share with Kitty. But she hid it in the garden. When she went to eat it, the inside of the tin was swarming with ants. Retribution for being selfish and greedy? Sasha knew better. It was proof, if she ever needed any, that God – or the devil – was always on Kitty's side.

PART ONE
September, 1850
Kitty

Chapter One

People called them 'the beautiful Hammond girls', though they were not equally beautiful.

There were four of them: Leah, Lavinia, Kitty and Sarah – called Sasha – who always felt as though she was straining against the family pecking order and minded dreadfully being the last of the brood. Sasha wanted to be twenty instead of only sixteen. She despised girls she knew who had learned to make themselves appealing as the baby of the family with feminine posturing and whining.

Miss Holloway had probably been the last of a brood. Sasha watched the tears well up in her governess's eyes. Miss Holloway was definitely the runt of a scrawny, sickly litter, with her whimpering, 'I shall tell your father.'

'Oh, tell my father then!' Sasha wriggled further on to the window ledge and leaned out over the street. Clinging to the frame with her free hand, she dangled Miss Holloway's shoe by its yellow ribbons. She was behaving appallingly. It's because it's so hot, she told herself; she certainly needed an excuse, she was too old for games of this kind. She pushed back her hair from her shoulders with the hand that held the shoe and caught a waft of stale foot-sweat. 'Pooh! Cheese! Ancient Stilton, I should think!'

She allowed herself to be distracted briefly by the traffic in the streets below Hanover Terrace. She could see cabs and carriages, and the docks at the bottom of Bristol's Avondon Hill, crammed with ships' masts. She had a strong desire to let go of the window frame, to leave the schoolroom behind and float away to join that bustling, noisy scene. Sasha had once convinced herself she could fly; she had stood on the lid of the grand piano and cast herself into the air . . .

'Shall I throw it down for the horses to piddle on?' she called, with the express intention of offending Miss Holloway's sense of delicacy. She glanced back into the room.

Miss Holloway, deeply distressed, stood on one foot; the other hung like a limp root vegetable; her white stocking was wrinkled round the heel and had yellow dye stains at the foot. She was trembling with the effort of trying to halt the tears that trickled down her face.

Sasha's better feelings rose to the surface. 'Oh, here you are. You shouldn't have taken it off to scratch your foot when you thought I wasn't looking.' She threw the shoe to her. At the same time she heard a voice thunder from the road below.

'Sasha? What in heaven's name are you doing?'

Her father stood on the pavement. He was not alone. Sasha's interest quickened at the expression of amusement on the face of the man beside him. It was an extremely pleasing face: wide-spaced lively eyes; a square-jaw; clean-shaven except for modest side-whiskers. The stranger gave her a faintly ironical bow. His hair was ash-blond like her own.

'It looks as though Father has brought someone home.'

'Miss Sarah, please come down from the window.' Miss Holloway hobbled towards her, struggling to put on her shoe and made an ineffectual attempt to reel Sasha in by her sleeve.

'A waif or a stray do you think? I can't tell.' A promising artist? The son of one of her father's friends or patrons? No. He looked too hot and shabby to belong to a patron. A fellow artist, Sasha decided. 'A stray, I should guess,' she said out loud. 'I bet Father met him at the West of England exhibition. He's *very* good-looking.'

'Another one for Miss Kitty to flirt with?' Miss Holloway's

attempt at dignified disapproval unfortunately came out as a sneer. She gave way to curiosity and peered from the window at the figures in the street. She withdrew her head quickly. '*Now* will you come down from there? Your father certainly doesn't look very pleased.'

Sasha slid from the sill and closed the window. Her heart was beating pleasantly fast at the prospect of a diversion. She threw an impish look at the other woman. 'Come on. Let's go and see what's happening.'

The men were taking off their hats and coats in the hall. One of the housemaids stood by to receive them and Sasha's mother stood at the foot of the stairs. The stranger seemed to be in a state of nervousness as he removed a top-coat that looked very new, and out of place on such a warm day; he could not get his arms out of the sleeves. Having at last rid himself of the offending garment, he bowed very gravely over Mrs Hammond's hand, and seemed for an instant to be going to kiss it.

Sasha leaned over the banister above the stairwell.

Miss Holloway hovered beside her. 'He's uncouth,' she whispered with an audible sniff. 'He has scuffed boots and a frayed collar and doesn't know how to behave.'

'Sshh!' Sasha did not smile. Thin and small, with large dark eyes and well-defined brows that contrasted markedly with her fair hair, she looked very serious as she felt a leap of sympathy for the stranger. Her father's waifs and strays were inevitably reduced to a state of nerves in the stately presence of her mother. She studied the stranger's profile and the way his hair fell over his eyes. 'I think he's sweet.'

Her governess turned away. 'You think they're all sweet. Anyway, this one's far too scruffy to entertain your sister.'

Which leaves at least half a chance for me, thought Sasha.

She and Miss Holloway were seated near the empty fireplace by the time the party arrived in the drawing room. It was a room that embodied all that was tasteful

7

about the Hammond household. Nothing had a place there unless it was pleasing to the eye, or, in Mrs Hammond's words, 'soothing to the soul'. Books featured largely, in two magnificent glazed bookcases flanking a large Venetian mirror. Various stringed musical instruments reclined among music stands in corners. Vases of fresh flowers stood beside a highly polished grand piano. The floor was richly but soothingly carpeted in shades of blue and gold, and the curtains and drapes fell in rich festoons of the same subtle colours.

Sasha too wore blue, a dusky shade, with broad sleeves that showed off her fine wrists. She was winding wool into a ball from a skein offered by Miss Holloway on her outstretched arms; the image was one of studied industry. The only jarring note was the figure of the governess, red-faced and impotent, looking like a badly made wooden doll in an ill-fitting yellow dress.

The Hammonds, fearing Sasha's excesses of temperament might be encouraged by other unruly girls if she attended a day school as her sisters had done, had employed a governess for her. Mrs Hammond sometimes thought the experiment had been a total failure. She met Sasha's innocent gaze, took in the governess's rigid pose and the wool, and raised her eyebrows in silent scepticism, as if to say, now what has been going on?

Mrs Hammond, more classically beautiful than any of her daughters, was far from being a conventional Victorian matriarch. She floated around, long before aesthetic dress was in fashion, in trailing velvets and richly embroidered gowns. Her philosophy of life had more of a hint of the radical freedom of the eighteenth century than nineteenth-century probity. She was an eccentric. But she was not vulgar. Mrs Hammond abhorred vulgarity above everything. She would have thrown up her hands in horror if anyone had suggested there was so much as a hint of ill breeding about herself, her household, or any of her daughters.

It was all the more surprising, then, that she was so tolerant of her husband's 'waifs and strays', who very often lacked breeding. This was not the first time Nathaniel had brought someone home. Sometimes he would invite strangers in simply for a chat. 'The fellow looked interesting. He had opinions.' Sometimes the interloper would be invited to come to dinner. Occasionally he would stay a week or more. Nathaniel might spend hours with someone in his studio if he thought he had artistic talent; he would lend him paint and canvas, offer free tuition. It was a highly unusual and stimulating way of life in a house where there were four young women. The Hammond girls had learned to judge character, to flirt, to cut their teeth, so to speak, on their father's protégés.

'What – is only one of my lovely daughters here to greet her poor old father when he comes home?' said Nathaniel with a mock sense of injury.

Sasha dropped the wool to the floor and ran to cover his whiskers with kisses. 'There! A hug from all of us! And another, and another . . . and *another*!'

Nathaniel turned to introduce the stranger, who stood smiling at the sentimental, domestic scene. 'This is Mr Elliman. I overheard him this morning at the Academy's exhibition, extolling the virtues of one of my paintings to passing strangers. We have been firm friends ever since.'

'My husband responds exceedingly well to flattery, Mr Elliman,' said Mrs Hammond in her deep, melodious voice.

'I do. I do enjoy praise. It's true. And it *is* very unusual to find a man of science so responsive to the arts.' Nathaniel beamed at his companion.

'So, you're a man of science, not an artist, Mr Elliman?' Sasha's interest deepened. 'Do you perform experiments with electricity like Mr Faraday?'

The stranger's voice had a trace of cockney in its intonation – Sasha at once decided that it was appealing. 'I'm afraid I'm no such genius as Mr Faraday, Miss Hammond. Chadwick is my hero. Edwin Chadwick. I was passing through Bristol and had time to kill. I'm on my way to compile a report in Penbury for the General Board of Health.'

'Mr Elliman has studied Medicine at University College in London,' said Nathaniel.

'I hope, in a small way, to be able to further Chadwick's work for sanitary reform.'

'Oh, why in a small way, Mr Elliman?' said Sasha. 'Why not in a *grand* and *spectacular* way?'

He laughed, and his smile was infectious, the look in his eyes engaging. 'Well. Who can tell? Anything might happen.'

'And who are your people, Mr Elliman?' said Mrs Hammond politely. She sat, and indicated that he should do the same. 'I mean, do your family live in London?'

'My father is in London. He's . . . a medical man.' The hesitation was slight but noticeable, and seemed to imply a dubiousness about his father's occupation. 'My sister keeps house for him,' he went on quickly. 'My mother died some years ago. But her family – my grandfather and an aunt – live in Norfolk. That is all the family I have.'

There was a pitying silence.

'You must come for dinner this evening.' Nathaniel rubbed his hands together and beamed at them all. 'Yes, yes. He must come to dinner.'

Mrs Hammond's eyes widened momentarily. She threw her husband a look of mild reproof as she echoed, 'Yes. Of course you must. We shall be delighted to entertain you.'

'And you shall meet the rest of the family,' continued Nathaniel blithely. 'Where the devil are they?'

'Leah and Lavinia are at their Ladies' Watercolour Society meeting,' Sasha said eagerly. 'Kitty is shopping.' She pulled a disparaging face.

'Daughters,' laughed Nathaniel. 'They'll ruin me, Mr Elliman. Fairly ruin me.'

'It will be a great pleasure, sir, to meet all of your daughters.'

'Now! You must come and look at the rest of my paintings.' Nathaniel nodded encouragingly and moved towards the door.

Mr Elliman stood. He shook everyone's hand gravely in

turn, including that of Miss Holloway, who, unused to the attention, blushed fiercely.

Mrs Hammond threw a glance heavenward after they had gone. 'Will your father never learn? Chadwick and the Board of Health! Water pipes and sewers!'

Miss Holloway repressed a smirk. She looked down with a superior smile at her hands and the skein of knitting wool in her lap.

Sasha flopped down in her chair and began winding wool vigorously. She released a sigh of delicious anticipation.

William Elliman believed himself a good judge of paintings. He knew what he liked, and the nearer a painting was to something in real life, the more he liked it. He pronounced all Nathaniel's paintings in his studio, particularly the views of Bristol and the Avon Gorge, 'very fine'.

'Are these all portraits?' He paused before a stack of canvases. There was a picture of Mrs Hammond in her youth, dressed in a shocking, diaphanous Greek costume; he attempted to regard it dispassionately. And there were various portraits of Sasha, the dark-eyed naughty girl downstairs. What had she been doing on the window sill? Were all Hammond's daughters so unruly?

'This is Leah.' Hammond pulled out a portrait of a strong-featured beauty with her head wound in a turban and her dress falling off her shoulders. 'And this one is Lavinia,' a pretty, fawnlike creature seated in a very romantic rose bower.

'Oh, that is excellent!' William said, enchanted.

'And this . . .' Hammond struggled with a large painting, heaving it from behind the others against the wall. 'This is Kitty.'

The portrait was of a girl in a dark, loose-fitting robe; she carried a water pot on one shoulder; her arms and neck were bare. A proud, Biblical image. William looked at it and knew that he had never seen anything more lovely.

★ ★ ★

11

Kitty dropped her parcels on the hall table. She was tall and willowy and fair. All the Hammond girls were fair. 'Like immortal goddesses,' someone had once said. Kitty looked at her reflection in the mirror, remembering the remark and the occasion with satisfaction. A party in London. Some of her father's friends. It had been one of the Rossetti crowd who had made the famous remark. Though the man had been too sozzled at the time to know a goddess from a chamber maid.

She took off her bonnet and straightened the tiny lace cap underneath, patting her chignon and tucking a stray lock of hair into place. She liked what she saw: the wide-spaced eyes above classically shaped cheek-bones; the wide, down-turned mouth, the swanlike neck. Kitty knew she was beautiful – more beautiful than her sisters. Sasha was too small and energetic; Lavinia too much like a piece of bone china. There was Leah, of course. But Leah spoiled her looks with her robustness and appalling dress sense.

'Hello, Holly.' Kitty spoke without taking her eyes off her own reflection.

Miss Holloway had come down the stairs. Her expression of disapproval hid entirely different feelings: envy, admiration, even a hint of adoration. 'Your father has brought home a stray. He's coming back to dinner later.'

'What a bore.'

'I think Miss Sarah has her eye on him.' Miss Holloway moved to stand beside her. She spoke with a peculiar familiarity that Kitty endorsed rather than discouraged. 'Your father won't be pleased. You spending all his money on clothes. They know where you've been.'

'I'm sure they don't, Holly.' Kitty winked at her.

This was one of the little games they played. Kitty hinting she had been to meet a lover. Miss Holloway pretending complicity. Miss Holloway was sure the game was extremely innocent, but it gave her a vicarious thrill to think that Kitty might one day confide in her about an admirer. Of all the sisters, the governess envied Kitty the most. Leah and Lavinia were older and more sensible, but

12

Kitty knew what was what, and she did not give a fig for anyone. Miss Holloway studied Kitty's reflection alongside her own pinched face in the mirror and wished she could appear as cool and as languid. She dropped her eyelids a fraction to try to emulate the look.

'Whatever are you doing, Holly? You look disgustingly drunk.'

Miss Holloway flushed deeply. 'I feel like turning to drink, and that's a fact. I really do.'

'Good heavens. What's brought this on?' It was the closest Miss Holloway had ever come to revealing a vein of humour.

'Oh – your sister, I suppose. Miss Sarah's such a wilful girl.'

Kitty turned away with a delicate yawn. 'Sasha's monkey tricks are becoming tiresome. It really is time she grew up.'

'It's all right for you. You don't have to try to teach her anything. Why aren't you interested in your father's stray? He's very handsome, even though he's scruffy.'

'I'm getting too old for the waifs and strays.'

Miss Holloway watched Kitty pick up her parcels. She noticed a faint blush colour Kitty's cheek and said with a gasp of revelation, 'That's not it! You're not interested because . . . you really *have* got an admirer!'

Kitty's composure wavered only briefly. She smiled and flicked the governess's cheek with the fingers of her gloves. 'That's none of your business, is it? You're getting above yourself, Holly, my dear.'

Leah and Lavinia seemed to Sasha always to have been grown up. They are already old maids, she thought, swinging with her back against the edge of the door to their room. She watched them change out of the plain dresses and over-smocks they always wore for painting. Leah was twenty-six and Lavinia almost as old. Sasha listened to their conversation as they dressed one another's hair; they were discussing the possibility of one day opening a gallery and selling their paintings to the public.

13

They would do it too. They always seemed to know what they wanted.

At least, Leah knew what she wanted, and Lavinia went along with her; Lavinia idolised Leah and tried to copy her ideas. Once, when they were much younger, Leah had decided she and Lavinia must go to a school in Switzerland. Their mother and father, swayed by Leah's determination, had said it would be a marvellous opportunity for them. If that was so, Sasha could not now see where the advantages of a foreign education lay. Her sisters had come back from the Continent, as unattached and as deadly serious about everything as they had been before they went.

Her sisters were not interested in marriage, Sasha reminded herself. They were self-reliant, independent, dismissive about the business of husband-catching that formed the chief preoccupation among their set. At least, Leah was scornful of such things; Lavinia sometimes seemed a little wistful about opportunities missed. She would marry in the end, Sasha was sure of it; Lavinia was the marrying kind. She wished she could be as sure about what she wanted in the future. How did one combine the pleasure of falling in love with wanting to do things and be independent? Sasha was almost certain she wanted a husband one day. People looked down so on women who stayed single. But how terrible it would be to marry somebody one didn't like simply to avoid being an old maid.

'Come in, if you're coming in,' said Leah testily through the hair pins in her mouth. 'And close the door. The servants will see us half dressed.'

'I'm not coming in. I only wanted to ask you something.'

'And what is that, darling?' crooned Lavinia, turning to flash a smile at her.

'Who is Edwin Chadwick?'

'Drains,' said Leah. 'He worked for the Poor Law Commission and set up the General Board of Health. He's put people's backs up by saying that everyone should

14

wash more thoroughly, and by getting local boards to clean up their towns.'

'Why should that annoy people?'

'Because it costs money, nincompoop.'

Sasha felt foolish. She was, in fact, far from being a nincompoop. She knew she was not as clever as Leah, who knew more Latin and Greek than any of them, and could quote from Shakespeare or Carlyle with equal ease. But Sasha was quick; she absorbed knowledge like a thirsty plant absorbs water. She was brighter than Kitty or Lavinia, and she knew she was cleverer than her governess.

'Why aren't you with Miss Holloway?' Leah regarded her critically.

'She's been particularly wet today. We called the lesson off.'

'You mean you've been tormenting her again.'

'She deserves it.'

'Poor baby,' said Lavinia with her gentle smile.

Sasha grinned back. She returned to the room she shared with Kitty, and thought about Mr Elliman and Chadwick, and their ambition to clean up the country. She reflected on the pleasures of bathing in a bath-tub: the delicious sensation of submerging herself in hot water, the smell of rose-scented soap, the bustle of servants hurrying in and out of the bedroom with towels and huge copper jugs. And she contrasted her father's house in Hanover Terrace with the houses in the streets closer to the Bristol docks, where several families shared a privy and probably never, ever had a wash. It was unusual for someone as lively and handsome as Mr Elliman to show such a very great concern for the poor. She hoped he was not going to disappoint her by turning out to be dull and preachy.

Sasha stood in front of the mirror in her corset and pushed handkerchiefs down the front of her chemise, tucking the corners out of sight. She did not put up her hair; her mother had strong views about a girl's hair flowing freely over her shoulders until she was eighteen, so she contented herself with tying it back in a ribbon and bit her lips to make them red. She had sneaked some boot polish from below stairs and dipped an old toothbrush in it to thicken her eyelashes.

'Father's young man is back, with knife and fork practically in hand,' said Kitty coming into the room.

Sasha thrust the toothbrush behind her back. But Kitty had seen the boot polish. She was on the point of saying something caustic, but failed. Sasha, pink with hurrying, looked lovely in her white frock. Feeling charitable, Kitty tightened the ends of the blue bow at her sister's waist. 'You look a stunner. He's all yours.'

'Miss Holloway says you've got a lover.'

Kitty moved away and clicked her teeth in annoyance. 'Miss Holloway ought to learn to hold her tongue. She's paid to din some decorum into you, not pry into my affairs.'

'Does Mother know?'

'I sincerely hope not.'

Sasha let the implications sink in. Kitty had a lover? Might she be the first to marry? She took mental stock of the young men who had been to the house in the past, but could think of none Kitty would seriously consider good enough for her. In any case, their mother would not allow any of the waifs and strays actually to pay court to her daughters; the girls had only been practising all these years for when they met the real, true love of their lives. Was that why their father cultivated the young men? It seemed very unfair. Several of them had fallen in love with Kitty. And even Leah and Lavinia had allowed a few to admire them from a safe distance.

Sasha watched Kitty change into a low-cut dress with a lace berthe that revealed her long neck and graceful shoulders. Jealousy and longing, and an inexplicable sense of loneliness, seized her.

Mr Elliman, looking heavenly in a black dress coat and white waistcoat, came into the drawing room. He had probably borrowed the clothes, whispered Miss Holloway, since they seemed to be too big for him.

Sasha found the notion of Mr Elliman's borrowed evening clothes endearing. Leah and Lavinia were introduced. Sasha, waiting her turn, realised she had laced her corset too tightly; she imagined the fuss there would be if she were to swoon, as heroines did in novels when faced with overwhelming emotion – though she had never fainted in her life and told herself that she was not about to start. The pressure of his hand was firm and manly as he said, 'Hello again, Miss Sasha.'

And then Kitty, looking regal, extended her hand languidly and smiled in that vaguely provocative way of hers. Was it unconscious, or did she know *exactly* what she was doing? Sasha saw Mr Elliman's glance flicker, his attention linger on Kitty's white neck and shoulders. Oh, Kitty, Sasha wailed inwardly. It isn't fair. It really isn't fair.

Seated next to Mr Elliman at dinner, Sasha was able to observe him more closely. He seemed overawed by Leah and Lavinia as they talked about painting and about promoting better education for women. But when Mrs Hammond asked him about his medical studies, he spoke rapidly and with great earnestness about the advances in medical science; he said he agreed with Leah that universities should allow women to study Medicine.

Sasha glanced at Kitty; she was not behaving at all as if she had a lover, but stared frequently at Mr Elliman, smiled with her eyelashes lowered, and encouraged him to tell them more about Mr Chadwick's recommendations for improvements. Even she seemed won over by Mr Elliman's combination of unsophisticated charm and enthusiasm for his subject. He talked of the shocking things exposed by Chadwick in his survey of towns up and down the country, of the bad air from town middens, and impure water supplies. 'I can envisage a future when every town will be served by closed sewers.' He waved his wineglass in his enthusiasm. 'With water closets to every home.'

Mrs Hammond's interest faltered. Her liberal-mindedness did not extend to the discussion of water closets at the dinner table. She decided to change the subject. 'Do you play a musical instrument, Mr Elliman?'

William had been brought up to believe that pursuits such as poetry and music were effeminate, and he looked slightly affronted. 'I . . . sing a little, Mrs Hammond.'

'The girls will play some music for you after dinner,' Nathaniel said. 'You'll be pleasantly surprised, Mr Elliman. Just you wait until you've heard young Sasha.'

The others turned to Sasha, and to her horror she began to blush. Mr Elliman's expression was uncomprehending as he looked from one to the other of the sisters with an amused half smile. He would be expecting the usual warbling sopranos and laboured pianoforte studies. Sasha said quickly, 'My sisters and I have formed a musical chamber ensemble, Mr Elliman. Leah and Lavinia play violin and viola. Kitty plays the cello.'

'And you, Miss Sasha?' He spoke with an ironical lift to his mouth that set her heart beating more urgently.

'I play the pianoforte.'

'Sasha is training under Lindau,' Mrs Hammond explained gently. And then, suspecting that Mr Elliman might not know that Julius Lindau was a pianoforte artist of world renown, added, 'He is very famous. He thinks Sasha has a future.'

'Why did you have to say that?' Sasha wailed when they left the men to their wine. She sat down heavily on the piano stool in the drawing room. 'Now he'll think he has to pay me special attention.'

'Isn't that what you wanted?' said Lavinia in her gentle teasing way.

'I hope none of you are taking this young man seriously.' Mrs Hammond frowned. 'He has a certain charm, I'll admit. But he is barely more respectable than a Poor Law physician.'

'It's time Father gave up his charity cases,' Lavinia said. 'They nearly always end up taking advantage.'

18

Leah went to sit beside Miss Holloway in the window seat. The governess worked silently at a piece of embroidery; it was not her place to make conversation or to comment in Mrs Hammond's presence. The Hammonds refused to treat a woman of intellect as if she were one of the servants; on the other hand, they had no conscience about a small degree of segregation; a governess could hardly be treated in the same way as family or guests.

Kitty stood by the fireplace, distanced from the others. She leaned her arm on the mantel and traced her forefinger idly along the veins in the marble as if deep in contemplation. Her profile in the mirror was serene, her eyelids drooped. It was impossible to tell what she was thinking – or whether she was thinking anything at all.

Sasha pushed up her sleeves from her elbows and spread her fingers over the piano keys; she felt stifled, and very conscious of Kitty's silent, languid presence. Kitty had a lover. A *real* lover. Would marry instead of following a career. Sasha thought of the way her sister had monopolised Mr Elliman during dinner, and the way he had looked, as if he couldn't drag his eyes from Kitty's face and bosom. Was it right of Kitty to encourage him if she was in love with someone else? Sasha lifted her hands and brought them down, hard, on the piano keys in a chord. Herr Lindau had begun to talk seriously about her having a career as a pianist. She knew it was only a matter of time before her mother consented to his plans for her. What then? When a whole concert hall might stare and talk about her? She began to play, feeling her aggression come to a peak, then leave her, as it always did when music flooded her mind. A Chopin study flowed swiftly through her hands.

'Very nice, Sasha dear.' Mrs Hammond applauded lightly.

'Too fast. I've heard you play better.' Kitty turned from the fireplace. 'Is that what you're going to perform for Mr Elliman?'

Sasha's gaze met hers, and she saw a strange expression in her sister's eyes, as if they had suddenly become

19

adversaries. She began to search through the music on top of the piano. 'I might. We ought to be deciding on something we *all* can play for him.'

Kitty reached across Sasha to pull several sheets of music from the pile. 'How about Mendelssohn? Mr Elliman looks like a romantic to me. Let's have something with a bit of feeling in it.'

While the girls played, Mrs Hammond explained in a whisper to William that Sasha had transcribed several of Mendelssohn's *Songs without Words* for the quartet; that Sasha was the one – though all four of her daughters were very musical – marked out for fame by her tutor.

William supposed it was all very serious, and that the feat of rearrangement was rather difficult. He understood that Sasha's talent was something phenomenal, and applauded very loudly, with enthusiastic calls of 'Bravo!'

'I never thought . . .' He turned to his hostess as the final chords died, and was at once distracted by Kitty. Her head rested against the neck of her cello as if she were drained by the music. Her eyes were closed, the eyelids seeming translucent. Her hair glowed in the lamplight; soft curls and tender wisps of gold lay against her neck and caressed her ear. She lifted her head with a look of triumph, then spun the cello on its spike away from her body and smoothed her skirts in a practised gesture.

Sasha knew that Kitty was play-acting. The exhaustion, the gestures, were purely for Mr Elliman's benefit. She can't help it, she realised. She does it instinctively. She must have a conquest. With a sense of having been betrayed Sasha clenched her teeth to hold back sudden tears of frustration. She believed that everyone was a witness to her humiliation at seeing the newcomer fall for her sister.

'Why don't you play us a solo piece, Sasha?' said her father.

'Oh, yes. Please do,' said William with a smile of encouragement.

Sasha bowed her head bitterly over the piano. She

would play them some Beethoven, something that would startle Mr Elliman into respect by its dark passions and the brilliance of its execution. So dramatic, so tragic would her playing be that he would forget Kitty and be fascinated by it; and, being fascinated, he would not be able to prevent himself from falling in love with her.

Herr Lindau had first played the '*Appassionata*' Sonata for her. She had almost fallen in love with him for playing so beautifully, even though he was older than her father and had bad teeth. Sasha forgot her desire to impress Mr Elliman. The sheer exhilaration of playing always made her lose all sense of time or nervousness about performing. And afterwards, when everyone applauded, when she was high on a tide of euphoria, she hardly noticed all the fuss. The drawing room, with its elegant furniture, faded away. The Venetian mirrors. The handsome prints and paintings and vases. The bow-legged sofas and their straight-backed occupants: Mr Elliman, seated between her mother and Leah; Kitty, serene and self-assured; Lavinia and their father smiling fondly at her; Miss Holloway, resentful because Herr Lindau's teaching was in a class beyond her own poor efforts in geography and Algebra and Latin prose. All those people who had seemed so important when she had begun to play, faded and became insignificant.

What was it about music that went straight to her *soul*? She could practise for hours, even scales and arpeggios, without tiring. Sasha did not believe there was anything in the world that could compare. Her mind and body were driven and pulled all ways. She supposed that people who had experienced religious ecstasy knew the same degree of passion – people always talked a great deal about the soul in the context of religion – but Sasha knew she had never felt, nor could feel, this way in church, not even under the spell of a charismatic preacher.

The piano fell silent, and she saw again that she was in the drawing room above Hanover Terrace, that they were all there still, perched on the uncomfortable sofas, smiling and applauding.

21

Her father dabbed at his eyes. Her mother nodded with a serene smile that acknowledged the superiority of Sasha's talent. But it was to Mr Elliman that Sasha looked for a reaction. He was applauding with vigorous movements of his arms, and did all that was enthusiastic short of bursting into cheers. 'Well done, Miss Hammond!' But he did not look at her in the way he had looked at Kitty.

Sasha remembered the expression in his eyes, and the exquisite weariness with which Kitty had raised her head from her cello. She felt a sense of resignation. If Beethoven could not inspire such admiration in him, there was nothing within her power that could affect him.

Chapter Two

'I'm in love,' William told himself as the coach rattled along the road to Penbury. He had hardly slept that night, lightheaded with the novelty of his situation. 'In love,' he repeated, the extra emphasis overcoming his lingering cynicism about affairs of the heart. 'She's the most adorable, the most wonderful . . .' He threw back his head, lost for adjectives. She had played like something divine. No one could have imagined . . . He glanced at his travelling companions who seemed to be dozing. They were all, without exception, lumpish and unattractive. How rarely the human form presented itself in a way that was appealing to the eye. Instead, it threw up bulbous noses, clogged pores, hairs that sprouted from ears and chins. And yet Hammond had managed to produce four seemingly perfect specimens of womanhood. 'You watch out for yourself, William,' the voice of reason said in his ear. 'Women like that have a reputation for breaking men's hearts.'

Not Kitty. Nobody could say that about Kitty Hammond. He had not known that such beauty, such pure loveliness existed!

He looked out of the window at the Somerset countryside, green and lush and pulsating with the heat, and reminded himself that he would be in Penbury, compiling a report for, at the very least, the next three months. Kitty Hammond would forget all about him. He wanted to do something energetic – jump from the carriage, run all the way back to Bristol and pace the street under her window. But he did not know which window was hers.

The thought of windows reminded him of Sasha, her face alive with devilment. He had enjoyed flirting a little. What a contrast in her when she had played for them. So fierce! As if she were possessed by a demon of a very different ilk. The whole family were out of the ordinary. He remembered Hammond telling him that his wife had been an artist's model when she was younger; the idea of a fellow marrying his model lent a delicious element of danger to William's encounter with the family.

They were approaching Penbury. The close air inside the coach was overlaid by the smell of bad drains. William was used to objectionable smells; the Thames was never pleasant, nor Westminster night-soil carts; and his recent association with the General Board of Health had brought him into contact with many aspects of the country's sewerage crisis. But never, he thought, had he met with anything so foul as the combined stench of Penbury's sewage and its tanneries and factories.

He looked from the window at the open ditch beside the road; it was choked with a black filth moving sluggishly beneath a green scum.

'You'll get used to it,' said one of his travelling companions, apparently undisturbed by the poisonous air. 'The tanneries and the glue factories are the worst.'

William nodded, his reply smothered by his handkerchief as he tried not to choke.

'It's better at the top end of town,' said a woman. 'There are some very nice houses up there.' She eyed William's clothes, mentally pricing them: the top-coat, under which he was sweltering, his new hat, and his official-looking document case. 'Oh, yes. It's very pleasant, is Penbury. Once we're past the lower end of town . . . Are you visiting someone, or passing through?'

'Neither. I'm staying at the Neptune.'

'You're not from round these parts.'

He explained that he was from London.

'You're the fellow sent by Whitehall!' said the man who

had spoken earlier. 'I'm right, aren't I?' He turned to convey the information to the other people in the coach.

William raised his voice above the heavy rumble of wheels on cobbles and said that, yes, he was in Penbury to compile a report. 'And, if I may say so, I seem to have arrived none too soon.'

The man beside him took his arm and began pumping his hand vigorously. 'You tell them in Whitehall. You tell them how bad it is, and that we need a local board of health.'

William smiled but said nothing. He became aware of dark brick factory walls, a glimpse through an open doorway of men and women scraping leather; the street ran with a stream of slime and sludge. The reality of his position hit him. He was a public health inspector. What prospects would he ever have to tempt a girl like Kitty Hammond into an attachment? Even if he went back to London and one day inherited his father's property, his prospects were no less horrible; he doubted whether serving in an apothecary shop was the kind of future Hammond expected for any of his daughters. Even in general practice, it would take him years to build up a respectable medical career. How could he ever aspire to the genteel ambience of Hanover Terrace?

The coach climbed the hill through the town and came to a halt outside an inn. William stepped down and reminded himself that he was not in medicine for the money. He had chosen the profession for the noblest of reasons: he was going to be a reformer. He noted a pleasant cobbled square, a tumbledown market hall, and a broad street leading to shops. His spirits lifted a little. The people around him were respectably dressed; their accents were countrified, but not coarse. A group of young women bent their heads together in excited conference. It was not disagreeable to be an object of attention and speculation. What was more, he observed that his travelling companions had been right: the smell was hardly noticeable at the upper levels of the town.

He was eating his supper in the parlour of the Neptune,

when a man walked in through the door; he regarded William with a speculative and pugnacious air.

'Are you looking for me?' William said.

'I don't know. You don't look like a government man.' William introduced himself. 'I'm Elliman.'

The stranger came forward and shook his hand warmly. 'I was told you had arrived. Has anyone else spoken to you yet? They were planning a reception committee.'

'I didn't write to say exactly when I would be coming.'

'Good.' The stranger sat down and rested his hands on his knees. 'I'm Brewer. Charlie Brewer of the *Penbury Gazette*. I wanted to get to you before they did.'

'And who are they?' said William cautiously, leaning back in his chair.

'The Town Improvement Overseers. So-called. They'll try to tell you we don't need reforming. They're all scared of losing face if you start pointing out their inadequacies.'

William had been briefed a little on the characteristics of the town and knew that the local officials had been dragging their feet over the issue of sanitary reform. 'I shall do my job without fear or favour,' he said with a convincing note of confidence.

'I hoped as much,' beamed Brewer. 'They need a boot up the backside, and I hope you're the man to give it them. People have to live like pigs in this town, Elliman. Like pigs. And there are men who could change things overnight but who do nothing, either because they're terrified of increasing the rates, or because their own soap and glue and leather factories are causing most of the problems. Lord knows, *I've* done my best. I've drawn attention to matters in my newspaper.'

William felt a surge of responsibility; if people were looking to him to do something to help them, he would not let them down. 'Have a drink.' He signalled to the potboy to fetch more beer. 'Tell me about the town overseers.'

Brewer listed the chief manufacturers, the land-owning gentry, and the traders in the town who formed the body of local government: those who were in favour of public

26

health reform, a small handful, and those who vigorously opposed any suggestions of change. 'They have almost all become complacent. Only a few of them attend meetings regularly, and even they have their own interests and profits at heart, so don't let anyone hoodwink you.'

'Who got up the petition for an inquiry?'

'I did. With the help of a few men who do want reform. Wotherspoon for one. He's the biggest of the manufacturers in the town. Be careful of Wotherspoon though. He'll try to fudge the issue. What he really wants is for Penbury to become a municipal borough. He wants to be mayor. Be even more wary of a fellow called Scrope; he'll pretend to be on your side over getting a local board of health, but he's really fighting for himself. He's dead against borough status. He knows he'll be booted out for sure if Penbury gets an elected council.'

'And what do you expect from me?'

'If your report says things are bad enough, Penbury will get its board of health. Who knows, we might even get a decent council. I'll be happy enough to see some of those villains thrown out. But don't get sidetracked. That's the important thing.'

'I shall make my report without any bias,' William repeated.

'Of course.' Brewer grinned at him. 'But I can see you're on the right side in the matter.'

William was aware that he was being drawn rather too quickly into the local politics. On the one hand, it was very satisfactory to know that his report could bring sanitation to the town. On the other, dealing with all the issues was going to be harder work than he had anticipated.

He thought with longing of the congenial way of life in the Hammond household. The Hammonds were wealthy and clever and cultured, superior to anyone he had ever met. And the girls – all so at ease, so musical.

If he was honest, music itself did not excite or move William so much as provide a pleasant and lively entertainment. He enjoyed a good tune; and he had liked the mellow, resonant sound of the cello; but it was Kitty's body wrapped around its contours that had thrilled him more than her playing. Her figure was sinuous, her expression had been absorbed. He could appreciate that there was a superior expertise, even a brilliance, in Sasha's playing – the girl was very accomplished, her appearance too was striking, with her dark eyes and pale hair – but she was young and transparent; she lacked the mystery that was Kitty's. William remembered the older girl's expression, remote, almost unassailable; and yet, he was sure too that she had smiled at him once or twice with a rare degree of warmth.

He had told the Hammonds that he sang. He remembered the blunder with horror, thankful they had not asked him to prove his singing talents; his repertoire was confined to a knowledge of supper-room songs, some of them very vulgar. 'I hope you enjoyed the playing, Mr Elliman,' Kitty Hammond had said, clearly expecting him to comment on their music.

'It was wonderful, Miss Hammond. You and your sisters are extremely accomplished.' Was that all he could think of to say? William remembered the glaring inadequacies of his conversation.

She had replied that they enjoyed playing; when one enjoyed something, it became easy. For herself, she would be a poor, restless thing if she did not have her music. Even women needed a purpose in life. Didn't he agree?

'Oh, yes. I do,' he had said. 'I'm not one of those fellows who believe young ladies should merely be decorative . . .'

Oh, but she was that. He could think of nothing else but Kitty's decorative talents as he paced the floor of his room that evening. In the last few hours William had become desperately committed to the idea of winning her. His glance fell on the pens and ink and paper he had laid out for the start of his report. In a fever of optimism he sat at the desk and dashed off a letter to Nathaniel Hammond.

28

He reminded him of the family's kindness to him and their encouragement to call again at any time. He wrote that he hoped he might, when next visiting Bristol, be permitted to call in particular on Mr Hammond's daughters, for whom he had formed 'the greatest respect'. He looked at the letter and added rashly: '. . . To be truthful, sir, it is your daughter, Miss Kitty Hammond, on whom I wish to call. If you would allow it.' There. He had come out with it as plainly as he knew how. And if Hammond told him he was a miserable upstart even to suggest such a thing after so brief an acquaintance, it was no less than he deserved.

William consigned the letter to the post.

Nathaniel read William's letter in surprise. Kitty? He considered the idea. Sanitary reform was hardly a subject to strike poetic chords in a woman's heart – least of all Kitty's. However, in Kitty's case, a bit of down-to-earthdom might do her a world of good. He would ask her opinion on whether the young man might be encouraged to call on her. He put the letter with a pile of papers on his desk in his studio, and promptly forgot all about it.

That afternoon, he attended an informal meeting of the local Academy members, to gossip with friends and discuss various art projects. Nathaniel had begun to feel lately, in a disquieting way, that his prestige among his friends was slipping. He boasted a little about Sasha, by way of a boost, and told them her music teacher was arranging for her to give a public concert at the Bath Assembly Rooms. In the course of conversation, he invited several of his friends along.

'You ought to paint your daughters together, Hammond,' someone said. 'The beautiful Hammond girls! What a painting that would make! Do it soon, before they get married and start bringing you grandchildren to dandle on your knee.'

Nathaniel was captivated by the idea. He stayed until the late evening, drinking wine and coffee, smoking cigars, and discussing the form the painting might take.

He was a little tipsy by the time he walked home. The world, bathed in moonlight, seemed a very pleasant place for a man at the height of his career, with several thousand a year income, a beautiful, loving wife, and four lovely and talented daughters. He paused for a moment to look back down the hill. It was late summer. The smell from the floating harbour was obtrusive; but the moon was reflected prettily on the water. The harsh strains of a fiddle drifted up from a public house near the docks. He remembered for a moment Sasha's playing. What a feather in her cap it would be if she were well received at her concert.

He leaned against the railings at the side of the pavement and gazed up at the sky where the moon, like an opalescent lamp, illuminated the night. How unequal life was. How unfair that the people who lived down there by the docks never had their chance to hear fine music. What terrible inequalities there were between rich and poor. The thought reminded him of his young friend Elliman. He would invite him to the concert, he decided. The fellow obviously appreciated music.

Nathaniel had no reservations about encouraging an impoverished doctor to visit his daughters. The distinctions of rich man, poor man, seemed to him a very crude form of classification. The Hammonds would admit openly to only one form of snobbery: they believed that artists – painters, writers and musicians – were superior to any of the social classes. The only distinctions they made were between people who had an instinct for the higher things in life, and people who had no soul. To be declared soulless was an expression of the highest condemnation in the Hammond household. Rich people without soul were beyond the pale.

Nathaniel went straight to his studio when he got home, and looked for a piece of paper on which to write down his ideas for the painting before they escaped his mind. As he searched through the muddle on his desk he came upon William's letter again. He wrote to him in a generous mood: 'You must come and visit us. Soon. Often. Come for weekends. My wife will be delighted. You shall become better acquainted with "The Beautiful Hammond Girls".' And he told William about Sasha's concert, and his idea for a new painting.

'Mr Elliman has written to me – and I have written back,' he said at breakfast the next morning. He glanced at Kitty. 'He would like to visit us again. I have said he may, but I thought I should ask your opinion on the matter.'

'Why should you ask my opinion on Mr Elliman?' Kitty looked alarmed.

'Nathaniel!' Mrs Hammond frowned. 'You might have discussed this with me first.'

'Mr Elliman is a man who appreciates culture. And he is rising in the world. He has asked to call on Kitty in particular. Well, child? Shall I give him my blessing?'

Sasha said nothing. Why Kitty? she thought savagely. Why did it always have to be Kitty? She tried to sort out the confusion of her thoughts. Why was it all so very important? And why did her breathing quicken when anyone mentioned Mr Elliman? She knew almost nothing about him, except that he was keen on public health – and, of course, obsessed by Kitty. He probably wanted to marry her. He might even fight a duel with Kitty's secret lover, whoever *he* might be.

There was a knot of pain in Sasha's chest that would not go away when she swallowed. Kitty had two admirers. And she could not attract even one! She pictured the eager look in Mr Elliman's eyes when he had applauded Kitty's cello-playing. She imagined Mr Elliman coming to call, Kitty smiling at him in her lazy, enigmatic way, letting him think she found him vaguely interesting, vaguely worth cultivating, holding out a straw of encouragement for him to cling to. Sasha tried to imagine the same look of worship, the same enthusiasm lapping around her. Was that what was meant by winning a man's love? Was that the goal every woman sought? It was a very odd thing on which to pin one's destiny. Her thoughts drifted ahead to the concert in Bath.

She was terrified by the thought of a public performance. Herr Lindau wanted her to attempt a tour as a soloist, with him accompanying her. She would have to take Miss Holloway as a chaperone. She thought about the world beyond the familiar frontages of Hanover Terrace and the Avondon woods and everything she had known from childhood. It was all changing too quickly.

'Have you any objections to the fellow?' Nathaniel continued, still on the subject of Mr Elliman.

Kitty considered the question. She had no objections to any man paying court to her, and Mr Elliman was very handsome; his attentions had been flattering. 'I have no feelings about him one way or another. I suppose there's no harm in letting him come.' She began to peel an apple on her plate, spearing it and turning it slowly on her fork. It might be fun, she thought. She would instil some soul into him and cure him of his fascination with drains.

The Three Bells Inn was crowded. The Penbury Improvement Overseers had called a public meeting and attendance was high.

'Everyone's come to get a good look at you,' murmured Brewer, who was there to report on the meeting for his newspaper.

Mr Scrope, the chairman of the overseers, introduced William to members of the committee, all of them relatively prosperous, shrewd-looking men. As the room filled, the mass of bodies cut down the air and light in the overheated inn; people leaned in at the windows from the street outside. William, feeling suffocated, was passed from overseer to overseer and shaken by the hand. Mr Wotherspoon said in a loud voice that he hoped William's arrival would 'herald a new chapter in Penbury's history'. This acted as a signal for the committee to push through the crush and take their seats. A place was found for William.

Mr Wotherspoon made a speech of welcome in which he repeated his hopes for a new chapter; and William was invited to outline his plans for his survey. He said he expected to be visiting all of the manufactories in turn. 'I hope I can count on the co-operation of the Board of Guardians and other officers. I shall be examining nuisances in the town, and the systems of drainage, sewerage and water supply.'

They assured him with varying degrees of enthusiasm that he had their full support.

'Tell them in Whitehall, we want all the Town Overseers thrown out!' shouted a voice. 'Those lazy so-and-sos were appointed to deal with nuisances more than *five* years since. When are they going to get on with it?' William recognised one of the men who had travelled with him on the coach from Bristol. A cheer of support greeted the challenge.

'We do what we can, bearing in mind the cost of improvements,' said Mr Scrope laboriously, with an air of having said the same thing many times before. 'And remember the outcry after every expense in the past? There'll soon be voices raised if we have to put up the rates again. And they *will* go up. You can be sure of that if we have a new authority.'

'We want a decent water supply,' someone shouted. 'What are you going to do about it?'

'The overseers have no statutory powers for providing a public water supply and sewerage system,' said Scrope.

'And that is precisely why we need a proper council,' interrupted Wotherspoon calmly. 'Our only hope of improvement lies in an effective local government.'

A supportive cheer rose in the room. It was taken up by the crowd outside.

'I shall examine all these issues very carefully,' William promised.

'We go round in circles, Mr Elliman, as you can see.' Wotherspoon, a bluff man with a cheerful manner, drew him aside after the meeting. 'People are set in their ways. Many of the overseers on the committee are afraid – some of them with good reason – that they won't be elected if we get a borough council.'

William remembered Brewer's warning not to be hoodwinked. 'I'm more concerned in getting facts than simply promoting your claim for borough status, Mr Wotherspoon.'

'You've been talking to the fellow from the newspaper.' Wotherspoon lowered his voice. 'You don't want to be taken in by Brewer.'

'He seems properly concerned about the needs of the town.'

'His own needs, more like. His only reason for supporting a public health bill is to stop local traders leaving rubbish outside his newspaper offices and to get the cattle off the street on market days – the beasts disturb him with their mooing when he's writing pieces for his newspaper.'

'I agree with him that the town needs public health reform above all else. A proper water supply. Flushed water closets. Sewerage and drainage systems.'

'Yes, yes. So do I. So do I. A local board of health. Splendid. I know some excellent men for the job. But it would have no muscle. Not without an elected council to back it up. A council would deal with the *whole* of local government, including public health.'

William hesitated. He had felt that he was keeping a sense of detachment, yet what Wotherspoon was saying made sense. He was evidently a popular employer – he had provided cottages for his employees – and he would probably be an effective mayor. 'It wouldn't do to commit myself to any party until I've made my report.'

'No, no. I can see you're a steady fellow, Mr Elliman. By all means, consider all the issues at stake. But remember, Brewer needs to sell newspapers. What better way than to promote the public health issue above that of full-scale municipal reform and create a controversial campaign? While I think of it – my wife would be obliged if you would come to dinner tomorrow evening.'

William raised his hat. 'That's very kind, but I have a prior engagement . . .'

'Another time. But I'll leave you to think on this: people may well agree that Penbury should have a local board of health. But once that's done, they'll get nervous about the rates going up, and forget about further reform. They'll settle for Scrope and his cronies running things like they've always done.'

'I shall consider all sides of the matter,' William promised. 'Good day to you, sir.'

He was surprised to find Mr Scrope waiting for him as he crossed the street to the Neptune.

'I hope you'll be reassured after you've seen conditions here for yourself, Mr Elliman,' Scrope said, skipping along beside him. 'I'm sure you realise that men of Brewer's calling tend to exaggerate. You know newspaper men. All for scandal and sensation. And I expect you've realised Mr Wotherspoon has his eye on a place on a municipal council. They try to make themselves popular, do you see? You mustn't listen to them.'

'You mean, I should listen to you instead?' William said with an ironical lift to his eyebrows, feeling that he was beginning to handle the situation pretty well.

'Judge for yourself, Mr Elliman. That's all I'm saying. Nothing more. Judge for yourself.'

'I shall do that. When I begin my survey.' William had reached the Neptune. He hoped the man was not going to follow him inside.

'Then I trust you will report in favour of leaving the Improvement Committee well alone.'

William halted.

Scrope smiled and stood his ground. 'I could make it worth your while, do you see? I suspect you're not a rich man, Mr Elliman.'

For a moment, William did not believe that he had heard what he had heard. But the man was still smiling and waiting. William's medical course and his briefing from the General Board of Health had not prepared him for this; in fact, they seemed to have little to do with anything that had happened to him since leaving London.

'I fully intend to make my report without bias, Mr Scrope.' He raised his hat. 'Good day to you.' And he turned and hurried inside.

William went straight to his room and sat on the bed. His heart was pounding in his chest. He had to confess he was shaken by Scrope's crude attempt at a bribe.

He needed to cleanse himself with those good, decent people at Hanover Terrace. A mental picture of Nathaniel Hammond, honest and solid, calmed him a little. And his wife, and the four beautiful Hammond girls. He lay with his hands behind his head and reflected on the encouraging tone of Hammond's reply to his letter. The family had invited him to attend a concert in a few weeks' time. He thought of the sisters travelling to Bath, and imagined meeting them at the Assembly Rooms. The picture was very pleasant – and the lovely, womanly image of Kitty was even more reassuring.

Kitty had told everyone she was meeting former schoolfriends in Bath. She had gone there early by mail coach on the day of Sasha's concert, and was taking a short cut through a side street when she came face to face with one of those very friends she was supposed to be visiting.

'Why, Kitty! Kitty Hammond!'

Kitty saw the light of curiosity in the other woman's eyes and introduced her companion as, 'A friend of my father's . . . Mr Randolph Portland. Mr Portland – this is my old schoolfriend, Miss Sophia Mannering.'

'The writer!' screeched Sophia. 'You wrote *A Woman of Noble Intent*. What a book! What a fuss it caused!'

'A little notoriety perhaps,' affirmed Kitty's companion with nervous bravado.

Kitty held Sophia's gaze without flinching. 'We're engaged to meet my father shortly, so I regret, Miss Mannering, there's no time to chat. We shall not have the pleasure of discussing Mr Portland's book.' She nodded to her and walked on.

'Did you have to be so damnably offhand?' muttered her companion as soon as they were out of hearing.

'Well, you *are* a friend of my father's, aren't you? And since you're almost old enough to *be* my father, she's hardly going to suspect anything.'

'Will she mention seeing us?'

'Not to anyone of any consequence, I hope.' Kitty smiled. 'Don't be such a coward, Porky. It's not very becoming in a lover.'

'Oh, you may well not worry,' he said as they turned into a quieter side street. 'But a stray word of gossip could make all the difference to me.'

She put her arms round him and pulled him into a doorway. 'Darling Porky. I have far more to lose than you do if anybody suspects us. You know I have. Now kiss me.'

The pressure of his mouth on hers drove out the panic that had made Kitty's blood run cold on seeing Sophia. She closed her eyes. Porky would lose nothing at all if they were seen together. His wife, renowned for her discretion, must already know what he was up to – Kitty had never made the mistake of thinking her a stupid woman. But for a young woman to be seen alone with a married man, and a notorious womaniser at that, was a different matter. Kitty shivered with the danger of it and because it was cold in the shadow of the buildings. She stood to lose everything: honour, respect, her right to mix in decent society.

He pulled her closer. 'Oh, Kitty. Charming, cruel, kissable Kitty. Let's go back to my hotel.'

'I don't know.'

'Don't know whether we have time to go back? Or don't know whether you want to?'

'Don't know whether I want to when you're so ashamed to be seen with me.' She grasped him by the coat lapels and kissed him, letting her mouth go loose, stirring him to the point where she felt him harden as he pressed himself against her. Then she pushed him away.

'You're a slut, Kitty,' he whispered. 'Silky . . . sultry . . . Come back to my hotel.'

'There isn't time. I have to be at the Assembly Rooms for Sasha's concert in an hour, and it must look as if I've been *strolling* by the river with old schoolfriends, not *rolling* on a mattress with my lover.'

He laughed and stepped out into the street. Glancing up and down to make sure that it was empty, he tipped his hat at a jaunty angle, and held his arm for her to take his elbow. 'In that case, you can damn well accompany me to the railway station as a penance for disappointing me.' He took hold of her hand and made her link her arm in his. 'Do you remember when we first saw one another?' he said as they walked along.

Kitty said that she did not, though she recalled every second of the encounter as if it were seared on her memory with a hot iron. As was every other time they had met, whether in secret in Bath, or, more rarely, those times when her family went to London. But he preferred not to meet her in London, on his own territory.

'Your father had invited me to address the Avondon Arts Society on the subject of the form of the novel, with particular reference to *A Woman of Noble Intent*.'

'You are so tedious when you reflect on past glories. When are you going to start another book, Porky?' Kitty halted. 'This is as far as I'm going.' Then, seeing the injured look on his face, 'You're right. It's too public. And I really shall be late for Sasha's concert if I walk all the way down to the station with you.'

'Why aren't you playing in the concert as well?' he said, swinging his cane. It had only now occurred to him that she would be doing something after he had gone, that she would continue to exist outside his own need of her.

'I told you. It's to be Sasha's début performance. Her teacher has aspirations for her. He thinks she should play professionally.'

'Don't your parents object to the notion of a Hammond beauty performing in public?'

'They're liberal-minded. Besides, her tutor is extremely venerable and trustworthy.'

'How far would Nathaniel Hammond's liberalism extend, if he knew about me, I wonder?'

'He would horse-whip you, Porky dear. He'd have you blackballed from your club.'

'I'm trembling in my boots.' He kissed her hand. 'Adieu, then, my love. Shall I see you again?'

Kitty felt a flicker of apprehension. What if he decided to call an end to their love affair? What if he had already met someone else? She knew that he had embarked on passing affairs with other women in his set, even while writing her love letters from London. Don't grovel, she told herself. Don't ever let him know that you would die for him.

'I can't say. I'll write to you at your club.' With an enigmatic half smile, Kitty watched him walk away towards the railway station.

'You're late! Kitty, where on earth have you been?' Leah, pacing up and down outside the Assembly Rooms, ran to her and seized her by the hand. Kitty could hear the din of the audience in the concert room as she was dragged through the entrance. She glimpsed her mother, standing anxiously in the front row, and the white-haired, alarmingly gnarled figure of Herr Lindau, talking to Sasha by one of the pillars; he looked, Sasha had once said, like a very ancient tree that had been struck by lightning. The analogy was a good one.

Relief lit Mrs Hammond's face, and she bobbed out of sight among the people already seated. There was a note of expectancy in the hum of gossip. The piano gleamed in isolation under the chandeliers. For a moment Kitty envied her sister: the youngest, the brightest, the one who had been given a chance to do more than be a Hammond beauty. Kitty, aware that her looks were her chief asset, perhaps her only passport to a financially comfortable future, told herself with a bitterness that would have astonished Sasha, that life was unfair . . . And then she saw William.

He was standing with her father and had not noticed her arrive. The light from the chandeliers glinted on his hair and threw his face into pleasing angles and shadows, making him look sleek and slightly wicked.

'Hurry *up*!' Leah pushed Kitty into a seat next to Lavinia.

'Where have you been?' hissed Mrs Hammond. 'Everyone's been going frantic. You know how upset Sasha would be if you hadn't come.'

'I had tea with the girls from school. Sophia Mannering wanted to walk to the river, so we came back the long way round. We didn't realise how far we had gone . . .'

She fell silent. Her father and Mr Elliman were walking towards her. Mr Elliman nodded to her, and Kitty's heart missed a beat. How thrilling it was, she thought, seeing the expression in Mr Elliman's eyes. What a sense of power in knowing one could provoke such a look of hunger.

Sasha had never before played for such a large audience. She had given drawing-room performances to biased acclaim, but she had never played for an unfamiliar audience. Of course, they were not all unfamiliar; there was her family, friends of the family and friends of her father, and Miss Holloway and Herr Lindau, and people who knew Herr Lindau here in Bath. She saw him take his place at the end of the front row of seats. He gave her a lopsided smile of reassurance and ran a hand through his thick white hair. He was pinning a lot on her performance, she realised. Next to him was a man with a notebook and pencil. A scout for an impresario? A newspaper reporter?

Fear leaped at Sasha's heart as she walked to the piano; it stood like a black outcrop of rock in the middle of the room. Beyond it, the blur of figures began to agitate their arms and hands and make a clatter of noise. It was some seconds before Sasha realised they were clapping, and that she was the cause of their enthusiasm. She felt sick. The piano would be out of tune – for it was a hot and humid evening. She would strike the opening notes and a horrible cacophony would fill the room. What were the opening notes? Sasha could not remember one bar of the work she had elected to play, nor the one to follow it. Was it the Mendelssohn, or the Chopin polonaise? Had she decided to end with the mazurkas or keep them as an encore?

She reached the piano stool and, with a swift nod and smile to the audience, sat down and stared at the keyboard. A silence fell upon the hall. Sasha's heart thumped in her chest as she flexed her fingers. She raised her hands and the hush deepened behind her. The effect of the silence was calming. She saw only the pattern of the keys in front of her, heard only the rhythm of the music in her head as she began.

Herr Lindau watched her with tears in his eyes. His pupil's playing was bright, dazzling, with a wonderful clarity even in the more difficult Chopin passages. Her absorption, her sincerity and total surrender to the music were very moving. He sighed for a past when he had been motivated by a similar love for music. But he recognised that Sasha was special, and felt a surge of tenderness for the taut figure in the white dress. There was an undercurrent of suppressed passion in her playing; it surfaced now and then and caused a leap of response that set one's emotional nerve ends jangling. The shock of surprise was thrilling for an audience. He had been right to make her include some Beethoven in the programme. He wanted the world to see that there was nothing she could not play.

Sasha did not know whether Herr Lindau was correct when he insisted she had a future as a concert player, but, as the programme came to a close and she stood to receive the applause of the audience, she could believe that such a future might well be a glorious one. She stood, small and wide-eyed, gripping the edge of the piano lid, letting the clamour of applause flow over and through her. It was exhilarating, delicious, the best thing in the world.

William had been invited to the celebrations at the house in Hanover Terrace. He was glad the concert was over. He had sat between Mr Hammond and a fellow who kept grumbling because there were no choruses and no orchestra. William was inclined to agree with him; the distraction of a chorus or two might have alleviated the torture of gazing at the back of Kitty's head and the perfect curve of one ear for two whole hours while her sister performed gymnastics on the piano. Afterwards, amidst all the congratulations, Kitty had seemed to be avoiding him. And then, on the journey back to Bristol to the Hammonds' house, William had been obliged to ride outside on one of the carriages, squashed beside the driver.

He felt his heart beat erratically as the guests drifted in at the doors of Hanover Terrace and up the stairs. In a moment he would be able to speak to Kitty. How would she behave? Would she be cool towards him? Or did Hammond's permission to call on her mean that she had some sympathy for his feelings? In the drawing room, everyone crowded round Sasha. Kitty stood a little apart from her sisters and, bliss, she glanced his way and smiled at him. He started across the room towards her.

'Mr Elliman. Let me introduce you to people.' Mrs Hammond intercepted him and steered him away from perfect happiness towards the open doors of an anteroom where food had been laid out for the guests. He turned and looked for Kitty. The distance between them was widening as Mrs Hammond introduced him first to one person, then another.

'I like to see colour,' she told him as she saw his glance rest on the supper table. 'One should dine with the soul, as much as the stomach, in mind, Mr Elliman. Don't you agree?'

William nodded, swallowing his disquiet; he had never seen such an excess of taste as was laid out on the white damask cloth. He stared at the maidenhair ferns, the flowers and grapes and vine leaves. And the food dishes! The ham and tongue and game, the fish piped with cod's roe; the salads, raised pies, pineapples, blancmanges, fruit compotes and pyramids of glazed pears. He was appalled by the fact that the display would have fed a whole street in Penbury for a week.

He could see Kitty in the drawing room; she was smiling with her head arched back, revealing her white throat and neck. A long-haired young man, who looked like an artist,

42

had drawn out his pocket book for her to write in. The party consisted chiefly of musical and artistic people, William realised. He felt himself to be a fish out of water and said as much to Mrs Hammond. She gave him an enigmatic smile, but said nothing to reassure him. After a few introductions, she left him with Herr Lindau and drifted away to talk to Miss Holloway. Did she really find that dried-up spinster's company preferable to his? The possibility that she did was a considerable blow to William's self-esteem.

'Do you play an instrument, Mr Elliman?' said Sasha's music tutor, looking at William expectantly. He had piercing blue eyes, a terrifying guttural accent, and a mop of thick, yellowish-white hair that William found embarrassing; so much hair seemed immoderate in a man of Lindau's years.

William admitted reluctantly that he did not play an instrument. He bit back the qualification that he sang a little.

Herr Lindau cleared his throat. A silence fell between them. The tutor looked irritably at the ceiling, as if searching there for a topic of conversation.

William, looking for an escape, saw – salvation – that Sasha had entered the dining room.

Not even William's obvious preference for Kitty could spoil Sasha's own happiness that evening. Fired by the brilliance of the music and the acclaim of so many people, she had decided she would be satisfied with nothing less than to become an international pianist.

Herr Lindau put an arm round her shoulders and said in his heavily accented way, 'This is my little genius, Mr Elliman. Not my pupil – my inspiration. She is going to be very famous one day.'

William smiled indulgently. 'I expect that's because she practises hard.'

'Discipline and practice do not make a genius, Mr Elliman. Merely a very proficient pianist. Sasha is that rare creature, a natural musician. It is a gift from the gods.'

'Herr Lindau exaggerates dreadfully,' said Sasha, laughing. 'Simply because I've had a good audience today.'

'And have met some very useful people. Introductions, Mr Elliman. A musician thrives on them.'

Sasha asked William about his survey in Penbury: was the work very exciting? What influence did he think it would have? How soon did he expect changes to take place? She was restless and bubbling over with her success. Herr Lindau waved an airy hand and walked away at the mention of sanitary reports.

'It's all a matter of getting things moving,' William said. 'The townspeople want reform. They can see it happening in other places – proper drains, clean streets, water companies, and they want it to happen in Penbury.'

Kitty was approaching. As she joined them, William continued more enthusiastically, 'I'm beginning to think those who are agitating for municipal reform *before* they attend to public health matters have the right idea. Nothing will change in Penbury until they have an effective town council. It seems no one will take responsibility for any decisions. For instance, the whole town is at present served by wells, which in most cases rely on land-soak. You can imagine – with all the emanations from the factories – that's a terrible situation for some parts of the town! It's a wonder typhoid hasn't killed off the entire working population. Or alcohol poisoning, since beer is the only fit substance to drink.'

'Good heavens!' said Kitty languidly. Sasha was pleased to see her stifle a yawn.

Kitty turned to Sasha. 'Oh – by the way. Mother wants us to play together for everyone. Do go and choose something, Sasha.'

'Oh, please do!' echoed William.

Kitty gave Sasha a meaningful look that said, go away and leave us alone.

Sasha hesitated. 'I shall choose something with an infernally difficult cello part,' she said in a low voice and walked away.

'She's jealous,' explained Kitty.

'Jealous?' William watched Sasha's retreating figure and shook his head in bewilderment.

'Because – you numbskull – my little sister has fallen in love with you, and yet you so obviously prefer me.' Kitty was laughing. She put a hand to her mouth to hide it. The gesture and the look in her eyes were very appealing.

'Your father spoke to you?' William said eagerly, feeling his face grow hot.

'He said you wanted to call on me. It sounded very quaint. "Sweet", Sasha would say. I am right? That is how you put it? You wish to call?'

'If that would be agreeable to you . . .'

'Oh, very agreeable, Mr Elliman.'

'Then I might visit you whenever I'm in Bristol?'

'You may. But right now I must join my sisters.' She laughed and added in a confidential voice, 'I hope you know what you're taking on.'

'You're not going to encourage that fellow, are you?' said Miss Holloway, scurrying across the dining room after Kitty.

'And why not, Holly dear?' Kitty paused.

'Because he isn't good enough for you. That's why. You're so fine, and cultivated, and sensitive and lovely . . . and he's so common and unrefined. Truly, I don't know what Mr Hammond is thinking of.'

'My father doesn't think, Holly. He simply follows his heart when it comes to his waifs and strays.'

'So you're not interested in Mr Elliman?'

'Did I say that?'

'Oh – Miss Kitty,' Miss Holloway wailed.

Kitty sighed. 'Holly. You surely don't think Mr Elliman intends anything serious after such a very slender acquaintance?'

Miss Holloway was confused. 'No?'

'No. Mr Elliman simply wants to be our friend.'

'Well, yes . . .' The governess was reassured a little. 'And, after all, he has no money.'

'Oh, his wealth, or lack of it, would make no difference, Holly . . . *if* I were to fall in love with him. Father believes only in love-matches. And so do I.'

'But—'

'Holly. I'm growing tired of this conversation. In fact, I really think you should mind your own business. Do, please, go away.'

Miss Holloway flushed scarlet. She walked away with as much dignity as she could muster. Her jaws and throat ached with the effort of not bursting into tears after being spoken to in that cold, sarcastic way. She did not care what any of them said. It wasn't right, encouraging a man to call. They could talk until they were blue in the face about platonic friendships between the sexes and not being prejudiced about class. If a man came calling regularly on a houseful of unmarried women, it could only mean one thing.

The girls played Sasha's arrangements of Mendelssohn for the Hammonds' guests with a poignancy that suggested a swansong. Afterwards Lavinia was in tears, sensitive to the emotion that flowed between the sisters whenever they played together. She did not know that the others felt as strongly, that not even Kitty could ignore the power of the music uniting and carrying them along.

'I am so proud of you. I'm proud of all my daughters.' Nathaniel threw his arms round Lavinia and Kitty. His eyes were moist with sentiment as he turned to his youngest child and pulled her forward to stand before their guests. 'But tonight, Sasha, you are the very brightest star in my personal heaven.'

Everyone applauded. The women dabbed at their eyes with handkerchiefs. Sasha leaned her head against her father's shoulder and felt her heart swell so full with love that she thought it would burst wide open.

Leah said with a generous laugh, 'How can we play our chamber pieces with you after today, Sasha? You'll soon become too grand for us altogether.'

'Oh, but we must,' Sasha said in distress. 'We *must*

46

always play our music together. We've *always* played together. Ever since I was little. Promise me.' She looked round wildly at the others. 'Promise that however famous, or old, or however grand *any* of us get, nothing will ever change.'

Lavinia promised willingly.

'Sasha, you know that's a crazy sort of promise,' Leah said gently.

'You've got to. You too, Kitty.'

So they promised, because everyone was waiting and because the sisters did not want to distress Sasha. But they all knew that the changes had already begun.

Sasha lay on her bed, hearing the sounds of the last of her father's friends leaving the house. She listened as the clock on the landing struck two, oddly dissatisfied now that the evening was over. She was muddled by her feelings. She had felt miserable and humiliated because Mr Elliman was in love with Kitty. And yet, she had almost despised him for being in love when he so obviously had more important matters – the poor and deprived townspeople of Penbury – to concern him.

She could hear Kitty snoring faintly. Would Mr Elliman be so devoted if he knew his beloved snorted like a pig? She wished her sister had choked at supper and spoiled her so elegant image. She amused herself by imagining Kitty's face swelling up and turning bright puce, and Mr Elliman watching, repelled. On the other hand, being a medical man, he might decide to rescue the choking victim. Sasha had seen a lady choke on a piece of meat at a dinner party once, and a doctor had jumped up and unlaced her corset. With everyone looking on! It had all been very exciting. Sasha imagined that if Mr Elliman were to unlace Kitty he might enjoy the experience, however revolting the circumstances.

Sasha got out of bed, opened the window quietly and sat on the sill. She could see lights on the river, and those of the town all down the hill. Herr Lindau had spoken to her parents that evening about doing a musical tour in the

47

North. She tried to imagine how it would be, far away from her family, from everything that was familiar, and from all hope of ever attracting Mr Elliman's attention. She would live only for her music.

She leaned her head against the wall, and a longing swept over her that she could not define. The same fitful yearning affected her sometimes when she played the piano, when she felt as if she were striving towards some hidden revelation in the music, and she knew she would never be satisfied unless she discovered it. Surely she could not be haunted merely by a desire for Mr Elliman to love her, and yet, she knew that Mr Elliman was connected with her discontent. If she found love, and was loved in return, would it compensate for that other longing, the craving in her soul for something beyond her reach?

She glanced down at the square and wished she were free to wander out there in the darkness, up and down the streets under the gas lamps and along the river – like the women one never talked about, not even in conversations about drains. But Sasha knew there would be nothing exciting, nor even free about being a woman of the night. A *whore*. There, she had thought the word aloud. Now the devil would come to take her away.

Most of all, she felt an urge to play her piano. She wished she could fly downstairs to the drawing room that minute and lose her restlessness in the solace of music, but she would wake the household. Her mother would think she was sick, or tell her she was inconsiderate. Besides, it *was* inconsiderate to wake the servants when they had already been obliged to stay up late. She closed the window and went back to bed.

'I'm afraid for Sasha after tonight,' Mrs Hammond told her husband as he climbed into bed beside her. 'Should we be encouraging Lindau's ambitions for her?'

'Don't you want her to develop her gift?'

'Yes. Of course. We must use the talents the good Lord gave us. But life is so hard on women who are blessed with a strong intellect or artistic talents.'

'Are you trying to tell me you regret giving up your painting?'

'No,' she quickly reassured him. 'I was glad to.' She silenced his doubts, pressing her lips against his. 'Glad to model for you and to become a dormant star in your personal heaven. I always knew you must shine the brightest. Besides, I could never have been more than a mediocre painter of flower gardens and landscapes. But I worry about Sasha. She's such a reckless child, so careless, so . . . immature. Yet, when she plays, there's something unearthly about her. It's almost as if she becomes the music. How is she going to reconcile herself to combining her love for the piano with marriage?'

'She's young. There's plenty of time.'

Nathaniel could never understand why women always had to create difficulties about everything. Their minds were too much at liberty to think up imaginary crises that the men in their lives were supposed to deal with. A pleasant feeling of superiority settled in him. He felt desire stir for his wife and he pulled her towards him.

'But what about when she's older?' Mrs Hammond persisted. 'She's not going to stay sixteen for ever. Will she be content, when she meets someone, to give it all up? Or will she try to divide her life between a musical career and marriage? Don't you see the dilemma, Nathaniel? What if she should have to forgo marriage and all the domestic pleasures?'

She stroked Nathaniel's neck as he moved against her. He had already, some seconds ago, stopped listening to her. She sighed and let her tenderness for him take precedence; but, though her body responded to him as always, a corner of her mind remained detached and continued to worry.

Chapter Three

Kitty paced the floor of the hotel room in Bath and waited for Porky. He was invariably late. He expected her to wait. People in his circle always waited for him, those friends and hangers-on who hoped the glitter of his reputation might rub off on them a little.

Kitty had never been intimidated by his literary fame as others were. He said he admired her lack of reverence, but she suspected he wanted her to be in awe of him. 'I like you for yourself,' she had told him. 'Not for what the world thinks of you.'

'That's as well,' he had replied. 'For half the world would not hesitate to call me a rude name or two.'

And they would be right, Kitty thought, glancing at the time by her fob-watch. And anyway, why should she respect him, merely because he had written half a dozen novels? Her own father had a more satisfactory reputation among cultivated circles; and her sister was about to make a name for herself as a musician. She thought for a moment with envy about Sasha's career. At least Sasha was going to escape. Kitty longed for a similar chance to travel – even if it *was* only to Manchester or Leeds.

She sat on the bed and glanced again at her watch. She would give him two more minutes and then she was leaving. She stared at the pattern of the carpet; it was cheap and nasty, and there was a burn mark near the fire, where a hot cinder had made a hole. She wished they could meet somewhere less seedy than a third-rate hotel every month. 'It's not that I'm being stingy, old thing,' Porky had said. 'But, anywhere more salubrious and someone might recognise me, even in Bath.' Kitty wished he did not have a wife. She wished. Oh – but where would be the fun in it? Kitty had enough self-knowledge to realise that much of Porky's attraction rested in his unavailability.

She heard footsteps on the stairs and stiffened, watching the door handle. Deliberately, she did not go to greet him when he entered.

'You're late. I was on the point of leaving.'

'I'm sorry, my precious, precious girl – abject apologies. I bumped into someone. I didn't want to raise their suspicions.'

'You could simply have said you had an appointment. There's nothing very suspicious about that.'

'True. But, you know how it is. We got chatting.'

No, I don't know how it is, Kitty thought. When she knew she was going to see him, every minute that held her up filled her with a savage impatience. She could not have chatted pleasantly on the street as if she were on her way to some vague engagement. He bent to kiss her, and she turned her mouth away and offered him her cheek.

'You'll be late once too often, Porky darling.'

He brushed her face with his lips. 'You don't mean that.'

'Oh, don't I? I have an admirer.' She was determined to needle him.

He smiled. 'My darling. You don't know your own attractions. I'm sure you have a thousand admirers in Bristol.'

'I mean, this one's serious. He has practically asked my father if he might court me.'

'And—?' He took off his hat and gloves and pulled the fingers straight before laying them on a chair.

She shrugged. 'And I have said he might.'

He raised his eyebrows, then came to her again and kissed her, holding her jaw with one hand so that she could not move and letting his mouth linger.

'I thought I might encourage him.'

He drew back a little and looked at her quizzically. 'Kitty? Are you by any chance trying to tell me something I should be taking seriously?'

'I'm tired,' Kitty said sulkily. 'Tired of all this hiding. I want to be with you all the time. Oh, Porky – why can't we run away together?'

'Don't be ridiculous.'

Kitty smarted under his look of amazed contempt. She wondered whether sometimes she hated him almost as much as she loved him. She could put an end to all this so easily. Ditch Porky, and harness Mr Elliman. The idea was not unattractive.

Porky was thoughtful. 'You know, this admirer of yours could prove rather useful. In fact – it's excellent! The perfect decoy to draw everyone off the scent.' He got up to hang his coat on a hook behind the door. 'You must capture him. Captivate, cultivate him.'

'Aren't you even a little bit put out?'

'Should I be?'

'He's very handsome.'

'In that case, I am passionately jealous, my darling.' He came back to the bed and flung himself down on his back beside her, smiling up at her. 'Where does the fellow live? Who are his people? I shall challenge him to a duel tomorrow. No. This evening. Tell me the blackguard's name.'

'Elliman.' She laughed. 'He's compiling a report in Penbury for the General Board of Health. It's all very boring and respectable.'

'The cunning devil. He must know I can't compete with a *respectable* occupation.'

She bent and kissed him, wishing that for once he would say something tender and kind, instead of pulling her down beside him. He kissed her more intimately and began to search among her skirts. She tried to imagine Mr Elliman's style of courtship, and knew that it would be earnest and affectionate, and that she would despise him for his consideration of her feelings.

52

Porky dragged back her petticoats over her thighs and whispered, 'Open your legs. I want to know what you're like from waiting for me so long. Mouthwateringly mossy, meltingly moist.'

She lay back on the pillow and with a gasp of pleasure he found the place quickly. 'Oh – my little muzpot!' His fingers slipped into her with scarcely a hesitation. She closed her eyes as her sexual agitation grew stronger. Mr Elliman would fumble, she told herself, and deliberately crushed the image of him as a lover. He would puff and pant and groan, taking his own pleasure, and then apologise for violating her. Porky was always leisurely in his lovemaking, and the notion of violation would not have occurred to him. He was skilled at knowing how to please her, knew that women *could* be pleased as powerfully as men. He had taught her so much in the months she had know him. She stopped thinking and let herself travel with the rhythms of her body as the sexual part of her being took over from her mind's consciousness.

Later, as they lay side by side and watched the afternoon shadows on the ceiling, he turned to her and said, 'Will you be here again tomorrow?'

'I can't.' She tried to sound indifferent. 'Father wants us all to sit for a portrait. I have to be at home.'

'Oh, Kitty.' He leaned on one elbow, tender at last, lifting her hair away from her face. 'My cruel Kitty. What frustrations you put in my way. Here am I. Free for a whole three days and you have to sit in front of your father's canvas.'

'Perhaps I could meet you later . . .'

'I hope you will.' His voice hardened. 'I hope you will, Kitty, because I can't afford to waste *my* time hanging about in hotel rooms if you are not going to turn up.' He sat up and began to dress.

'Porky. Be reasonable.'

He stood by the fireplace, fastening his shirt buttons, watching her, but without speaking.

'Promise me you'll be nice to Mr Elliman.'

'I might be nicer than you think.' Kitty watched him

53

dress, wanting to beg him to make love to her again. 'I *might* decide not to turn up at all.'

'Don't be silly, my precious girl.' He came back to her and kissed her. 'We don't want to spoil all this, do we?'

Nathaniel Hammond's studio was on the top floor of the house in Hanover Terrace. It was a large, draughty room with several sky-lights; the stove at the centre of the floor barely took the chill from the air. 'It's not good to be too warm when one is working,' Nathaniel maintained. Normally the kindest of men, he had scant regard for his sitters once he had embarked on a painting, though he would have been horrified to know that they were suffering.

The girls did not complain. They recognised the need for stoicism, and that their own comfort must come second to the requirements of their father's genius.

Sasha was flanked by Kitty and Lavinia. Leah stood behind them, leaning inwards as if to read over Sasha's shoulder the book spread on her lap. Sasha looked at the blur of text. It was a volume of poetry. Appropriately – for symbolism was apparently important to the painting – the book lay open at Tennyson's 'A Dream of Fair Women', a catalogue of women who had made their mark on history. And had caused considerable mayhem in the process, thought Sasha. Had their father looked beyond the title for his choice? Sasha wondered which of the 'Fair Women' she might be. Cleopatra, Queen of the Nile, spirited, powerful, who went all to pieces when she fell in love? Or Helen of Troy – beautiful, sensual, fair, with lots of suitors? On the whole, she thought she would rather be Helen. The poisonous asp was a distinct obstacle to the role of Cleopatra. Kitty, of course, would have to be Iphigenia, marked out by her father for sacrifice to Mr Elliman. Sasha smothered a laugh. She saw her father frown.

'Are you bored, Sasha?'

'No, Father.'

He stepped back from the easel. At the same time they

heard the sound of people on the stairs. 'Ah – I had forgotten to tell you. That will be your mother with our young friend.'

Sasha's heart gave a violent leap. She knew that her father had offered an invitation to Mr Elliman to look in on a sitting. She had thought she was almost cured of her feelings for him since the concert, but her heart began to pound at the sound of his voice in the corridor, and she was overwhelmed by a melancholy hope that he might notice she was central to the composition of the portrait.

Nathaniel went to the door. 'Come in, my dear fellow. You've arrived at the perfect moment. The girls are in need of someone to relieve the tedium of sitting.'

'I have never known my daughters remain still for so long, Mr Elliman,' said Mrs Hammond. 'Don't you agree my husband has discovered the most splendid idea for keeping an eye on them?'

'A splendid idea altogether,' said William.

'You notice, Mr Elliman, it is the younger ones who are seated,' said Leah. 'My father has no ideas about age before beauty.'

William, confused by notions of chivalry, declared heartily, 'You *all* look very lovely.'

'Flattery, Mr Elliman, will go a long way to easing our aches and pains,' smiled Lavinia.

'At the moment, I need all the girls together,' Nathaniel said. 'Until the painting has set in my mind, you understand. Soon I shall be able to work without needing them all in the studio at once, but for now . . .' He returned his attention to the canvas.

Mrs Hammond smiled and with a finger to her lips bowed discreetly out from the studio. William, feeling abandoned, and excluded from his host's thoughts, decided to take a seat. He smiled at Sasha, who smiled back at him eagerly. He hardly dared trust himself to look at Kitty's figure in the clinging, muslin gown, but Kitty seemed to want to engage his attention.

'We haven't seen you since the concert, Mr Elliman. Have you been very much occupied by your report?'

'I fear I have, Miss Hammond,' he said quickly. 'There is a fair amount of pen-pushing, as well as visiting the various institutions.'

'Do you inspect schools and hospitals?'

'And factories, Poor Law Unions and the like.' He leaned forward, turning his hat in his hands. 'Yesterday, I was investigating the possibilities for a public water supply.'

'I am sure you win converts by your enthusiasm,' said Kitty softly.

Sasha looked at her in amazement. Why could no one else see that Kitty was being utterly, sickeningly false?

'I hope your converts are prompted by their own consciences, Mr Elliman, as much as by your own undoubted enthusiasm,' said Leah. 'For when you're gone, who will inspire the townspeople to carry out the reforms you hope for?'

'Ah – but it could well be I shall not leave Penbury after all when my report is ended,' William said energetically.

His thoughts returned to Penbury and to pleasant conversations with Wotherspoon; he recalled the dinners at Wotherspoon's house, the comfortable evenings over a glass or two of fine old port. 'I'll be plain with you, Elliman,' Wotherspoon had said. 'If this town gets an elected council and I am made mayor, I shall support you one hundred per cent in every public health reform you can think of. There! That's a promise. I'll go further. I'll see you set up in one of the best practices in Penbury.'

William had laughed. 'I'm not a wealthy enough man to buy into a prosperous practice.'

'Ways and means, dear fellow.'

Had it been a bribe? Not so obvious as Scrope's attempts perhaps, nevertheless . . .

'Think of the possibilities,' Wotherspoon had added. 'You could have a place on a local board of public health. You would personally oversee the reforms. Instead of going back to London, you would be sure that Penbury was engaged in the hard work necessary. Everyone here would have a sense of dedication, because you would be one of us, Elliman, a Penbury practitioner.'

Could it be called a bribe, when the town would benefit from all the advantages he was pressing for? If he recommended borough status, the town would get its public water supply, well-regulated markets, clean streets, sewerage and drains . . . and Wotherspoon as mayor. William dismissed his unease. A strong mayor and a vigorous council was exactly what Penbury needed.

He glanced at Kitty. 'It's possible that a practice in the town, a very thriving and well-paying practice, could become available – should I decide to settle in Penbury.'

'But how wonderful!' said Lavinia. 'Isn't it, everybody?'

'Yes . . . wonderful,' agreed Kitty.

William searched her face for the delight he had hoped for when he had imagined how he would tell them about his good fortune. Hammond looked up from his easel and tipped back his smoking cap. 'Capital! Capital news.'

'It means waiting for the present incumbent to retire, but . . .' William shrugged, to show that this was a minor obstacle.

'You will have seen many discouraging sights in the course of your work, Mr Elliman,' said Lavinia.

'Yes, Miss Hammond. I have. I wouldn't want to burden you with them, but dirt and poverty are a terrible scourge on our towns and cities.'

Kitty said with a yawn, 'I often wish we could do something to help alleviate the suffering of the poor.'

'Perhaps you can.' Nathaniel looked up from his painting. 'You know, I was listening to some poor fellow scraping away at a fiddle the night I decided on this portrait, and it occurred to me what little opportunity the poor have to take their minds off their unhappy circumstances – to see good paintings or to hear good music.'

'You mean you might put on an exhibition of your paintings in Penbury?' said Kitty.

'No! Father means a concert!' said Sasha. 'We could play our music for the poor people of the town.'

'Exactly!' Nathaniel turned to William. 'What do you say?'

Kitty looked briefly appalled. But William was already warming to the idea. He imagined showing Kitty the more attractive features of Penbury, the good houses at the top of the town, winning her over to the idea of living there.

'An excellent suggestion!' he exclaimed. 'I've already thought of a venue! Penbury has some decent-sized schoolrooms. I could arrange transport for you all. And for your instruments. But I don't know about a piano, Miss Sasha.'

'We will arrange for a piano to be transported,' said Nathaniel.

'I think it's a very beautiful idea,' said Lavinia. 'You'll arrange a suitable programme, Sasha?'

'Oh, yes.' Sasha looked at William and her heart gave a bound. His gratitude was written in his eyes, and, in that brief moment, his eyes were locked on hers. Her voice dried with emotion.

'I shall put my heart and soul into organising a programme.'

William could not get Kitty out of his mind on the journey back to Penbury. Had she been pleased by his chance of a permanent move to the area? It was so hard to tell what she was thinking. She had not exactly leaped for joy at her father's idea of putting on a concert in Penbury. What if Kitty were to decide she did not want to be a doctor's wife?

He had already made up his mind to propose to her. It was only a matter of time, a decent period of courtship, before he would ask her to be his wife. And, with the prospect of a medical practice in his pocket, that courtship might not have to be too lengthy.

He was glad to see that the square was almost empty as he climbed from the coach outside the Neptune. Scrope had been in the habit of coming to the inn in the evenings to ask how his investigations were progressing, hovering in the parlour and plying him with drink.

William went straight to his room, unwilling to risk Scrope waylaying him. He looked at the neat pages of notes and questionnaires on the desk by his bed; they listed in detail his observations about the insanitary courts and alleys in the town: the constant presence of fever, the absence of effective sewerage and the lack of good water. His work here would be over by Christmas. He thought of Scrope's veiled threats of writing to the General Board of Health to the effect that he was ignoring the excellent work of the overseers; that he was in the pay of Wotherspoon to make a bad case against them. There was some truth in the accusation, thought William, and his conscience troubled him again. As well as the invitations to Wotherspoon's home, there had been offers of the use of his carriage, and a gift of six pairs of very fine kid gloves.

Scrope had pointed out issues for him to raise in his survey, jabbing the table with his finger. 'Put that in your report. Tell them we appointed a surveyor to deal with obstructions and for scraping the streets. I don't think you understand the situation, Mr Elliman. Now, if you would let me add some particulars. Drains, for instance. We've covered over the drains with paving. Oh yes. They were *all* open before the committee took a hand.'

Never mind that the paving had fallen in, that the broken paving slabs had blocked the sewers and prevented them from working. Never mind that nobody had directed anyone to repair them . . . But it was all there in William's notes, the negligence, the idleness of the overseers.

There were notes too on William's inspection of Wotherspoon's workers' cottages; he had been appalled by the cramped living quarters. When he had pointed out the poor quality of the cottages, Wotherspoon had agreed without embarrassment. 'I regret the haste in which they were built, my dear friend. But I intend to make improvements. Don't worry about that. When we have a new corporation, Elliman, all these matters will be dealt with. But one step at a time. Rome wasn't built in a day.'

William looked down at the orderly pile of papers. He believed Wotherspoon's good intentions, but what were

Wotherspoon's chances of becoming mayor if names were named and the damning pages about the sub-standard cottages went into the report? He sifted through his notes and read them again. He weighed the pages in his hand. With Wotherspoon as mayor and himself as principal physician, reforms would be underway in no time. What a team they would make, working to make Penbury a model town! And Kitty would be his wife, would grace his house, ride in his carriage beside him. All in all, didn't he owe Wotherspoon something?

He was thoughtful for a moment longer, then he tore the pages on the cottages in half, and again in quarters, and put them on the fire.

'Elliman!' Brewer shook William's hand. 'How is your report progressing? I haven't seen you for weeks.'

'I've been heavily engaged in Bristol,' said William, swinging his cane over his shoulder, and falling into step beside the newspaper editor. What a fine November day it was, with the last of the leaves shining pale gold in the sunshine, and the smell of bonfires, factory chimneys and a touch of frost in the air. 'To tell the truth, Brewer, I expect to be even more heavily *engaged* there in the future.'

'A young lady?'

'Oh, Brewer! The most enchanting you ever saw.' William had a strong urge to confide in a friend. He wanted Brewer to share in the pleasure of knowing Kitty, to understand how he was feeling. 'And you shall meet her. That's the joy of it. She and her sisters have promised to play in Penbury in a Christmas charity concert! They are all four talented musicians. You must save a page in the *Gazette* for a report.'

Brewer smiled at his enthusiasm. 'And what about your own report?'

'Almost finished.' William hesitated. 'I've decided to make a strong recommendation for the town to be granted municipal status. The right men in positions of power. It's the only way forward.'

Brewer regarded him more thoughtfully. 'Are you sure about this?'

'Never more sure of anything.'

'Well, then. You're the expert.' They had reached the office of the *Gazette*. Brewer again shook his hand. 'I look forward to meeting your lady musicians. As for borough status . . . I'm behind you, Elliman. And so is the paper. I'll prepare a piece for this week's edition. We'll fight this campaign together.'

The landlord of the Neptune knocked at William's door that afternoon and handed him a letter. It was from his sister, and was very short and to the point:

'You must come home, Will. Father is very ill. Best not take too long about it. Your devoted sister, Lily Elliman.'

William was in London by the following morning.

His father's apothecary shop stood at the corner of a row of terraced workmen's cottages, bridging a space between respectable artisan housing and the kind of London streets that Dickens had already made infamous in his novels. William had read Dickens's stories in his youth: *Oliver Twist* had gone some way towards influencing his early aspirations to do something about the living conditions of the very poor.

Here, as much as anywhere, was a need for reform, William thought, as he turned into the yard and caught the smell of privies on the night air. On the other hand, he did not necessarily want to make great strides for the future of mankind on his own doorstep. The realisation of how little improvement had been made in the years since men like Chadwick had been pointing out a need for reform depressed him in a general way; but, more particularly, he was affected by a personal sense of hopelessness. However much he mixed with the Wotherspoons or the Hammonds of this world, William knew he would never escape his roots here, among the dingy bricks and the communal courts and alleys that had been so much a part of his childhood.

He paused at the back door. Was he out of his mind to

think he might ever marry Kitty Hammond? What if the family were only being kind by inviting him to the house and with all their talk of putting on a concert in Penbury? A terrible thought struck him. Did the Hammonds view *him* as a charity case?

Lily was in the kitchen. Her dress was dark and plain, as if she were in mourning. She would have taken pleasure in wearing true mourning, thought William. She was probably hoping for a good funeral after their father was gone.

'So, you got my letter.' Lily spoke in a hoarse whisper, the words coming out in bursts, as if she had temporarily lost control of them, though she tried manfully to maintain a grip. She returned her attention to pouring mixture from a bottle into a bowl of hot water. There *was* something oddly masculine about her, despite her frail physique, thought William. She held herself very erect. Her thick, prematurely greying hair was scraped into a knot. And there was an almost military air in the way she always barked out her whispered comments.

'I came as soon as I could.'

'Well, he's worse.'

'If he took fewer of his own remedies he might feel a lot better,' William said bluntly.

'Now don't you start despising the shop the minute you've come home. Not when it's fed and clothed you all these years.'

'They're quack cures and you know it.'

'Learned that at the university, did we?'

'There's nothing in there to do him any good,' William protested.

'Nor harm, neither. So, it won't make any difference if he takes them, will it?' She picked up the bowl, ignoring William as he opened the door to the stairs for her.

He stood with his hand on the edge of the door. 'Welcome home, Will. It's nice to be back, Lily,' he murmured.

He considered going up to see his father. He could hear

62

Lily talking in the room above and the old man's grumbling reply. He closed the door to shut out the sound.

His father had been very bitter about his work for the General Board of Health. He had never wanted him to study surgery, had always expected him to take on the shop after getting his licence from the Apothecaries' Society. Most of all, his father resented the fact that William's mother's side of the family, the Sparrows, had paid for his education. It couldn't have been easy for Grandfather Sparrow to keep paying his fees, William realised. He put the kettle on the stove, telling himself he ought to be more grateful. He ought at least to have visited his grandfather and Aunt Georgie from time to time. Told them his plans. Let them know he was aware that he owed everything to their generosity. He ought too to be more compassionate towards his own father. He ought. He ought. He was full of good intentions and guilty omissions.

He picked up the empty medicine bottle from the table and read the label: 'Elliman's Antibilious Mixture. For foulness of the stomach and bowels.'

Lily came downstairs again. She had her coat and Sunday bonnet in her arms.

William held the bottle to the light. 'What's in it? Crabs' eyes and dried snakes' skins?'

'He believes in it. That's what matters.'

William considered telling her now about the chance of a general practice in Penbury. He was half afraid of her sarcasm. Lily had always been sceptical about his ambitions. 'Anybody can be clean and decent if they make the effort,' she had once said. 'It doesn't take legislation and commissions and medical boards.'

'You're off to Chapel?' He watched her tuck her hair out of sight under her bonnet.

'I can, now you're here.'

She ought to have been a widow, he thought. She would have enjoyed that. Never a wife, of course. But widowhood would have given Lily the kind of status she had always wanted; there was a dignity about it that did not come so readily with spinsterhood. Widows evoked sympathy. There was little about Lily to evoke a natural sympathy.

'I'm going to work in Somerset permanently,' he said, watching her expression in the mirror. She stared at him open-mouthed, and William felt his nerve fail him. 'There's a practice near Bristol. Someone's retiring soon.'

'So, you've become too high and mighty for people round here, now you've got your doctor's letters after your name.'

'It's not like that at all. It's a tremendous opportunity to do some good in the world.'

'Rubbish! You're leaving us behind, Will. Getting on. It's got nothing to do with good works.' She marched out of the parlour into the shop and began banging jars of liniment and boxes of pills around, pretending to tidy them on the shelves.

William followed her. He thought of the Hammonds in Hanover Terrace, and the picture of genteel living clashed with that of his father's apothecary shop. It made him want to weep.

'Why did you write? Why send for *me* because he's sick? What do you want me to do about it?'

'You could try behaving like a son instead of looking down on him.'

'I don't look down on anyone – but he's a quack. You must have known I wouldn't stay here for always. Even Father must have known that.'

'Who's going to go on minding the shop when he's gone? Who's going to pick up the pieces after?'

William looked at her in horror. He had never in his life seen Lily cry, but she was crying now. Her mouth expelled ugly, harsh sobs, and her nose was running. He gave her his handkerchief. She blew her nose loudly and handed it back.

'I think you've been very selfish, William,' she said with dignity, turning away from him to pick up a bottle from one of the shelves. She shook it furiously until he was afraid the cork would fly out and spray the shop with

Elliman's Antibilious Mixture. She pushed the bottle into his hands. 'Here. Take this up to him. He wants it neat.'

His father lay with his hands gripping the bedcovers against his chest as if he were afraid someone might steal them from him. His heavy face looked waxy and yellow. The smell in the room was fetid and his nightshirt had dark stains down the front. He showed no emotion on seeing William. 'She said you were back.'

'She's gone to Chapel to pray for your soul. You'll have to make do with me for company.' William put the medicine bottle on the table beside the bed and instinctively moved away. 'How are you feeling?'

'I'm dying.'

William looked at him uneasily. He went to the window, opening it a crack. 'You need some air in here.'

'You can shut that again. Don't think I don't know those tricks.'

William closed the window. 'The room needs air.'

'You're after the shop when I'm gone.'

'If you must know – it would be very inconvenient for me right now if you're planning on dying.'

William felt his control begin to slip. That was all he needed. To start shouting at a dying man. What sort of a physician would he make if he could not even practise his bedside manner on his own father? He lowered his voice to a reassuring tone. 'I'm sorry. I'm very sorry things have got worse.'

A spasm of pain made the old man wince. He gestured to the medicine bottle, and William poured some into a glass and held it for him to take a sip. His father lapsed into grim contemplation. 'Who's going to look after Lily when I'm gone?'

'She can look after herself. She'll have the shop. She can sell groceries or something.'

'I'm leaving the shop to you.' He ignored William's protest. 'I want you to promise me something. I'm not much longer for this world . . . No.' He silenced him. 'I can feel it this time. And Lily knows it. Promise me you won't get so much above yourself that you won't look after her. I mean – you'll take her in. There's no one else. Lily hasn't got a head for the business. She won't be able to manage.'

'Nonsense. She's as tough as . . .'

'I mean it.' He sank back into the pillow. 'I shouldn't rest easy six feet under if I thought you would let the workhouse take her.'

'Of course it won't come to that.'

'You're not to abandon her!'

William promised. He sat with his father until the old man fell asleep, and then went to the inn at the end of the street for his dinner. The fact that his father was dying, was leaving him the apothecary shop, threw out ripples of hope in his mind; he calculated the value of the business. He would be a man of *property*. If he had some capital behind him, he would be in a position at once to ask for Kitty's hand.

When he returned to the house Lily met him at the door. Her face was puffy, as if she had been crying again. 'Where were you? You should have waited for me to come back from Chapel.'

'He was asleep,' William said.

'Well, he isn't asleep now.' Her face puckered and she fell back against the kitchen wall. 'You couldn't even be there!'

William stared at her. 'He can't have . . . I was talking to him only an hour since.'

Lily was trembling. She clenched her hands against her breast as if forcibly restraining herself from hitting him. 'You . . .! Call yourself a doctor!'

'A sad day, William.' Grandfather Sparrow and Aunt Georgie had travelled from Norfolk for the funeral. 'I suppose I shall be the next. We have to face these things. In the midst of life . . . Yes, boy. It's true enough.'

'Lily's put on an impressive tea,' said William, desperate for something cheerful to say.

'She's a good girl,' their grandfather acknowledged.

66

William tried to think of Lily as a girl. She had always looked as she looked now, a middle-aged spinster; she had never been out of black since their mother had died six years earlier. What would Lily do now? He remembered his promise to his father that he would look after her. The old man need not have worried. Lily could certainly look after herself. He watched her tight, dried-up figure scurry to and from the kitchen with a huge teapot in her hands. She was bearing up, enjoying being at the centre of things.

'Lily's had a cross to bear all these years,' said Grandfather Sparrow with a shake of his head.

William scanned the parlour for his Aunt Georgie, unwilling to dwell on Lily's sacrifices. His aunt was only a few years older than Lily, and of the two, she looked the younger. Small and round-shouldered, she twisted nervously at her fingers and chatted to the woman next to her with timid movements of her head; the little exertions threatened to topple her frizz of curls, fastened with numerous pins and combs. She caught William's eye and bustled towards him, black ribbons flying and her shawl trailing in her wake.

He kissed her. She smelled of soap and camphorated oil. 'Aunt Georgie.'

'I'm pleased to hear you're doing so well for yourself these days, William. So, when are you going to find yourself a wife?'

She laughed, and covered her mouth with her hand in a gesture that reminded him oddly of Kitty. He remembered his mother saying that Aunt Georgie had been pretty and flirtatious as a girl. She had been the youngest in her family and was obliged to look after her father when the others left home. He imagined how she must have watched her chances of marriage slip by; and he wondered which of the beautiful Hammond girls would be the stay-at-home old maid. Sasha? Leah? He recalled Kitty's cool beauty and pictured her as his wife, on his arm, in his bed. Distance and the ugliness of death lent a stronger enchantment to his images of her. And yet, he thought with frustration, he had made so very little progress in his courtship, had so few opportunities to see her, let alone talk of love.

'You're never thinking of marrying already, boy?' asked Grandfather Sparrow.

'He's twenty-six. High time he turned his mind to such things,' said Aunt Georgie.

'He needs to make some money, get himself a solid practice somewhere, instead of wasting his time with sanitation. That's what it's all about, boy. Making money. I didn't pay for you to become a doctor so you could inspect cesspits.'

'He's right, for once,' Aunt Georgie whispered. She smiled up at him. 'You'll have fallen in love ten times over before long. You get yourself a nice solid living, ready to marry the right one when the time comes.'

'Now then, will you be all right?' William asked for the third time, feeling an obscure anxiety about Lily after everyone had gone. She seemed to have run out of energy and to have shrunk into the chair where she sat by the fireplace.

'Of course I'll be all right. Go on back to Somerset. Don't mind me.'

William placed his coat and hat on the table, reluctant to leave her now the time had come. But he had to talk to her, get things straightened out, and it might as well be now. He drew a deep breath. 'I suppose we could sell the shop.'

Lily looked at him sharply. 'It didn't take you long to figure that one out. And Father hardly cold in his grave! Then what? You with your nice tidy capital. Me with nothing.'

'I only thought . . .' What had he thought? That he would not need Wotherspoon's help? That his conscience could rest easy?

'You only thought of yourself,' said Lily. 'You only thought you could turn me out and make some money.'

He held up his hands in appeasement. 'All right. We won't talk about it now.'

68

'You think I can't run a shop? I've been running it all the time he's been up there in bed.' Lily put a hand to her mouth. Pressing it against her teeth in a desperate attempt to stem her emotion, she began to weep with hard dry sobs.

William felt an exasperation with her. 'It was you who said you didn't know who would look after things . . .' He gave up. 'There, there. You'll miss him for a while.'

He comforted her by patting her shoulder until her sobs had subsided. Fetching the half-empty port bottle from the kitchen, he poured some into a glass. He watched her drink it greedily, and cursed himself for handling the situation so badly.

'Well, well, well. It's *good* to see you, Mr Elliman!' Nathaniel shook his hand warmly. 'Come up to the studio. I should like your opinion on how the painting is progressing.'

William followed him, listening for the sound of female voices, but there was no sign that anyone else was in the house, except for a discreet murmur from the servants' quarters downstairs.

'They are all out. Choosing clothes,' Nathaniel explained. 'Sasha has got everyone all boiled up and in a lather about your charity concert. They talk about nothing else. And the practising!'

'Miss Kitty has gone too?'

'With Kitty any excuse for buying a new dress will do. Now then . . .' Nathaniel directed him to stand by the easel. 'Quite an improvement, don't you think?'

'A triumph, sir.' William was struck at once by the life in the painting. Hammond had brought out the beauty of all his daughters – Leah's strong classical features, Lavinia's gentle, solemn eyes, Kitty's aloofness. But the focus of the painting rested in one figure. Much as William might have wished that Kitty would shine out from the canvas, he had to admit it was Sasha who gave the picture its energy. A smile hovered at her mouth; her eyes were alive with feeling.

'Of course, we have a long way to go. And I shall need them to sit for me again, but you get the idea?'

'It's marvellous, sir. Truly . . . I am moved.'

'What more can an artist ask than that, eh?'

'Indeed.' William remembered the purpose of his visit. He cleared his throat. 'To be truthful, sir, I had come here today to ask *you* something. The fact is, I shall shortly become a man of property. I mean to say – my father has died very recently . . .'

'My dear fellow. I'm sorry to hear it.'

'My father has died,' William continued doggedly, 'and he has left me the family business. At the moment it's managed by my sister . . . and I'm content with the situation for the present. But when my survey in Penbury is ended – and it is going very well – I hope, in time, to be able to sell up. I think I could count on capital of four hundred and fifty pounds. I am twenty-six – an age where a man begins to consider marrying. I am at last in the happy position of being worthy of a woman's affections. I should like to become engaged to your daughter Kitty.'

'Does she know?'

'Not yet.'

'Four hundred pounds is not enough to keep our Kitty, Mr Elliman.'

'Four hundred and *fifty* pounds, sir. I don't intend marrying now, you understand. I only hope to become engaged to be married. When I'm established in a practice, a very considerable practice . . .'

'Of course. Plenty of time. You ask her. I shall be delighted if she accepts you, dear boy.'

William could hardly believe his good fortune. Hammond would be delighted to have him as a son-in-law? He might walk out with Kitty, be seen with her in public? He could even be invited to the Hammonds' house for Christmas. The bliss of spending that festive and comfortable season in such perfect company was almost overwhelming when he thought of the alternative, Christmas with Lily. At once he was plagued by a mental picture of her slumped in the kitchen chair. He had no idea where she would go if he sold the apothecary shop over her head.

There were sounds of movement on the stairs and, a moment later, Sasha came into the studio dressed in a fur-trimmed cloak and dark bonnet. Her cheeks were flushed with hurrying. 'Father, you'll be amazed. We have been buying the most elegant . . . Mr Elliman! What a lovely surprise!' Sasha stared at William, delighted to be the first to know he had called on them. 'You've been looking at Father's painting?'

'Oh, yes. It's *very* lovely.'

'We have been shopping. We have bought *bunting*, Mr Elliman, in preparation for your concert.'

'Take Mr Elliman downstairs, Sasha,' interrupted her father. 'I believe he has something to say to Kitty.'

Sasha's stomach gave a lurch. So, he had come today to propose. She knew it. She could see it in his face, and in her father's expression. Her spirits sank, and she was struck by a thought: he would be her brother-in-law! Sasha led the way down the stairs, telling herself that Mr Elliman for a brother-in-law was better than no Mr Elliman at all. I shall never marry, she thought. If I can't have him, I'll have nobody. There. I've decided. Besides, I have my career to consider.

She turned to smile at William, a sisterly smile, the smile of a woman with higher goals than marriage. 'We are going to rehearse some music in the drawing room, Mr Elliman. You must listen.'

'I hope my visit isn't inconvenient.'

'Mr Elliman! When could *you* ever be *inconvenient*?' Sasha halted. 'Oh, it's so nice to see you. Did I tell you about my tour? Herr Lindau has contacted his friends in various musical associations in the North of England. Contacts,' she quoted. 'A musician thrives on them. It's all a long way off, but I feel so *impatient* to begin.'

William, soothed by this welcome, felt his heart begin to beat erratically as they neared the drawing room.

Sasha lowered her voice. 'You must tell Lavinia she is *not* playing flat. Her pitch is almost as perfect as Leah's. But she has so little self-confidence. So, you must tell her.

Say how good she is. Would you do that?'

William nodded. His throat had dried. In a moment he would see Kitty. He had been visiting schools that morning, and was sure the smell of unwashed children still clung to him. He was sure that other, more pungent smells of drains and soil heaps must linger too. He could not get them out of his head.

The contrast, as Kitty came forward to greet him, was like seeing a flower come into bloom. The sudden impression of loveliness dominated his senses. It was as if her perfection could temporarily erase all the sordidness in the world.

'Mr Elliman! Have you travelled all the way from Penbury this afternoon simply to come and see us?'

'It's not many miles, Miss Hammond.' He saw that she had been teasing.

She was alone. He was relieved to see that Mrs Hammond was not in the drawing room; he had a strong feeling that Kitty's mother did not quite approve of him.

'Mr Elliman is going to hear us rehearse,' Sasha said. 'And you must tell us how your survey is progressing. Is it almost finished?'

'I think Whitehall will accept my recommendations. And Penbury is very firmly behind a campaign for municipal status, with petitions and the like. The future looks very bright.' William cast a cautious glance in Kitty's direction.

She smiled and said in a low voice, 'Do we really have to discuss drains every time you come to see us, Mr Elliman?'

Sasha went to the piano and banged out a number of cords. 'We are sending a piano over to Penbury. I hope it will be in tune.'

'Would it really matter if it wasn't?' said Kitty lazily. 'It's hardly going to be the Victoria Rooms.'

'I think you will find it's a pleasant enough hall,' William said quickly. 'Though I regret the audience won't be as discerning as some, Miss Sasha.'

Sasha flashed a look of fury at Kitty. 'If you dare to give

a less than professional performance, I shall throttle you with my bare hands!'

William was alarmed by her change of mood. 'I'm sure that Miss Kitty didn't mean . . .'

'Sasha – why don't you fetch Leah and Lavinia?'

There was silence. Kitty stared at Sasha pointedly.

'Oh dear. I hope we didn't upset her,' William said as Sasha marched from the room.

Kitty yawned. 'Sasha gets very temperamental if she feels anyone is attacking her music. You'll get used to it.' She sat at her cello and caressed the strings with the bow. 'You know, I'm rather looking forward to this concert.'

William's breath rose harshly in his chest. 'I'm glad, Miss Hammond. I'm so glad.' They were alone. She had given him the perfect opportunity to frame a proposal. But somehow, it had been easier to make his approach to Kitty's father than it was to ask Kitty herself. He had rehearsed his opening words: my dear Miss Hammond . . . *dear* Kitty – during these past weeks and months you have become *very* dear to me. Would you consider . . .? He remembered that she had once said she could not tolerate people who dithered.

'How can you bear to work every day among poor and dirty people?' Kitty said, striking a few notes on the cello.

'Well.' William felt discouraged. 'I hope that by doing what I'm doing, I might reduce the dirt and misery.'

'How very worthy you are.' She regarded him with a mocking smile and her head tipped back. She gave a sudden shudder. 'I couldn't do it. Such . . . horrid wretchedness.'

'No. Well, you don't have to. You have a wealthy father to cushion you.'

'My, my, Mr Elliman.' She was laughing at him. 'Do I detect a spark of criticism?'

'I'm sorry.' He crossed the room and pulled a chair close to where she sat at her cello.

'Don't apologise. I was beginning to think you might never disagree with me. I know, deep down, that you're

73

doing excellent work, and that someone has to be public-spirited.'

'You seem to ridicule it so.'

'No, I don't. Not really. But you and your kind make our own lives seem so *un*worthy. I would treat you as badly if you were an employer who cared very deeply for his workers, or a particularly well-meaning parson. In fact I have been known to treat parsons with extreme contempt.' Though she still mocked him, he felt he had penetrated the indifference she always affected. He thought he had never drawn so close to her before.

'Kitty—' He was alert to the possibility that her sisters might at any moment walk in through the door. 'I don't know if you're aware of my feelings for you.'

She did not answer.

'I mean, I don't know whether the fact that I worship you might be enough to move you in any way. If I said that I adore you, that—'

'Why don't you simply say what you really want to say?' Her tone, if not her words, was gentle.

'Marry me, Kitty.'

She laughed. 'You would have to do more than minister to the sanitary needs of the poor.' She regarded him steadily. 'I mean, you must make a little *money*, William.'

'I know, and I fully expect that in a year or two I shall have established a practice.'

'Yes.'

'In Penbury,' he said hopefully.

'I'm not talking about your practice. I mean, yes, I'll become engaged to you, if you like.'

William stared at her. 'Great God in heaven!'

She laughed again. 'Is that how a man who has been accepted is supposed to respond?'

'You really mean it?'

'Yes, Mr Elliman. I mean it. We shall announce it publicly at the concert.'

'May I kiss you?' The nearness of her made his stomach feel as if it were turning somersaults. I have just become the happiest man on earth, he told himself.

74

She reached out her hand that held the bow and tipped it behind his neck, pulling him closer. Her lips touched his. He closed his eyes as a sexual heat shot through him. 'Oh . . . Kitty!'

They drew apart, hearing footsteps approaching.

Sasha swung open the door with Leah and Lavinia close behind her; she saw Kitty and William in an embrace and knew at once from William's dazed look of rapture that he had asked Kitty to marry him. Leah and Lavinia exclaimed in surprise as Kitty broke the news that she had agreed to an engagement.

Sasha braced herself and met Kitty's eyes. She was surprised by an expression of wariness in them. She has no intention of going through with it, Sasha thought. She is still in love with someone else. She's wondering if I will tell the others, or, worse, tell Mr Elliman. She is asking herself, how strong is sisterly loyalty?

Quite strong enough, Sasha realised, as she went towards them. She put her arms round Kitty and embraced her lightly. Then she turned and kissed Mr Elliman on the cheek. Oh, the shock of the touch of a man's face against her lips, after dreaming about it for so long. She felt a wild and almost unmanageable urge to plant her mouth on his and rub out that smile of contentment. She stepped back and gripped the top of the piano.

'I hope you will both be very happy.'

Chapter Four

Sasha fidgeted in her chair. It was freezing in the studio, lit by a wintry sun, but she longed to give way to the little thrills of excitement that seized her imagination. Herr Lindau had confirmed her concert tour of the North of England the following summer. She wanted to fling out her arms and dance around the room instead of sitting rigidly for hours and hours.

'Only a little longer, Sasha. Five more minutes, and I can do the rest from memory.'

Sasha looked at her father, at his paint-splashed coat and unruly whiskers and the faded little velvet hat he always wore when he was painting, and she felt her heart pitch into an uncertain area of emotion. She would miss him dreadfully, and her mother, and this beautiful, beautiful home. But she was ready for a change; she wanted to escape the loving, cloying safety of family. It was all too comfortable, too agreeable. She needed a single focus for her energies instead of a diffuse affection towards her sisters and her parents. She had thought she had discovered someone to absorb her energies when she fell for Mr Elliman . . . but he had chosen Kitty. Poor Mr Elliman. He had seemed so romantic, with his streak of crusading spirit towards the poor. Sasha was sure she might well have devoted herself to him satisfactorily if he had fallen in love with her. She would have shown him a tender intimacy and become the perfect wifely figure at his side.

Hang *wifely* figures. She was never, ever going to fall in

love with anyone. She was going to become a concert performer, an *artiste*. It sounded much more exciting, and vaguely sinful, even though dear old Herr Lindau would be acting as her protector, and Miss Holloway would be trailing along behind as a chaperone.

'Sasha, sit still!'

Sasha straightened her back automatically. Next summer! she reminded herself. No more a Beautiful Hammond, but cast adrift in a world of music, alone!

Well, not quite alone. She thought again of her governess and wished she could dispense with her services, for Miss Holloway was no earthly use to anyone travelling; she got sick headaches and was overcome by the heat. I shall ignore her, Sasha decided. I shall put her firmly in her place as extra baggage.

Miss Holloway walked through Avondon, intent on the purchase of some new gloves for the concert in Penbury the next day. The December cold pinched her face and she had the beginnings of a headache. She took a mental stock of her medicine supplies and, being close to the chemist's in the Mall, went inside to buy an extra tin of health salts.

As she came out again, she recognised a young woman walking past the store. 'It's Sophia Mannering, isn't it? You went to school with Miss Kitty.' The two women walked companionably side by side along the pavement.

'How is Kitty? I haven't seen her for such a long time,' said Sophia. 'Not since I met her last summer in Bath.'

'I remember. You had tea together one day. Were you at the concert?'

Sophia gave her a puzzled smile. 'Concert? We didn't go to a concert. And we didn't have tea together either, Miss Holloway.'

'I'm sure she said—'

'I bumped into Kitty in the street. She was with a friend of Mr Hammond's – Randolph Portland. You know. The writer.'

Miss Holloway's expression had stiffened and a veiled

look entered her eyes. 'Yes . . . I've heard of him.'

'He's a friend of Mr Hammond's.'

Miss Holloway's mind was working quickly. 'That's right.'

'He wrote a *terribly* wicked book.'

'I know Mr Portland,' Miss Holloway said as calmly as she could. 'He's an old friend of the family. And I'm sure the book is not as wicked as people say.'

Sophia shrugged; but Miss Holloway had seen the look of uncertainty in her eyes. What was she thinking? What *should* she be thinking? That Miss Kitty had been walking out alone with a married man? What if the girl should start spreading gossip? Kitty's reputation would be at risk. Kitty, so proud and lovely, would not dare to be seen in society, would not be able to walk through Avondon without someone pointing a finger, whispering and wondering. No. No, thought Miss Holloway, there had to be an innocent explanation.

'Good day to you, Miss Mannering,' she murmured. 'I have to pack. I'm going to a concert tomorrow, you know. The whole family is going. Mr Portland may even come with us,' she added with a stroke of inspiration. 'He often visits.'

Miss Holloway hurried back to the house in Hanover Terrace. She climbed the echoing stone stair holding on tightly to the iron balustrade. Her headache was worse; the glass chandelier hanging from the high ceiling dazzled her eyes and her mind hurt with the confusion in her brain. Without pausing to take off her cloak and bonnet, she scurried along the corridor to the room Kitty shared with Sasha and knocked. There was no reply. Miss Holloway went inside closing the door behind her.

The room smelled of scent and feminine clothes. A taffeta dress was laid out on Sasha's bed and one of the wardrobes was standing open. Miss Holloway wandered up and down, touching Kitty's dresses on their hangers and the hairbrushes on her dressing table, uncertain what she was looking for, but sure that it was there to be found if she looked hard enough. She heard someone in the corridor and leaped away from the dressing table.

'What the devil are you doing in here, Holly?' Kitty took off her bonnet and cloak and threw them on to her bed. Her hair was untidy, noted Miss Holloway. Her eyes were bright, her lips full and red.

Miss Holloway's throat closed in anxiety. 'Where have you been?'

'That's none of your business,' Kitty said angrily. 'I want to know what you're doing in my room.'

'I had to see you. I've been talking to Sophia Mannering.'

'So?'

'She said she saw you. Last summer. She said you were with a man.'

Kitty went to the dressing table mirror and sat on the stool. 'Stop playing silly games, Holly, and get to the point. What's all this about?'

'Randolph Portland.' Miss Holloway's breath rose harshly in her chest and her voice came out in a whisper as she saw Kitty's expression alter in the mirror. 'You've been meeting Randolph Portland. Oh – say it isn't true!'

'No. Why should I deny it? Especially to you.' Kitty began to rearrange her hair, appraising herself in the mirror. 'You can keep a secret, can't you, Holly? And it's not really so very terrible. He's awfully nice. You'd be charmed by him.'

Miss Holloway's eyes were wide with terror. 'Whatever are you saying?' she wailed. 'A *married man*. How could you? Don't you know that when you die, you'll go to hell?'

'I'm already there,' Kitty said with a bitter laugh. She put down her hairbrush. 'You don't know what you're talking about. But you wouldn't, would you, Holly? I dare say a man has never even touched you.'

It was true that no man or woman had ever assailed Miss Holloway, with either friendship or love on their mind. It was a cold, unwelcome realisation on top of the shock of Kitty's admission. 'You wicked girl, to talk like that about touching and . . . and . . . Oh, you *wicked* girl!'

'Shall I tell you what it's like, Holly? Is that what you want? It's really very pleasant, not at all disgusting like you think. People tell you it's disgusting, simply to stop you doing it. Doing what? you ask. Poor Holly. I don't suppose you even know.' She paused, enjoying the look of outrage on the woman's face, wanting to say something that would shock the wits out of her. 'Well, there's more to it than kissing, I can tell you. A man has this *thing*, you see – I mean, it's attached to his anatomy. And when he pushes it up inside you—' Kitty rolled back her eyes in mock ecstasy. 'It's all terribly exciting for him. But the best bit, Holly – and the bit nobody dares to tell us in case we go off the rails – is that it's exciting for a woman too. When Porky . . .' She watched Miss Holloway's face express disgust and finally become a mask of revulsion, and Kitty realised she had gone much too far. She returned her attention to the mirror. 'That's enough, I think, for a first lesson.'

Miss Holloway did not answer. She made an odd choking sound and ran from the room. The Beautiful Hammonds, people called them. She should have known it was all a counterfeit. She should never have taken a position in the house of an artist. Friends had warned her they would be tainted with immorality. Paintings of naked women. Peculiar friends. Scruffy young men to dinner. So much for their fine airs and importance in the area. Miss Holloway was weak with the thought that for the past five years she had been living in a house of sin. She felt like an avenging angel, as if she were on a divine mission. Throwing open the door to the drawing room, she came to a sudden halt.

'Miss Holloway!' Mrs Hammond half rose from her chair. Sasha was leaning with her elbows on the piano, staring out of the window.

'Whatever is the matter, Miss Holloway?' said Mrs Hammond. 'Are you unwell?'

'I am well enough,' the governess said in a strangled

voice. She turned as Kitty burst into the room behind her – beloved Kitty, so pure, so superior – and a sob broke in her throat. 'I have come to denounce that Jezebel!'

They stared at her. No one laughed, though there was something more comic than tragic in Miss Holloway's proclamation.

Kitty was the first to move. She seized the governess by the arm and said in a low, harsh voice, 'You stupid woman – be quiet!' She altered her tone. 'I was only teasing, Holly. You *mustn't* say anything in front of my mother.'

'What is this all about?' Mrs Hammond said coldly.

Miss Holloway shook Kitty from her arm. 'Your daughter is no better than a harlot!'

'I don't know what you are talking about, but you are dismissed, Miss Holloway.' Mrs Hammond's voice cracked like ice. 'Go to your room and I shall come and talk to you directly, when you've calmed down a little.'

Sasha tried to still her excitement. Oh, the delicious scandal of it! Miss Holloway thrown out! And was Kitty going to get her come-uppance at last?

Miss Holloway continued to stand there, unmoving. 'A harlot!' she repeated, pronouncing the two syllables distinctly. 'Lord, deliver me from this house of sin. Poor Mr Elliman. Poor Mr Elliman!'

Mr Elliman? Sasha threw a wild glance at Kitty, seeing briefly a look of terror in her eyes, and a peculiar helplessness in the way she stood there.

Mrs Hammond turned to Kitty. 'What is the woman talking about?'

'I don't know,' Kitty stammered. 'She was in my room. She became hysterical.'

'Don't behave as if I'm half-witted. She must have a reason. Miss Holloway has never said boo to a goose before today. Have you done something you should be ashamed of? If you've compromised yourself!'

'Women like that!' spat out Miss Holloway. 'She belongs with those vicious creatures among the lower orders. They are forced by circumstances to follow their loathsome occupation. But she is ten times worse. She has *chosen* her path of sin.'

'What is this about?' Mrs Hammond repeated. 'I *will* have an answer.'

'Kitty has been the plaything of a notorious womaniser, Mrs Hammond. What's more, she was quite open about it. She was seen flaunting her behaviour in Bath last summer.' Miss Holloway gripped her hands together and nodded. 'There! And I know his name. It's Randolph Portland.'

Sasha's mouth dropped open with disgust. 'Porky Portland!' Her thoughts whirled back to a party, when the family had been to Portland's house in London, full of literary people and artists. Her father, laughing, had once said Portland was a rake. And he was old! Kitty, how could you? Sasha thought silently. The scandal would rock the whole family. Her mother and father would be horribly wounded. And what about poor Mr Elliman? How would he be able to bear the humiliation?

Kitty had begun to cry. 'I love Porky, Mother. I love him. But I knew I could never have him.'

Her mother stared at her. Without a word, she hurried forward and bundled Miss Holloway from the room.

'He loves me too,' Kitty shouted defiantly. She sat down hard and folding her arms tightly began to rock herself to and fro with little moaning sounds.

Mrs Hammond directed the weeping Miss Holloway towards her room upstairs with a fierce promise that if she uttered another word, she would personally force down her throat the contents of the tin of salts she was carrying, together with the considerable stock of castor oil in Miss Holloway's medicine cupboard. Feeling satisfied with the effect of her threats, her outward appearance only a little ruffled, Mrs Hammond went to her husband's studio and told Nathaniel everything.

Sasha could not bear to look at Kitty. She hovered briefly and then sat at the piano, but she did not touch it. How odd, she thought. I feel so much stronger than Kitty. And all because of a man. Oh, I have certainly done the right thing in renouncing love for ever.

Suddenly Kitty stopped rocking. She dried her face on her sleeve and went to her cello. Wrapping herself around it, seeking its comfort, she played a series of vigorous scales. 'I suppose you're very pleased about all this,' she said after a while.

'No. But I don't know how you could pretend to love poor Mr Elliman, when all the time you were carrying on with Porky Portland. Why did you have to encourage him? Why let him think you might marry him? It's so – so *unkind*.'

Kitty hesitated. 'I'm in love with Porky, Sasha. I mean, really, horribly in love. And, believe me, it's not what you think. It's not disgusting – but nor is it a delightful, enviable feeling. It's wretched and humiliating.'

'But to get engaged.'

'I liked Mr Elliman a little.' Suddenly Kitty laughed. She was in control again, the old Kitty, cool and impassive. 'Oh, who knows? I might even have gone through with it. I knew I could never have Porky. His wife is healthy enough for another thirty years or more. Besides . . . I had quite taken a fancy to the idea of becoming a doctor's wife. I was going to persuade Father to give us a handsome dowry and William could have bought a well-paying practice in London. That way I would still have been able to see Porky.'

'But what about poor Mr Elliman?'

'He would have had me to parade on his arm – which is all he wanted when it came down to it. And I wouldn't withhold the other, the conjugal side of things.'

Sasha stared at Kitty in disbelief, and felt a sudden hollow fear for her; though she did not know why she should feel sorry for Kitty, when it was Mr Elliman who had been injured. 'I can't believe you can be so horrid.'

'Life *is* horrid, Sasha, my darling.'

Mrs Hammond returned to the drawing room. She sent Sasha away, and questioned Kitty closely and harshly until she had satisfied herself that she had not compounded her disgrace with a pregnancy.

'I suppose this means my engagement to Mr Elliman is off,' Kitty said casually. 'I shall tell him I've changed my mind.'

'Be quiet, you silly girl!' said Mrs Hammond. 'Don't you see? Mr Elliman is the least of our problems. If Miss Holloway talks to anyone else . . .'

Kitty's eyes widened. 'She wouldn't . . .'

'She may well do just that.'

'I'll throw myself on Porky's mercy. He'll look after me.'

'That scoundrel! Your father is at this very moment writing to Portland to let him know he is to be regarded as *persona non grata* in this house. If he ever tries to get in touch with you again, your father will shoot him – and if he doesn't I will!'

'He won't take any notice. He'll come for me! He loves me!' Kitty's protest was a despairing one. She knew Porky would go to any lengths to avoid open scandal.

For a brief moment Mrs Hammond's expression was pitying. 'Oh, Kitty! Why Portland? The good Lord knows I wasn't over the moon about your engagement to Mr Elliman, but I never expected this!'

'Porky made everything seem alive and exciting.'

Her mother hardened her heart. 'Well, you're going to find matters a little less exciting from now on. Your father has suggested Switzerland.'

Kitty stared at her in dismay. 'No. Not to the Wormington-Prossers?'

'Mrs Wormington-Prosser is a very good friend.'

'She's a dragon! Leah and Lavinia said she eats people alive! No, I won't go,' Kitty said fiercely. 'I'm not going to be hidden away in Switzerland.'

'You'll do exactly as you are told.'

'I won't go!' Kitty screamed, her control finally snapping.

But Mrs Hammond's had broken too, and she slapped Kitty hard.

★ ★ ★

Shortly before four o'clock the Hammonds gathered in the drawing room, as if the custom of meeting for afternoon tea must be kept up at all costs. Leah and Lavinia talked by the window in low voices. Mrs Hammond paced the carpet, glancing from time to time at the clock and at her husband, who was slumped in a chair, until the maid arrived with a tray of tea things.

Kitty stood near the door, half poised for escape. She was pale, her complexion so colourless it was almost transparent. The fight had gone out of her, and she was resigned to Switzerland.

'Miss Holloway will not be with us this afternoon,' Mrs Hammond told the maidservant calmly.

'Yes, ma'am.'

The servants know, thought Sasha. They have overheard something; and they are as frightened as we are, excited by the whiff of scandal in the air, but nervous as well in case everything should come crashing down.

The family waited in silence for the maid to leave. 'What are we to do about Miss Holloway?' Mrs Hammond said as soon as they were alone. She stopped pacing the floor. 'The wretched woman will have to go. But there is a strong risk she might talk.'

'We shall pay her,' said Nathaniel.

'*Blackmail*!' said Sasha with a sense of drama, almost beginning to enjoy the situation.

'A pension,' her mother corrected sharply, frowning at Sasha for the interruption. She turned to Nathaniel. 'She's been a loyal servant. It wouldn't look untoward to give her a pension. We would probably dispense with her services anyway after Sasha's tour.'

They looked at Sasha. Until that moment, no one had given a thought to her tour and the need for a chaperone.

'My tour,' Sasha wailed. 'Who will come with me on my tour! Herr Lindau has made all the bookings.'

Her mother drummed her fingers on the piano.

'But that's too bad!' Sasha turned on Kitty with a bitter fury. 'Now look what you've done. At least I could

85

manage Holly. Now I shall probably have to take someone even *worse*.'

Leah glanced at Lavinia, and a silent communication passed between them, a look of inquiry that Lavinia acknowledged by a nod of confirmation.

'Why shouldn't Lavinia and I act as chaperones?' Leah said quietly.

'You?'

'Why not? Would we be *worse* than Miss Holloway, do you think?'

Mrs Hammond considered the idea and nodded, relieved to have solved one of their problems.

Lavinia put her arm round Sasha. 'You see? Not everything is spoiled.'

'It is for poor Mr Elliman perhaps,' said Nathaniel.

They were all very sober.

'We've got to tell him something,' said Leah. 'The concert is tomorrow.'

'Kitty must write him a letter,' declared Mrs Hammond.

'And tell him everything?'

'No, no. Of course not. But a letter breaking off the engagement.'

'I'll take it to him,' said Sasha.

'Yes,' exclaimed Nathaniel. 'That is best. Sasha can explain, break it to him more kindly. Say Kitty is unsure of her feelings. It was all a little too hasty.'

William had arranged for the Hammonds to stay at the Mansion Hotel, a larger, and more magnificent establishment than the Neptune and situated on the outer fringes of Penbury. He had checked the bookings on the day of the concert, and had been to the school-rooms to make sure everything was in order.

He took off his coat and shoes, flung himself on the bed with his hands behind his head and concentrated on the cracked and yellowed ceiling. In another hour she would be here. He would show her off to Brewer, and to men like Wotherspoon, and they would all look at him with a fresh respect. He had the pile of papers that made up his

86

report ready for despatch to London. And then Christmas! Christmas with the Hammonds. He had bought Kitty a brooch inscribed with his name and hers. They would be united in reality before long. A few months for Penbury to get its charter of incorporation in the Municipal Reform Act, a few more until Dobber, the Penbury physician, retired.

William's reverie was broken by a knock at the door.

Sasha had been walking up and down outside the Neptune Inn, trying to pluck up courage to go inside. She was beginning to attract the attention of passers-by, but she could think only of the news she had to break and the impossibility of guessing Mr Elliman's reaction to it. At last, she followed a small group of men and women into the inn and tried to look as if she were attached to their party.

It was very dark inside. There was a choking smell of beer, and pipe smoke, and of food being cooked. She dared not follow the people into one of the crowded bars, but waylaid a potboy and told him urgently to see whether Mr Elliman was at the inn and ask him if he would come out to talk to her. She waited in the corridor, squeezing herself against the wall as people went in and out. After several long minutes she saw Mr Elliman come down the stairs towards her.

'Is anything the matter, Miss Hammond? Is it about the concert?'

In her agitation Sasha seized his arm. 'Mr Elliman. I must talk to you . . .'

'Is Miss Kitty with you?' William looked eagerly towards the street. 'She isn't ill?' His heart leaped with anxiety.

'Yes. Yes, she's ill,' said Sasha. 'At least, that is what we must tell everyone. She won't be coming to the concert.'

'My poor Kitty. How ill? Why didn't anyone tell me sooner? You could have written.'

'Listen!' Sasha lowered her voice. 'Listen to me.' She

felt too hot and her heart pounded with the enormity of what she was doing as she saw William's look of bafflement. 'Mr Elliman, could we go outside, do you think? It's very close in here.'

They walked into the square and as they moved away from the crowded inn Sasha began to feel perfectly calm. Now, she thought. Now he will see how shallow Kitty was. He will realise there is only one person who could truly love him.

'I have something very unkind to tell you, Mr Elliman, and I want you to be very brave when you hear it.' She took a deep breath. 'Kitty had no right to accept your proposal of marriage. She already had a lover. She has been seen with him in public.'

There was a long pause.

'You are a naughty girl, Sasha, to spread such stories.' William looked at Sasha with mistrust. He could hear people enjoying themselves in the inn behind him; the sound of laughter came in waves on the cold air and seemed to add their mockery to the message from the girl in front of him. He saw her expression and felt a chill of anguish. 'This is simply malicious gossip,' he blustered.

'Kitty was deceiving you,' Sasha said earnestly. 'She thought she could marry you and keep the love affair going. You see, there's something else you don't know. Kitty's lover is a married man.' She flinched at the expression of pain and intense dislike in William's eyes.

'You seem to have taken a lot on yourself for a child of your years,' he said at last.

'No one else knew how to tell you. They got Kitty to write a letter and wanted me to deliver it. They wanted her to say she had changed her mind, but I couldn't bear them to be so cruel.'

'Do you think this isn't cruel?'

'No. Of course not.'

'To be told by her sister, a mere child still . . .'

'I wish you would stop calling me a child,' Sasha said with a touch of indignation.

William narrowed his eyes. 'Do you know – I don't think I believe you.'

Sasha pulled Kitty's letter from her coat and gave it up to him. She watched miserably as he read and re-read the terrible sentences: '. . . a misunderstanding . . . too hasty . . . nothing more than friendship between us.'

William's heart was thumping as if it would force its way out of his chest. He drew himself up and said with dignity, 'Miss Hammond. I should like you to ask your father to release me from my engagement to your sister. There will of course be no announcement after the concert this evening. And you may tell Miss Kitty . . .' He paused in confusion, unsure what anyone should tell Kitty and unable to trust himself to say anything more without breaking down.

Sasha laid a hand on his arm. She felt as if her heart would break for him. 'Kitty is going to be sent to Switzerland, Mr Elliman.'

'So far away?' he almost whispered.

'They are sending her away because of gossip. And in case her lover tries to get in touch with her.'

'Her lover!' William said in a strangled voice. 'Her lover!' It was all over. His dream had turned to ashes. He could not bear Sasha's childish pity. She had made him feel a fool. He looked at her with distaste. 'Please. Go away, Miss Hammond.'

Sasha walked up the hill and away from the town. It was cold and crisp, and the road was empty of traffic; the ruts of mud were frozen hard, and her boots made a crunching sound.

She had hoped William would turn to her in his heartache. Instead she had humiliated him, and now he would hate her almost as much as he hated Kitty. She had lost what little hope she had ever had of his affections. The sound of a church clock drifted up on the clear air. The concert was waiting, to be endured somehow. She must dress in her white concert frock. Leah and Lavinia would be waiting for her.

She turned back and was presented with Penbury laid out below her. The view could not compare with those of Avondon or the gorge and the beauty of Leigh Woods; but the countryside with its traceries of bare tree branches was certainly very pretty in the afternoon sunshine. Even the factories with their tall chimneys and plumes of smoke looked picturesque; there was no evidence of insanitary ditches, or unholy smells at this distance.

Sasha picked out the Neptune Inn among the buildings and wondered how Mr Elliman would bear to attend the concert and meet her sisters and parents. And she would have to play the piano as if nothing had happened. She could not escape seeing him again. Sasha set her face to the town and walked back down the hill.

Leah and Lavinia were waiting for her in the hotel bedroom. 'You're late!'

Sasha's spirits lifted. How very unimportant Kitty's behaviour seemed all of a sudden. 'I told Mr Elliman!' she said dramatically. 'He was horribly upset.'

Lavinia began unbuttoning her day-dress for her. 'You've been running. It isn't ladylike to perspire.'

Leah smiled. 'Who wants to be ladylike, eh, Sasha?'

It occurred to Sasha that Leah would always regard the prospect of a single life as no great tragedy, a great deal more pleasant, in fact, than that of tying herself to some man. Leah did not have a very high opinion of men. Perhaps she has a point, Sasha thought, reflecting on how easily Mr Elliman had been duped. How unfriendly he had been towards her when she had only been trying to protect him.

'I wish I hadn't chosen to play Liszt,' she murmured.

'He's popular,' said Leah. 'People love to believe it's all a struggle.'

'It's pure histrionics and no real *feeling*. One thinks, is it never going to end?'

'Poor Mr Elliman. He will be at the concert,' murmured Lavinia, remembering.

'Oh – hang Mr Elliman!' said Sasha. 'He escaped, didn't

he? At least he isn't going to *marry* her. And it was all his own fault in the first place!'

She pulled her dress over her head. She would copy Leah's example; she would embrace the life of a spinster gratefully. What did anything matter except playing well? After tonight she would devote her life to music; she would stir people to feelings deeper than courtships and engagements and betrayals.

William did not know how he was going to get through the concert. He alternated between lying on his bed to stare at the ceiling, and walking up and down in his room, kicking up the rug under his shoes and wishing he had never been born.

Towards four o'clock he dressed slowly and meticulously. A number of people were already making their way towards the schoolrooms as he left the Neptune. He saw Brewer inside the entrance, and shrank from the thought of telling him what had happened.

'I hear your fiancée is ill. They tell me the young ladies have changed their programme.'

'Yes,' William said bleakly.

The room was filling with a deepening roar of sound, of raucous voices and laughter and boots scraping the floorboards. A hundred or more of the town's factory employees had accepted the invitation to a concert; they looked forward to the free music and, it was to be hoped, some rousing songs from local singers. The rest of the audience was made up of traders and farmers and various town dignitaries and their families, including Wotherspoon and Scrope.

Nathaniel Hammond was coming down the room towards William. Out of the corner of his eye, William could see Leah and Lavinia by the door, and Sasha, dressed in virginal white; they made their way towards the piano. He wished he had never thought up the idea of offering the town a concert. He imagined turning to everyone and making an announcement: 'I'm sorry, you can all go home now. It's off. It's over. None of this is what it seems.'

'Mr Hammond,' said Charlie Brewer. 'I hope you'll allow me to write a piece about your daughters for my newspaper. Perhaps you would let me have a few details that might interest my readers?'

William waited in an agony of embarrassment until Brewer had finished making notes. He squared his shoulders to face Nathaniel, and when he finally greeted him it was with an expression of hurt disbelief.

Nathaniel's voice broke with emotion. 'My dear fellow . . . what can I say?' He was unable to go on; shaking his head, he turned away to escort Mrs Hammond to the front row of chairs.

Mrs Hammond did not speak until she passed William, then said in a low, sympathetic voice, 'I very much regret any embarrassment my daughter's behaviour may have caused you, Mr Elliman.'

It was almost too much for him. 'Not embarrassment, Mrs Hammond. No, not that. But Kitty has done me a great injury.' Choking back tears he walked away.

The air vibrated with the sound of the viola and violin being tuned. Sasha moved to the piano, and the clack and gabble of voices died as William too went to the front of the hall. The only sound was the occasional cough and scrape of a boot.

William held the written programme. 'Ladies and gentlemen . . .' He was surprised by the natural sound of his voice, and continued more strongly, 'Ladies and gentlemen, I thank you all for attending our concert, in which Miss Sasha Hammond, Bristol's own charming lady pianist, has consented to contribute music by Mendelssohn, Chopin and Liszt, accompanied by two of her sisters.' He looked at the paper in his hands and the blur of ink became recognisable words. He read out the programme of entertainment: the songs and glees, the piano trios transcribed by Sasha, and the solo pieces – the first a study by Liszt. Encompassing Sasha with a gesture of the programme in the manner of a theatre impresario, he sat down.

William tried to retreat into the blank misery of his

thoughts, but he jumped with alarm as the Liszt study began. It jerked him to attention. The violence of the piano was awesome, terrifying; the figure seated at it seemed too small to produce the volume of sound that crashed towards him. Sasha's fingers ran up and down the keys producing cascades of notes following furiously, one upon the other.

William sat gripping the programme. For the first time in his life, he felt himself moved by music. There was no Kitty to gaze on, nothing to distract him. His head filled with the runs and blistering successions of chords.

The audience too was spellbound as the pace of the music seemed to build, faster and faster. William heard the applause all around him when it ended; people stamped their boots in appreciation. He pretended to study the next item on the programme – and tears flowed down his cheeks.

PART TWO
June, 1851
Leah and Lavinia

Chapter Five

Everyone said it always rained in Manchester, but they were wrong: the afternoon sun shone gloriously through the window to light up the faded red wallpaper and the picture of a fat old Georgian gentleman in a gilt frame next to the dust-coated mirror on the wash-stand.

Sasha was in heaven. She poured some water from the ewer into the bowl and as she washed her face, she could hear Leah and Lavinia laughing and talking in the next room. 'Hey you! Girls! Keep the noise down in there!' She thumped on the wall with the flat of her hand. They were laying plans of some sort. Ever since leaving Bristol, they had been full of suppressed excitement. And so had she. It burst out from time to time. They had sung in the railway carriage, every song and round they had learned as children, and Herr Lindau had joined in, sitting cross-legged on the seat to sing 'When I was a Tailor', and doing all the actions to 'Dashing Away with a Smoothing Iron'.

Sasha bounced on the bed and rolled on to her back. A wave of pure joy swept through her. She raised her arms above her head and flexed her fingers, longing for a keyboard within reach so that she could release the passion bubbling up inside her. She sat up. A piano! What if they could not find her a decent instrument! Herr Lindau had made all the written arrangements at the various towns, but what if there was not a decent piano to be had in the whole of the North, and all she had to play were battered uprights from the nearest supper rooms with cracked keys and broken pedals? She gave a little moan of agony. She could not bear it. There was a whole hour before Herr Lindau called to fetch her for a rehearsal at the concert rooms.

'Excited, Sasha?' Herr Lindau checked through his musical programmes beside her in the carriage. His absence of concern was almost as infuriating as it was reassuring.

'I wish there wasn't so much waiting. I wish we didn't have to rehearse. I wish it could all happen now.'

'Ah, Sasha,' he said with an air of wistful melancholy. 'Such impatience with life.'

He looked so like an ancient sage that Sasha wanted to hug him for being simply perfect. Everything was perfect, or almost so: the rehearsal went smoothly; the piano was in perfect pitch. They had chosen a programme of Chopin, Thalberg, Mendelssohn and some Beethoven; the other performers were local singers, and a cellist and violin player; they did not play as well as her sisters in the trios, and Sasha was tempted to say so.

'I wish you were playing with me,' she said to Leah, when, back at the hotel, they were dressing for the evening performance. 'You are every bit as good.'

'Don't be silly. I'm a painter, not a performer,' Leah said. 'And I, for one, wouldn't fancy dressing up in a white frock with a dozen petticoats and a corset that kills, and being looked at by hundreds of people. I'd sooner put on my walking boots and get out into the countryside with my easel.'

'You never minded playing at home.'

'At home, in one's drawing room, in front of one's family's friends is very different. And well you know it.'

'Yes, it is,' Sasha said with a little shiver of excitement. 'It's so much more thrilling in front of strangers. Friends are always complimentary. Here, I feel as if I have to *make* people love me – or, if they won't love me, at least they must love the music.'

'They'll love you *and* they'll love your music,' Leah

said, putting on a little black velvet waistcoat she favoured for evening wear.

'I'm so scared that if I don't win them they might start booing. It's terrifying, but it's thrilling as well.'

'They wouldn't be so boorish as to boo,' laughed Lavinia; she gave the strings of Sasha's corset a final tug.

'No. But there's always that chance,' Sasha insisted, relishing the risk, not wanting Lavinia to dispel the drama.

The audience did not boo. Sasha, after two encores, felt as if she were dancing on air.

The next morning they travelled from Manchester to Liverpool, and then on to Preston and Blackburn. Sasha repeated her success in every town where she played. Sometimes Herr Lindau conducted, sometimes he was persuaded to play as well, and Sasha was sure she could never be as good; Herr Lindau played as if he were in love with the piano as well as with the music.

They had fun too; there were the private parties among people who knew Herr Lindau, where he played Leah's violin immoderately to Sasha's piano accompaniment. His mop of hair tossed vigorously and afterwards everyone stamped and cheered as he handed the violin back to Leah saying he should stick to the keyboard. And then Leah and Lavinia were persuaded to play with Sasha, and it was almost like old times – except that Kitty was not there.

They rarely talked about Kitty. It was as if she had ceased to be part of their lives once she had been despatched for Switzerland. She had written, saying she was sorry for all the trouble she had caused; she had begged them to let her come home. Their mother had read the letters out to them, as if delivering a cautionary tale, clicking her tongue and shaking her head over Kitty's complaints. Afterwards she would fold the letter carefully and take it to her room. She emerged an hour or more later, her eyes suspiciously red, her smile a little too forced.

Sasha avoided even thinking about Kitty. It was easier to pretend she did not exist any more. Easier, until the sisters played together, and then, however frivolous the music, she could not keep a note of sadness from their playing.

They travelled from Lancashire into Yorkshire. The weeks passed, and Sasha was giving concerts almost every night, until she began to look tense and pale. Leah insisted they must rest for a few days, to recuperate and breathe clean country air. She made Herr Lindau turn down all further invitations to impromptu concerts and evening parties. They spent the days walking and sleeping, and finally stayed at an inn close to the north-east coast and the town of Eskton, where Sasha was due to resume her concerts.

'A final day's holiday,' Lavinia said, throwing back the windows to their room. 'Shall we ask Herr Lindau to find us some transport to Eskton, Sasha, and see if we can discover such a thing as ribbon to trim your dress for tomorrow?'

Leah leaned her elbows on the window ledge. Somewhere a curlew was calling, and there was a fresh wind off the moor. 'I think I shall reject the search for ribbons and take my sketchbook for a walk.' The road wound away past the inn yard and into the distance; a bloom of purple lay on the horizon. The stone walls, very pale, reflected the light below an overcast sky. Leah's mind itched with the restlessness that came with a new painting. She knew she must capture the particular quality of the moor here, before it eluded her.

Leah was thrilled by the landscape: the vast expanses of tussocky heather cut by deep valleys; the streams tumbling over boulders; the unexpected little farms sheltering in hollows, and whole villages built of autumn-coloured stone, clustering for protection around squat-towered churches. She watched Lavinia and Sasha drive off to Eskton with Herr Lindau, and set out carrying her paint-box and sketchbook.

A strong sense of freedom lifted Leah's spirits. Her skirts brushed the heather with a swish and crackle; it sprang and crunched under her boots and a warm dry scent swirled up into her face. She had gone some miles

100

before she found the place she wanted, a bowl of moorland scooped out of the surrounding hills; it was cut by a stream that wound among rocks and stunted oak trees. A dark cluster of farm buildings nestled in the distance, halfway up the valley. She scrambled down to an outcrop of rocks some way from the track and bunched up her skirts as a cushion. Resting her sketchbook on her knees, she began to draw.

Not for the first time Leah gave a mental prayer of thanks to Miss Holloway for causing such a rumpus over Kitty. She wondered idly whether Kitty was bluffing about being a reformed character; she would need to be convincing to fool their mother's friends, the Wormington-Prossers. Poor Kitty. But she had brought it on herself. A married man. What joy was there in that? Leah saw, with a degree of self-understanding, that she could never, unconditionally give herself to a man – married or single. Her mind and senses were not drawn to the alien touch of a man's body. She thought again of Kitty, beautiful Kitty, debasing herself for that vulgarly conceited Porky Portland. If there was something lacking in her own nature, making her unresponsive to the kind of love a man like Portland offered, she did not regret it.

She and Lavinia had talked at the start of Sasha's tour about settling in the North, convinced it was time to leave home and live by themselves. They had even, in one town and another, begun a search for the perfect accommodation while Sasha was at her rehearsals with Herr Lindau. Leah had no illusions about Lavinia's ambitions: she knew her sister would marry one day and abandon her, but until then they would be independent – or as independent as any woman could be who lived on an allowance from her father. They would paint, and establish a gallery and sell their sketches. How idyllic that sounded.

And how beautiful and raw was the landscape here. Leah quickly pencilled in the rocks and stream and the outline of the moor beyond. It was so much more majestic than the woods and combes of Somerset. The moors were very inspirational. How much more interesting it would be to live in such natural splendour instead of in a town. Why not here? She had seen several cottages in the area. She would talk to Lavinia. Leah opened her paintbox and bottles of water, and pushing back her bonnet from her hair, began painting with broad strokes.

She had been working for some ten or fifteen minutes when a sound drifted on the wind behind her. Leah lifted her head, startled to hear the strains of a violin. The music was haunting in the empty landscape. It was not the effort of some scraping fiddler; the notes were true and pure. Nor was the unseen musician playing some rustic dance tune. Leah recognised snatches of Mozart in the intensely sweet and soaring notes.

She stood and looked about her, but the land was empty except for the farm some distance to her right. The music continued. Packing up her painting, Leah scrambled up from the stream and crossed the heather. Was she imagining it? Had the beauty of her surroundings gone to her head? She called out, feeling slightly foolish, 'Hello? Is anyone there?'

The music ceased abruptly.

Leah had always maintained a strong scepticism about the supernatural and felt a distinct sense of relief. A musician who stopped playing as soon as he knew he had been overheard seemed to be of a satisfyingly human origin.

'Where are you? There's no point in hiding from me.' In a way typical of the Hammonds she had assumed a natural proprietorship of the moor.

A boy rose from a hollow in the heather some distance from where she was standing. His violin still rested on his shoulder, as if at any moment he would resume playing.

'Come here.'

He walked towards her. 'I didn't know anyone was there, ma'am. You popping out of the heather like a rabbit.'

'I am nothing like a rabbit, young man. And you were the one who was hiding. Who are you?' She regarded him critically, seeing a long-legged boy in shirt and waistcoat

102

and patched trousers. His looks were out of the ordinary, very wild; but his complexion was good, almost delicate; his eyes, a deep brown, gazed steadily at her, and his dark hair, long and curling, clung damply to his forehead.

'I'm Gabriel . . . Gabriel Ridgeway. I live over there.' He pointed to the farm buildings.

'Well, Gabriel Ridgeway. You play divinely. How old are you?'

'Thank you, ma'am. I'm fifteen, but I shall soon be sixteen. It was my Great-uncle Jacob learned me.'

'*Taught* you. You mean he taught you,' Leah corrected automatically. 'How is it that your great-uncle knows how to play Mozart?'

'He's dead now. But he always went to hear all the music he could when he was living. He was educated. But it wasn't him taught me the piece. I learned that all by myself. I go to the concerts in Eskton when I can save up the money out of my wages. I once went to Leeds for a concert.'

'You mean you were playing by ear?'

'I can't read music. I can read books though,' he added defensively. 'Father sent me to school. A proper school in Eskton.'

'Did he now?' Leah smiled. An idea occurred to her. 'Would you like to go to a concert tomorrow, Gabriel?'

He frowned a little. 'I would that, but I haven't got the money.'

'I have some tickets.' Leah pulled them from her pocket, imagining the sense of power a conjuror must feel when he produced bouquets of flowers from his sleeve.

The boy laughed. 'Fancy that!'

'Would you like to go to the concert?'

He shook his head. 'It wouldn't be right not to pay for them.'

'Why not? They're mine to give.'

Gabriel considered the ethics of the situation. He studied his would-be benefactor shrewdly. He saw a tall, determined figure with a straight nose, corn-coloured hair, a humorous mouth and very beautiful eyes. She was dressed in a brown silk frock with a black braided jacket, and the bonnet hanging round her neck was trimmed with blue silk flowers: the clothes of a gentlewoman, but her boots were those of a farmer. He decided he liked her. She looked severe and honest, and she was very handsome; she was just about the most handsome woman he had ever met.

'I'd have to give you something in return.'

'What if you were to play me another tune?'

'Don't be daft. That's not enough.'

'A glass of milk from your farm, then. *And* another tune. I could meet your family, and they would see I'm not going to spirit you away from them with my tickets to a concert.'

'That sounds fair enough to me.'

As they made their way across the heather Gabriel told her about himself. His family had always been farmers, he said. In the winter, things were pretty bad up there on the moor. His brother John would take on the farm when his parents got too old to do the heavy work, but his own heart wasn't in farming. He wished he could play in an orchestra, but he knew that the dream was a daft one.

Several things were 'daft', according to Leah's young companion. Wishing for what he couldn't have, for a start; but so was slaving all year on the land for very little reward. His brother John was courting a woman from Runsby. Gabriel knew he would have to get his own farm one day or stay on and work for them. He did not relish either prospect. He was not made for labouring, he said, and he sometimes wished his family would recognise as much. When he was a small boy his mother had encouraged his Great-uncle Jacob to teach him mathematics and how to play the fiddle, but now, if he came out on the moor to play his music, she said he was lazy. His great-uncle had said he might some day make a living from music, but Gabriel didn't see how. 'Unless I join a fair or a circus. Mother says that's all I'm fit for.' He laughed good-naturedly. 'But I don't rightly fancy that.'

Leah told him about Sasha's concert tour and how they

were travelling around Lancashire and Yorkshire with Herr Lindau who was a famous German pianist.

'But your family must be rich, Miss Hammond,' he said with a hint of bitterness edging his good humour. 'It's easy for your sister.'

'Oh, I don't think Sasha will find life easy as a concert performer,' Leah said. 'Far from it.'

'No, but she'll have had the best people to help her.'

They had reached the farm. Ignoring the mud and slurry, Leah lifted her skirts above her boots and walked across the yard.

The kitchen was low and dark. It smelled of animals. Hens pecked at the cracks in the flagstone floor and clouds of flies buzzed and banged against the ceiling. A girl of seven or eight sat at the table peeling potatoes; as she finished each one she dropped it into a cooking pot, reaching up to slip it over the edge. She looked round and grinned at her brother, then scrambled to her feet, alarmed by the sight of Leah.

A woman was standing by the stove. 'Gabriel! You might have warned us we'd got company.'

Gabriel put his violin on the table and went through a low doorway into a room beyond the kitchen. He called over his shoulder, 'I've promised this lady she might have a drink of milk.'

The woman bobbed a curtsey. 'Excuse us for not being up to visitors, ma'am. It's a bit forsaken round here. Mary! Get away from that stool and let the lady sit down.' She pushed her daughter aside, clearly irritated by the arrival of a stranger – a woman at that – in her kitchen.

The boy returned with a mug of milk. Leah took it and solemnly exchanged it for a concert ticket. She sat on the stool and drank the cool liquid while Gabriel explained to his mother about the concert and their bargain on the moor.

'Perhaps you would like to have a ticket as well, Mrs Ridgeway?' suggested Leah.

'Me? Get on with you.' The woman laughed. 'I've never been to anything like that!'

'My sister will be playing the piano at the concert.'

'Is that a fact?' Mrs Ridgeway regarded her with her hands on her hips, smiling, but not visibly impressed. She glanced dismissively at Leah's paintbox and sketchbook. 'You're an artist, are you?'

Leah showed her the painting she had begun. 'I shall finish it back at my hotel.'

'It's clever enough. I recognise it. From down the valley.'

'My father does much finer pictures. But my sister Lavinia and I are looking for somewhere to settle down, to paint and perhaps open an artists' gallery.'

'Fancy. Gabriel's the clever one in our family.' Mrs Ridgeway turned back to the stove.

Leah looked round the kitchen, seeing the hens, the limited furniture and rag rugs by the fire, and the violin beside her on the table; it was old and scuffed at the edges, but as lovingly polished as her own.

She finished the milk. 'Thank you, Gabriel. And now you must play some more for me as we agreed.'

The sweetness of the violin was intensely moving in the enclosed space of the kitchen. He played more of the same sonata, distorted by memory, but recognisable, and with perfect pitch. When he had finished, Leah shook hands with him and with his mother.

'I shall look forward to seeing you at the concert, Gabriel.' She pulled a flower from her bonnet and gave it to the little girl, then turned again to his mother. 'Gabriel's is a wonderful talent, Mrs Ridgeway. You should nurture it.'

'Should I now?' said the other woman as she watched Leah stride away across the farmyard. 'And how does her ladyship propose I should do that?' She turned to Gabriel and moved to clip him across the ear, but the boy stepped nimbly aside, ducking her hand.

He picked up his violin and nursed it moodily. 'I reckon she knows what she's talking about.'

'Leah! Your boots!' Lavinia met her in the inn yard.

'I've been visiting a farm and tasting the local milk.'

106

Leah sat on the tail of a dog-cart and tugged at one of her boots with both hands.

'I'll fetch your shoes,' said Sasha. 'You look as if you fell in a midden.'

'I've had an adventure,' Leah said when they were in the bedroom.

'So, you *did* fall in the midden.'

'Sasha! Do you have to be so down-to-earth?' protested Lavinia. 'How are we ever going to turn you into a civilised grown-up?' She took a brush from her trunk and began to attack the dirt caking the hem of Leah's skirt.

'Listen!' said Leah impatiently. 'I've met the strangest boy, a heavenly child, with hair like a gypsy's and the most beautiful eyes. He has learned to play music – Mozart, all by ear! – from saving up the wages his father pays him on his farm and listening to concerts. He lives in the middle of the most awful squalor – hens, flies, ugh! a red-faced mother! There was I, sitting in the heather, painting, when I heard violin music coming across the moor. He plays like an *angel*, and, guess what – his name even is *Gabriel*. I've given him a ticket for the concert tomorrow night.'

'You expect a poor farm boy to travel all the way to Eskton to hear me play?' Sasha sat on the bed and began stitching fresh blue ribbons on her white frock. 'You must be mad.' She laughed. 'Or *he* must be mad, if he thinks of coming simply to please you.'

Gabriel walked the ten miles to Eskton the following afternoon after he had finished his work on the farm. His mother had made him slick down his hair with water, but by the time he was on the road it had already dried and was curling and springing as waywardly as ever. He wore his brother's good coat and trousers, lent for the occasion, a clean shirt with a Sunday collar, and a black neckcloth stolen from a drawer when no one was looking. He felt buoyant, as if somehow his fortunes might be about to change since meeting the woman on the moor; it wasn't every day someone gave him a free ticket to hear some music.

He let himself wonder a little about his new friend – the fair Miss Hammond. And she was fair, in all the meanings of the word. She had not behaved like gentry usually behaved; it was easy to see she had really meant it when she said he played well. Gabriel knew, without any false modesty, that it was true. He loved to lose himself in the violin and to translate into sound the music he remembered. The violin seemed to become part of his body when he played, as if he were singing the most beautiful notes in his head – more beautiful than he could ever make with his voice – and the song was taken up by the instrument for him to hear. He tried to explain it sometimes, but his family did not know what he meant. They thought he was touched. Perhaps he was. He knew he was not like them – and that he was destined for more than planting potatoes and herding cows. It had been a magical thing, to see Miss Hammond there in the heather as if she had sprung out of the ground like a creature in a fairy-tale. He remembered she had said she was travelling with two of her sisters, and that they each of them played an instrument. A trio of fairy, musical creatures.

His boots rang on the dirt, hard and dry from a week of fine weather. He walked more quickly, so as not to miss the start of the concert. It was good to sit among people who liked music, even if it was only for a few hours. Feeling for the ticket in his pocket, he was reassured by its firm edge – his passport to a world of enchantment.

Gabriel was moved by the sight of the girl standing by the piano in the Exchange Rooms. Miss Hammond's sister was not much older than he was, he realised in surprise. She was thin and small and pretty; her hair looked like gold thistledown spilling on to her white frock; but her eyes were very dark and lively, and her colour high, like a country girl's. He looked eagerly for her sister, his friend from that morning, and saw Leah next to a man with white hair, who he guessed must be the famous German. He felt a stab of envy as he saw how easily Miss Hammond was talking to him, as if it meant nothing to be a world-famous musician.

She had not seen him arrive. Gabriel handed over his ticket at the door and slipped into a seat at the back of the hall. He rested his hands on his knees and craned his neck eagerly, waiting for the girl to begin her concert.

Sasha had chosen Chopin – a study, very fast and energetic. Gabriel had not heard it before, but a chill went through him as she began to play. He recognised at once what was happening. It was not the music, nor the girl's skill at the piano that was awesome, though she seemed to master the difficulties of the piece with perfect ease; he saw that she and the music had become from the outset a united, living thing. She was transfigured; her hands and body were one. It was as if she had given herself entirely to the spirit of her playing even if it should break her.

He understood. Gabriel too felt as if his heart was being torn from him when he played. And now, as he listened, he felt possessed by the music. Did no one else feel it, that excitement driving on and on? He was consumed by the experience. He wanted it to last for ever.

'Sasha, I want to introduce you to Gabriel,' Leah said, eventually drawing Sasha away from the people who had been crowding round to congratulate her at the end of the concert.

'You mean the pauper? He came? You must have created quite an impression.'

'He has walked all the way.'

'Oh, the poor boy.'

Sasha's scepticism turned to sympathy as she recalled Leah's description of the farm and pictured the child's wretched circumstances. She remembered Mr Elliman's charity concert in Penbury and his work to alleviate the miserable conditions of the poor. How satisfying to know that her playing could reach out beyond the gentry in places like Penbury and Eskton.

'We must do something for the boy, Leah. You could

give him something to take back to his family.' She was exhilarated by her recent success and still awash with energy.

'I think you've given him all he wants. I'm sure he enjoyed your playing.'

'I mean *do* something,' Sasha repeated, still searching for Leah's pauper child. Her gaze met that of Gabriel standing a few feet from them; he had overheard their conversation, and his face was flushed with a dark embarrassment.

Leah introduced him.

'Miss Hammond.' Gabriel nodded to Sasha, swallowing his injured sensitivities. He held out his hand.

Sasha did not notice it; she had seized Leah's purse and was fumbling in it for some money. 'Here. You poor boy. You *walked* all that way! Take this for your journey home.'

Gabriel faltered and his expression hardened. He glanced at Leah for support. 'I was meaning to tell you how much your playing . . .'

'May we get you some supper? Oh, but we must – please, let us pay for some supper for you.'

'No, thank you,' he said stiffly. 'And I'm used to walking. Folks round here think nothing of ten or twenty miles of a day.'

'But your poor feet.' Sasha looked down at his heavy boots, half expecting to see them in holes, and was surprised by their sturdiness.

Gabriel turned to Leah. 'I must be off. It's a fair walk back, used to it or not. And my mother frets once it gets dark. Thank you, Miss Hammond, for the ticket to the concert.'

Leah hurried after him; she caught up with him by the door. 'Gabriel – don't take offence because of Sasha. She misunderstood. That's all.'

'Yes?' He regarded her with a disappointment that seemed older than his years. 'I suppose country people all seem the same to you, Miss Hammond. But we're not destitute. And I'd be glad if you don't tell folks we are.'

110

'I should like to call on your family again, if I may?'

'What for?'

Leah had resolved her thoughts over the past few days. 'I'm thinking of coming to live in this area. I shall be looking for a cottage. Your father might know of a cottage somewhere?'

'He might be willing to ask around.'

'May I call again?'

He hesitated then accepted her hand. 'Well, then. I'll be glad to see you again, Miss Hammond.' And, at last, his scowl softened.

Leah was moved by the warmth of his handshake and the wonderful depth of his smile, glad that she was forgiven. She imagined his lonely journey on the moorland road. The half-light on the moor was an eerie thing; shapes rose out of the mounds of heather, clumps of trees and bushes became sinister masses. She wanted to protect him from the night drawing in. Why had she talked about living near here? she wondered, as she returned to the others. She had no idea whether Lavinia would agree with her that it was the perfect place to set up a base for their painting. How could she explain that she had fallen in love with the austere beauty of the moor and a boy who played heavenly music?

'He was not much like an angel. More like a sour devil,' Sasha said crossly. She fell silent, at once forgetting the farm boy, beguiled by the picture of Lavinia coming towards them on Herr Lindau's arm accompanied by a gentleman in a very superior blue velvet coat. Herr Lindau introduced the stranger as 'Mr Pickersgill'. He was about thirty, had nice eyes, a solid figure and rather prominent ears, the tips of which had gone pink.

Lavinia too was blushing. 'Sasha, Mr Pickersgill's father would like you to play at an evening party at his house.'

'If you would be so kind,' added Mr Pickersgill. 'If you *could* bear to extend your tour. Herr Lindau tells me you were almost ready to return to Bristol.'

'Oh, I think we might stay a little longer without any difficulty,' said Sasha, taking her cue from Herr Lindau

who was nodding in agreement. 'Introductions,' she murmured to Leah with a knowing look at Lavinia. 'A
musician thrives on them.'

The Pickersgills' invitation was one of several that
followed the concert, and for the next few days the
sisters were thrown into a whirl of social occasions.
Leah, hoping to visit Gabriel's farm again, and wanting
too to talk to Lavinia about settling in the area, found it
difficult to engage her attention on the subject; Lavinia's
concentration was being increasingly absorbed by Mr
Pickersgill. Leah did not in the end return to the
Ridgeways' farm. She was obliged to accompany
Lavinia and Sasha on drives with the Pickersgills, to
luncheon at the Pickersgills' manor, and to walk on the
Pickersgill estate – where Lavinia and Mr Pickersgill
had eyes and ears only for one another. Discussing
what? Leah and Sasha speculated. His mother's singing? The Squire's taste in music? Both of which they
agreed were horrible. The whole of their remaining
time in Yorkshire was taken up with the Pickersgills by
day, and a succession of suppers and concert parties in
the evenings, requiring hours of dressing up and making
small-talk, and endless discussions with strangers about
Sasha's promising career.

Leah was growing tired of Sasha's career; she wanted
to concentrate on her own future. She was becoming increasingly impatient with Yorkshire provincial society. But
Sasha was in her element; she seemed to generate an air of
excitement around her; she was enthusiastic about everything; she played with exuberance whatever anyone
requested, flirted mildly with the young men who paid her
compliments, and involved herself deeply in even the
most idiotic conversations, as if everyone, whether or not
they had the Hammonds' definition of 'soul', had something important to say. Sasha was growing up – and
quickly – away from the protection of home. She had
always thrived on attention, but she was becoming more
poised, beginning to temper her reactions in public. She
was learning to bite her tongue a little, to slow down and

use her intuition. Everyone fell in love with her.

Everyone, that is, except Mr Pickersgill, thought Leah with amusement; Mr Pickersgill had clearly fallen in love with Lavinia, and she with him. Leah considered the possibility of Lavinia marrying earlier than she had expected. What would her own ambitions for the picture gallery be worth then? Her dream of a cottage on the moors receded a little, and she felt a surge of frustration. Did everything have to go wrong quite so soon?

Leah's ambitions receded even further – and Lavinia's with them – when the sisters returned to their hotel one evening to find a letter from their mother waiting for them.

Leah read it aloud and came to a tersely expressed message:

'. . . I am afraid Miss Holloway has proved incapable of holding her tongue any longer. She has been very indiscreet. I regret that life may become rather unpleasant here in Avondon.'

'Miss Holloway has finally blabbed about Kitty all round everywhere,' Sasha interpreted.

'We should go home,' said Leah gravely. 'I think we should leave at once.'

Lavinia and Sasha stared at her. She was right of course, thought Sasha. The family must close ranks and show a united front. But to leave now, when she was so much enjoying the concerts and all the musical parties. '*Damn* Miss Holloway! And damn Kitty.'

'Sasha!' protested Lavinia mildly, but she felt like echoing Sasha's opinion. Tears of disappointment pricked at Lavinia's eyes as she thought of the perfect atmosphere of the past few days. How amiable and cheerful everything had been: the little walks and rides and games of cards; the musical evenings, when Mr Pickersgill sang in his pleasant baritone voice, and she and her sisters had played their music. The elder Pickersgills were not, it was true, as musical as their son, but they *were* extremely appreciative. And they

113

had liked her. She was sure his mother had approved of her. And now Mr Pickersgill would forget all about her. She began resignedly to pack.

Damn Kitty. Damn Kitty. Placid, gentle Lavinia was surprised by the violence of her emotions.

Chapter Six

Sasha wandered round her father's studio while he talked to her about 'good taste'. He had begun a new painting, a landscape reminiscent of the style of his earlier paintings. As he worked, he described the Great Exhibition in London, which he had hated. The Hammonds deplored the kind of good taste dictated by manufacturers and advertisers.

Sasha halted in front of the half-finished portrait *The Beautiful Hammond Girls*; it leaned abandoned against the wall. Shortly before Kitty's disgrace her father had decided to turn it from a picture with vague allusions to Greek myth into one with intimations of a medieval allegory, though it had not been very clear which one. Perhaps he would never finish it now. His heart had gone out of the project.

'You should have seen it!' – the Exhibition in London again – 'Like some great greenhouse! Splendid enough. Amazing the wonders of science! But as for works of art – nothing but rubbish! Chairs like gothic cathedrals. Cherub-infested writing tables. Winged inkstands. Silver-plated fish knives! Plaster fruit stuffed under ugly glass domes . . . When you marry, Sasha – for you will one day marry – reject all furniture, glass and china that is ornamented purely for ornamentation's sake.'

I should like to go to London one day, Sasha thought. I should like to make an impression on the conductors and critics there.

'I shall never marry, Father,' she said casually.

Nathaniel stared at her with his brush-hand poised, distressed by the note of certainty in Sasha's voice. 'Don't talk rubbish, child! Of course you'll marry. Now Leah . . . If Leah had told me . . .'

'No. I shall never have a home of my own in the way you mean. I shall live alone. And everything *will* be honest and beautiful and gratifying to the eye, and of course soothing to the soul. But I shall never share it with a man.'

Her father frowned. He pretended to be occupied with a detail in one corner of the painting. After a while he said, 'I saw our friend Elliman while you were up north.'

Sasha laughed. She wondered whether her family had always been so transparent. Or was she getting wiser? She put her arms round his neck and kissed his whiskers. 'No, Father. I am definitely not going to marry Mr Elliman.'

'He seems to be working very hard in Penbury. He has the medical practice he once talked of, and is working besides for the Poor Law. He has become a very serious young man.'

Who wouldn't feel a little serious after Kitty had done with them? thought Sasha. She tried to revive her romantic image of Mr Elliman, but the thought of impressing London critics was more exciting.

It was true that Miss Holloway had spread scandal about Kitty all round Avondon. Mrs Hammond had been cut dead in the street by people with whom she had once dined. On the Sunday after their return from Yorkshire, the girls went to church. Sasha sensed curtains twitch at windows all up the hill. People stared as the family reached the Green. A group of women turned their backs.

Sasha's cheeks burned with indignation. She threw up her chin and stared back at those who were bold enough to look at her in church. 'How dare they!' she cried when they reached the privacy of the house in Hanover Terrace again. She threw her arms round her mother. 'How dare they sit in judgement on the rest of us!'

116

'We shall ride out the storm,' Mrs Hammond said with her usual equanimity. 'And, for myself, I shan't mind a little less need to be polite to people we don't care a jot for. Our real friends have remained loyal. But it will be difficult for you girls.'

'We've decided you must all get away from the unpleasant atmosphere here for a while longer,' Nathaniel told them. 'I've been talking with Herr Lindau. He's going to make arrangements for you to perform in Germany and Switzerland, Sasha.'

'Germany!' echoed Sasha. Her heart leaped with excitement. 'Another tour!' She thought of the applause and the excitement and the parties. Wherever she played, it was as if the music were enough to satisfy her whole being, but in public, when people surrounded her with admiration, that too seemed as if it could make her emotions spill out in an explosion of joy. 'Thank you! Thank you for letting me go away again so soon.'

Sasha saw a look pass between her father and mother and her heart sank again. Of course. They had said Germany and *Switzerland*. The only possible reason they could want her to go to Switzerland was for Leah to check up on Kitty.

She went to her room and stood looking down at Kitty's empty bed alongside her own. It all seemed so long ago: Miss Holloway's unholy outburst, the concert in Penbury, Kitty going away. It was difficult to picture Kitty in Switzerland, languishing with the Wormington-Prossers like a princess locked away in a tower. Sasha remembered Kitty fastening her dress for her the first night Mr Elliman came to dinner, promising her, 'He's all yours.' She took off her bonnet and looked at herself in the mirror.

She will spoil the tour, she thought. Somehow, Kitty will manage to ruin everything for me.

Lavinia was very quiet during the discussions about the trip to the Continent. Herr Lindau was getting on with things, sending letters, securing his introductions. It

117

seemed as if the tour would take up the whole of the winter.

'Lavinia has fallen in love,' explained Leah to her mother when Mrs Hammond worried about Lavinia's low spirits.

Mrs Hammond gave a weary moan of despair. 'Oh, no. Not another one?'

Leah laughed. 'Mr Pickersgill is a gentleman. His father owns half the land in Eskton, he rides to hounds and is the perfect country squire. His mother looks like a walrus and sings like one. In fact the whole family is rather walrus-like. Extremely respectable creatures. I think Lavinia is very much in earnest. And so is he . . . He has written to her.'

'Has he indeed?'

Leah conquered her own self-interest and closed her mind to the art gallery project. 'It would be a good match. I think you should encourage it.'

Mrs Hammond regarded her shrewdly. 'They are the right sort of people?' She trusted her eldest daughter's judgement implicitly.

'Very much so – though they may lack a little *soul*.'

Lavinia, when questioned on the subject, declared that Mr Pickersgill was the most excellent person she had ever met.

'And do you think he feels the same way about you?' Mrs Hammond glanced at Leah who was nodding confirmation.

Blushing furiously, Lavinia said she thought Mr Pickersgill had grown as fond of her as she was of him during the time they had spent with the family. She could not imagine experiencing a deeper regard and affection for any man.

'Very well – I shall write to the family,' suggested Mrs Hammond. 'I shall thank them for their hospitality towards you all, and establish a friendship between us . . . I shall make it clear we approve of a correspondence between Mr Pickersgill and yourself.'

'You would do that for me!' gasped Lavinia.

'My darling girl. What are mothers for?'

Mrs Hammond sighed a little, accepting Lavinia's embrace. She remembered a time when she had been in love with Nathaniel. Could she have talked of *regard* and *affection*? She had burned with the need to have him and no one else. Now, thirty years on, she might describe her love in less urgent terms – but weren't the young supposed to feel a little passion? She thought of Kitty, and supposed she should be thankful that Lavinia at least was not likely to cause her any great heartache.

What about Sasha? She was growing up so quickly. Were they doing the right thing in sending her out in society? Mrs Hammond worried about her daughters far more than they realised. Her mind closed in terror at the thought of what Kitty might become. She worried least of all about Leah. 'Leah will find her niche,' she and Nathaniel always said. Without acknowledging the precise way in which Leah was different from her sisters, they knew that she was strong; she would withstand whatever knocks the world had to offer.

Leah did not feel strong as she contemplated Sasha's tour on the Continent. She felt taken for granted. Was she always going to be a surrogate mother, or governess or warden to her sisters? I am not patient and willing like Lavinia, she protested silently. I do not want to go abroad. I do not want to be at the family's bidding. I want to live on the moors and paint. Will I never have a life of my own?

Gabriel had waited in vain for his friend Miss Hammond to return. Some evenings, when the farm work was done, he took his violin as far as the road to Eskton and sat by the crossroads, playing tunes taught him by his great-uncle many years before, watching the few travellers pass. Some of the ladies and gentlemen in carriages thought he was a beggar and threw him coins. Gabriel scooped them up after they had gone and took them home to store in a jar for the next concert in Runsby or Eskton. He thought of

Miss Hammond's sister wanting to give him money for his supper. He should have accepted.

The money in his jar mounted steadily. After a week or two Gabriel played with the sole purpose of coaxing money out of the pockets of passing travellers. Irish tunes were the favourite, but sometimes he would toss in remembered fragments of Mozart or Beethoven, and people would stare as they rode past. Sometimes they were so taken with his playing they forgot to throw money in his hat.

One morning Mr Runicles, the landlord of the Rose and Crown in Eskton, rode by. He said he had been hearing about Gabriel's skill on the fiddle. How would he like to entertain his customers? After that, on Saturday evenings, Gabriel walked to Eskton to play at the Rose and Crown. Sometimes he was joined by an accordionist, and sometimes people would sing. Everyone who came made a fuss because of his playing. They bought him glasses of ale. Runicles gave him supper, and Mrs Runicles made a proper pet of him.

Once, at the Rose and Crown, Gabriel fell in with a man who said he came from down south. The stranger was very tipsy and spoke with a foreign accent. He applauded loudly when Gabriel was playing. 'You could be a professional musician,' he told him afterwards. 'Another Paganini, another David, another Joachim. You ever heard of Merrill?'

'I've heard of Paganini.'

'No – Karl Merrill – the concert promoter. He's got up a series of chamber concerts. There'll come a time when everyone takes notice of Merrill in the same way as they're beginning to notice Hallé in Manchester. If you ever get down south . . .'

'If ever!' Gabriel said laughing.

'I mean it. Listen . . . I've worked with Merrill. You tell him . . .' He fumbled in his pocket and produced a piece of paper on which he scribbled with a stub of pencil. 'Tell him, if you ever meet him, tell him I've recommended you.'

The note read simply: 'I tell you, Merrill, this fellow is a genius.' It was followed by an indecipherable signature. The man's comment about him becoming another Paganini impressed Gabriel more than his personal recommendation; he put the note away in his money jar.

The money he had saved was mounting higher. He was able to go by train to concerts farther afield than Eskton. Sitting in the solid warmth of theatres and halls in Leeds and York, Gabriel dreamed of performing to real audiences.

Sometimes he dreamed of Mrs Runicles, who was large and soft and buxom. On his sixteenth birthday she had let him kiss her; he had put his hand inside her bodice and held one creamy silk breast. His mother grumbled about the company he was keeping; she worried about the barmaids and the ale; but Gabriel worried about nothing – except avoiding the attention of Mr Runicles, and saving enough money to escape from the farm.

Sometimes, when he played his violin, Gabriel remembered Leah and her sisters. He thought about the advantages that came with learning. What did he know, beyond what he had heard at school or could glean from other people's conversations? People told him he should get himself an education if he was going to follow the great performers. Strangers told him about famous musicians, many of whom were self-educated.

He began to spend money on books.

His choice was confined to music at first: the lives of composers, and the theory of music, hunted for in Eskton's secondhand bookshop. The farm was busy with autumn ploughing and the studying was slow and difficult. He began to work more systematically, turning to works of literature he had heard of: Scott's *The Lady of the Lake*, novels by Dickens, and Boswell's *Life of Johnson*. He collected old music scores and wrestled to understand them. He bought, from 'Wallace's Scientific Library', books on geology, botany and other branches of science.

The books filled the space under his bed. On Sundays

he was allowed to work in the best parlour. His family approved of reading. They were proud of his learning, pleased that he was trying to better himself. His mother began to boast that Gabriel was destined to become a school teacher or a parson.

But there were people who knew him better. Some in Eskton, observing the profound effect Gabriel's good looks had on the ladies and girls of the town, said he would be ruined by drink and debauchery long before he became a parson. Some of those who had heard him play – and particularly the women – said they were sure Gabriel was destined for musical fame, so spellbinding were his talents. Others were more pragmatic; they said they doubted Gabriel would live much past Christmas if the landlord at the Rose and Crown found out about him and Mrs Runicles. Let him fiddle his way out of that.

By December Sasha's tour had reached Baden-Baden. They spent Christmas with friends of Herr Lindau. Afterwards, Sasha's tutor discussed their plans.

'It's time you had a proper rest again, Sasha. Those dear, clever fingers will be worn down to the bone.' He glanced at Leah. 'Why don't you young ladies go on to Switzerland without me?'

Sasha saw the look that passed between Leah and Herr Lindau, and knew there had been little spontaneity about the suggestion. He was not offering them time for a rest, so much as time off for snooping on Kitty.

Herr Lindau waved goodbye to them on the railway platform. Sasha watched until he was no more than a thin, dark smudge in the snow, and then the smoke from the train swirled past the window and blotted him out altogether.

'On at last to Basle,' said Leah settling back in the railway carriage seat.

'What a long way we have come from home.' Lavinia looked tired and slightly wistful. Sasha guessed she was thinking of Yorkshire and Mr Pickersgill rather than Hanover Terrace.

'It's Sasha's birthday after New Year. You'll be eighteen, Sasha.' Leah spoke as if there were some particular significance about her birthday.

Sasha puzzled about it for a while.

'I mean,' Leah said, 'after you are eighteen, you should be thinking about hiring a travelling companion. Mother agrees.'

'You'll be going back home soon?'

'No, no. Of course not,' said Lavinia gently; she looked at Leah for confirmation. 'But later . . . if you take on summer engagements, Sasha. Leah and I have decided we shan't come with you on your next tour.'

Sasha nodded. 'Of course,' she said, to let them see she had understood they could not always be there. She remembered the promise she had once extracted from them, that nothing between them would ever change and they would always play music together. But Kitty had altered all that. Sasha felt tears prick at her eyes and she turned quickly to look out of the window. She did not blame them for wanting to give up touring with her, but she would miss them. She would miss them terribly.

'Leah and I have decided we are going to live in Yorkshire.' Lavinia was sensitive to Sasha's mood. 'You can come and stay with us, when your concerts take you up north.'

'You're going to marry Mr Pickersgill?' Sasha forgot her despondency.

'Sasha! Of course I'm not. He hasn't asked me. And I hardly know him . . .'

'I know you will. Mother has been writing to the Pickersgills.'

Lavinia blushed a fiery red and pulled at her gloves. 'We are going to Yorkshire chiefly because Leah has fallen in love with the moors. She is going to make the arrangements as soon as we get back. We shall lease a cottage and paint landscapes, local scenery, perhaps make trips to the coast. The Yorkshire coast is said to be very congenial for artists.'

'And *then* you'll marry Mr Pickersgill,' Sasha persisted with satisfaction. 'Oh, admit it. You're so obviously made for one another.'

'Sasha!' Lavinia protested, trying to keep a straight face and failing.

Sasha beamed at Leah. 'She *will* marry him. I'll stake my life on it.'

The Wormington-Prossers had sent a carriage to meet them at the railway station. It sped them, wrapped in fur blankets, with bells clanging and the red tassels on the harness flying, through the snow and out of the town. After a few miles they saw a large, turreted house on the slope of the hill, rising like a miniature castle from among pine trees. Sasha gasped at the fairy-tale aspect of it, picturing Kitty locked away somewhere inside. So, she really was like a doomed princess! She felt a touch of pity for her sister.

Kitty came to the door to meet them. She wore a navy wool frock with a white lace collar and cuffs, and a black cashmere shawl pulled round her shoulders. Her hair was scraped back from her forehead, almost hidden under an elaborate lace cap. She looked like a rather stylish Puritan, thought Sasha.

Mrs Wormington-Prosser stood beside Kitty, a large, handsome woman with a high complexion and eyes that seemed to bore through one's smile of greeting and into the thoughts that lay behind it.

'What a gaoler!' murmured Sasha to Lavinia as they climbed from the carriage. 'And what a gaol!' She looked up at the high turrets. 'Mother couldn't have chosen better.'

'Hello, Sasha—' Kitty's smooth cheek touched hers, warm and fragrant; her voice was husky with emotion. Her blue-grey eyes filled with tears as she embraced each of them in turn. 'It's so wonderful to see you all again.'

'Come in! Out of the cold,' commanded Mrs

Wormington-Prosser, drawing them all inside to a large reception hall. A broad stone stair led to several balustraded galleries above. An icy chill lay on the air.

The girls tried not to shiver as they handed their cloaks to the maidservant. They waited in the hall while their trunks were unloaded and carried upstairs, looking longingly through open doors into a room beyond, where a log fire blazed in the fireplace.

A nod from Mrs Wormington-Prosser signalled that Kitty might at last take them to their room. Kitty led them along one chilly corridor and then another and finally showed them into a bedroom. Three iron bedsteads stood in a row and a fire burned in the hearth.

'She's put you in here. My room's along the corridor next to hers. *He* hardly ever comes home. He's always away on business.'

Sasha ran to the fireplace and spread her hands to warm them. 'Oh! I'm so cold! I think I'll die!'

Kitty sat on one of the beds and threw back her shawl over the foot-rail as if she were unaffected by the cold. She watched them begin to unfold dresses from their trunks. Her expression was serene, enigmatic.

'How are you?' Leah looked at her critically. 'You seem thinner.'

Kitty pulled a face. 'The food is awful. The worst of English menus combined with the very worst of Swiss cooking.'

'Don't you ever have visitors?' Sasha imagined months shut up in that fortress, with no one but Mrs Wormington-Prosser and servants for company. She felt a reluctant stab of sympathy.

'Oh, they have musical parties and people to dinner. But it's all very boring.' Kitty looked down at her hands in her lap.

'Are you keeping busy?' said Lavinia. 'Are you reading – painting? You have your cello.'

'Oh, yes. I have my cello. And the Prosser keeps me occupied. I go on *cultural* trips with her to Berne and Neuchâtel – if you can call looking at lakes and mountains

125

and playing the cello for their boring friends culture. She treats me as if I were a child and watches over me all the time. She even sends a servant to spy on me if I go into the garden.'

'I expect she's doing her best – for Mother's sake,' said Lavinia gently.

'It's no more than you deserve.' Leah pushed her half-emptied trunk against the wall for the servants to finish unpacking. She stood by the fire with her hands on her hips.

'They know everything,' Kitty said. 'Mother told them everything. Can you believe she would be so disloyal?'

'Of course the Wormington-Prossers had to know why you were sent here,' Leah said harshly. 'Mother was only thinking of your welfare. Once you've proved you're never going to do anything like that again, you can come home.'

Kitty's expression altered. She gripped the foot-rail of the bed and her eyes pleaded with Leah's. 'You must tell them at home how much I've changed,' she said feverishly. 'I've got to get away. Tell them I'm truly sorry for upsetting everyone. It's hateful here. The Prosser won't even let me go shopping unless she's lumping along beside me.'

'Oh, Kitty,' said Leah wearily. 'You know they won't believe it. And nor do I, frankly. You'll go straight back to meeting that horrible Randolph Portland again.'

'I won't. That's over, I promise. He hasn't even written to me.'

'You tried to get in touch with him?'

'Only at first. I was so horribly miserable. I got one of the maids to sneak out a letter. Oh, Leah. You don't know what it's been like.'

Lavinia, full of sisterly pity, looked at Leah and tears filled her eyes. 'Perhaps we could talk to Mother when we get home.'

'Oh, please! Leah, *please*!' Kitty said with such an air of pathetic helplessness that even Leah was shaken.

'You can't come home yet,' she said more gently. 'Miss

Holloway gossiped about what she knew. It's all over Avondon. Quite honestly, I don't know what's going to become of you, or how you can ever show your face there again.'

Kitty's expression crumpled. 'I was hoping so much . . .'

Sasha remembered how, when they were children, Kitty had never revealed when she was upset or hurt; she could bear any pain without a sound – even, once, the setting of a bone in her arm, white-faced, her teeth clenched to prevent herself crying out. This business over Porky Portland has really vanquished her. She's changed, thought Sasha. Perhaps she's *really* changed.

'At least let me come to Basle with you one day,' Kitty pleaded. 'They won't let me go anywhere. They're so afraid I'll do something to embarrass them.'

Leah hesitated.

'Of course you shall come to Basle with us.' Lavinia hurried to Kitty's side and put her arms round her, looking up at Leah with an expression of sentimental appeal that would have melted the hardest of hearts.

Leah sighed. 'Very well – I shall persuade the Wormington-Prossers you've been here long enough to earn a little more freedom.'

Kitty dropped her eyes meekly. She leaned her head against Lavinia's shoulder. 'Thank you. You don't know how comforting it is to know you're all here with me.'

Leah and Lavinia fitted easily and resignedly into the rigid regime of the household. The Wormington-Prossers had once kept a friendly eye on them when they were at school in Switzerland; but to Sasha everything was new and foreign. She understood why Kitty hated their hostess, who watched over them like a humourless headmistress. Their mother and Mrs Wormington-Prosser had attended a ladies' seminary together – for they had been girlhood friends. Sasha tried to imagine them going for walks and discussing admirers, but gave up the attempt.

Mr Wormington-Prosser returned soon after the girls'

arrival. His wife had arranged a musical party in honour of his homecoming. Sasha was surprised at the quality of the musicians invited to the party – as good a standard as many of the people they had encountered on their tour of Germany with Herr Lindau. She had not expected the family to have high cultural aspirations: Mrs Wormington-Prosser had declared an aversion to the theatre, placing it with street entertainment, the circus and the playing of concertinas as being seed-beds for all manners of vice.

To Sasha's astonishment, the opera singer Werner Backhaus and other performers had been invited to the party. She nudged Leah.

'Mother wouldn't have had time for the Wormington-Prossers, if they didn't have respect for at least some of the arts,' said Leah.

Lavinia yawned, bored already with the evening. 'I wish Herr Lindau would finish with his relatives in Germany, so that we might move on from here.'

Leah tapped her fingers on the back of Lavinia's chair. 'I, for one, detest these large parties. And I'm growing rather tired of being polite to the Wormington-Prossers.'

Sasha wandered away from her sisters, unwilling to associate herself with Leah's tetchiness and Lavinia's ennui. She wanted to enjoy the evening in spite of the awfulness of their hosts. There were people here who had met Mendelssohn; they spoke of him with reverence, as if they were talking about a god. She stood near the fireplace of the crowded drawing room, shivering in the white muslin dress she usually wore for concert performances. She was glad of the weight of her hair warming her neck and shoulders; she rubbed at the goose pimples on her bare arms. Something exciting was going to happen this evening; she could feel it in the air, and in the rising tide of sound.

She heard Kitty's voice above the din: 'May I introduce you to my sister . . .?'

'So, you are the lady pianist?' Sasha turned at the softly clipped accent, thinking for a moment with pleasure that the speaker sounded like Herr Lindau; but the man beside

Kitty was much younger than her tutor; she guessed about thirty. He made her a formal bow.

'Sasha, have you met Herr Backhaus? He is Mr Wormington-Prosser's cousin.' Kitty was smiling at her and looked very beautiful in a blue satin dress with a full berthe of soft white lace threaded with blue ribbon. Her hair was looped up, and fell in large, heavy ringlets on either side of her head. Here, in the company of so many people, her familiar poise had returned.

'You're Mr Wormington-Prosser's *cousin*? But he is English and you are not.' Sasha's surprise made her forget normal etiquette; she realised that she was staring at the opera singer in too ingenuous a manner. She noted his dark eyes and hair and sensual mouth, and saw that he was amused by her.

'I am German,' he said. 'Mr Wormington-Prosser is English. It's true. But, a long time ago, our mutual grandparents did come from Switzerland.'

Kitty touched Sasha's arm confidentially. 'I shall leave you two to talk.'

She drifted away, like a deep blue flag iris blown by a light breeze among less graceful blooms. Kitty drew people's attention naturally; and for a moment the singer too followed her with his eyes. But almost at once he turned back to Sasha.

'I do not like these entertainments. For me, I like the natural dignity of the opera house. Or perhaps a simple song in a *Bierhalle* . . . And of all these things, I think I prefer the *Bierhalle*.'

Sasha laughed. 'I enjoy the opera. But I've never been in a *Bierhalle*, and I'm sure Mrs Wormington-Prosser would die if she heard you even suggest it.'

'It's a special thing for me,' he said in his softly clipped way. 'You must try it. It's very amusing, Miss Hammond.' He glanced round at the assembled gathering. His attention rested on a woman by the piano who was preparing to sing. 'God in heaven! Miss Hammond, can you imagine? Grand opera at a party!'

'But it's good to hear singers of quality.'

129

'She is not knowing how to perform in a small room. Opera singers know only how to sing in a grand auditorium. We bellow and *project* the voice. The effect is overpowering outside a theatre.'

The woman sang a little-known aria with many trills and embellishments. When the song had ended Backhaus turned to Sasha. His eyes held hers in amusement. 'Am I not correct? Oh, Miss Hammond,' he added, unheard by anyone else amid the applause, 'I am wishing you and I are in that *Bierhalle* instead of at my cousin's dull party.'

Sasha caught her breath. Her senses leaped dramatically at the rash expression in his eyes. She felt a tug of response and said clumsily, 'Ladies don't drink beer.'

He laughed. 'Then, I shall get you some wine.' His manner was again very correct.

Beer halls! The Wormington-Prossers would have a fit. Sasha considered whether she ought to escape before he returned. She could see Kitty by the piano, talking to a very handsome man with a moustache. Kitty seemed to be relishing her freedom; the Wormington-Prossers had evidently relaxed their guard. There was an empty chair beside Leah and Lavinia. It would be easy for Sasha to retrace her path among the guests, let Herr Backhaus discover her with her sisters and be forced into polite, and safe, conversation, instead of talking about beer halls. She hesitated, then stood her ground and looked impatiently for his return.

People were clamouring for Backhaus to sing. They called his name with shouts of enthusiasm. He came towards Sasha and pulled a rueful expression as he handed her a glass of wine. 'They are wanting me to be a performing monkey.' The shouts were becoming more insistent. People were looking at them, waiting. Seizing Sasha by the hand, he said, 'Miss Hammond, you will sing with me?'

'I don't sing,' Sasha said in alarm. 'I never sing, except for myself at the piano.'

'You are not drinking beer, and you do not sing? Then you must play for me.' He held her hand more firmly and

130

pulled her towards the piano. 'Do you accompany?'

'Of course,' said Sasha indignantly. Had no one told him she had performed in German salons and theatres where Chopin and Mendelssohn had once played? But she could not sustain her indignation. The contact of his hand on hers sent shocks of exhilaration through her. She tried to make sense of the change that had come over her in the space of less than half an hour. One moment she had been trying to warm herself near the fire, and the next she had felt as breathless and invigorated as she did when she was playing a concerto.

Kitty leaned over the piano, searching through the music books to help them select a sheet of music. 'I think you've made a conquest,' she murmured in Sasha's ear.

Sasha looked at her swiftly for signs of sarcasm, but found none. She sat at the piano, took the music Backhaus had chosen and read it quickly before she began to play.

The song was supposedly sung by an old woman lamenting the way the world had gone to the bad. Backhaus performed it in a comic vein, wavering on the high notes. Even in comedy, his voice had a power over his audience that held them poised between laughter and admiration.

Sasha felt a prickling sensation run through her as everyone applauded. She looked for Kitty, but she was at the far side of the room with the man she had seen earlier, and Sasha was again alone with Werner Backhaus.

The song had dispelled the sober atmosphere of the party; but Backhaus was not finished with them yet.

'Let us have the *Erlkönig*,' he whispered to Sasha. 'The story of the poor father, who is riding, riding to save his son's life? Ah . . . but all in vain. Let us stir them just a little.'

Sasha played the accompaniment at a rattling pace. His voice was thrilling, dramatic and intense, with a suggestion that its full power was held in reserve. When they came to the end, and he sang, almost in a whisper, the tragic words that the boy was dead, Sasha played the final chords with a heartfelt flourish.

'Oh, you have stirred them, Herr Backhaus!' she said in triumph. 'You certainly stirred them.'

He laughed. 'And you, Miss Hammond. I should say you are never playing Schubert so well in your life!'

Mrs Wormington-Prosser announced that there would be dancing. The hired orchestra began to tune up. People were pushing back chairs for the servants to roll up the carpet.

'Will you dance with me?' Backhaus took her hand. 'We have sung, and we have played together. Please, Miss Hammond, say you will now dance with me.'

He detained her for three waltzes in a row. There were no dance cards here, as there were at home; Sasha could not make the excuse that the next dance was already taken. Nor did she want to refuse. She felt as if she were caught in a whirlwind as he spun her around the floor. Dizzy, enraptured, suddenly and violently in love, she sank at last on to a chair.

He sat beside her. 'Ah, forgive me. You are exhausted. I shall dance a waltz with your sisters.'

'No,' Sasha protested. 'I'm not tired. I have more stamina than anyone supposes. It's because of playing the piano. Don't go!'

But, with a smile that seemed to promise that his return would be more eventful than anything that had happened so far, he left her. She watched jealously as he spoke to Leah and Lavinia, and then spun Lavinia on to the floor. Sasha watched more closely when he danced with Kitty. She watched Kitty's every move, waiting for the languorous, flirtatious looks from under lowered eyelashes, Herr Backhaus's inevitable dissolution into spoony helplessness. But Kitty danced only one waltz with Backhaus before she drifted away towards the handsome man with the moustache, her skirts fluttering a blue path among the dancers.

Werner Backhaus then danced with Mrs Wormington-Prosser, and Mr Wormington-Prosser partnered Sasha in a mazurka and a waltz; he was an immaculate dancer and swung Sasha round and round. It seemed that at every

132

turn she was confronted by Backhaus, laughing and dancing, then talking with a crowd of admiring ladies, but always catching her eye and smiling. Sasha seethed with a fierce impatience to be alone with him again.

'Are you enjoying our little party?' said her host, holding her close, his hand in the small of Sasha's back.

'Oh, yes!' Sasha closed her eyes, not knowing whether at that moment she felt miserable or jubilant. And then Mr Wormington-Prosser had released her and Herr Backhaus was again by her side.

'Shall we go into the hall? It's very hot in here.'

Sasha's body was on fire as he tucked her hand into the crook of his elbow and she felt the solid mass of his forearm through his coat-sleeves. Her heart was pounding violently.

'I was wrong, Miss Hammond. They are human after all,' he said, when they had found a quiet space beside a potted camellia under the echoing stair. 'They are all very happy, and jig about like peasants on a holiday.'

He sat beside her and released her from his arm. Sasha immediately felt abandoned. She wanted to hold his hand against her breast so that he could feel the heavy thump, thump of her heart; but he was consulting a pocket book from his waistcoat. 'So – when can you escape the notice of our good hosts?'

She stared at him. 'I'm not sure. I don't know what you mean.'

'I mean, when can I see you again?' He looked up from the page of his pocket book and his eyes held hers. 'I have to see you again. Surely you know? You have held my heart in turmoil all evening. Oh, Sasha . . .'

Sasha felt her stomach somersault at his tender use of her first name. '*Your* heart has been in turmoil . . .?'

'Without question. Oh, Sasha – when? When?'

'I don't know,' Sasha said again. She wished she could think of something sophisticated to say, instead of behaving like a child who had been offered a choice of an outing and did not know what to ask for.

'I can come on Wednesday,' he said urgently. 'I can

meet you. My cousin's family will not know.'

'Mrs Wormington-Prosser is going to visit friends . . .'

'It is good. Can you walk in the garden?'

'I think so.'

Sasha's heart pounded with the enormity of what she was doing. He wanted to meet her alone. It was the sort of proposition Kitty might have agreed to, but Kitty was different – pathetically governed by her nature. Sasha told herself she was too strong-minded to go along with such a thing. Besides, it wasn't proper. It wasn't *done*.

'Then we are agreeing to this? On Wednesday afternoon at three o'clock?' He pencilled it in his pocket book, as if it were an official appointment. 'Do you know the lake?'

'Yes. It's frozen. It's very pretty.'

'And so are you,' he said softly. 'You have captured my heart, Sasha. I feel . . . so happy.' He was looking at her with a gentle look in his eyes. 'I am picturing it already. The sun on the ice. You waiting by the trees. So beautiful.' He snapped shut the pocket book and put it away. 'Will you be meeting me there?'

Sasha came to her senses. 'I don't know. You must see it's not quite . . . not very proper. I'll tell you later.'

'Before the evening is ending?'

'Yes. All right. Before the evening is over.'

They returned to the drawing room and mingled with the other guests; the orchestra was still playing, and they danced again. She should have said no at once. Why give him hope that she might be there? Had she gone mad? Yet, each time she stole a glance at him, each time she caught his eye, each time he smiled at her, Sasha felt her breath come quickly again.

She had made a solemn vow, she reminded herself. She had promised herself she would never again let anyone affect her in the same way as Mr Elliman. What a ludicrous vow to have made! What an absurd comparison! This was nothing like her feelings for poor Mr Elliman. This was so different that she could not understand what was happening to her. There were the

134

oddest of contradictions in the sensations in her body: her spine prickled with cold, and yet her breast felt so restricted and hot that she longed to tear away the strings of her corset. She thought of the look in Herr Backhaus's eyes and the shape of his lower lip when he smiled; she thought of his insistence about meeting her on Wednesday, and shivers of delicious, terrifying anticipation ran through her.

Before the evening was over, she had given him her promise.

Chapter Seven

Sasha put on her cloak and boots and slipped out from the house. The light was thin and grey, the trees heavy with snow, crowding in on her with their silence as she hurried down to the frozen expanse of the lake. She glanced behind her to be sure she could not be seen from the house and saw that the lake was completely hidden. Herr Backhaus must know his cousin's estate intimately; he had chosen the perfect place for a meeting.

Sasha stamped her feet and swung her arms across her chest, wondering if he would come. Had he been amusing himself with her – a droll diversion for the evening? He would tell his friends about her sometime: 'It's very easy to make a conquest. Simply pick out the youngest and most stupid-looking girl in the room . . .' A singer like Werner Backhaus must have met hundreds of women, far more enlightened than she was about the way to behave when a gentleman suggested meeting by a lake, on a freezing cold winter's afternoon, without anyone knowing about it.

Sasha did not know what the time was, but she was sure it must be well after three. She turned angrily away from the trees. Throwing back the hood of her cloak to let the air numb her face, she marched down to the very edge of the lake, frightening a huddle of starlings into the air. Thick ridges and lumps of snow roughened the surface of the ice. She dug at the edge with the heel of her boot, trying to crack it. 'You stupid girl!' she muttered fiercely. 'You stupid, stupid idiot!'

She had made a small gouge-mark and stopped, panting a little. She sensed rather than heard that she was not alone and looked up in alarm. A figure stood by the trees. He came towards her swiftly.

'I am sorry. Oh, are you very angry with me? I can see that you are. But I had to be sure no one is seeing me on the road.'

'Why?' Sasha said, shivering with tension. 'Why must no one see you. Why all the secrecy? Why not simply call on Mr Prosser your cousin and meet me openly at the house?' She threw back her head. 'Are you married?'

He burst out laughing. 'You funny child. What an idea!'

'You haven't answered me yet.'

He became very serious. 'No, Sasha. I am not married. Do you think I am asking you to meet me if it is so? Do you think so badly of me?'

The expression of candour and intimacy in his eyes made Sasha's breath rise quickly to her throat as it had on the night of the party.

'No. I don't think badly of you at all. I think – I think you are . . . very nice.'

They walked along under the trees. Nice? thought Sasha. *Nice*! Was that all she could say to someone who, simply by a look or a word, tightened all her senses until she felt as though she were strung with piano wires?

'I am asking you to meet me here because they will watch us too closely. You are seeing the way they watch your sister.'

'You know about Kitty?' she interrupted. 'Do you know why she was sent here?'

'Of course. We all know these things.'

'You must think us a very peculiar family.'

He did not answer.

'Of course, you might think us less peculiar because of Kitty's indiscretion than because my family reacted so harshly to it,' Sasha continued. She walked swiftly, swinging with her hand to dash snow from the branches as she passed.

137

'It does seem a little harsh, to send your sister away from the ones she loves best.'

The ones she loves best? thought Sasha. Oh, Herr Backhaus, how little you really know.

She cast little sidelong glances at him, trying to be objective, deciding how much she liked of what she saw. She admired his compassion for Kitty, even if she could not share his opinion about her. She adored the way his lower lip made a prominent edge below the upper one. She was full of concern because the cold made his complexion so pale; but she was reassured by his indisputable vigour: every now and then he reached out to pull a handful of snow from the branches and, rolling it into a ball, sent it gracefully skimming across the lake. Sasha found the combination of movements intoxicating.

They walked halfway round the lake and back again through the trees, talking about the composers they most admired, and a little about what had attracted each of them to the life of a musical performer.

'The sad part about touring is that everything is so transitory,' Sasha said. 'I make new friends and then have to move on.'

'And so – we must make the most of the time you are here. What do you suggest? Some place not so secret, since you are worrying about my moral intentions.'

'No. I trust you. I really do.'

'But, we will make an outing. Yes? Perhaps with your sisters?'

'It's my birthday next week . . .'

'Excellent!' He seized her hand and swung it against his breast. 'The theatre. They are making a performance of *Iphigenie auf Tauris* in Basle. I shall accompany you and your sisters.'

Sasha shook her head. 'Mrs Wormington-Prosser wouldn't allow it. She hates the theatre.'

'Even when it is Goethe?' he was thoughtful. 'I shall suggest it. A cultural outing of the highest order. My cousin's wife cannot possibly be objecting to *Iphigenie*. But you must say nothing. You must behave as if you are knowing nothing about it.' He looked into her eyes and, still holding her hand, rolled back the woollen cuff of her glove to kiss the inside of her wrist.

The light touch of his lips sent shivers of sexual excitement coursing through Sasha's veins. She closed her eyes and let the sensation of pure delight linger.

'Farewell, sweet Sasha,' he whispered. 'Until we meet again.'

Kitty stopped Sasha in the upstairs corridor two days later. She was in a fever of agitation. 'Did you know they are planning a theatre visit for you? They were talking about your birthday. It seems Mr Wormington-Prosser's cousin has offered to escort you and Leah and Lavinia to Basle.'

Sasha's spirits soared at the thought that Herr Backhaus had been true to his word.

'But they won't let me go, Sasha,' said Kitty. 'The Prosser thinks the theatre might corrupt me. They'll allow the three of you to go with Mr Wormington-Prosser's cousin, but they say I must stay behind.'

'Oh, that isn't fair.' Lavinia, coming out from the bedroom had overheard. 'I shall talk to them. I'll ask Leah to talk to them. They have to let you come as well.'

'If only I *could* go to Basle with you.' Kitty looked longingly out of the staircase window, as if freedom lay only a step away from the snow-filled gardens. 'You've no idea what even the smallest pleasure means to me after all this time. If you could persuade them I can be trusted.' She turned her soulful eyes on Sasha. 'If *you* were to ask Mrs Wormington-Prosser, she might agree.'

'Oh, do, Sasha,' Lavinia said. 'It's your birthday.'

Sasha remembered Werner Backhaus's ready compassion for Kitty; how unkind she had become towards her sister; and all because of Mr Elliman, who was nothing to her now. She felt a wave of generous sentiment go out from her and encompass Kitty – poor Kitty, who had lost Porky Portland, her lover, and been shut up here in this ghastly house for months and months, and now almost seemed sorry about all the trouble she had caused.

'We'll *all* talk to them,' she said.

The Wormington-Prossers were won over. Kitty was allowed to see *Iphigenie auf Tauris*, because the story was 'classical' and by Goethe. The sisters all promised to take full responsibility for Kitty's behaviour.

Kitty cried with happiness; she flung her arms around Sasha as if there had never been any ill-feeling between them. But Sasha hugged her secret about Herr Backhaus to herself. She tried out his first name secretly with a thrill of pleasure. *Werner*. He was in love with her, and she would have the whole evening in his company. She thought of the warm darkness of the theatre and imagined him sitting beside her in a close, wholly sanctioned intimacy.

On Sasha's birthday Kitty gave her a present of a purse she had made, saying, 'I know I have been horrid in the past, Sasha, but I hope you can find it in your heart to forgive me.'

Kitty had grown very calm since the longed-for outing had been granted. In the evening she dressed slowly and meticulously in a sober frock, and selected a sensible plaid wool cloak with a fur shoulder cape. She was very pale except for two spots of high colour on her cheeks.

'Oh, dear. I hope she's not going to be ill,' murmured Leah as they went downstairs.

Lavinia vowed that when they returned to England she would plead for Kitty to be allowed to go home. 'What does it matter if people in Avondon gossip? Anything has to be better than being incarcerated in this house!'

The thought of returning to England depressed Sasha a little. She tried not to think beyond the evening's outing to the theatre. She turned a corner of the stairs and saw Werner waiting for them in the hall. His glance took in the four of them. Sasha smiled at him with a special gratitude for being so clever and arranging the outing.

He did not acknowledge her look but behaved as if she were a stranger as they exchanged greetings and he wished her a 'happy birthday'. Sasha felt a twinge of disappointment. But of course, she told herself, they had to be discreet. They did not want the Prosser suspecting they had met one another since the party.

Werner sat next to Leah in the carriage as they travelled to Basle; he chatted amiably and with great charm. When they reached the theatre he sat between Leah and Lavinia. Sasha felt isolated next to Kitty, who seemed lost in a world of her own. Sasha was restless with frustration as the curtain rose. It was her birthday, but Werner was paying so much attention to her sisters that he had barely said a civil word to her. She stared straight ahead at the lighted stage, bored already with the play though she pretended to be engrossed by it. Her grasp of German was adequate, thanks to Miss Holloway; she knew enough to follow the play easily. In any case, she was already familiar with the story: father promised to sacrifice daughter; daughter, rescued by the gods, escaped to foreign parts. Just like Kitty, Sasha thought, and was tempted to share the joke with her.

At the start of the first interval, as they got up to walk about and ease their cramped limbs, Werner whispered in her ear, 'Say you are too hot. I must talk with you.'

Sasha's sour mood was instantly dispelled. She felt obligingly overcome by the heat and allowed Herr Backhaus to escort her outside.

'I shall walk with your sister in the snow a little,' he told Leah, taking hold of Sasha firmly by the arm.

They walked along the street, away from the theatre, and Sasha began to laugh. At last, weak with happiness, she had to stop and lean against the wall.

'How old *are* you?' Werner said, laughing with her.

She looked at him, suddenly sober. 'Eighteen.'

'Ah,' he sighed. 'Sweet child.'

'Don't say that,' she said quickly. 'Don't say that.' She dared not ask him how old he was. She had guessed at thirty and did not want to hear that he was older.

He drew her into the darkness of the wall. 'Sasha, *süsse* Sasha. One kiss?'

141

Sasha gave herself to that first ever kiss. She reached upwards and was filled with an intense yearning. His lips were warm in spite of the night air. His arms folded her to him, imprisoning her in the armour of his body, so that she could not escape. She felt she must either be absorbed by him or else her feelings would overwhelm her; it was as if she had been swallowed alive by a vast, voluptuous darkness.

He was the first to break free from their embrace. He tipped her chin in his hands and murmured, 'Perhaps not such a child after all. Ah, Sasha. What is it I am doing to you? Forgive me?'

Sasha did not see why she should forgive him for making her so happy; but she could see no hope ahead, beyond the interminable *Iphigenie*, the next weeks of her tour, the journey back to England, and then black despair. 'What are we going to do?'

'I shall think of something,' he promised, turning her towards the lights of the theatre and directing their steps that way. They reached the auditorium in time for the second act. Werner halted.

'I am seeing an old friend. I shall join you in a moment.' He left her to find her own way to the auditorium.

'Where have you been?' hissed Leah as she stood up for Sasha to get by. 'Where is Herr Backhaus?'

'Talking to a friend.' Sasha stumbled past her and past Lavinia and slipped into her seat. The seat beside her was empty. 'Where's Kitty?' she whispered, as the lights were dimmed.

'Gone to look for you,' hissed Lavinia. 'Really, Sasha. What was Herr Backhaus thinking of, keeping you outside so long?'

Sasha did not answer. She sat in the darkness, unconscious of the drama taking place on the stage as she lived over and over again the sensations of their kiss. She wanted to tell the whole audience and the theatre players that they could halt the performance, that nothing had any significance any more, except the fact that she was in love.

Five minutes passed, and Sasha began to feel more

142

concerned about Werner's absence. She looked at Leah and Lavinia in the darkness, and at the empty space between them. Kitty had not returned either. Leah was leaning across the vacant seat and speaking urgently to Lavinia; after a while she got up and left the auditorium.

Sasha tried at last to concentrate on the play, but a feeling of unease nagged at her. Why had Kitty not come back yet? And why, if Kitty had gone to look for her, had they not met in the vestibule of the theatre?

She remembered Kitty's peculiar fervour when she had begged them to seek permission for her to come to Basle. She remembered now that Kitty had talked about Basle on their very first day with the Wormington-Prossers. Why had it not occurred to anyone that Kitty had got exactly what she wanted? Kitty *always* got what she wanted. Why Basle? Suddenly Sasha understood.

Leah had returned. She was whispering across the seats, 'Get up! Get up! Something terrible has happened!'

Basle – with its main line railway station! Sasha was jolted into action. She scrambled from her place and pulled Lavinia to her feet with her. The people in the row behind began to grumble loudly. Pausing only to snap at them, 'Oh, do be quiet! It's only a stupid play!' Sasha hurried after Leah to the back of the auditorium.

The theatre staff stood in the brightly lit vestibule, looking perplexed. Leah's face was white.

'She's gone! She's left us this note.'

'What do you mean – gone?' echoed Lavinia. She took the sheet of paper from Leah and read it very slowly, as if she could not make out the message it conveyed.

'Leah means Kitty's run away,' Sasha said quietly. 'And Herr Backhaus has gone with her, hasn't he? *Hasn't* he!' She kept her voice calm, though she wanted to scream at Leah to tell her it wasn't true.

Lavinia handed Sasha the note with a look of bewilderment. It was brief and to the point: 'Werner and I have been planning this for a very long time, so there's no point in trying to find us. I am sorry, Sasha. Truly I am.' The word 'truly' was underlined.

Leah cast a swift, searching glance at Sasha and saw the pinched look of misery in her face. She walked towards one of the staff and asked for their cloaks. She put Sasha's cloak round her shoulders for her and fastened it at the neck.

It was snowing again as they waited for a carriage. Sasha said nothing at all on the journey back to the Wormington-Prossers. She endured in silence the inquest that followed, but her heart ached from the double betrayal. She should have seen; she might have known Kitty could not be trusted; but Werner . . . She remembered the way he had kissed her, the caressing warmth of the things he had said. All lies? Even the kiss? Could it really all have been lies?

Leah was tight-lipped, furious with Kitty, and with Sasha, but most of all with herself for allowing the disaster to happen. She explained to their hosts as much as she knew. For Sasha's sake she did not show them Kitty's note. She said she would take all responsibility. The Wormington-Prossers must in no way blame themselves. At last, the girls were allowed to go to bed.

Sasha undressed in silence, glad the questioning was over and that her sisters were too shocked and exhausted to talk about what had happened. At least the Wormington-Prossers need not know she had fallen in love with Werner. At least she would be spared the agony of a public humiliation.

Even so, Sasha's humiliation was terrible. She lay in the darkness, and covering her head with her pillow to smother the sound, she wept for an hour without ceasing; in the end she did not care whether Leah and Lavinia heard her or not. At one point Lavinia stirred, and with a cry of anguish threw back her bedclothes to go to comfort her. Leah thrust out her arm to restrain her, and Lavinia lay down again.

Sasha stopped crying. Her nightdress was soaked with perspiration, and the mattress felt wet against her neck. She sat up and turned the pillow over, pulling it down to cover the tear-soaked sheet; then she turned down the top sheet, smoothing it over the blankets with her hands, glad of its coldness against her wrists. She lay down and tried to lose her jangled nerves in sleep, burying her face in the cool, dry comfort of the pillow. But the knot of hurt and anger in her chest would not shift, her eyes were salted and sore, and she lay, exhausted, unable to sleep.

In the morning, everyone tried to resolve exactly what should be done. It was agreed that Sasha should wait with the Wormington-Prossers for Herr Lindau to arrive, and then continue her tour. Leah and Lavinia would return at once to England and explain Kitty's disappearance to their parents.

The Wormington-Prossers avoided mentioning Werner Backhaus by name, as if, by distancing him, they could avoid all connection with Kitty's seducer. They said they would put out inquiries, they would leave no stone unturned until they found her; but everyone knew there was not much point; the lovers could have been anywhere.

Sasha waved goodbye to her sisters from the gate, drained of all feeling, except for a swift homesickness when she thought of her parents. She was a long way from home. She felt a brief need for the security of Hanover Terrace and thought instead of her tour. She still had her music. No one could ever take that from her.

Two things at least had become clear, she thought, as she turned back to the house. Love was nothing but a cruel confidence trick . . . And Kitty had triumphed again.

Leah felt a lump of tenderness rise to her throat at the sight of Sasha, her hand raised, standing at the Wormington-Prossers' gate. She watched from the carriage until the small, determined figure turned back through the snow to the house. But she held the image of Sasha for a long time on the journey home, seeing her wrapped in a shawl to still her shivering, flakes of snow falling on her hair and shoulders.

Leah was aware that Sasha had given her heart and had it thrust back to her, badly bruised. It would mend, she

145

thought. She's still very young. Her own heart quickened as they neared the railway station. She thought of Yorkshire, and freedom. At last! At long last her life was going to be her own.

Gabriel found it difficult to choose his favourite from among the seasons. His father would have regarded the cycle of the year in purely farming terms: the winter was the harshest, with livestock always to feed, but there was the compensation of long evenings by your own fireside. Spring was new and green and full of hope for a good year. The summer was always chancy – too wet or too dry. The autumn was the best, once the crops were in: the year's work nearly over; pork and bacon lying salted; the satisfaction of animal feed stored for the winter.

But Gabriel did not look at the seasons in farming terms. He was invigorated by all the moods of the year. The summer brought torrential storms, long hot days that lifted the delicate smells from the moor, and the air was full of cricket song. The autumn was the saddest of the seasons and the most beautiful; the colours ran into one another, brown and purple and gold, and the rain smelled of decay. Winter was cruel, but there was the compensation of the peculiarity of the light on the snow-covered moor, the clean cold smell of frost in the air, the crunch of ice under his boots.

Spring was the best of all. He liked to walk in the rain, feel the sun on his face or let the wind buffet his ears. He would throw out his arms to the sky, with violent inward cries of 'Blow, winds! Rage! Blow!' borrowed from reading Shakespeare, but with a fierce sense of being alive that was unique to himself.

He stood looking down on the road to Eskton one afternoon in April. It had been raining and every detail of the landscape was very clear; he could see the coast, the grey stone church and houses of the next village, and the red-roofed cottage on the edge of the moor, where the workmen had been busy for weeks. He watched as the carrier's wagon he had followed with his eye all along the road rolled and rumbled along the track. He held his breath, waiting for its occupants to climb out. So, he had been right. With a leap of exultation Gabriel put his violin to his chin, felt it mould itself to him and the bow become an extension of his arm. The music drove through him; he heard it in his head and on the clean air. Would she remember?

He saw one of the figures halt as the men carried the trunks and boxes and furniture from the wagon into the cottage. He played on. She had come back. She had said she would come, and now she was here!

Leah raised her hand to command Lavinia to listen.

'It's him! The angel Gabriel! Isn't it wonderful!' She whirled round to scan the moor and saw the figure among the rocks. She felt a thrill of pleasure as she recognised the music he was playing.

Lavinia, hot from the journey and tired after supervising the carriers from the station, pushed back her hair from her sweating face with an impatient hand. 'As if we haven't got better things to do! As if *he* hasn't either!' She hurried inside after the men.

Leah threw a last glance behind her and raised a hand to the solitary figure. Early that evening she put on her mantel and bonnet and announced she was going to call on their farming neighbours.

'Oh, Leah! Can't it wait until tomorrow?' Lavinia was unpacking their books, stacking them on a set of shelves behind the sitting room door. 'There's still so much to do.'

Beneath her shield of intense domestic activity, Lavinia was a dithering mass of insecurity. She looked round the sitting room with strong feelings of unease. Beyond it there was nothing more than a bedroom and a scullery; outside lay a garden and a few outbuildings. They would keep hens, the sisters had said in their enthusiasm. They would turn one of the outhouses into a painting studio. They would keep a pony for journeys to town. But would they ever make it look civilised? What about when their mother came to visit? Or the Pickersgills?

Mr Pickersgill had aided them in their plans, assuring the Hammonds by letter that he had vetted the spot. Lavinia had thought only of being near him when she had agreed to Leah leasing the cottage; but did Mr Pickersgill think it a little eccentric of her to want to live on the edge of the moor instead of in Eskton? She did not know whether he would even like her after all this time. Nor, indeed, whether he had any feelings about her at all. He *had* expressed delight at the move to Yorkshire, and she had tried to find a reading between the lines. But he had said nothing that was explicitly sentimental about their friendship; his letters were rather formal. Did he believe she had come as a companion to Leah, or did he imagine – Lavinia blushed at the thought – that she had come because she was in love with him? If challenged, she would have had to admit it, for she was incapable of lying, but she would rather die than have him suspect that she was chasing him.

'*You* may be able to wait until tomorrow to go visiting,' Leah said. 'I shall visit the Ridgeways today. We shall be needing milk and bread, and there are other matters to discuss.'

'Ask them if they would lend us a pony and trap,' Lavinia called after her as Leah went out of the door.

Gabriel came towards her as she crossed the farmyard. 'I knew you were coming back. Father heard the cottage was being got ready for two ladies from down south. I guessed it was you.' He grinned. His face was wide open with happiness. 'And I thought you'd gone and forgotten us.'

'After I'd heard you play? How could I?'

Gabriel led the way into the farmhouse, calling out, 'Mother, we've a visitor.' He signalled to Leah to step inside the kitchen.

Leah remembered the animal smells and the smell of the dairy. There was a stronger scent overlying them, for Mrs Ridgeway had been baking bread; she came through from the room beyond and stood, wiping her hands on her apron. She gave no sign that she recognised Leah from their meeting the year before.

'You'll be one of the ladies from the cottage.'

'It's Miss Hammond,' Gabriel told her impatiently. 'The lady who gave me a ticket to a concert last summer.' He sensed that she was being obstinate for some reason known only to herself.

'I've come to ask if you can supply us with bread and milk, Mrs Ridgeway,' Leah said, in her way of getting straight to the point. 'My sister and I intend living here for some time. We shall need to impose on you for produce. Oh, and if you could lend us a horse and trap until we get organised . . .?'

'We're not a jobbing stables, Miss. We only have the one cart. But we can let you have milk. And I can sell you bread and eggs and a few vegetables until you get yourselves sorted.' She softened a little. 'We go to market in Eskton, Thursdays. You're welcome to ride along with us then, if you've a need.'

'I'm much obliged. I expect we shall soon be better organised. We plan to keep a few hens. And we shall grow vegetables.'

'I thought you were here to paint, not to farm.'

Mrs Ridgeway saw that she had betrayed the fact that she remembered Leah very well. Too well. She remembered that she was clever and wealthy and beautiful, and that she had turned Gabriel's head with her talk about how well he played the violin.

'Yes. We shall paint.' Leah regarded her steadily and wondered why the woman so clearly mistrusted her.

Mrs Ridgeway dropped her gaze. 'Well, then. I'll fetch you a loaf.' She returned to the room beyond the kitchen.

Gabriel looked at Leah with a shy smile. He was taller than the last time she had seen him. Less of a child.

'Will you come and play your violin to us sometimes, when you've some time to spare from the farm, Gabriel?' she said on impulse. 'My sister and I play the violin and the viola. It might be amusing for us all to play together.'

149

'I should like that.' Gabriel's thoughts ran ahead with pleasure. To play his violin with real musicians who knew more about music than his Great-uncle Jacob! It was a dream come true.

His mother brought a loaf of bread and filled Leah's jug with milk, covering it for her with a net.

'Father's let me have space in one of the barns for studying since I saw you last,' Gabriel said as he went out with Leah across the yard.

Leah sensed the barely suppressed desire to swagger a little. 'Would you like to show me?'

'If you like.' He was suddenly diffident.

The cow-shed had a cobbled floor and a door at either end. The stalls were empty; the animals were out in the field. The stall at the farthest end was wider than the rest; and someone had extended the height of the partition to meet the timbers of the roof, dividing it off more positively. Daylight flooded in through the open door. Within this space, some six or seven feet square, next to the smell and darkness of the cattle housing, an attempt had been made to create an area of comfort.

'I was bothering John with reading at night,' Gabriel explained. 'Mother was all for me using the parlour, but Dad reckoned I should have a place of my own. I've got an oil lamp, see? And a table. And the animals kept it warm through the winter.' He stepped back against the wall so that she might admire everything more clearly.

'It makes a splendid *study*,' Leah said, deliberately dignifying the space with the term, moved by his attempt to create an atmosphere of learning in what was to all intents and purposes still a cow byre. There was an inkstand on the table, a heavily ink-stained blotter, and a pile of manuscript ledgers of irregular sizes.

'Are these your books?'

A number of laden shelves ran along the back wall of the cattle stall. She read the worn book-titles. There was a volume of Shakespeare's plays; a few of the Waverley novels and a few modern works of Dickens standing beside *Ideas for the Young Naturalist*, *Whateley's Elements of Logic*, and *Lives of the Great Composers*. She scanned them all and looked at Gabriel with a sense of respect. 'But how have you managed to read all these?'

'I told you, I went to school until I was fourteen. I lodged with an uncle in Eskton. But I've been teaching myself the rest.'

Excitement banged at Leah's ribs as she looked at the titles. 'Would you like to borrow others? Lavinia and I have books of poetry and literature, and several books on music.'

'Would I!' He fell back against the wall with an exclamation of joy.

Leah laughed at his unaffected exuberance. 'Oh, Gabriel. I'm so glad you and I have met again.'

An excitement of her own took hold of Leah as she swung her way across the heather to the cottage. A germ of an idea, planted in her mind over a year ago, had begun to generate a distinct plan. What a triumph it would be to feed the boy's thirst for knowledge and watch it develop. He was obviously a natural for learning. There would be a vast amount for him to catch up, but she and Lavinia between them had plenty to offer; they were both well grounded in mathematics and Latin and Greek.

She told Lavinia about her scheme that evening.

'I hope you know what you're doing.' Lavinia was hanging curtains at the low window.

'Does that mean you don't have any objections?'

'If you want to amuse yourself by playing tutor to the boy, I'm not going to interfere.'

Lavinia's nerves were feeling considerably soothed; the cottage was beginning to look almost charming; a smoky fire burned in the grate; and a message had come by servant that evening to say Mr Pickersgill wished to call on them the next day.

Mr Pickersgill arrived on horseback. He looked stouter than ever and very pink about the ears after his ride. He inspected the cottage and exclaimed at the air of domesticity the sisters had achieved in the space of twenty-four hours.

'Charming. Utterly charming,' he said for the third time, so that Leah felt a strong urge to squash him. 'But you need a servant, ladies. And my mother knows just the girl. Strong and willing. She is fourteen years of age, can cook and clean and comes highly recommended from the parson near here.'

'We *were* going to inquire in the village . . .' Lavinia said, anxious to let him see they had not entirely neglected the matter of servants.

'There. I have done it for you. The girl will come up every day from eight until three o'clock. Now, as for transport . . . You'll need a carriage. I shall help you to select a pony at the market on Thursday.'

'Thank you, Mr Pickersgill, but we were going to drive to market with Ridgeway the farmer to purchase a pony and trap,' said Leah, disliking Mr Pickersgill's assumption that they could not function without his masculine guidance.

'Oh – but Leah! If Mr Pickersgill is willing to recommend a pony for us . . .'

'I shall meet you there on Thursday,' said Mr Pickersgill.

A warning look from Lavinia prevented Leah from protesting further and she fell silent. If she was honest, Leah was glad to offload some of their domestic duties; she had no doubt that Mr Pickersgill was a good enough judge of horse-flesh.

'Lavinia, why don't you show Mr Pickersgill the building we thought to use as a stable?' Leah wanted to be alone, finding Lavinia's meekness and Mr Pickersgill's mild dictatorship tiresome. She thought of the challenge she was about to set herself in educating Gabriel, and shut the door on the conversations of the couple outside. Going to the bookshelves, she knelt on the floor to select the material she would need. How long? she wondered. How long, Mr Pickersgill, before you gather my sister to your manly bosom, whisk her away on your white charger to nuptial bliss in Eskton,

152

and I am left to fend for myself?

She was surprised by how attractive the notion of self-reliance seemed.

Gabriel came to the cottage carrying his violin the following evening. He was nervous about playing to them at first. Leah set up the music stands, talking all the time about the music she and Lavinia had played with Sasha and Kitty when they were all much younger.

The mention of Kitty set Leah wondering what had happened to her. They had heard almost nothing since she had disappeared with Werner Backhaus. There had been a brief note from Frankfurt to say they were not to worry about her, and Sasha had written from Strasburg with news that the runaways had been heard of travelling through France, but nothing more.

How could you, Kitty? thought Leah. How could you give up everything for a man? She looked at Gabriel, seeing the youthful bloom on his jaw and the deep-set, dark-fringed eyes. The mixture of strength, sensitivity and innocence was one that had a peculiar appeal. She imagined, fleetingly, what he would look like when he was older. Would women fall at his feet too? She thrust the question from her mind.

They played Mozart and Beethoven that evening: duets, solo pieces for one another, improvisations. When Gabriel had gone, the sisters sat back and smiled at one another, exhausted by sheer delight.

'You were right,' said Lavinia.

'I know. He has such a marvellous combination of natural flair and an eagerness to learn.'

'He needs tutoring. He needs to learn to read music. But he has a gift. He's like Sasha.'

'He plays better than Sasha,' said Leah quietly. 'He has more feeling.'

Leah raised the subject of Gabriel's education on the way to Eskton that Thursday. The front of the cart was loaded with farm produce, and Mrs Ridgeway, seated amongst spring cabbages and baskets of eggs and cheeses, was occupied with the business of watching that nothing spilled or rolled away as they jolted along the track. Leah and Lavinia were perched on the narrow seats on either side of the open cart, dressed in bonnets and shawls, 'like a pair of country bumpkins,' Lavinia said.

'I should like to tutor Gabriel, Mrs Ridgeway,' Leah said, when they reached the smoother, downhill road to Eskton. She raised her voice above the rumble of wheels. 'I think I could teach him mathematics and the classics to a fair standard.'

'Miss Hammond. Folks like us can't afford for him to have a teacher,' Mrs Ridgeway said, so quickly that Leah wondered whether she had been expecting something of the kind. 'Besides, we need him on the farm until his brother marries.'

'And what then? What is Gabriel's future to be?'

Mrs Ridgeway did not answer, but her thoughts flew to the hours Gabriel wasted in the inn at Eskton; and the notion of her son becoming a parson nudged into her mind.

'I mean,' said Leah, 'I would educate him for nothing. It would be a pleasure to me to see him learn.'

'Why?' Mrs Ridgeway lifted her head and regarded Leah, woman to woman.

Leah met her gaze, aware of the element of conflict, jealousy even, in the confrontation. 'Because he has a talent which *must* not go to waste. We must release it. I mean all of us. You and your husband, and Lavinia and I. Gabriel loves music, and he loves learning. He has a fine intelligence. It's criminal to keep it hidden here on the moor. There is *so much* Gabriel could do if he were given an education.'

Mrs Ridgeway, torn between the desire to see her son better himself and a reluctance to hand him over to another woman's care, saw her ambition become a possibility. 'Like go for the church maybe?'

'If that is what *Gabriel* wants. Or perhaps he might become a lawyer, or an engineer, or develop his musical talents.'

'No.' Mrs Ridgeway set her mouth in a line of resistance. 'I'll not have you stuffing his head with any more of that nonsense.'

'At any rate, he *must* be allowed to further his knowledge.'

'The lad must choose for himself,' said Mr Ridgeway, who until then had remained silent. The farmer shifted his attention briefly from the horse and the road, and turned from the driving seat to look at Leah. 'We won't stand in the way of Gabriel getting an education if you think you could make a scholar out of him. And we thank you. Thank you, Miss Hammond, for saying he can be pupil to you. He'll come when his work's done tomorrow night. I'll tell the lad.'

This was a long speech for Ridgeway. He seemed so much surprised by his own eloquence that he was quiet for the rest of the journey.

His wife, however, became more talkative once her husband had made up his mind. She was not convinced the Hammond sisters were to be trusted, but hadn't Squire Pickersgill's son, down in Eskton, taken up with the younger one himself? She chatted along the way about the various well set-up families in the area.

'. . . The Pickersgills are the best-connected people round these parts. They're well respected by everyone, rich and poor alike.'

Lavinia flushed with pleasure at the commendation.

'I believe young Mr Pickersgill came to call on you the other day,' Mrs Ridgeway added. 'He's such a lovely fellow.'

'He's going to help us choose a mare and pony-cart, Mrs Ridgeway.' Lavinia hoped the weightiness of choosing a horse and cart might dispel any hint of romance about the encounter. It would be unfortunate, at this early stage, to become a subject for local gossip.

But Mrs Ridgeway's opinion of Mr Pickersgill as a 'lovely fellow' still echoed brightly in Lavinia's ears when they reached Eskton. The object of this praise was waiting for them by the market hall. How handsome he looked among the old farmers, in their smock frocks and leggings, and the younger, country and working men. He wore a green riding coat of a cut-away style that showed off his sturdy figure, while his green and yellow striped waistcoat, and a very stylish, wide-brimmed felt hat, seemed to Lavinia to emphasise a dashing quality about him, which, she had to admit, had not been evident before. She felt briefly unsettled, remembering the artists who had come to her father's house dressed in yellow striped waistcoats. Had Randolph Portland worn something similar? Then she decided that a touch of the swell did nothing to detract from Mr Pickersgill's excellence.

Lavinia's heart beat erratically as he raised his walking cane in a greeting and came towards the Ridgeways' cart. She felt a further flutter of excitement as he handed down each of the women in turn. He bowed low to Mrs Ridgeway with a sweep of his hat; and the farmer's wife began to flutter too and busied herself with unpacking her produce.

'Shall we proceed first to the horse sale, ladies?'

They agreed that it would be a shame, through dallying about the town, to miss the best of the animals, and, parting from the Ridgeways, Leah and Lavinia walked with Mr Pickersgill through the market. Cattle stood patiently at the sides of the road. Men shouted greetings and bartered, and the baa-ing of sheep and whinnies of horses joined the general babble of sound.

'You must visit us again, Miss Leah and Miss Lavinia,' Mr Pickersgill said. 'My mother has been so much looking forward to your arrival. She asks if you would come over to tea tomorrow?'

'I'm afraid I must refuse,' said Leah quickly. They halted as they reached the horse traders. Leah ignored Lavinia's very obvious dismay. 'I've promised to tutor the farmer's boy. His first lesson has been arranged for tomorrow. But my sister may come to tea, Mr Pickersgill. Lavinia will make my apologies to your family.' She turned and linked her arm in Lavinia's, smiling at her swift recovery of spirits. 'What an adventure, Lavinia! You shall go in the new pony and trap.'

Leah stood outside the cottage in the late afternoon, watching for her first sighting of Gabriel as he came over the moor. It was mild, and the sun was warm on her neck and face. She was glad Lavinia had gone to Eskton. Much as she valued her companionship, she was discovering as each day passed that there was infinitely more pleasure in being alone.

It occurred to Leah that she did not behave as most women behaved; she did not seek out feminine company and, even less, that of men. She leaned against the stone wall of the cottage – *her* cottage, as she already thought of it – and folded her arms. She knew she was no longer apprehensive about Lavinia marrying – for she was sure now that matrimony was in Mr Pickersgill's mind. Leah surveyed the folds in the open moor. Already she felt as if she belonged here, in this severe but lovely landscape. Tomorrow, she would begin painting. She closed her eyes against the golden light of the sun. She would spend the summer days painting, and in the evenings she would cultivate the mind of the youth who was about to come to her for his first lesson.

Leah snapped her eyes open as she heard a shout. Gabriel had seen her and was waving. He began to run, books tucked under his arm and his coat edges flying in the wind. He reached her and came to a triumphant halt. He smiled, eager, a little uncertain, and Leah felt a jolt of excitement seize her.

'Well, Gabriel,' she said, bringing a school-ma'am tone to her manner. 'I thought we would start straight away with some Latin. I managed to find some texts in a bookshop in Eskton yesterday. If you decide you want to go to university in two or three years' time, you will need to have studied the classics. We have a hard task ahead. Do you think you would like to learn Latin and go to a university?'

Gabriel looked at Leah. All that day he had gone about

his work and had imagined the long hours, reading under her tuition. He had felt dizzy at the prospect. He felt heady now with anticipation.

'Do I?' he grinned. 'I think Providence must have sent you to me, Miss Hammond.'

Chapter Eight

Sasha stood beside Herr Lindau at the deck rail of the steamer and felt a pull of emotion as she saw the English coast loom into view through the mist; she bit her lip, feeling the threat of tears.

'Are you *sorry* to be going home, darling Sasha?' said her tutor.

'Oh no,' Sasha said fervently. 'It's the White cliffs, and the sea mist, and the *smell* of coming home that makes me want to cry. I can't wait to see the green hedges and trees of England.'

She glanced at Herr Lindau, and was sorry for him. Did he feel the same way about his native Germany? Was it a terrible wrench for him to come back to England? He looked very frail these days. His hair was blowing about like wisps of cotton flax. She reached up and tucked his scarf more firmly round his neck.

'You won't miss all your admirers?' he teased.

She laughed. 'They can all go hang themselves in despair.'

'You're a hardhearted young woman.'

'I know.'

There *had* been a few flirtations, in spite of her vow to renounce love for ever, Sasha acknowledged. But she had not given her heart again. She would never ever give her heart to anyone in the way she had given it to Werner Backhaus that winter. She was convinced these days that no man possessed the combination of character, romantic appeal, and trustworthiness to satisfy her. Something else too, she was sure, was necessary, something she could not quite define. She would know it if she ever came upon it, but . . . Sasha reminded herself that she had no desire to encounter any aspect of love again.

'If only they were all like you,' she said, tucking her arm through her tutor's, believing for a moment that she could be happy living with Herr Lindau, who was so cultured, so kind, so . . . satisfactory. She imagined how it would be if they were married, instead of being tutor and pupil. They would be returning to a home that was, even now, being prepared for them. It would have a grand piano, of course, and gracious rooms like the ones in Hanover Terrace, and an atmosphere of dignity. The idea was pleasant. She dwelled on it, considering for a moment the general assumption that a young girl and an elderly gentleman travelling together were free from all suspicion of impropriety. Herr Lindau's distinguished age and her extreme youth precluded all possibility of an attachment in the minds of decent society. Her mother had no qualms about her dispensing with a paid companion for the journey to England.

And yet, Sasha had to confess, there had been moments on her tour when she guessed her mother might have felt a pulse of alarm. Strange, disturbing moments, when she felt a strong desire to put her arms about her old friend, or, with a quickening of her heart, to touch and explore the lines of his thin face. She had often speculated about the history of love that lay behind those pale, fiercely passionate eyes.

The men who had brought her flowers and courted her seemed pathetic fare in comparison. 'They are all so insubstantial', she had written to Lavinia, after hearing that her sisters were installed in their Yorkshire cottage. Sasha pictured Mr Pickersgill, solid in every conceivable sense of the word. She smiled. Oh, yes, Mr Pickersgill was a man worthy of a woman's heart.

'Now what is amusing you? First you are sad. Now you laugh.' Herr Lindau bent towards her and patted her hand.

People would suppose he was her grandfather, or an uncle, or an eccentric old family friend. 'I was thinking what a waste of time love is.'

'Oh, yes, Sasha. You are right. Such a squandering of our emotions.'

'Music is so much more worth while.'

Herr Lindau acknowledged the fact with an ironic smile, knowing that while music could satisfy some of the senses and was a great consolation to an old man, it would not be enough for Sasha when love one day took possession of her. Memories flooded his mind of friendships with the great names of his youth: Kalkbrenner, Hummel, Ries. He remembered his first meeting with Beethoven, not yet totally sunk into the misery of his deafness; and other memories, both bitter and sweet, of pretty women in flimsy, clinging dresses that showed off their breasts and thighs in a tantalising way, women without corsets, without false modesty. He could remember a few who had shown no modesty at all. He was content these days to do no more than look, to admire Sasha's spirited beauty, sigh a little for his lost youth, and dream of what might have been, had he only been thirty or forty years younger.

It was not comfortable to be the only daughter at home. The house in Hanover Terrace seemed too large and empty; it echoed with the ghosts of her sisters' feet running along corridors, and of music playing in the drawing room. Her father had taken up the portrait again: *The Beautiful Hammond Girls* dominated the attic studio. He shut himself up there every morning and afternoon and seemed obsessed by the painting. It was as if he were trying to recapture something: an image of them as they once were, pure, united, innocent. But perhaps even that was an illusion, thought Sasha, watching his brush caress the sheen on Kitty's hair. Had they ever really been innocent?

They did not talk about Kitty. 'Where is the point?' said her mother. 'She's lost to us now. She has chosen her path.' Mrs Hammond had found consolation in the minutiae of domestic life, in church on Sundays, and visits, and 'at homes' among those friends who had stayed loyal.

Sasha felt impatient with them; she had forgotten how dull life in Avondon could be. She took up as many invitations to play as were offered in Bristol and Bath, and she found herself looking forward with longing to the series of concerts Herr Lindau was planning for the autumn and winter in London and the provinces.

'I shall not come on tour with you on this occasion, Sasha,' Herr Lindau told her, when he arrived one day to discuss where she would be playing. 'I am getting too old for travelling. My physician tells me I must slow down for the sake of my heart.'

'You're ill?' Sasha exclaimed with a leap of terror at the possibility that he might die.

'I am old, Sasha. It comes to us all in time. And you are becoming a celebrity without my assistance. People are asking to hear you play. I have talked to your father about a musical agent in London. Ross, a friend of mine. If you like him, he will arrange your concerts in future. And then, darling Sasha, think of what awaits you. Won't it be simply wonderful?'

'But you won't be there!' Sasha imagined the future ahead: the concert tours, travelling alone, or with an agent, or with a suitable travelling companion. Why did a sense of bleakness envelop her?

She played a little Bach and Beethoven with Herr Lindau; for a while, she was his pupil again and could pretend that nothing had changed. But, as they played a duet, she was so overwhelmed by sadness that at the end she found herself weeping.

'Sasha, you are a young woman now,' Herr Lindau said with a hint of brusqueness as he packed up his music. 'The world does not stay still.'

'I know.' Sasha scrubbed at her eyes with a handkerchief. 'But I shall miss you.'

'And I shall miss you. More than I can say.'

He stood, leaning with one hand for support on the piano. She remembered she had once likened him to a tree struck by lightning. She had so admired his vigour, and his charismatic, spellbinding enthusiasm for music. Now she saw that he was fading, and knew in that moment that he had been preparing her. He *was* going to die. Not next week, perhaps, nor next month. But could she be certain about next year – or the one after that?

'Come, Sasha.' He regarded her kindly. 'It's not all over yet. And you have your whole life ahead of you.'

'Promise you'll see me during the summer, and you'll let me come to play for you at your house in Bath. Promise we shall play duets together. I need help with counterpoint still,' she said desperately. Don't abandon me, she wanted to say. Don't leave me. I'm not ready.

'We have the summer,' he promised.

Lavinia's romance with Mr Pickersgill moved ponderously along the lines of regard and affection that summer. Between visits to the Pickersgills, she and Leah painted landscapes and turned one of the outhouses into a painting studio. In the autumn they captured the warm, sun-tinted brown and gold of the trees, the bronze of the bracken and the rusty purple of the dry heather. After a search, they found a shop to rent in Eskton and prepared to open a gallery.

'I've never known any women like you,' Gabriel said one evening, listening to the sisters talk excitedly about the builders and decorators they would engage and the way they would lay out the gallery. 'No one round here behaves the same way as you two.'

'That shows what a small world you live in,' Leah told him. 'And it confirms my heartfelt opinion that we are doing the right thing in weaning you away from the women at the Rose and Crown and broadening your horizons.' She laughed at his look of consternation.

'How did you know about the Rose and Crown?'

'Your escapades are the talk of Eskton,' Lavinia said. 'Your poor mother's hair will be turning white.'

'I don't play so much at the inn any more.' He felt himself blushing furiously, and hoped they had not heard all the rumours.

'Those poor young ladies of Eskton must be breaking their hearts because you've abandoned them. Poor things,' teased Leah.

'I can't help women's hearts,' he said roughly.

'Not even a few? Come, that's not how I've heard it.'

'I'm done with girls,' he protested. 'I've no time for anything but studying. You and Miss Lavinia have taught me so much since last spring . . . I shan't ever manage to pay back all I owe.'

'Tut! tut!' said Lavinia. 'It's cost nothing except time – which Leah never begrudged anyone.'

'And *patience*,' interrupted Leah. 'A great deal of patience.'

'We won't hear another word about anyone owing anything. Shall we, Leah?' Lavinia put on her cloak. 'I'm going out to the studio to paint while you work through tonight's lessons.'

Gabriel sat at Leah's feet, turning the pages of the Latin translation he had made while she read out her own version and explained points she felt he should have been aware of. When they had finished she asked him to throw another log on the fire.

Gabriel watched the flames spark and crackle, and returned to sit by her chair. His gaze followed her movements as she selected a book of French poetry from the pile of books on the table. He wished she did not know about the females in Eskton being after him. He wanted her to think well of him. Remembering his one-time lusting after Mrs Runicles' breasts, he felt weak with mortification. The thought that Leah might somehow discover his true nature, seemed more terrible than anything he could imagine.

Leah asked him to read to her; she had been teaching him to speak French. She never laughed at his efforts, only praised where she felt he had succeeded.

'That was very good tonight,' she said when he had

finished. 'You've made such strides, Gabriel. Remarkable strides after only six months. It's so thrilling for me to see the changes that have taken place. And in the violin as well.' She smiled. 'But that's our dark secret.'

'That's the best of all about coming here,' he said. 'Nobody else but you and Miss Lavinia understand what it's like to make real music.'

Leah smiled and began to read from Verlaine while he listened. He did not understand all the meaning, but the sound of the French verse was hypnotic and it set up a response in him, similar to that when he heard music played. He laid his head in her lap.

Leah did not stir, but continued talking; he felt the vibrations of her voice through her body, like the notes through the strings of a violin. He drank the feminine smell of her, like the farm-dogs did when they came to him for comfort and put their heads in his hands.

'You owe me nothing, Gabriel dear,' Leah said, stroking his hair, wanting to tell him that she sometimes imagined he was her own, that his eagerness to learn had brought her more joy in the past months than she had known in the whole of her life.

'I love you, Miss Hammond!' He seized her hand and kissed it, pressing his lips against the cool dry skin. He felt her fingers stiffen and curl; they shrank away from his mouth. He buried his face deep in her skirts. 'I love you, and it hurts.'

Leah was very still for a moment, feeling a desperate tenderness towards him; then she straightened and eased the weight of his head from her lap. She said, looking into his eyes, 'I am your tutor, Gabriel. And I have always looked on *you* as my pupil. That is how we are to one another. That is how it will always be. Do you understand?'

He nodded. But his body trembled with an ache that did not go away. When she stood and went to the kitchen door and said, 'Here comes Lavinia. It's getting dark,' he felt that she had deliberately thrust a barrier between them. He saw that it would remain. From now on she would be on her guard.

165

'I think it's time we took a holiday,' Leah said when Gabriel had gone.

'But what about the gallery?' Lavinia protested, meaning, if she had been honest, 'But what about Mr Pickersgill?' The truth was, Lavinia was beginning to despair of her friendship with Mr Pickersgill ever developing into more than a respectful understanding. She was half afraid that if she were to go away at this point, he might even put her out of his mind altogether.

'The decorators know what to do at the gallery,' Leah said. 'It will take them three weeks or more to get everything done. It will do us good to take ourselves off for a while.' Leah paused. 'Besides, it will do Gabriel good too. He needs a break from his lessons. I'm afraid they may have become too concentrated for him recently.'

'He *is* very clever.'

'Yes. I thought I might talk to Father about him. Do you think he would help me send him to a university?'

'A waif and stray? The idea might appeal to Father, but would the Ridgeways let Gabriel go?'

'He'll be eighteen this time next year – old enough to rebel a little and make his own decisions.'

'Oh, but I should miss him,' protested Lavinia.

'It's a long way off. Meanwhile, what about this holiday? I've been wanting to do some paintings of the harbour at Runsby.'

'Runsby,' Lavinia echoed.

'Didn't you say Mr Pickersgill has an aunt who lives in Runsby?'

'I believe so.'

'Well then, Mr Pickersgill might well make up the gentleman in our little party . . . simply to see that we come to no harm on the wilds of the North Sea coast.'

It was high time Mr Pickersgill proposed to her sister, thought Leah. Having generated the idea, she had decided to give it a push in the right direction. 'I shall ask the Squire and his wife if they can spare their son to escort us. Are you agreeable to the proposal?'

Lavinia turned pink at Leah's choice of the word, which

may or may not have been accidental.

'Oh, Leah. You know I am. You always have the best ideas.'

Mr Pickersgill's aunt, Miss Ferrers, lived alone with her cat, her books and her garden. She was a woman of no more than forty, brown-eyed and prettily feminine, with a manner that was very candid and direct. She was also very well read, Leah discovered.

'I am no musician, Miss Hammond,' she said. 'But I do know about things. I can tell good music and a good painting when I see it. I know the plants that will grow well in my garden despite the salt air. And I can sing.'

The last remark was no mean boast. Miss Ferrers had a pure, soprano voice with a vibrato that sent a thrill of exhilaration running down one's spine. Leah and Lavinia spent pleasant evenings in her sitting room, which overlooked the town across the harbour estuary, where they and Mr Pickersgill had taken lodgings. With the curtains drawn against the sound of the wind, they entertained one another with solo pieces, duets and boisterous choruses of popular songs.

Leah left Lavinia alone with Mr Pickersgill on every possible occasion where it was convenient and decent to do so, and enlisted Mr Pickersgill's aunt in her matchmaking campaign. The two women talked pointedly of the coming winter, a time for *dormant ideas* to be mulled over pleasantly; they said the early spring was an ideal season for *long-matured plans* to come to life, to *blossom*, so to speak. At last, growing tired of overburdened imagery, they spoke more plainly of weddings.

During the day, while the lovers explored the narrow streets of the town around the harbour, Leah and Miss Ferrers went for walks along the cliffs and shore. They talked easily, as if they had known one another for years instead of only a few days. Leah told Miss Ferrers about her paintings and her ambitions for the gallery; Miss Ferrers talked about her garden, and about the history of Runsby.

167

'Don't you *admire* the seafaring people, who have fished this coast for centuries, Miss Hammond?'

They had climbed the steep cobbled way to the church; the graveyard lay below them, its headstones standing in rows, blank sentinels watching over dead sailors and looking out to sea. The November wind buffeted Leah's bonnet against her ears, making the ribbons flutter violently like pennants on a boat's rigging. She looked down on the town and harbour. 'I admire all men and women who have had to struggle against nature for their livelihood, Miss Ferrers. I thank the good Lord I was born a Hammond.'

'And I, for being a Ferrers, and a woman of independent means,' said her companion emphatically. 'The Ferrers have been doing very nicely for three generations.'

'Do you come from a large family?'

'My sister, Mrs Pickersgill, is the eldest, and somewhat older than myself – more like a mother to me than a sister before she met Squire Pickersgill. She brought a considerable sum to that marriage, and her husband did very well when he married her. Lavinia will do very well too if she hooks my nephew.' Miss Ferrers threw a mischievous glance at Leah. 'And we are going to make sure that she does. I also have a brother. He has continued the family business, of which I'm a shareholder, and makes boilers. I am the youngest – the old boiler left on the shelf.' She gave a peal of laughter. 'I'm not dissatisfied with the position. Life has treated me very well so far.'

'Life is so very *unequal*,' said Leah, thinking of Gabriel, as the women made their way down the hill again.

'Oh, we are *very* fortunate,' Miss Ferrers was earnest again. 'When I take up arms against the salt air and the north-east gales so that I might raise a tender peony, or a delicate lily, in my very pleasant garden, I never lose sight of my good fortune in not having to make my living by battling against the sea or selling fish from the harbour quay.'

Leah talked about the Ridgeways' farm, and about her ambitions for Gabriel to break away.

The other woman listened intently. 'You've become very fond of him.'

'Yes,' said Leah. 'I have. He's like a son. An adopted son.' She laughed. 'It's the only sort I shall ever have.'

'You don't ever want to marry?'

'Marriage seems a poor choice to me. To be at the beck and call of one's lord and master for a lifetime. What a prison sentence!'

'Oh, I couldn't agree more.'

Leah told Miss Ferrers then about Sasha's career. She talked as well about Kitty and the catastrophic adventure in Switzerland; she revealed more about Kitty than she had revealed to anyone.

'It's as if my sister was searching for something. But why like that, Miss Ferrers? Why such bad choices? I can't help feeling she knows the men she falls in love with won't make her happy. It's almost as if she wants to ruin herself.'

'Some women choose such odd partnerships.'

'I don't think they *are* partnerships,' said Leah. 'There seems little notion of equality when a man takes possession of a woman's wits. It's all so *pathetic* . . . for a woman to give up all her pride for a brute so generally ignorant of what a woman wants or needs.'

'Only women can understand women, Miss Hammond.'

Leah halted on the path, aware that Miss Ferrers had hit on the truth of the matter. Her companion turned to smile at her; her cheeks were flushed by the wind, her eyes bright with enjoyment under the rim of her bonnet; it was as if the remark had united them in some way.

'Of course, Lavinia needs marriage,' said Leah. 'She could never survive alone.'

Calling remarks to one another as they descended the hill in single file, they jokingly compared their opinions on the progress they had made in their campaign to secure an engagement. They were rewarded when they returned. Lavinia and Mr Pickersgill came back from their walk; Lavinia, looking pinker than usual, fluttered about the sitting room. She removed her bonnet and shawl, placed

169

them on the sofa, picked them up and then discarded them again, like a bird that knows it is nesting time but has not yet decided where to begin laying down sticks and feathers. Mr Pickersgill stood by the fireplace with his hands behind his back and said, several times: 'What an agreeable afternoon.'

'You look as if you have something more to tell us about than the agreeable aspect of the afternoon,' said Miss Ferrers at last. She threw a conspiratorial glance at Leah.

Mr Pickersgill looked at Lavinia and they giggled. The effect was strange in the sturdily built Mr Pickersgill; like a chubby, smiling baby, thought Leah, glancing at her future brother-in-law with some alarm.

'Tell them, Martin.' Lavinia blushed more deeply at her bold use of his Christian name.

'We must ask your father's approval . . .'

'Oh, our father will approve. Don't you worry about that,' said Leah quickly.

'Well then, Miss Hammond. Your sister has, on this very *agreeable* afternoon, consented to be my wife.' Mr Pickersgill held out his arm, and Lavinia ran to him and took her place by his side.

Leah's eyes met Miss Ferrers' in amusement. She was surprised by the degree of warmth she felt towards the other woman, and was startled by the look of affection she received in return. Miss Ferrers held her gaze for a fraction of a second longer. A heat passed over Leah's body. She dropped her glance, but her heart was beating rapidly as a pleasure of extraordinary strength shot through her.

Lavinia's engagement caused a flurry of excitement at Hanover Terrace when she, Leah and Mr Pickersgill travelled down from Yorkshire so that Mr Pickersgill might formally ask for Lavinia's hand in marriage. Mrs Hammond drifted about the house making plans for the wedding reception to be held in this room or that; she talked of honeymoons, and wedding clothes, and visits to

Yorkshire to meet the Pickersgills. The engagement was announced with buoyant celebration; and if anyone's thoughts turned to Kitty and a previous engagement celebration, no one mentioned it.

Leah did not lose time in putting her case to her father for Gabriel to go to a university. He leaped at the notion of a waif and stray by proxy, wanted to meet the boy at once, and insisted on putting up all the money.

Sasha was touring the South-East when the family were busy celebrating; she read her mother's letter about Lavinia's visit and felt an odd empathy with Kitty. We are both excluded from the celebrations, she thought: I by my music, Kitty because of her *grande passion* with Werner Backhaus. There was no question of going home during Lavinia's visit; Sasha's performances were booked through the rest of the winter, with scarcely a gap of more than one or two consecutive days in her programme.

Afterwards, when the tour was ended, the constant drip of news about Lavinia's wedding plans made Sasha nostalgic for the company of her sisters. She wrote to Leah to ask if she might visit for a few days in April.

Was Lavinia's a *grande passion*? wondered Sasha, thinking of Kitty. She wiped a patch in the condensation on the railway carriage window and looked out into the darkness of the final lap of her journey north. She remembered the way Lavinia had sighed and languished over Mr Pickersgill in Basle. Oh yes, Lavinia was 'in love', with all the feelings that entailed. But was it passion? Sasha felt a prickle of tension run through her as she remembered Werner's mouth on her lips and his hands on her waist . . .

Her thoughts often returned to Kitty these days. How cruel she was, to have cut herself off so completely, and yet, Sasha supposed, Kitty could never return after the things she had done – things considered criminal in a place like Avondon. *Twice* she had let herself be ruled by her passions.

Sasha puzzled over a moral dilemma: if Lavinia had been guided by fleshly instincts when she chose Mr

Pickersgill – and however much one cloaked it in sighs and romantic words, marriage *was* a *carnal* union – why did it all suddenly become decent and honourable, simply because she had elected to abide by the social rules?

Rules were rules, and Kitty had broken them, Sasha told herself, turning from the carriage window. She no longer envied her sister. She thought her a fool to have ruined her life for the sake of a man with a soft persuasive accent and confidence in his own powers of seduction. Yet, the sensations Werner had roused in her still lingered in Sasha's memory: a mutual look, an awareness of currents running powerfully beneath the surface of ordinary protocol, had swept away all her reason. If it had happened once, might it happen again?

Leah had come to meet her with a pony and trap; she waved and jumped down from the seat, and her figure was reassuring in the darkness outside the railway station.

Sasha ran to hug her. 'Oh, it's been such ages!'

'Let me look at you.' Leah stepped back and critically surveyed Sasha's thin figure and huge dark eyes in the light from the street lamps. 'You look exhausted. It can't simply be the effects of the journey. Have you been eating properly?'

Sasha laughed. 'You're worse than Mother!'

'Oh, far more attentive, I promise you. Mother goes about in a dream and doesn't seem to notice even where meals come from these days. How we all survived such neglect, I can't imagine.'

There were hen droppings on the seat of the trap. Leah's boots were scuffed and soiled. She looked healthy, but coarsened by life in the country.

'Lavinia is at home. She is baking a cake for supper.' Leah glanced at Sasha sideways as she brushed the seat with her gloves. 'Our humble cottage is rather basic. We have a servant, but she only comes to do the heavier work in the mornings.'

Sasha tried to imagine the dainty Lavinia in an apron and with flour on her exquisite hands, mixing a cake. She gave up the attempt and gripped the side of the carriage

172

seat as they bounced along the road. She tried to make out the shape of fields and the lines of dry-stone walls, ghostly in the wavering beam of the carriage lamps.

'You must tell me what you've been doing,' Leah said. 'Tell me about the amazing life of a concert pianist.'

Sasha told her about her recent tour, but try as she might she could not make it sound exciting. She told Leah how she had been playing in concerts almost constantly since January, that she was building contacts through Algie Ross, her musical agent; a programme of summer concerts was already half planned. Yet, she felt little enthusiasm for another tour. She *was* tired, she admitted to Leah.

'It's not so much the playing that's exhausting, but the travelling from town to town, the rehearsals with players I hardly know, and temperamental conductors, and dealing with less than perfect pianos.'

'It sounds to me as if you need a good rest in the country. We shall begin feeding you up. Lots of vegetables. Fresh butter from Gabriel's farm. But first and foremost, lots of rest.'

'Yes,' Sasha admitted. 'How *nice* it will be to stay still for a few days, out of sight and touch of a piano!'

Was she growing tired of her music? Sasha was shocked by the thought. She knew, after two years of public performances, that music would satisfy only part of her soul. The love of an audience was not enough. Something was missing. The admiration of strangers was thrilling, but she could not hold it close to her; it did not touch her intimately.

Lavinia, looking as fresh and graceful as ever, and not at all coarsened by country living, came out to meet them when they reached the cottage. She embraced Sasha with little exclamations of happiness. Sasha followed her into the tiny sitting room, where a well-risen Madeira cake took pride of place on the table. 'You shall try some,' promised Lavinia. 'But first, you must unpack and rest.'

They were full of all they had been doing: the wedding

plans, the painting gallery in Eskton, the crops Leah had planted in the garden.

'And I have bought a hand plough!' laughed Leah. 'Gabriel has helped me to use it.'

There it was again, thought Sasha: Gabriel. Gabriel's farm. Gabriel was teaching her to plough. A neighbour, she supposed. But Leah had spoken the name with a fondness in her voice. Had Leah, insusceptible Leah, fallen for a farmer? Sasha looked at her sharply, noting how Leah's skin looked weathered; her beautiful hair was the colour and texture of bleached straw. Sasha sensed a wholeness about her.

'Are you happy, Leah?' she said spontaneously. 'Won't you be lonely when Lavinia marries?'

'Not at all. I have my painting. And since, against all my advice, they've opted for a *year's* engagement . . .' She flashed a smile at Lavinia. 'I have plenty of time to get used to the idea. And there's my garden, and the livestock . . . and I've made friends round about.' She thought with gentle pleasure of the repeated visits to see Miss Ferrers in Runsby since Lavinia's engagement. 'I have the moors on my doorstep, wonderful sunsets in the evening, and my violin. What more could a woman want?'

Oh, so much more, thought Sasha restlessly. She said nothing, but she wanted to ask, what about the other things? What about love? And children? Didn't Leah feel a longing for all the things Lavinia was going to embrace?

And what about me? Sasha asked herself. Had Lavinia's engagement and wedding plans weakened her own resolve to keep love out of her life? Was that why she felt so unsettled?

'Gabriel helped us with the recipe,' Leah said as Lavinia cut the cake and handed round slices.

'*Who*?' Sasha was provoked at last into asking. 'This Gabriel seems to be a man of many talents.'

'Not a man,' smiled Lavinia picking a crumb from the table.

'He plays the violin.' Again there was a note of affection in Leah's voice. 'Oh, Sasha, you *must* remember.'

'Must I?' Sasha said, and then she recalled . . . 'That boy? The satyr who played like an angel?'

'He's my pupil. And his playing is more divine than ever. He would like to play in an orchestra, but Father and I have other plans for him.' Leah beamed. 'I shall tell you all about it.'

Sasha woke the following morning to the sun shining into the sitting room, where her sisters had made up a bed for her on the sofa. She scrambled over the covers to the window and leaned over the back of the sofa with her chin on her arms. She could see the moor, vast and empty, the road, lightly dusted with frost, and the sun, still low on the horizon. The sound of church bells drifted on the air, for it was a Sunday.

Neither Leah nor Lavinia had talked of going to church. She wondered whether they would make the journey to the nearby village on foot. Or would Mr Pickersgill come for them in a carriage, and would they all rattle off to Eskton in style? Sasha felt lazy and comfortable. It was tempting to lie down again among the covers on the sofa, but she needed to visit the outside privy. She wrapped the top silk coverlet round her shoulders over her nightgown and put on her stockings and shoes. Unlatching the door quietly, she went outside and down the garden past the hen shed.

The sun was rising higher; the sky was huge in proportion to the land, a blue, grey and gold cloud-mass of blowsy splendour. Sasha walked to the edge of the garden on her return, and leaned against the dry-stone wall. It was cold and damp and there was a sharp touch of winter still in the air. She was shivering, but she had to stay. A lark was rising from the heather slope. The sweetness of its song made her catch her breath. Without warning tears filled her eyes. She tipped back her head, following the bird's path until her eyes stung with staring at the sky and the lark was only a faint speck against the clouds. But still the song continued.

'You're right. It's the sweetest sound in the world.'

Sasha turned in alarm. She brushed the tears from her face with her hand.

Gabriel had come up the path at the front of the cottage. He stood by the door to the scullery with a couple of loaves of bread and a cloth satchel in his arms. 'It makes *me* want to cry sometimes, it's that lovely.' He looked up, searching the sky for the bird.

'The sun made my eyes water,' Sasha said.

He brought his gaze back to her. 'I suppose it did. Mother asked me to bring the Miss Hammonds these.' He held out the bread. 'I was going to put them inside, but you can take them in if you like.'

Sasha hesitated, then walked across the garden towards him. She held out her hand for the bread. 'Thank you. I remember you. You're Gabriel.'

'I remember you too,' he said noncommittally.

He looked different, thought Sasha. He wore a leather jerkin and a striped shirt, no hat, and his sleeves were rolled to the elbows; but he gave an impression of restraint, as if he were waiting for her next move before he made up his mind how to react to her.

When Leah had told her how she and Lavinia had been teaching Gabriel Greek and Latin, and about her plans for him to go to a university, Sasha had decided her sisters had lost their wits. 'He's a farm lad,' she had protested. She was sure the boy was using Leah, preying on her good nature for some purpose of his own, to better himself, or with an eye on the Hammonds' money, taking advantage in the way that their father's waifs and strays had occasionally taken advantage in the past. She decided it was time someone warned him off.

'My sisters tell me they have been giving you lessons.'

'They've been very kind. Miss Leah's been helping me learn to read music.'

Sasha frowned, impatient to make her point. 'I don't know what you want from my sisters, Gabriel. But if it's money . . .'

He did not answer at first. 'Miss Hammond, I brought Miss Leah and Miss Lavinia some bread. Why should I be

176

after money, except to pay for it?'

'I simply meant . . .'

'Miss Leah's been good to me. She's a good, generous person.'

'I simply meant . . .'

'I know what you meant. But we're not all made of the same stuff, Miss Hammond. And, I'm bound to say, your sisters seem to be made of a kinder and more generous metal than yourself.'

Sasha was dismayed by the inference that she was somehow inferior to Leah and Lavinia. 'You don't know anything about me.'

'I know you seem set on mistaking me for a beggar every time we meet. I know you're nothing like Miss Leah. There's no one like her. Miss Leah's the handsomest woman in the world.' A flush of passion had suffused his face.

'You're in love with her!' Sasha was shocked by the discovery. 'Oh, my goodness.'

Gabriel turned away. 'Don't say that. You've no rights to say that when you don't know the first thing about it.'

'You're in love with her,' Sasha repeated. 'But you're only a boy! A farm boy. It's perfectly horrible.'

He reached into the satchel he carried and thrust a bundle of papers into her hands. 'Please, give her this for me.'

Sasha stared after him as he walked away. She glanced down at the paper in her hand. It was an essay. She read the first paragraph, then read it again in astonishment. She glanced at the figure striding away up the road. That crude, graceless boy had written an argument on the tragedy of pride in *King Lear*.

Leah was in the scullery. 'I thought I heard you talking to someone.'

'I met your prodigy in the garden. He's brought you some bread. He seems to have penned you an essay on Shakespeare.' Sasha placed both items on the table and stared at them. After a while she picked up the essay again, reading casually, as if she had nothing better to do. The script was large and confident, the language persuasive.

'Surprised?'

Sasha put the papers down again. 'I think he's in love with you.'

'I know,' Leah said quietly. She turned to put the kettle on the hob, and Sasha could not see her expression. 'But it's puppy love. He has a lot to learn. He'll get over it when he goes away.'

'You really mean it? You're going to pay for his education?'

'He doesn't know yet, but I've discussed it with Father, and he thinks it's a worthwhile venture.' Leah looked at her and smiled brightly, with a note of warning in her eyes. 'So, the less you say about it, Sasha dear, the better.'

They drove to church in Eskton and, afterwards, to lunch with the Pickersgills.

Sasha tried not to think about the farmer's boy. Leah had often provoked an adulation among their father's waifs and strays: young men, too intimidated to come under Kitty's particular spell, who wanted to be mothered. But Leah had always spurned that kind of attention in the past and privately mocked her 'boy slaves'; she had never actively encouraged them, nor had she talked of them with particular affection.

Sasha puzzled over the nature of love as she sat at the Pickersgills' luncheon table. Did Gabriel really adore Leah in spite of the appalling fact that she was years older than he was? And had Squire Pickersgill once adored his silly wife as devotedly as young Mr Pickersgill clearly worshipped Lavinia? It was hard to imagine. And it was embarrassing too to watch Lavinia, to witness the compliments and glances exchanged with her fiancé, the chances seized upon to place their heads together or accidentally brush hands. Sasha fervently renewed her vow never to fall into such a gluey trap.

The family's interest in Sasha's musical career drove out

her worries about Leah. She would not let the visit to Yorkshire depress her; she talked about her forthcoming summer concerts, determined to revive her enthusiasm. She would go to see Herr Lindau in Bath when she returned home. He could always make her see that the only thing worth while in life was her music.

'It's a grand thing, for Martin to be marrying into such a talented family,' Squire Pickersgill declared. 'We're looking forward to your parents' trip north this year. We've yet to see your father's paintings, but I hear they are very much admired.'

'Leah and Lavinia have done some charming landscapes, too,' said his wife. 'That's one of Lavinia's, framed behind you. She did it for us for Christmas.'

'And now, here you are since last we saw you, Miss Sasha, more celebrated than ever.' Squire Pickersgill beamed at Sasha. 'May we prevail on you to do another recital for us while you're in Eskton? The townsfolk would think it such a tribute.'

Sasha, suddenly longing for escape, said that she regretted she would be staying in Yorkshire no more than a few days, so there was no time to arrange a concert.

'Well then, you must play us some Chopin after luncheon,' Mrs Pickersgill pleaded. 'Chopin is so *comme il faut*, don't you think?'

Sasha said that she did; she had become practised at matching people's banal observations with platitudes. She had learned too how to manipulate audiences by using virtuoso quirks and flourishes, appealing to the public's need for sensation. What would the Pickersgills say if she told them she did not consider Chopin *comme il faut*, nor any music, for that matter? Chopin was amazing, fearsome, beautiful. His music could and should touch the soul, not charm the ear as a drawing-room *morceau*. But they need not be alarmed; she would give them a pretty little mazurka or waltz, if that was what they desired.

She played a number of piano pieces. Then Leah and Lavinia took everyone on a jaunt to their painting gallery in Eskton, a dusty shop, crammed with their own and other artists' work. They squeezed inside and walked about examining the pictures, and spilled out again on to the pavement. The sisters parted at last from the Pickersgills.

'Can you imagine! By next spring Martin and I shall be married and living in our own house in Eskton!' Lavinia exclaimed as they drove home. 'Will you break your concerts, Sasha? You *must* break your programme and come to the wedding. You do want to come to the wedding?'

Sasha detected the apprehension in Lavinia's voice. Could it be possible she wanted her approval over the marriage! Had her own scepticism shown too clearly? Sasha hugged her with a fierce determination to reassure her. 'Of course I shall break my tour. And I know you're going to be so very happy.'

The following days passed quickly. Sasha was force-marched on her sisters' favourite walks, driven to the coast, and presented with the local views and beauty spots to exclaim over. Lavinia fed her with country produce and Madeira cake, and in the evenings the three sisters played and sang together.

Leah had vowed that Sasha must hear Gabriel play the violin to them, but he had not been back to the cottage since that first morning of Sasha's visit.

Sasha had already decided the boy was avoiding her; she was relieved he was nowhere about after they had walked across the moor to call on the Ridgeways' farm; she did not want to be forced into complimenting him for scraping away at an old fiddle simply to please her sister, however talented he might be. Sasha disliked Mrs Ridgeway, with her hard stare and coarse manners; she was repelled by the farm's lack of refinement. Gabriel was 'over at Eskton', his mother told them.

Leah did not hide her disappointment. When they walked home she fretted about Gabriel's visit to Eskton, saying she was sure he would be at the Rose and Crown.

Was she really fond of the boy? Sasha wondered. It was so unlike her. 'Mrs Ridgeway seemed to disapprove of you,' she said cautiously. 'In fact, she didn't seem to like any of us.'

'She doesn't like musicians,' said Leah. 'She thinks music is a waste of time. I'm so afraid she'll turn against the idea of Gabriel's education altogether. She's been more hostile recently. I think she knows I've been teaching him to read music.' She turned on Sasha. 'I hope you didn't say anything to upset him the other morning.'

Sasha was silent, and Leah regarded her impassive expression with suspicion.

'You must have said something,' Leah decided that evening, brooding about the fact that Gabriel had not come for his lessons.

'I told him I thought he was taking advantage of you,' Sasha admitted at last. 'Well, it's true, isn't it?'

Leah gave a gasp of anger, and even Lavinia looked shocked.

'No, it's not,' Leah said coldly. 'And you had no right to interfere!'

'You've let him take up all your time and energies. Look how you've so obviously neglected your gallery project. Pictures all higgledy-piggledy. No sense of organisation. Lavinia can be excused, she's in love. But you, Leah – you're almost old enough to be his . . . well, too old, anyway!'

'Be quiet!' Leah snapped. She added more calmly, 'It's truly none of your business.'

They spoke no more about Gabriel. The sisters played and read to one another before they went to bed, but the incident had soured their last evening together.

In the end, Sasha was glad to escape. The visit had provided the rest she had needed, but they had all travelled too far along separate paths to restore the companionship of Hanover Terrace. They were no longer 'the Beautiful Hammond Girls'. Sasha was nineteen, with the hard and lonely work of a career ahead of her. Lavinia was soon to be 'Mrs Pickersgill', a married woman. And Leah was becoming an eccentric spinster with eccentric preoccupations.

And what of Kitty? Sasha wondered as the train drew out from the station and she waved to her sisters from the carriage window. Not once had they spoken about Kitty or even acknowledged her existence.

Sasha settled back in her carriage seat and heard the engine expel a long, melancholy hoot; it seemed to echo her own mood. Did there have to be such a sense of loss about growing up?

'I'm truly sorry Sasha was so rude to you,' Leah said when Gabriel came for a lesson a few days later. 'You mustn't take too much notice of her. She's impulsive. She jumps to conclusions.'

'It makes no odds.' He concentrated on unfastening the satchel in which he carried his books.

'That's a gambling term,' said Leah disapprovingly. 'It's time you gave up your friends at the Rose and Crown. If you're going to go to a university . . .'

He looked up with an eager expression. 'So, you think I could do it?'

Leah told him that her father had agreed to put up the money for his board and education. 'Of course, he'll want to take a good look at you first. He's coming on a visit to Yorkshire very soon.' She smiled. 'But I think he'll like what he sees.' She watched his desire to accept her father's generosity struggle with his notions of charity. Leah's heart ached at the thought of his leaving her. She did not want their lessons to end.

'I'd pay back every penny,' he said at last. He thought of his mother. 'They mightn't like it at the farm.'

'I'll ask my father to meet your parents. He'll persuade them. He can talk anybody into anything.' She reached out a hand and touched his hair where the light caught it from the window. 'Oh, Gabriel, dear. How shall I bear it?'

'You won't abandon me?' he made her promise. 'Say you'll still want me to come here in the holidays, and we shall read the books together, and play the violin like we've always done?' He seized her hand and pressed it to his mouth.

'I shall always be your friend,' she promised. She moved away from his too tender grasp. 'But now we must talk more seriously about your future. I know you want to be a musician, Gabriel, but your parents will certainly never agree to let you go if they think that's the case. And it would do no harm to take your other studies further. I was wondering . . . I've written to the London University for you, and they say they think we have been following the right subjects and they would like to meet you. My friend Miss Ferrers and I will come with you to London – to see you don't lose your way or get into any bad company. We shall let Lavinia stay here and watch over Mr Pickersgill.' She gave him a sly smile. 'Well – what do you say?'

Chapter Nine

Sasha was shown into a sunny room in the house in Bath where Herr Lindau lived, alone except for his house-keeper and a retinue of servants. How frail he looked since the last time she had seen him. The bones of his face poked under the skin as if they could almost pierce it. He was wrapped in a thick rug, though it was a warm day in May and a good fire burned in the hearth.

'Are you sick today?' Sasha sat beside him and kissed his hand; it was cold against her cheek.

'Better for seeing you.' He smiled at her with faded eyes from which the vigour was almost spent. 'Tell me, how is it with you, my darling Sasha? How was Yorkshire with your sisters? How were London audiences? You say so little about your public when you write to me. Only what you have played, and who else has played, and that you prefer Schumann these days to everyone else. Your agent has to write to tell me how everyone adores you.'

'Oh, I don't think they do. Not really. They simply enjoy an evening at the theatre or concert hall, away from their humdrum lives.'

'But they stand and cheer. I read about you in the *Musical World*, and Chorley praises you in the *Athenaeum*.'

'Well, perhaps I don't really want their adoration,' Sasha said moodily, releasing his hand. She told him about her trip to Yorkshire, about Leah's peculiar obsession with educating a farmer's boy, and about

Lavinia and the Pickersgills.

After a while he said, 'What is it, Sasha? What is wrong?'

'Oh, I've been thinking such silly things lately . . . restless, unhappy things, as if music somehow wasn't enough.' She looked at him, shrugging her shoulders as if to say, I know I'm being ridiculous.

'And what do you want me to say?'

'I want you to tell me I'm wrong, to say that playing the piano is all that matters.'

'But you are not wrong. And there is far more to life than playing the piano.'

'But you've always told me!' Sasha protested. '*Music* is the most important thing. *Nothing* else matters.'

'That was simply talk. To make you practise when you were a little girl.'

She stared at him, feeling betrayed.

'It never was enough for me.' He smiled.

'But if my music fails me, what will there be to put in its place?' The tears welled in Sasha's eyes and spilled over. Why wouldn't he reassure her?

'Men and women need to fulfil all sides of their natures to be truly happy,' he said, handing her a clean handkerchief.

'But how? I don't know what I want any more.'

'You will fall in love, of course.'

'Never!'

'Sasha. You are only nineteen. You are made for love.'

'No. It always goes wrong. Love doesn't make anyone happy. Look at what happened to Kitty.'

'So, your music makes you happy, eh?'

'Yes! While I'm playing. I feel alive and fulfilled, and I know nothing could be more wonderful. At least, that's how I used to feel.'

'Now you're not so sure?'

She shook her head violently then blew her nose.

'That's because you are no longer an innocent child, Sasha. You have other needs. I can't talk about these things to you. I'm an old man. And it wouldn't be right.

But you need more. Believe me. Everyone needs something more than their art.' He patted her hand. 'Now – play something for me.'

Sasha went to the grand piano. She played Beethoven's *Appassionata* Sonata. She played it with every ounce of feeling for Herr Lindau, because it was the first music he had ever played for her and because she loved him, and he had given her so much.

When she had finished he smiled, and nodded, saying, 'For an old man at the end of his life, music is enough.'

Sasha heard a few weeks later that he had died. She had been performing again in London, and was in the apartment rented there for her by her father; she was practising at the piano, when the girl engaged as a travelling companion handed her a letter from her mother.

The Hammonds had recently been to Yorkshire – where they had charmed the Pickersgills and, apparently, the Ridgeways as well: Mrs Hammond's last letter had been full of Leah's plans for Gabriel to go to London. Sasha slit the envelope and scanned the news casually, expecting to read more of the same. Then, because she had not wanted to believe it, she read the letter again. 'No,' she murmured. 'No. I'm not ready yet. He can't abandon me.'

At that evening's concert she played Beethoven's Sonata *Les Adieux*, altering the programme a little to suit it. Afterwards, her agent Algie Ross rode home with her in the cab to her apartment.

'I have never heard you play better than tonight, Sasha. He would have been proud of you. Will you be all right?'

'Oh, yes,' Sasha said. 'You don't have to worry about me.'

She went into the sitting room. The maid had left the gas burning and a tray of food by the fireplace; the companion had gone to bed. Music lay in untidy heaps on the piano lid and on the floor where Sasha had left them.

She was so desperately tired: weary of the life she had chosen, weary of travelling, and the exhausting nature of concert performances. Sasha knew she had played from her heart that evening, but she was conscious too these days of the exploitation of her gift for other people's gain. She resented the unrelenting demands on her energies, and the assumption that audience applause was the highest confirmation of her talent. After two years of concerts, she knew that the rewards of being a public performer were hollow.

Sasha walked to the piano and fingered the keys lightly. She wanted to play something more for him, to pretend Herr Lindau could still hear her, but her mind felt numb. Leaning her arms on her piano, she buried her face in her sleeve and cried as she had not cried since the night Kitty had run away with Werner Backhaus.

Nathaniel had finished *The Beautiful Hammond Girls*, and had submitted it that year for the Royal Academy's annual Exhibition in London.

Sasha had been depressed by her father's painting, particularly by his portrayal of her. Her hair was painted very nicely, she had acknowledged: very romantic and poetic, and tumbling over her shoulders, but she thought she looked too girlish and animated, too unsophisticated by far. Besides, one only had to look at Kitty's dreamy soulfulness – suggesting she was hiding beautiful and mysterious thoughts – to know that the painting no longer told the truth.

People in the art world did not share Sasha's disappointment in her father's painting. Nathaniel was fêted and congratulated on his triumph. A paragraph in *The Times* stated that the picture marked the pinnacle of his career, and contrasted his work with that of the Pre-Raphaelites, whose 'exaggerations' still made the new school of artists suspect in some quarters.

Leah, sitting in Miss Ferrers' walled garden, read out loud the reports from the various papers:

'. . . Mr Hammond has excited nothing but admiration with his depiction of feminine beauty, though the countenance of one fair maiden may be said to be too severe for comfort and another seems pinky and schoolgirlish and reminds us not at all of the celebrated pianist who lately has been said to "call up angels" with her musical talent. One figure succeeds however, in its expression of pure womanhood, saintly rather than worldly, poetic, tender and affecting, fixing upon the mind's eye the true characteristics of beauty . . .'

'They can't have heard about Kitty and her lovers.' Leah put down the newspaper in her lap. 'Oh, Felicity. Poor Father, to have all the attention drawn to Kitty like that. And the critics have totally failed to see how much he has in common with Millais and the others – reviving the past, going to nature for inspiration. Father has been painting pictures like that for years.'

'We shall go and view it,' said Felicity, breaking off a thread in her mending. She looked at Leah over her spectacles. 'We shall take Gabriel to see the exhibition when he goes to London next week.'

'He has become very enthusiastic about the idea of going to the university.'

'You sound almost disappointed.'

'It's silly, I know, but I shall miss him so dreadfully that it makes me feel ill when I think about it. I'm sure even his mother doesn't feel as badly.'

'From what you've told me, he's a very personable young man. I might have fallen in love with him myself, if I were only twenty again.'

'I'm not in love with him,' Leah said with an indignant surprise. 'And neither am I a girl of twenty.'

Felicity smiled, shielding her eyes from the sun, enjoying teasing her a little. 'Not a teeny, weeny bit?'

'No.' Leah hesitated then said in a rush. 'If I love anyone, Felicity . . . it's you.' She waited, her heart beating painfully.

Felicity put aside her sewing. 'And I love you too, Leah dear. I have hoped and hoped all these months . . .'

There were tears in her eyes but she was smiling. 'I'm so glad you've asked me to go with you to London instead of Lavinia.'

But I do love him, Leah realised, as she sat in the railway carriage and watched Gabriel with sidelong glances. Lanky and immature though he was, hot and twitchy in the confined space of a railway carriage, and drinking in every detail of the journey. She did not love him in the way she loved Felicity, not in that spellbinding, heart-stopping way she had discovered in the weeks since their conversation in the garden, but she felt a deep tenderness for him that made her question the nature of physical love.

Felicity's skirts rested against hers, their elbows brushing occasionally as they turned the pages of their books. Leah thought of the adventure in London, sharing a room and lying all night in one another's arms. And the picture filled her with happiness and an impatience to reach their destination.

'What do you think of it?' she said, when they stood in front of *The Beautiful Hammond Girls*. The Academy had hung the portrait on the wall farthest from the door; it was surrounded by a patchwork of paintings that filled the space from floor to ceiling, as if each were bent on cancelling the effectiveness of its neighbour. Yet, amidst all the jostling for attention, *The Beautiful Hammond Girls* commanded respect.

Gabriel stared at the portrait. He thought he had never seen anything more lovely. The women's dress was sensual, medieval: the rich reds, blues and greens of the fabrics, the detail of the embroidery, the braid in the girls' hair, and their hair itself, like waves of ripened corn, glowed from the canvas. He wanted to run his fingers through it, to trace the curves of flesh under the drapery and feel the warmth of their skin. I want always to be enthralled by such beauty, he thought. Never to tire of the wonders there are in the world. I want to surround myself

189

with women who are as lovely as Leah and her sisters, and with beautiful clothes and paintings, and music and books.

'What do you think?' Leah repeated.

He turned to her and said seriously. 'I should like to own that painting one day.'

Nathaniel had been apprehensive about the portrait's reception. He remembered his early ambitions for the painting, when the girls were to have been symbols of purity. He knew he had captured something of their beauty; Leah's gravity and Lavinia's grace gave the picture weight and dignity. Sasha supplied it with vitality. Kitty's apparent calm added an element of mystery. But he was aware that people who knew Kitty's story would regard the painting with a private – or worse, a public – scepticism; they would ask themselves how 'the Beautiful Hammond Girls' could signify purity when one of them had transgressed all the laws of decency. There were some fathers who might have painted her out of the picture, announced that Kitty was no longer his daughter; but Nathaniel was not capable of doing it. He still loved her, and his heart ached for his wayward child.

Sasha had been easy to paint; and Leah and Lavinia had been persuaded to sit for an hour here and there when they visited Hanover Terrace; but he had painted Kitty from memory, and from earlier portraits. The final figure had a sense of distance that intensified his heartache.

Nathaniel wondered whether there was something in his own make-up that had made Kitty as she was. He cast his mind back to the transgressions of his youth. There had been moments that he remembered with an uncomfortable clarity. But he was a man. A measure of excess was expected of young men.

Sasha had met her parents in London when they came to view the painting. How altered she was since the death of Lindau, thought Nathaniel. As if all her vitality had been knocked out of her. They arrived at the exhibition towards the end of the afternoon. People were moving around in ones and twos; their voices were muted, as if they were growing tired of commenting about this artist and that.

'There it is.' Nathaniel was pleased to see that the portrait hung in a place of prominence. 'Ah, my four lovely girls. My beautiful daughters. If only . . .' He pulled out a handkerchief and blew his nose with a sudden emotional urgency.

Mrs Hammond took his arm. 'I am very proud,' she whispered.

Sasha said nothing. As soon as they entered the room, she had recognised one of the visitors; he stood with his hat in his hand, tapping it against his leg as if to a silent rhythm.

Her mother, sensing Sasha stiffen, looked to see what had caught her attention. 'God defend us,' she murmured. Her eyes widened. 'Whatever are we going to do?'

'We are going to acknowledge him, of course,' hissed Sasha.

William had read about the painting in the newspaper. He had waited for several weeks before deciding to come to London to view the Royal Academy exhibition. A mixture of fear and mistrust had held him back, but in the end the memory of Kitty was too powerful. He had persuaded himself that if he saw the finished painting, it might put the final lid on that episode in his life.

His gaze had sought, and found, the image of Kitty, her long neck, her slender figure and her hair loose to her shoulders. 'Oh, Kitty!' He heard himself murmur the words out loud and was startled by his own lack of constraint. People close by were discussing the paintings; they had not noticed his involuntary cry. He took in every detail of her cool beauty: her lips half parted, as if about to reveal a thought that would account for the melancholy expression in her eyes. She was as beautiful as ever. What man, looking at that painting, could have guessed that she would be so false? William sought justification for his gullibility. Was he still in love with her? He sighed. He supposed he was.

'Mr Elliman! What a surprise to see you here.'

He blanched a little. He had been so captivated by the painting he had not noticed Sasha. 'Miss Hammond—'

'I hope you like the finished portrait.'

'It is very uplifting,' he said gravely. 'Art has that effect, don't you think? It is so—' He had been going to say 'uplifting' again and changed it to, 'So inspiring. Like music – but I don't need to tell you that.' He paused. 'I've heard you are becoming quite famous.'

He looked pale, Sasha thought. She supposed he was overworking. The passage of time had thrown William into a nobler light in her imagination; she imagined him effecting great changes of a sanitary nature on the poorer parts of Penbury.

Her parents were approaching. William greeted them with some embarrassment.

'Mr Elliman, I do hope you are well.' Mrs Hammond extended her hand as if she was not the least agitated by the encounter.

'I am in very good health. I thank you, Mrs Hammond. Mr Hammond.' William shifted his hat from hand to hand. 'Congratulations, Mr Hammond, on a fine painting.'

He did not look particularly well, Sasha thought. His pallor lent him a kind of dignity; his gravity masked the boyish smile of former times. Both suited him, she decided.

'And what are you doing these days?' Nathaniel said. 'How is the great campaign for sanitary reform progressing? They could do with reforming the Thames, don't you think? *There's* a project for someone to take up – the cleansing and dredging thereof!'

'I agree, sir. But I'm rather glad to say I shan't be spending long in London. I have a practice . . . quite a substantial practice now in Penbury. I came to London . . .' He glanced at the painting, remembering why he had come to London, and faltered. 'To see my sister.'

'You must visit us in Bristol, Mr Elliman,' said Nathaniel. 'You must. You must. For old times' sake.'

'Yes,' William said uncertainly, wondering whether the family had forgiven Kitty and she was back in England. 'I mean to say – perhaps not. I'm very busy these days. The practice . . . You know how it is.' He smiled apologetically.

'Really, Nathaniel!' said Mrs Hammond when they had parted. 'What a foolish thing to say! As if the poor man wants *old times* brought up.'

Sasha was quiet. Poor Mr Elliman. She saw now that he had gone to see the portrait because of Kitty. Though she deplored the indignity of his devotion, she could not help pitying him a little.

William had seen Sasha's expression of sympathy. He remembered how hard he had been on her long ago when she had broken the news of Kitty's betrayal. He felt ashamed. The poor child had been nursing tender feelings for him, and he had thought only of his injured pride.

When the Hammonds left the exhibition, William went back to the painting. He took note of Sasha at its centre; it occurred to him that without her, the portrait would have no focal point. Sasha was no longer a child, he realised. Even Hammond had been forced to acknowledge her womanly shape; the figure in the painting wore a soft red gown, tied at the waist with a knotted braid. Flowers, wound into a wreath, bound her hair low on her forehead. He compared her warm attentiveness with Kitty's enigmatic, shrouded expression, and with the graceful dignity of her older sisters; his spirits lifted involuntarily in response to the expression of mischief in Sasha's eyes. Hammond had painted the child in her; but he had recorded something besides. William looked at Leah and Lavinia; they, like Kitty, held something back; they offered nothing more than an invitation to contemplate their beauty. At last he understood: Sasha's expression did not say, you may admire, but that is all; she engaged the person looking in.

He walked along with a spring in his step, more uplifted by his experience at the exhibition than he could have anticipated. He walked in through the door of the former apothecary shop and banged the bell on the counter. No one came. There was an atmosphere of neglect, dead flies on the shelves, boxes stacked in corners, old newspapers on the floor. He went through from the shop into the parlour and called Lily's name.

The house smelled of drink, bad food and slops, and there was no fire in the stove. It was far worse than on his last visit, he realised grimly, remembering his discovery that his sister was becoming a drinker. Something had to be done about it. The shop was losing money. He supposed he could sell, but the question still remained: what was to be done about Lily? He remembered his promise to his father to look after her. He was in no position to honour his word; he had his reputation to maintain and a drunken sister would be a terrible embarrassment in Penbury.

Lily came into the parlour. She wiped the back of her hand against her mouth to remove the smell of port when she kissed him. 'You never said you were calling.'

'I was passing through London. I wanted to see how you are.'

'You mean you wanted to check on the shop. Keeping an eye on your interests?'

'It's your livelihood, Lily,' he reminded her. He ran his hand along the layer of grease on the table. 'There was no one minding the counter.'

'The girl's left me. It's not easy being everywhere at once.'

'No. I'm sure it's not.' William went to the fire and began to lay it with sticks and paper. He felt a wave of pity for her and saw that their father's death had been hard on her – life was hard for any woman on her own. He made a decision.

'I think I should stay for a little while and help you get things sorted out.' He fixed her with the look he used when he told patients, 'Now you are going to take my advice.'

To his surprise, Lily did not protest. She seemed to

collapse inwardly; her face crumpled a little. 'Anything you say.'

In the next few days, he cleaned up the shop, threw out the empty wine bottles, and extracted a promise from Lily that she would not let things get out of hand again without writing to him for help. They parted with more family sentiment than either of them had expressed in years.

William's house and practice in Penbury were at the better end of the town, not far from the Neptune Inn and convenient for most of his patients. It was a cold, ugly, Georgian building, with its main rooms set solidly on either side of the front door. But it was spacious, and it had 'possibilities', and Wotherspoon had worked some influence so that he got it at a generously low rent. There was a good annexe which held the dispensary and surgery; a large drawing room for entertaining, and a dining room that overlooked the garden. A heavily balustraded stair-case led up from the flagged hall to four first-floor bedrooms. The attic rooms on the second floor would be convenient for 'the servants' and for 'the children'. William looked forward to both in the plural: he had ambitions for a more comfortable style of living. He was optimistic about there being a day when Bertha, the general servant, would be augmented by a cook and a housemaid, and when the gloomy atmosphere of the house would be brightened by the activities of a family. All in good time, he had told himself. After his experience with Kitty he was not going to get burned again quite so easily.

But the house seemed to echo with unfulfilled promises when he returned to it from London. The dying heat of the day made the timbers crack in the silence. The sun streamed through the windows, lighting up vacant rooms and empty furniture.

That night he slept fitfully. Images of Kitty haunted his dreams; they became confused with the painting and the portrait of Sasha. She smiled at him. Her red dress had a

195

strange incandescence and its folds flowed like fire over her figure.

'All in good time,' he reminded himself the next morning. 'Rome wasn't built in a day.'

It was a phrase of Wotherspoon's. William had noticed lately that he frequently adopted sayings used by Wotherspoon.

'You must be tougher on him, Elliman. You're on the local board of health. Use your authority,' said Brewer that lunchtime, when they were seated in the Neptune over a glass of ale. 'Complacency is the chief curse of this town. Complacency and greed.'

'Of course, now that Wotherspoon's Mayor . . .'

'Now that he's Mayor, he has an even better reason for sitting on his hands.'

'You think so?' William said anxiously.

'The trouble with Wotherspoon – good fellow though he might be, and very impressive in his mayoral chain – is that he is too fond of procrastinating. What about the sewage scheme and the waterworks? Has the council done more than turn down every plan anyone's put forward?'

'Some with good reason,' William protested. 'The council means to deal with public health issues, I'm sure of it. And plans for the gasworks are already underway.' Wotherspoon had promised. Of course he was reliable.

'The council means to spend the rates on a splendid town hall in the borough, Elliman.' Brewer raised his glass to him. 'But we'll shake them up, won't we? You and me? I thought I might run a few articles about building the town hall. I've seen the plans.' He tapped the side of his nose. 'Formal dining rooms, council chamber, fancy pillars and balconies. Very lavish. Very costly on the rates. Next to each article about the commodious nature of our councillors' town hall, I thought I might print a running report on how the reforms are coming along: with people in these times of progress and invention living and working in utter squalor, open sewers running under floorboards, and families living in one room; the only water to which poor families have access coming from wells

196

polluted by cesspools . . . What do you think?'

William agreed, but without much enthusiasm. It was all very well for Brewer to talk. All he had to worry about was stirring up good stories for his newspaper. The trouble with Brewer was he went at things like a bull at a gate. But William had his career to think of, and a doctor who went round stirring things up would soon find himself short of patients.

There were strong arguments against a waterworks, William had discovered. The best site was several miles away; the piping would be very expensive; poorer people should not have to pay extra rates for a public water supply, when they could get it for free from nearby wells. Wotherspoon could be very persuasive. There were alternatives: other sites, springs that might be tapped; William and the board of health had put forward several ideas.

William was reflecting on the progress in Penbury one afternoon some weeks later as he walked along the Strand in London. Wotherspoon's plans for an ornate town hall were certainly disturbing; and Brewer's articles had created quite an uproar in the town; it had been a matter of great anxiety, keeping his own name from being linked too closely with either Brewer's or Wotherspoon's party. Why was life so complicated? All one wanted was for everyone to live a decent life, with enough to eat, a solid roof over their heads, and running water and flush water closets. Was that too much to ask?

More personally pressing was the problem of Lily, but at least she was drinking less heavily; she seemed to be keeping her promise.

William determined that he needed cheering up. Whatever entertainment appealed to him among the theatres and halls, be it an improving lecture or a farce, he would treat himself to an evening out. He halted by the nearest billboard and saw that the programme at the Exeter Hall was a concert of music including a solo performance by . . . he read the name of the soloist with slow recognition. 'Sasha!' he exclaimed, a delight stealing through him as he remembered their meeting at the art exhibition. He went inside at once and bought a ticket for the evening performance.

William found himself looking forward to the concert with immoderate pleasure; he dressed with attention to the finer details of clean cuffs and collar, a well-brushed hat and polished boots. He ignored Lily's acid inquiries about where he was going and left the house with a spring in his step. He would not declare his presence until after the concert, he decided, as he walked again along the Strand. He would sit among the audience, and afterwards he would find her and congratulate her on her playing.

The concert was stimulating; William enjoyed the stirring effect of a massed orchestra. When it came to the solo performance his heart swelled with pride for Sasha. The grace and simplicity of her dress, the charm of her golden hair and her face and figure amongst all those dark-coated male players produced an odd effect on him. How small she looked, and vulnerable as she took her place at the piano; it seemed to William that she needed someone to take care of her.

William had come to several conclusions about women. His sister was one kind of female: a stoic, devoid of charm, hard-working when she was sober, and innocent of much that went on in the world. Then there were women like Kitty: advanced, rebellious, fascinating, but not, after all, the sort of woman a man married if he wanted to cut a place for himself in society. And then there was the ideal, women like Sasha: sweet, defenceless, utterly feminine, and in need of a man's protection.

He was less charmed by the brilliance of her playing – which, even to William's untuned ear, sounded mechanical, a little too brittle. But he stood and clapped his hands violently when she played an encore and took her bow.

He hurried then, pushing his way out from the Hall. It took him some time to find his way to the rear of the building, and when he did, Sasha was already leaving on the arm of a middle-aged gentleman. She was about to step into a hackney carriage when he called to her: 'Miss Hammond! Wait!' Her face was very pale in the gaslight.

'Miss Hammond. It's me. William Elliman.'

Sasha spoke rapidly to the man beside her; she nodded insistently when he protested, made him climb into the cab without her and came quickly towards William. 'Mr Elliman. How nice it is to see you again.'

'Yes.' He beamed happily. 'I heard your performance.'

A bunch of orchestra players came noisily out of the Hall. They raised their hats to Sasha, including William in the greeting. They called out, 'Good night, Miss Hammond,' and strolled in the direction of one of the nearby public houses. William saw Sasha's glance follow them. It occurred to him that if she had been a man she would have gone with them, but her sex cut her off from such fraternisation. He became acutely aware of the loneliness of the profession she had chosen.

'May I take you to supper?' he said on impulse. 'That is – unless you think it wouldn't be proper . . .'

He was not at all sure of the propriety of the situation, whether Sasha, by 'going on the stage', had already become a slightly ambiguous figure. He found himself wondering, whatever is her father thinking of, to let her wander the streets of London? And who was the fellow with her? Echoes of Kitty rang a strong warning in his mind.

'I should be very happy to have supper with you,' Sasha said. She walked along the street beside him. They went into a restaurant and took a seat among the crowded tables.

As they waited to be served William managed to say casually, making conversation, 'Have you heard from Kitty at all?' He breathed out slowly; it had been easier to say her name than he had anticipated.

'To be truthful, Mr Elliman, I've no idea where my sister is. The family has had no word from her for more than a year.' Sasha regarded him closely. How much was he still moping for Kitty? She hesitated before saying as gently as she could, 'She ran off with an opera singer in the end, Mr Elliman. You were well rid of her, if you had but known it.'

He digested this information slowly and realised that he was not in any way surprised.

'I hope she is happy, but I somehow doubt it,' Sasha said.

William was embarrassed into silence.

Sasha began to talk: about her concerts, about her musical agent – the man he had seen with her – and about their plans. 'Algie arranges all my concerts; he's a miracle of organisation. He deals with the concert directors, the tickets, the piano tuners, the men to carry the piano. He knew Herr Lindau,' she told him with a catch in her voice. 'He died earlier this summer.'

'I'm very sorry,' William said automatically.

'I was very fond of him. Nothing has been the same really since then.' She was silent, then said brightly, 'And how are you, Mr Elliman?'

'I'm very well.' He leaned forward, aware that their long acquaintance and her sympathy over Kitty gave him a freedom to confide in her. 'I have such high hopes of doing good in Penbury. Brewer – you remember, the journalist? He is helping push the cause of sanitation. We are making great progress in the town . . . the council has passed plans for a gasworks . . .' He tailed off. 'There's plenty of reforming work still to be done in Penbury, Miss Hammond. It will take some years.'

He smiled, and their eyes lingered briefly, regarding one another with memories of times past.

'Miss Hammond . . .'

Sasha's gaze faltered. There was a look of brief confusion in her expression.

William's voice trembled a little as he said, 'Miss Hammond, would it be agreeable to you . . . could we meet again?'

'Yes, Mr Elliman. I think I should like that,' Sasha said steadily.

'I'm so glad.' He reached out impulsively and laid his hand on her arm.

Sasha remained still. She saw in the simple gesture a possible end to the loneliness of the life she had chosen;

she contrasted the demands of concert performances with the promise of comfort, of friendship, of broadening her interests away from music, nothing but music. Was this, at last, a turning point? She longed to believe that it was. She was aware that the feelings she had known when she was sixteen could, with encouragement, perhaps be revived. As she looked at him and saw his altered expression, she did believe it.

'My programme takes me to Brighton tomorrow, but I shall be back in Bristol for much of the autumn.'

'Perhaps we could meet then?'

Chapter Ten

They were married early in January, even before the final arrangements had been made for Lavinia's wedding. There were no guests at the simple church ceremony except for Sasha's parents. Mrs Hammond was disappointed; she said she had wanted them to have a 'proper wedding'. Sasha did not care; it seemed so much more satisfying to marry and not to wait. Lavinia wrote with only a slight hint of pique, saying that Sasha had done it on purpose to steal all the attention. Nathaniel was delighted and gave them a dowry of three hundred pounds.

'Think of the expense and fuss we have saved you,' Sasha told her mother. 'You will have enough of all that when Lavinia marries in June.'

Sasha had no misgivings about the match. William was honest and affectionate – and hadn't he been her first ever love? What did it matter that he had once been bewitched by Kitty?

She had no misgivings either, no doubts at all, that marriage and children were all she had ever wanted, when she put her arms round her husband three months later and told him that she was pregnant.

Sasha took to the role of a provincial doctor's wife with a determination to perform it well. She generated activity, involved herself deeply in the household, storing up incidents and minor miracles of economy she had achieved, to share with William in the evenings. She told herself that she truly did not care about giving up the money earned from her concert performances, nor did it matter that William earned only a fraction of her father's income. After years of spending without wondering where the money would come from, she took a pride in acquiring housekeeping skills. And, from the start, she was determined to involve herself in every aspect of William's life.

'I don't know much about you, do I?' she said one evening, sitting on her heels on the floor by his chair and throwing back her head to look at him. 'You came into our lives, a handsome, dashing young doctor, passionate about drains, and I fell desperately in love with you, but I still know next to nothing about your family. I still haven't met your sister Lily, or your Grandfather Sparrow, or your Aunt Georgie.'

William thought of crabby, alcoholic Lily, of giddy Aunt Georgie and his garrulous grandfather, a trio of embarrassments. He pulled her up from her knees on the floor and kissed her. 'All in good time.'

'We shall invite the whole tribe to the christening,' she decided.

'As well as people in the town?'

'Everyone.' She sat on his knee and put her arms round his neck. 'I shall have to get the house straight of course, make it look less like a bachelor's retreat.'

He laughed. 'I'm so proud of you. My perfect little wife.'

'And I am proud of you, my clever husband.'

Yet, sometimes – and only in weaker moments – Sasha was subject to feelings of uncertainty. She wondered, when William grumbled about her occasional extravagances, or when he talked all evening about his patients or buried himself in medical and public health committees, whether her husband was not so much handsome and dashing as handsome and rather dull. She wondered how far William's reforming energies and his air of authority were really taking effect; he seemed unnecessarily overawed by Wotherspoon and men like Councillor Scrope – who had once been an enemy, she recalled, but was now a patient, so they must not offend him.

As for domestic matters: she wished he would not praise her only for saving money, and never for the changes she was making to his home. Sasha's ideas of economy were limited to distinct areas of household management: she was happy to make do with one servant and insisted that she enjoyed cooking – the pleasures of preparing meals for William without the constraints of a cook were novel and satisfying. But good taste could not be thrown over so easily as convenience; Sasha could not forgo a piece of fine furniture for the drawing room, nor deny herself a beautifully worked carpet, nor a pair of folding doors of 'good' panelling – absolutely necessary for isolating the house from the corridor to the surgery and dispensary.

But, as long as her father's dowry and the money she had brought to the marriage from her concert performances lasted, Sasha truly believed she was 'managing'. In those early days, she also believed she was happy.

What surprised everyone most, while acknowledging that it was only right and proper, was that Sasha had given up her musical career apparently without a backward glance.

'Mr and Mrs Elliman make a very handsome couple,' Mrs Pickersgill acknowledged at Lavinia's lavish wedding in Bristol, comparing the six months married Sasha and William with the newly-weds. 'But it was all *very* sudden. Sasha was so attached to her piano playing.'

'Sasha has stayed true to her womanly destiny. Matrimony suits her. She looks blooming.' Squire Pickersgill cast an admiring eye over Sasha, unaware that her softening figure had added to his wife's suspicions of a too hasty wedding.

Sasha did indeed look blooming, thought Leah, watching her sister mingle with the other wedding guests outside St Andrews Church; Sasha was dressed in a tartan *clochette*-style dress, with a small, very fashionable bonnet set well back on her pale gold hair; she had lost the tense, harassed look of the past few years.

'Don't you miss it, Sasha?' Leah asked when William was out of hearing.

'The concert tours? The rehearsals in draughty halls and theatres? No.' Sasha laughed. 'Not a bit.'

'You're really content, simply to be a wife?' Leah was aware of a sense of disappointment. While she had always known that Lavinia was made for marriage, she had expected so much more from Sasha.

'Not *simply* a wife,' Sasha said. 'William is determined to do good in the world, and I'm as determined to help him. I shall protect my husband from the tiresome business of keeping a house together. You've no idea the work there is in being married to a doctor.'

She laughed at Leah's look of scepticism. Poor Leah, thought Sasha. How peculiar she was becoming these days, with her old-fashioned bonnet, her hair dressed anyhow and a funny little knitted jacket over her dress, with wrong stitches showing. She would probably never know the satisfaction of giving up one's independence for the greater pleasures of marriage.

'Truly. I'm very happy. And there's Baby to look forward to.' She patted her waist.

'But is it going to be enough?'

'William would not have been happy for me to go on playing in concerts,' Sasha said more seriously. 'And, in all honesty, how could I have done it? Besides. I was tired of all that. It wasn't *fulfilling* any more.'

Sasha thought momentarily of Herr Lindau. He had known all along that she had needed more than her music could give her. How wise he had been. She wondered whether Leah would hate being alone now that Lavinia was leaving her to live in her new house with Mr Pickersgill.

'And you, Leah? How's the gallery? What about your pupil, the farmer's boy? Are you still going to turn him into a man of science or letters?'

'He spends all his spare time from his university studies learning the violin and piano under Franz Drossel.'

'He's *that* good?' Sasha was surprised. She had met

205

Drossel only once, but she knew that he had been taught by the violinist composer Louis Spohr.

'I told you. He's not called Gabriel for nothing. It's a shame you never heard him play.' A forlorn expression crossed Leah's face. 'He has such a good brain. There are so many things he could do if he wanted. I'm one hundred per cent certain of his ability. Less so about his steadiness. He falls in and out of love with catastrophic ease. Though, to be honest, Sasha, I don't hear from him very often. He's arranged this business with Drossel by himself. I suppose he's got some employment to pay for it. He writes to thank me for money when I send it, but otherwise, he has cut himself off.'

Sasha restrained herself with great difficulty from saying, I told you so.

Leah fell silent, remembering Gabriel's last letter, the most hurtful one of all: 'I can't be dependent on charity, Miss Hammond. One day, I shall repay all the money I owe you and your father.'

'And the gallery?' Sasha said.

'Oh, yes, I've been giving much more time to the gallery. Lavinia still has a part interest, but she's content to let me run things my own way.' Leah paused and said casually, 'I've been thinking I might give it up and open another one . . . in Runsby.'

What a strange idea, thought Sasha. Then she remembered. 'That's nice. You'll be near your friend, Mr Pickersgill's aunt.'

'Miss Ferrers,' Leah prompted. 'Felicity.' She gave Sasha a quick smile, suppressing the sense of joy and excitement that flooded her senses. 'She has asked me to share her cottage.'

No one thought of Kitty, or if they did – it was very much in private. Having ignored the fact that she existed, the shock was all the greater, Sasha supposed, when everyone returned to Hanover Terrace after the wedding ceremony and the butler told the family in a whispered, urgent conversation that he had not known what procedure to follow, but had shown 'Miss Kitty' up to the drawing room. Having delivered his news, the man stepped back with a look of anguish.

The guests were already spilling out of their carriages. Mrs Hammond turned to Sasha and William and gripped their hands tightly. 'Delay everyone – for a few minutes. Don't let anyone into the drawing room! And for mercy's sake don't let Lavinia know anything's wrong.' She hurried up the stairs with Nathaniel close behind her.

It did not seem possible that Kitty knew about Lavinia's wedding. Even more amazing – that, having heard about it, she would decide to come. How could she be so insensitive to everyone's feelings! Sasha was furious as she halted the guests on the steps outside. Lavinia was coming towards them from the bridal carriage on Mr Pickersgill's arm. She looked from Sasha to William with a breathless, questioning smile.

'What is it? What's happened? William, you look as if you've seen a ghost.'

'Come inside,' urged Sasha. 'William, Mr Pickersgill – hold everyone back as long as you can.'

Sasha left her husband and the groom standing with their arms spread like a couple of policemen and hurried Lavinia into the house. She considered how to break the news and saw that there was no gentle way. 'Lavinia – Kitty has decided to give us all the surprise of our lives by turning up to your wedding.'

Lavinia immediately burst into tears.

'What good is *that* going to do?' said Sasha in exasperation.

Lavinia could not answer; shaking her head and bunching up her skirts, she fled upstairs.

Mr Pickersgill, who had been watching his wife anxiously over his shoulder, immediately gave up his police duties; he hurried inside and ran after her.

William could be heard saying calmly, 'Only a moment or two longer, ladies and gentlemen. A slight delay with the wedding breakfast.'

Leah pushed her way past him into the hall. 'Well, it's

typical, anyway,' she said when Sasha told her what had happened. 'Kitty always did have a sense of high drama.'

'Can you console Lavinia, persuade her to behave normally?'

Leah was already halfway up the stairs. 'I'll do my best.'

Sasha gave orders to the servants not to allow anyone but family into the drawing room. She rescued William, and watched as the guests, unaware of the crisis, pushed upstairs in a wave of sound and laughter. 'How could Kitty do that? How *could* she?' William did not answer. They followed the tide of guests, then veered away towards the drawing room where Mrs Hammond came to meet them.

Nathaniel sat in a chair; his hands and mouth trembled. 'It's true, Sasha. She's come back to us. Like the prodigal. Our Kitty's come back to us.'

Kitty stood by the window, at a small distance from her mother and father. She looked as beautiful as ever, in a blue and grey striped dress with a hooped skirt trimmed with restrained elegance. But the air of languor had hardened; the weariness in Kitty's eyes seemed neither dreamy nor contrived; she had a look of fatigue.

'How did you know about the wedding?' said Sasha harshly.

'Someone in London – a friend told me.' She glanced at William. 'But I didn't know about you two. I must say, that was quite a surprise.'

Sasha turned to William; he was ashen, and he avoided looking at Kitty; she felt a surge of jealous impatience with him. 'For goodness sake. Why are we all being so civil? You might at the very least have warned everyone, Kitty!'

'Still the same old Sasha,' Kitty said with a little smile.

'Girls, there will be time for explanations later.' Mrs Hammond reminded them that for now duty counted above all else. 'We have our guests . . . Nathaniel, we must join them. William – Sasha?'

Sasha shook her head. 'I'll follow you in a little while.' She went to the piano when the others had gone, and caressed its lid for comfort. She thought of Werner Backhaus, and remembered the misery of being betrayed as a raw girl of eighteen. 'Where are you living?'

'In Frankfurt. I have a very nice apartment.'

'So why are you in England?'

'I've been playing with an orchestra.'

'You?'

'Yes, me. You're not the only one. I'm quite a novelty – a lady cellist among all those men! We were playing in London when I heard about Lavinia's wedding. Guess what – I met an old friend of mine. A very dear friend.'

'Not Porky again!' Sasha said wearily. 'What happened to Werner? Didn't he marry you?'

'No, he didn't marry me. Oh, people called me Mrs Backhaus for a while. I wore a ring. But he had his *career*. Let's face it, he got bored. It's funny. They all get bored after a while. You'll find that out for yourself. Marrying them doesn't give you any special claim.'

'William's different.'

'Yes. Probably,' Kitty said seriously. She laughed. 'Fancy you catching him. Just what you always wanted. You could have knocked me down with a feather.'

'William and I met again by accident. We became good friends.'

'Oh, that's the best. That's certainly the best. Far tidier than passion. Stay good friends and you can't go wrong.'

'So – what about Porky Portland?'

'We met by accident as well. I thought it was all going to be wonderful . . .' For an instant Kitty's expression was bleak. 'Anyway, when the band went back to Germany I stayed because of Porky. What a simpleton!'

'He didn't want you.'

'Something like that. You mustn't tell Mother . . . I came to England to play the cello. That's the story. And anyway, it's true. But what fools we women are, Sasha.' She laughed. 'Oh, I'm sorry. Not you. You were sensible. You married William.'

'What are you going to do?' Sasha interrupted. 'Why did you get in touch after all this time?'

'I suppose I believed some of the old clichés: family ties, blood being thicker than water.'

'They are none of them true. You don't belong here any more.' Sasha went to the door. 'And don't even think of putting in an appearance among the wedding guests. If you do anything else at all to hurt Mother or Father . . .'

She left the room.

Kitty sat in the window of the bedroom they had given her and watched the last of the guests leave the house. It was late. No one came to see how she was after the party. No one cared. Can you blame them? she thought with self-mockery. All the same, Kitty considered she had behaved very well; she had not upset anyone, she had kept out of sight all day – and a very boring day it had been too, listening to the party going on down below. Her mother had bundled her up to a spare bedroom and said they would have to see how things went. Kitty had understood her to mean she might stay.

Leah had arrived at one point, to slam doors and deliver a tirade of abuse. The newly-weds had avoided her as if she had a disease and they might catch it; they had escaped to Scotland without even saying goodbye. At least her father had remembered she might be hungry; he had slipped her morsels of food during the day and a glass or two of wine.

The worst, the very worst, Kitty realised, had been knowing Sasha was married to William. Not seeing Lavinia with her fat Yorkshireman – by all accounts a wealthy one – but Sasha, like a sleek cat who had taken all the cream, blooming, *pregnant*. She could have accepted Sasha's success as a musician; she knew about the short-comings of the life. But Sasha happy, and in love – that was a shock that was peculiarly hard to bear.

Kitty pressed her forehead against the cold window pane. She could hear people calling farewells to one another, the slam of carriage doors, and the grinding of wheels on cobbles. She remembered Werner, parties,

210

theatres, the joy of being free to go where they wanted; singing and playing in the salons of Paris; days and nights of pure indulgence; and, finally, living in Frankfurt. Then had come the excuses; his embarrassment over whispers of gossip; his evasions when she had said, believing he loved her, 'If you're so afraid of what people are saying, why don't we get married?' At least she had kept enough of her pride to leave him before he told her to go.

She pictured Porky, remembering their reunion, and the joy, the sheer relief of seeing in his face that he wanted her back. Kitty banged her head against the window. Why? Why did it never last?

The next day, William and Sasha prepared to leave for Penbury.

'Your father has said I might browse a while in his library and borrow a few books,' William told Sasha after breakfast, as she was putting the final touches to her travelling outfit. 'Can you bear to delay half an hour?'

Sasha laughed. Relief that the wedding had gone off smoothly, that they were going home and could escape the problems of Kitty's homecoming, had made them both less edgy. 'Come here.' She kissed him. 'Take as long as you like among Father's dry old books.'

William had been buried in the library for some ten minutes when he heard the rattle of the heavy curtain that excluded the draughts at the door. He had found a volume of Grant's *Lives and Thoughts*, and was sitting in the alcove made by the fireplace, hidden from anybody entering the room. He heard the rustle of a woman's skirts, the pad of feet on the polished floorboards. Glancing up from the page, he peeped round the edge of the alcove, expecting to see Sasha.

Kitty walked across the room without noticing him. She seemed set on reaching a particular bookcase. Feeling like a voyeur, and intensely flustered, William decided he must declare his presence. He coughed.

Kitty swung round with a cry of surprise.

211

'I was about to leave,' William said in his embarrassment. 'I simply felt . . . I thought you should know I was here.'

'Thank you, William. But I'm sure you were not about to leave at all.' Kitty stood with her hand pressed to her breast. 'Stay where you are. I promise I shan't disturb you.' She turned back to the bookshelves and ran her glance along them. 'I'm merely looking for something to help me pass the long dreary hours today.'

Confused, genuinely wanting to browse further through the pile of books he had collected on the seat beside him, William sat down again in the alcove. He continued reading uneasily, his heart beating quickly at the unpleasantness of the situation.

'The parents want me to stay,' Kitty said after a while. 'It's very touching – after all I've done to upset them.'

'It's a *damned* sight more than you deserve!' said William with feeling.

She laughed. 'I always knew you had a spark of spirit in you somewhere. Or is that Sasha's influence? I suppose I should have known she'd get you in the end. She was very soppy about you when she was sixteen.' Kitty reached up to pull out a book. He saw the whiteness of her arm as her sleeve fell back.

'Sasha is a wonderful wife.'

'A wonderful wife,' Kitty mimicked. She checked the title of the book in her hand and walked towards him. 'But do you *love* her, William? Do you desire her . . .' she sat in the seat on the opposite side of the empty grate '. . . as you desired me?'

'If you think I still . . .'

'Oh, but I do. I can see it in your eyes. Those feelings don't go away because of time passing, or because someone has treated you badly.' She laughed. 'Believe me. I know from experience.'

'You seem to have had rather too much of that for a young woman of your class,' William said piously. 'Women like you – women of refinement – are supposed to set an example.'

212

'How pompous you are becoming, William. I shall confess something to you now: I was beginning to feel envious of Sasha. Yes, I was. She looks so happy; there's the prospect of a baby to look forward to, and no doubt several more after that . . . But, you know, I'm really not so sure I've missed very much.'

'I thought you felt nothing for me at all,' William said bitterly. 'It has always seemed to me that I was some kind of a pawn in your game.'

'Oh, William. It wasn't a game. Truly it wasn't. Once I'd married you we could have been happy enough.' She was thoughtful, her lips curling a little at the memory. 'And I *would* have married you, if Miss Holloway hadn't caused such an uproar.'

'And I would have been none the wiser about your lovers, I suppose?' William tried to appear stern and self-possessed, though his heart was pounding furiously.

Kitty bent her head and flicked through the pages of the book in her lap. 'Would that have hurt you?'

'You *did* hurt me. You hurt me abominably! I couldn't believe it.' William thrust a hand through his hair, immediately destroying his impression of composure.

'Well, you should have believed it.' She looked at him, and for a moment an expression close to compassion crossed Kitty's face. 'You are such an innocent, William. But I don't suppose you would have fallen so hard if you weren't.'

'I thought you were so pure, so exquisite . . . I loved you.'

'No, you didn't. You were taken in by the myth about the fair sex and all that rot people talk.'

'Why?' he said in despair. 'Why do you have to destroy what is lovely and good?'

'Poor William. Is Sasha lovely and good, do you think? How very ignorant you are about women.' Kitty put down her book. Her gaze held his, and William felt a leap – an anguished kick of sexual desire.

She moved swiftly, switching from one side of the fireplace to the other and placing her arms round his neck,

213

all in one action. 'Kiss me and I'll soon show you what's lovely, and worth more than a lot of hot air about keeping oneself pure.'

Sasha came into the library, unseen and unobserving until she was at the centre of the room. She saw Kitty before she saw William, recognising the striped silk of Kitty's skirts; they were bunched up round her knees; one leg was extended, in a gesture half balletic, half abandoned; the shoe dangled, about to fall, but not quite releasing its hold on Kitty's toes. William's arm was buried in Kitty's petticoats; the other was around Kitty's waist. He was kissing her, holding her with a desperation, as if his life depended on every second; and Kitty's body was wrapped around his, her arms round his neck . . . like a snake crushing a rabbit.

Sasha released a sound, half cry, half moan.

They separated – mouths, then bodies. Kitty unwound herself from William's neck and moved from his lap to the other side of the fireplace. William could not look at Sasha. His head fell back with an expression of agony, that may in part have been produced by the impact of his skull against the wall.

'Don't . . . say anything,' Sasha whispered. She turned on Kitty as she opened her mouth to speak. 'Don't either of you say a word!'

William shook his head to clear it. He pressed the back of his hand against his mouth, as if he could wipe out the last five minutes.

Sasha swung violently away from them, half blinded by tears. She walked quickly to the door.

Recovering her self-possession by an effort of will, she said in a tight voice: 'Everyone's waiting, William. We're ready to leave.'

Kitty stood on the edge of the family group while Sasha's and William's overnight boxes were carried down to the hall. Sasha ignored Kitty as she said goodbye to Leah and her parents. William picked up Sasha's hatbox. She ignored him too, pretending he was one of the servants. Mr and Mrs Hammond looked at one another and smiled wryly; they assumed Sasha and William had quarrelled over something trivial; it would be over before they reached home.

Sasha swept out to the carriage in front of William. They did not speak until they reached Penbury.

Then, 'Sasha—' William said brokenly. 'How can I ever make it up to you?'

'You can't,' she said coldly. 'So don't even try.'

They went into the house. Sasha had forgotten to change the flowers before they left for the wedding, and she had given Bertha a holiday: the hall seemed dark and dusty. There was a blue Chinese vase filled with arum lilies by the foot of the stairs; the dead-white flowers formed thick curling funnels on long green stems that plunged into the neck of the vase. They looked sinister without any foliage; they hinted at corruption. The water would stink when the vase was emptied.

William sat on the bottom step. 'I don't know how it happened.' He began to weep. 'I honestly don't know.'

Sasha watched him for several seconds, feeling a slow emptying dread; even without Kitty's betrayal, she saw – in his tears, in the decaying flowers and the dreariness of the hall – that her marriage had been a mistake.

'No,' she said pityingly. 'I dare say you don't.'

Some weeks after Lavinia's wedding, Mrs Hammond wrote to say that Kitty had gone again. She had left a note: 'It is impossible. I cannot go back to being a dutiful daughter.' She had taken fifty pounds from her father's desk.

The prospect of a grandchild did much to soften their disappointment, wrote Mrs Hammond in a rare moment of confidence to Sasha; there was the hope that the mistakes encountered in one generation would be cancelled by the promises offered by the next.

Sasha took the message to heart. There was no going back. Mistakes – especially one's own – had to be lived with. She decided to ignore William's lapse from grace. There was no doubt that he had suffered for it. He went around with an expression of having committed a heinous crime, and was so pathetically grateful for every crumb of communication between them that, while not obliterating the incident entirely, she 'forgave' him, and put the blame on Kitty. Sasha put her energies into her pregnancy and, that September, into the birth of her first child.

They held Meredith's christening the following January, almost exactly a year after they had married. William invited Brewer and Wotherspoon, and several other local names, as well as his and Sasha's family.

Sasha was disappointed because Leah and Lavinia did not come. Lavinia was pregnant as well by then; she said she dared not attempt the journey. Leah sent a christening spoon and wrote that she would not be coming south because Gabriel was visiting her and Miss Ferrers. 'I do believe he has grown out of his childhood infatuation,' she added. 'He no longer has hopes of becoming my lover!'

Sasha thought the remark was in decidedly bad taste. And she felt the spoon was offhand. She told William that her sister was becoming increasingly peculiar in her old age.

The christening was not a success. Meredith was a fractious baby who cried all the way through the ceremony. Mayor Wotherspoon allowed a dispute to spill out of the council chamber and into Sasha's dining room; and William's Aunt Georgie fluttered and trembled so violently that she spilled a whole tray of teacups.

Sasha had a cold. She was exhausted by Meredith's crying, and by preparing mountains of food for more than thirty guests with the help of one, inexperienced maidservant. She was annoyed at William's apparent indifference to all her difficulties and his penny-pinching over the celebration; she felt irritated by her mother's fussing over the baby, and by the invasion of her home by strangers, who, she decided, had only come there to snoop. She had also taken a strong dislike to William's Grandfather

Sparrow, who seemed to think Norfolk the centre of the universe, for he talked of its virtues to the exclusion of all else.

On top of everything, Sasha was almost sure she was pregnant again. During a lull in the party, she escaped to the kitchen and, leaning on the top of the range to try to get warm, she found herself weeping.

She swung round at the sound of a voice, and saw William's Aunt Georgie hovering in the kitchen doorway.

'Oh dear. Oh . . . I'll go away. I didn't mean to pry.'

Sasha dried her eyes. 'No. Please don't go.'

Aunt Georgie sidled into the kitchen. She stood, drumming her fingers on the table, looking about her and casting sly smiles of reassurance at Sasha. In her own imagination Aunt Georgie was forceful and decisive; but to the outward observer she was a dithering assembly of nervous energy, giving an impression of moving in all directions at once, even when she was standing still. 'I know what it's like when you need a good howl and there's nowhere to go except the privy.'

Sasha smiled weakly. 'I really don't know what made me cry. I feel as if I've been burying everything under a mountain of activity for so long and have only today come to a halt.'

She paused. It was true; it was as if everything that had happened recently . . . No, not recently, not even since that ghastly moment when she had discovered William with Kitty. It had all begun after that concert one evening in London – she had been at a low ebb after Herr Lindau died, and William had seemed so comforting and nice.

'It's almost as if events have run away with me. There was no time to think about things – about marrying William, about babies, and the move to Penbury. Of course there *was* time; it simply seems as if there wasn't.' She stopped. She was being disloyal. Sasha looked at Aunt Georgie, whose life must be slow and lonely and uneventful. 'How silly I'm being. Of course being married to William and having babies is what I always wanted.'

Aunt Georgie nodded sympathetically.

Sasha doubted the other woman knew what she was talking about. 'I think I'm going to have another baby, you see,' she explained. 'I expect it's made me weepy.'

Aunt Georgie nodded. 'There are some advantages to being a spinster,' she said with a smile.

They did not hear William's sister Lily come in, until she announced, 'I'm looking for the privy.'

'It's across the yard.' Sasha waved her arm in the general direction of the back door.

Aunt Georgie said when Lily had gone, 'Do you think she's going there for a good cry?'

They laughed, and Sasha dried her eyes again and blew her nose. She felt soothed by Aunt Georgie. 'We haven't had time to get to know one another, have we?' she said. 'You're not quite what I expected.'

Sasha compared the diminutive figure of Aunt Georgie with the upright, slightly military Lily, dressed in black bombazine: like a stick, Sasha thought when Lily came back from the yard, a stick with a little gnarled head to it.

'Have you been blubbing?' Lily said in a tone of sharp accusation. She walked unsteadily to the stove and sat down very suddenly in the rocking chair Sasha had bought for five shillings at a local sale: a gesture of economy after William had expressed concern over her rash of spending on furniture. Lily began to rock herself to and fro; she glanced round the kitchen with its polished brass pans and the glowing range. 'You've made it very pleasant for William here. I expect that comes from having an artist for a father.'

Her speech was slurred. Sasha, who had begun to wonder whether William's sister was ill, saw with a slow realisation that she was drunk; though anyone less like a drinker was hard to imagine; Lily looked as if she had been fed on a diet of lemon juice and Chapel sermons.

'You've made everything very *nice*,' said Aunt Georgie quickly, recognising her niece's condition at the same time as Sasha.

'You've impressed *them* in there,' sniffed Lily. 'William will be pleased. William has always had firm ideas about

218

being refined, and going up in the world.' She tipped her head on one side and regarded Sasha. 'I expect that's the reason he married you.'

'Why didn't you tell me about Lily?' Sasha said, waylaying William in a corner of the dining room a few minutes later.

'Where is she?'

'In the kitchen. Don't worry. Your Aunt Georgie is keeping an eye on her. If only you'd confided in me that your sister likes the occasional tipple, I might have been more careful with the port.'

William glanced round to make sure that Wotherspoon had not overheard the remark about Lily's drinking and said, 'I'm afraid it's worse than that.'

They went back to London with Lily.

Sasha looked round the cheerless parlour of the apothecary shop. 'I had no idea . . .' She had not given a thought to where William had lived before she had met him. It was so mean, so horrid and dirty. No wonder he had never wanted her to go with him on the occasions when he visited his sister.

'How long has it been this bad?' They talked in hushed voices, aware that Lily, upstairs taking off her hat and mantle, might return at any moment and overhear.

'Too long. I honestly thought she had managed to stop the drinking. I wouldn't have let her come to the christening, but she promised to behave. I don't know if she can go on,' William confessed. 'The business has fallen right off, and I can't be here to do anything about it. Apparently she insults all the customers. She quarrels with everyone.'

'Why didn't you say?' Sasha jogged the sleeping Meredith in her arms. 'Ages ago. Why didn't you tell me?'

'We were so happy, and you were expecting the baby. And then . . .' He looked at his feet. 'There was that business with Kitty. There never seemed a right time. The

219

thing is, I promised my father on his deathbed that I'd see she was all right.'

'She'll have to come to us,' Sasha said making a decision. 'Lily must come to stay with us in Penbury.'

William felt a mixture of relief and doubt sweep over him. He had not dared to hope that Sasha would want to help.

'For a little while,' Sasha continued. 'Until we find somewhere for her to go.' She looked down at Meredith in her arms and wondered how she was going to tell William she thought she was going to have another baby.

'She'll have to stop drinking, of course,' said William. 'We can't have her knocking back the port. But it would be wonderful to be able to sell the shop.'

Lily came downstairs. Her hair was loosely knotted and hung in wisps against her face; she had not bothered to tidy it after taking off her bonnet. She picked up the teapot and peered inside to see if it was empty. There was a dull look in her expression, but as Sasha and William fell silent and she guessed they had been talking about her, interest glinted in Lily's eyes. She looked from one to the other.

'What's going on? You've been acting peculiar ever since we left Penbury.'

'I think it's time we sold up,' said William.

'We want you to come and stay with us, Lily,' added Sasha.

'Never.' Lily slammed down the teapot; the lid bounced on the table and rolled to the floor with a clatter.

'You liked it in Penbury. You said yourself – it's very pleasant.'

'I'm sure it is,' Lily said with heavy sarcasm, but the glint of interest had returned. Something about the idea had caught her imagination. She remembered the comfort of Sasha's kitchen, the people in Sasha's drawing room, who had asked her all about living in London and called her 'Miss Elliman', as if being William's sister had given her a special importance. She stared at the teapot without its lid. 'I'll make us a cup of tea.'

'She'll come round to the idea,' Sasha said confidently, as Lily went out to the scullery to fill the kettle.

William bent to pick up the teapot lid. He was ashamed to feel tears start to his eyes.

Sasha helped unpack the medicines from the apothecary shop several weeks later. Delving into the boxes in the room built on to the side of the house that was fitted out as a dispensary, she pulled out bottles, one after the other, from the packing straw. She read the labels as she handed them to William, who stacked them on the dispensary shelves.

'*Tartar emetic, Ipecacuanha, Laudanum, Rhubarb and magnesia.*' She dived into another box. '*Life Pills*! What on earth are these? *Elliman's Worm Lozenges, Elliman's Ointment*?' She looked at William with an amused smile.

William took the box of proprietary cures from her and put it on the dispensary table. 'I thought you realised my father was a quack. I ought to have thrown them out really. God in heaven only knows what's in here.'

He plunged in both hands and pulled out a handful of pill boxes. At the bottom of the box lay a jumble of papers and bound notebooks; the covers were stained with white patches and soft with mould. 'Old recipes. His pharmacopoeia.' He picked up a notebook and turned the crumbling pages. 'A cure for the ague. A cure for the indiscretions of youth. Genuine Jesuit Drops: A cure for . . . This is definitely *not* for a lady's ears.'

He pushed the box to the back of a cupboard. 'Where's Lily?'

'Settling into her room.'

William nodded. They fell silent, brooding on the realities of living with a difficult spinster, now that the thing was done.

'We have the money from the shop,' William said, searching for consolation. Less than he had expected, but still . . .

'Lily will be a help with the children,' Sasha said brightly, hopefully. She picked up a duster and began wiping the bottles on the shelves, adding, 'Now that there's another baby on the way.'

He stared at her.

'It's true,' she said. 'Are you pleased?'

William did not know whether he was pleased or not. He knew that he *should* be pleased, but his head kept filling with calculations based on the sale of the shop, his income, and on Sasha's decreasing capital. He decided to put a good face on it.

'Yes, of course. It's wonderful news.'

'Sasha has a little girl. Like Lavinia,' Leah said to Gabriel. He had come home to the farm to see his parents late that summer, and was visiting her again in Runsby. They walked together along the foreshore with the heavy roar of the sea in their ears.

'I'm pleased for your sisters,' Gabriel said, feeling in truth very little at all for Sasha, whom he remembered vaguely as a haughty sort of girl, whose only saving grace was a remarkable talent for music.

He had altered, Leah thought with a thrill of pride. His looks had matured in the last two years, and he was losing the broadness in his speech and the roughness in his manners. He would almost pass for a gentleman. She suspected he would not take the idea as a compliment.

'And how are you, Gabriel dear? Are you horribly in love?' Leah tucked her arm in his. He had begun to confide in her more freely on these occasions when he came to see her, and even in his letters; Leah was flattered when he asked her advice. She in turn discussed him with Felicity as if they were talking about a wayward son. They worried about his sudden enthusiasms, late nights and drinking parties, and – they suspected – his reputation as a flirt.

'I'm finished with women for ever!' He picked up a pebble and threw it along the beach. 'Except for you, of course, and Miss Ferrers.'

Leah knew the reason for the vigour of the remark. His affections had been violently engaged most recently by a girl called Amelia. The affair had been discovered. Amelia's father, a music professor in London, had forbidden them to meet. A few months ago, Amelia had allowed herself to become engaged to a man of more obvious promise, who had a career with the East India Company.

'She's gone to India,' Gabriel said mournfully. 'Whether she spares a thought for me ever in the heat of Calcutta, I wouldn't care to say.'

It was likely that she did, thought Leah. One could not be acquainted with Gabriel for long without fond memories lodging in one's mind.

'So, I'm done with women for good.'

'Until the next time,' Leah prompted.

He did not argue.

'Sometimes, my dear, I have fears of you becoming dissolute in the full tradition of a Byron or Shelley.'

'A Romantic would call me cold and sensible,' Gabriel laughed. 'After all, I haven't dashed out my brains on a rock or drowned my sorrows in drink or opium since she threw me over.'

Leah was thankful for that restraining streak of reason. But she knew he was not cold. Gabriel cared passionately about everything; about love – when he was in love – about beauty and art, and people and freedom, and about music.

'From this moment on, Miss Hammond, you are my first and only love,' Gabriel vowed. He swung her round on the sand and pulled her by the hand to the edge of the sea; he stopped short of the waves with their network of foam like thick, cream-coloured fishing nets. There was a haze of sea mist and spray on the wind. Across the estuary, the houses climbed the hill, row upon row, as if they were straining to reach those at the top and the squat brown church on the skyline.

'I love it here,' said Gabriel. 'And it suits you. I'm really happy for you.' He bent down and took off his boots.

Leah watched him for a moment, then did the same. They walked on, barefoot, saying little.

Gabriel noted that she had fine feet with long, even

toes. He wondered whether Miss Ferrers admired them. He would have liked to kiss Miss Hammond's long white feet, and to caress them with his own; he would never lose his awareness of Leah's beauty. He always wanted to touch – beautiful furniture, a cloak or skirt made of velvet, to stroke the surface, to feel the cool, or supple, texture. And as for the softness of white skin, the silk smooth sensuality of tumbling hair . . . Had he been rich he would, he supposed, have fulfilled some of Leah's fears by becoming a rake or a dilettante. But he had been saved from idleness by the desire to make his way in the world, and she had offered him the means to do it. He knew he would always be in her debt.

He smiled at her. Gabriel liked the company of women. When he fell in love he was always consumed by a heightened sense of being alive. He loved Leah for her generosity, but he was no longer in love with her as he had been when he was a boy. He recognised now that she was barred to him as far as sexual interest went; he even understood the attraction between Leah and Miss Ferrers, and was not shocked by it. It seemed right that the women should have found one another.

'What next, Gabriel?' Leah said, as they sat on a rock to put on their shoes and stockings.

'There's another year. Plenty of time. I've been playing second violin in a band in the evenings for a few miserable pounds a week; not much better than fiddling in the tavern at Eskton – we play in pleasure gardens and dance halls – but I go to hear all the professional concerts when I can.' He turned to her. 'I heard Joachim play at a house where I had a letter of introduction from Drossel. I was *stunned*, Miss Hammond. If I had half that talent!'

'Drossel has been getting you introductions?'

'He believes I have a future. But the foreign soloists take all the glory. One has to make an impression somehow. He thinks I should learn the piano as well, and get a formal grounding abroad.'

Leah thought of Sasha, and how little satisfaction her sister had found on the music circuit; and she felt afraid for him. She knew how good he was these days, how fiercely passionate his music. She felt a strong sense of terror when she heard him play the violin; it tore her emotions to shreds and made the hair rise at the back of her neck; he exposed his soul too willingly.

'Are you sure? It's such a haphazard, unsettled way of life.'

He laughed. 'You were the one who first encouraged me!'

'I know. But so uncertain a future!'

'I'm twenty. Who wants to be certain of things at twenty?'

'Have you the self-discipline?' Leah said wryly. 'You know how impatient you are with rules and routine. Could you really stick to dry, dull old theory without me to nag you? The money's no problem, I know Father would help. But what do your family say?'

He kicked up the sand and did not look at her as they set off back towards the cottage. 'They think I'm wasting everyone's time. They say they'll have nothing more to do with me if I become a musician. But the fact is – Drossel thinks I should do it, and so do I. The fact is, Miss Hammond, I see no prospect of happiness at all from a life that is not devoted to music.'

PART THREE
August, 1861
Sasha

Chapter Eleven

'I hope she is going to fit in,' murmured Sasha as she crossed the lawn with William. 'She's so different from Lily.'

Aunt Georgie was working at some article of sewing – it was hard to tell what from across the lawn. Her attitude was one of nervous industry. At the same time, she watched the children in the vegetable garden where Cope the handyman was letting them play with the watering can. Their shrieks of laughter set her head nodding energetically. One sensed she would have liked to join them.

Lily too sat under the lilac tree. As always she was dressed in black: dusty, crumpled, she appeared to be asleep. Was it really six years since she had come to them? And now Aunt Georgie as well. Sasha saw the future stretching before her, crowded with William's dependants.

Aunt Georgie was dressed in sugar pink; she looked like a faded piece of fondant confectionery. Defying convention, she had refused to wear mourning for more than a few weeks after Grandfather Sparrow had died. She had brought less capital with her than William had hoped; but, as he had said, what could he do? She was his aunt. Someone had to look after her.

They approached the two spinsters, William's aunt and his sister, and William let his arm slip from around Sasha's waist as he might when the housemaid entered a room where they were sitting or talking. Sasha stifled an urge to tell him to put it back where it was. What did it matter? Why such consideration for two old maids' sensitivities? She thought of the other constraints: the stifling of pleasure, the difficulty of containing the creak of the bed-frame. There would be two women now in the room next to theirs. Would they lie awake, listening? Would Aunt Georgie perhaps make some giggling comment to Lily? Or would she adopt her room-mate's pretence at ignorance about 'delicate' subjects?

Sasha reached the shade of the tree. William, with a nod of his head, left the three women together and walked on a few yards to talk to Cope. Sasha smiled a greeting at Aunt Georgie and sat in a vacant chair beside her.

'There's no need to do that, you know. We never expected Lily to take on the mending.'

'I like to feel I'm doing something useful.'

Aunt Georgie laughed nervously, drawing up her shoulders. Her hair was dressed in a frizz of henna-coloured curls, fastened with numerous pins and combs under her lace cap. Sasha found herself counting the ones she could see. Aunt Georgie threw a sidelong glance at their sleeping companion. Lily's head had lolled in the chair and she snored a little. One of the lappets of her morning cap had fallen over her face, hiding the whiskers on her upper lip; the lace stirred with each puff of breath.

'It's the heat,' Sasha said. 'It always makes her sleepy.'

'Did she get over that other business?' Aunt Georgie jerked her head; she waggled her hand as if tipping a glass.

'Oh, yes,' Sasha said quickly. 'In fact, she's grown very temperance-minded. She doesn't seem to miss it.'

'Lily has given up on life,' Aunt Georgie said with surprising assurance. 'You'd never guess she was my niece and younger than I am! Falling asleep in a chair! William's too good to her. Too good to me too. And she can't even bring herself to darn a few stockings!'

'William promised his father.'

Aunt Georgie paused in her sewing. She looked at

Sasha with a directness that was unnerving. 'He never made any promises about me. I don't have to stay. We can call this a trial visit.'

'I didn't mean . . .'

'All the same. I don't have to stay.'

'We want you here. And where else would you go?' Sasha, too late, tried to hide the obligation in her voice.

'I can find a position somewhere. A governess. Or even a housekeeper. I'm only fifty-one.' Aunt Georgie's voice trailed off. 'I shall try to adapt to your ways, Sasha. And if I don't, you must turn me out.'

Sasha pulled a face. 'Now you sound like Lily. You don't want to stay where you're not wanted.'

'You see? I already know the jargon.' Aunt Georgie gave a nervous shiver. 'How tiresome old maids can become.'

It occurred to Sasha that she had misjudged William's aunt, and was too ready, like everyone else, to dismiss her as silly or simple.

The children were running across the garden, Meredith banging the watering can after him. Every now and then he swung it round and sent a spray of water into the air, aiming at various targets: rows of cabbages, a sundial, a clump of dahlias. His sister Pippa ran alongside him, shrieking, 'Me! Me! Let me do it, Merry!'

'What fun they're having,' said Aunt Georgie. 'It makes me wish I was young again. I hope you'll let me help with the children, Sasha. I can see Meredith's becoming a handful.'

Sasha was about to suggest that Aunt Georgie was hardly likely to find Meredith easy to handle, since William already considered the child was becoming too much for his own mother; but she saw a look almost of pleading in Aunt Georgie's eyes. How terrible it must be, to dwell on the fringes of other people's lives. What a cold world it was for women who had not found a man on whom to pin their destiny; without a man, how did any woman acquire a home and status, or the blessings of a family? Oh, Sasha, what a fortunate woman you are, she told herself half severely, half mockingly. She leaned forward and kissed the other woman's cool cheek. 'Aunt Georgie, I think you and I are going to get along very well. And there'll be *absolutely* no talk of turning you out.'

Lily gave a grunt and stirred. The noise of the children had woken her. She sat bolt upright and brushed the lace lappet from her face rapidly, thinking it was an insect. 'What's happened? What's going on?'

'It's only the children . . .' Sasha watched Meredith whirling the watering can round. He was getting too excited. In a moment someone would have to curtail his enthusiasm. He reminded her so much of herself as a child, with his blond curls and talent for getting into trouble. She raised her voice to call to him, 'Not there, Merry—' and halted in mid-breath. He had begun spinning more wildly towards them. Sasha watched her son and the watering can as if in a state of mesmerism; it was as if she knew what was going to happen but was powerless to prevent it. An arc of water flew from the can, sparkled in the sunlight, and hit Lily squarely in the middle.

Lily shrieked. Her voice rose to a piercing note of indignation and she scrambled from the chair, tugging at the bodice of her dress. 'I'm soaked! Oh! Oh! Look what you've done!'

Pippa stood perplexed. Meredith held the can at an angle, letting the contents trickle on to the grass until Cope took it from him.

Lily shook off William's conciliatory arm. With an accusing glance at Aunt Georgie as if suspecting she had somehow put Meredith up to it, and with a turn of speed that surprised everyone, she gathered her skirts above her ankles and ran into the house.

William watched her with an anxious frown. He turned to Aunt Georgie who had caught some of the water from Lily's soaking. 'Are *you* all right, Aunt Georgie? What a thing to have happened on your very first day with us!'

'A drop of water never hurt anybody.' Aunt Georgie

threw a reassuring smile at Meredith.

Lily's head and shoulders appeared at one of the upstairs windows. 'I'm soaked right through to my *drawers*!'

'I'm sure she's exaggerating,' William murmured.

'All the same, I'd better go after her.' Sasha went into the house.

'Everything's wet. Everything!' Lily stood in the middle of the room with her arms folded across her breasts. She had stripped off her petticoats and corset and stood in her chemise. Her papery, whiskered face was puckered as if she were about to cry.

Sasha began gathering up the discarded corset and flannel petticoats from the bed. 'They're only damp.' She felt a reluctant pity stir in her. 'I'm sorry, Lily. I'll get you some dry clothes from the linen cupboard.'

Lily sensed the vein of sympathy and rejected it vigorously. 'I can fetch my own clean drawers, thank you very much. I'm not senile. Only wet.'

'Well then—' Sasha cast a glance round the room. Lily's bed-linen was squared at the head and foot, with neatly executed corners and the white sheet folded over the blanket, measured precisely. In contrast, Aunt Georgie's bed was covered by a pretty counterpane; her dressing table was already littered with hairnets, ribbons, and bottles and jars. 'Well then,' she repeated. 'If you're sure.'

Lily took the pile of damp clothes from Sasha and hung them over the window sills to air. 'That was no accident. Meredith is getting out of hand. It's time Will did something about it.'

'I shall reprimand Merry myself. And so shall William. He doesn't neglect his paternal duties, but he's very busy with the practice. With such a large household to maintain he has to work very hard.' She bit back an instinct to turn the exchange into a confrontation and left the room.

Sasha pictured the two spinsters in the room next door as she got ready for bed that night, seeing Lily like a matchstick in its box, Aunt Georgie's fussy head on a plumped pillow. Did they resent being dumped on William's charity? Were they unhappy, lonely? Would they become allies or enemies? She remembered the room she had once shared with Kitty, and wondered where Kitty was now.

'What are you thinking about?' William was watching her; he lay propped on one elbow as he waited for her to put out the lamp.

Sasha came to with a start, her hairbrush poised in her hand. She stared at herself in the mirror. Her hair looked lank – beige-coloured rather than ash-gold in the lamp-light. She would be twenty-eight next birthday. Were those age lines round her eyes?

'I was remembering when I was a girl.' She had been so jealous of Kitty, she remembered, and head over heels in love with William – or had thought she was. He was as handsome today as then: marriage had made little differ-ence to him in that respect. He was as tall, fair, a little heavier perhaps, though his jaw was as obligingly manly as ever; several of his female patients were in love with him. But he had acquired a polish that was less beguiling than the eager idealism of those early days. William had adopted the professional manner, the artificiality, the measured charm and gravity of the solid physician – not with ease, nor from a sense of admiration for other men who were professionals, but out of necessity, because being charming, solid and respectable paid the bills.

The money Sasha had brought to the marriage early on, her earnings, her dowry, had long since been whittled away, and so had the money from the sale of the apoth-ecary shop. The house and the practice were a constant, and to Sasha surprising, drain on William's income. They *had* installed a water closet upstairs, and piped water – what confidence could anyone have in a sanitary reformer who did not have the latest technical advances in his own home? Their plumbing was a show-piece for Penbury's new water company. Though what a struggle that had been. If it had not been for Charlie Brewer . . .

She continued brushing her hair. 'You were courting Kitty. And I was desperately in love with you. I thought you were amazingly handsome.'

'I was. I remember it distinctly,' he said quickly, unwilling to be reminded of Kitty; they had a tacit agreement not to mention all that business. 'We ought to be discussing what to do about Meredith.'

Sasha remembered her own unruly childhood, similar high spirits and scrapes. 'Not tonight.' She turned from the dressing stool. 'William, you were so *alive* in those days, so full of ambition and ideas. I thought you were a knight in shining armour. A crusader.'

He thought he recognised the train of her thought. 'There's no point in charging around putting people's backs up. Look at Brewer. He made so many enemies he had to leave.'

'He got things done.'

'And so do I,' William protested. 'We all mellow as we get older.'

'I don't want us to mellow. I feel so afraid sometimes. I see us becoming something other than I expected . . . *less* than I expected.'

William looked at her. How vulnerable she still seemed at times – and desirable, with her hair down on her shoulders like a girl's. The years between, the pressures of the practice and irritations of married life dropped away. He thought of the career she had given up to be a doctor's wife and the manager of his home, the readiness with which she had forgiven him over Kitty. She had never expressed any regrets about marrying him, and he was grateful.

'How I love you.' His voice softened in the way that made Sasha's senses heighten.

She turned down the lamp, climbed into bed and lay beside him. 'And I love you. But I'm not a girl any more, and you're not the young man I was in love with before you became a small-town doctor.'

'Nor we are.' William adopted a flippancy to cover his hurt at the casual phrase 'small-town doctor'. It sounded

235

faintly damning. He took her in his arms and kissed her neck, felt her respond as he unbuttoned her nightdress, and was relieved when they were on familiar ground. But, for a moment, he had been aware of something lurking, something that threatened their happiness. Aunt Georgie? Was another spinster in the house going to prove too much?

Sasha too was thinking of Aunt Georgie. She could remember what it was like to be lonely; she thought of the isolation of touring. Had she married William out of expediency, for no other reasons than because she had been terrified of spending the rest of her life alone?

'Hold me.' She kissed him over and over, wanting the closeness of sexual intimacy to drive out the doubts in her head. She relaxed as he pulled up her nightdress, heard his swift intake of breath, and stifled her own gasp of pleasure. She clung briefly to control, and then she lost herself in delight. Who cared about the bed creaking or the sleepers in the next bedroom?

Stepping round William as he shaved the next morning, patting his back, letting her hand linger briefly on the muscles above his waist, Sasha remembered her peculiar mood the previous night. She wondered if she was pregnant again: she always felt unsettled when she was expecting. She threw a prayer to the gods that she was not.

'You're very happy this morning, Mr Elliman.'

He had been whistling; he paused in his shaving and they exchanged an intimate, conspiratorial smile. 'I'm seeing Wotherspoon today,' he said after a while. 'I thought I might get him to pay his bill. You might take Aunt Georgie round the town and introduce her to a few of the women. Lily's friends. You know the sort of people.'

'Yes. Of course.' Sasha discarded her plans that afternoon for jamming blackcurrants with the cook and Bertha. 'Lily is going to a Chapel Tea this afternoon. Perhaps we could take the children.'

'Splendid. It will be good for Merry. Kill two birds with

one stone.' He took the towel Sasha handed him and dried the soap from his face.

Sasha could hear laughter from the room above. 'Aunt Georgie has asked if she might lend a hand with nursery duties. It would give me a chance to concentrate on Merry's lessons.'

'I've been thinking about Merry . . .'

'Yes. I know. He needs more discipline.' She wiped a smear of soap from his cheek slowly with her finger. 'So, that's settled then. I shall go and tell Aunt Georgie.'

The sound of the children had become muted as Sasha climbed the attic stairs to the children's room. She saw Aunt Georgie sitting on Meredith's bed with Pippa on her lap; she was brushing Pippa's long mouse-brown hair. Merry was showing her his scrapbook; Aunt Georgie was listening intently to his explanations about each picture without diverting her attention from the child on her knee.

Sasha watched them for several seconds until they looked up and smiled at her; their expressions of surprise, of tranquillity and ease with one another gave an impression of solidarity.

'Go on. Run and play,' said Aunt Georgie. 'I want to talk to your mother.'

Meredith closed the scrapbook; Pippa slid from Aunt Georgie's lap; they both ran downstairs.

'They're good children.'

Sasha laughed. 'How can you say that after yesterday?'

'High spirits. That's all that was. You know it's true.'

'Yes. I do. I was exactly the same. My parents employed a governess to keep me in check, but she was hopeless.' Sasha leaned on the banisters and looked down into the stairwell. A shaft of light from the oval stained-glass window above her head struck the black and white floor far below her and jewelled it softly with fairy colours. She was beginning to love this house now that they had almost completed their additions to it: she loved the stained-glass windows, the green Venetian blinds in the drawing room, the geranium and yellow stair-carpet, and the twin oak bookcases in the dining room; she was proud of the paintings by Leah and Lavinia, and the portrait of her mother on the stairs – one of her father's paintings. She would have liked *The Beautiful Hammond Girls* to hang downstairs in the hall if her father had not sold it to Algie Ross after exhibiting it. Perhaps it was for the best. The painting would only have reminded them all of Kitty. Even now, Sasha tried not to think too often of Kitty. She recalled her mood the previous evening. Shreds of it still lingered: a sense of lost opportunities, something missing.

Aunt Georgie wandered along the attic corridor, looking in each of the rooms where Sasha stored trunks and hatboxes. 'You could easily get my bed into one of these.'

'But this is the attic. It's where Bertha and our cook, Mrs Ash, sleep. I mean – it's servants' quarters.'

'You don't mind your children sleeping near the servants.'

'What I mean is, we want you to feel welcome.'

'By putting me in with Lily? I should rather you pushed me up here in the attic.' Aunt Georgie looked round the little room. 'It would be nice to be closer to the children. I could attend to Pippa if I heard her in the night. I'm a light sleeper, and Lily snores. Dead to the world. I doubt a steam train going through the front garden would wake her.'

'Very well. I shall ask Mrs Ash and Cope to move the bed.'

Sasha felt an inexplicable sense of satisfaction. So, there were going to be changes, she thought, as they went downstairs. Silly, ineffectual Aunt Georgie was going to stir them all up a little.

Lily had grown very diligent about Church and Chapel since going to live with Sasha and William, and attended the parish church with them every Sunday morning. She did not dislike the Anglicans; the curate was dour enough for her taste, and he was the president of the Penbury Total Abstinence Society. But the church services had become 'High' of late; a new vicar had arrived, and Lily suspected him of wanting to introduce the rituals practised by those slaves to Catholicism, the Puseyites. She watched for the tell-tale signs – the lighting of candles, the bowing and scraping – and vowed that when it all got too much, she would turn her back on the Anglican Church for good. Meanwhile, she evened the balance by going to the Baptist chapel on Sunday evenings. She went to Temperance meetings with great energy, and all the Chapel prayer meetings and Chapel Teas. Lily looked forward to introducing Aunt Georgie to these satisfying routines.

The little group entered the Baptist Rooms as the town hall clock struck four that afternoon. Heads turned to look at them as they moved down the room. Pippa clung to Aunt Georgie. Meredith wriggled free from Sasha's hand, conscious of being too old to need the protection of females. The wives of local farmers, manufacturers and tradesmen nodded greetings to Sasha with a measure of reserve. She was not popular among the Chapel wives. They were conscious that she had once been a 'musical performer'. The image this conveyed of a sophisticate provoked a certain degree of mistrust.

Sasha's background was a barrier for most of the women in Penbury; those who remembered her performance there as a girl and did not suspect links with the stage or music hall, feared she might be a 'blue stocking'. It was rumoured that she was 'stuck up'. There was the possibility of being patronised if one was invited to the Ellimans' house, with its stylish furniture, the cultured pictures and educated books, and a grand piano filling the drawing room. People were torn between admiration and a desire to find some fault that might tip the doctor's wife firmly and satisfyingly on her face.

The women felt no such spite towards William; the doctor was attractive and dignified, a knowledgeable physician and a sound chap, who had helped make Penbury a good place to live. They could take to Lily too; Miss Elliman, plain and sour, was the sort they understood, though she was a Londoner and an outsider; she did not give herself airs.

Lily introduced Aunt Georgie to the other spinsters in the room: Miss Hewett, who ran a Bible class for young men; the Misses Vaughan, the Baptist minister's three unmarried daughters; and Miss Scrope, who had recently opened a school for pauper children and whose brother, Councillor Scrope, was a Chapel deacon.

Sasha disliked the sanctimony that lurked under the cheerful cover of Chapel teas: the sermonising speeches, the reading of the Chapel accounts, to which everyone listened very intently.

She surveyed the meeting room. The Chapel wives had laid out long tables with white cloths on which plates of bread and butter and plain and currant cake formed lonely islands. Sasha knew that the old people, given free tickets, relished the good butter and the superior quality of the cakes; but as for the rest – it was such a waste of energy.

Sasha had an aversion to organised enthusiasm, and particularly when it was applied to religion; she recalled the *laissez-faire* attitude to attendance at St Andrews in Avondon; the whole family had trooped off on Sunday mornings, and over Sunday dinner they would pull the sermon to pieces. It had been an enjoyable intellectual exercise; there was never any earnestness about it.

'How nice to see you here, Mrs Elliman.' Mrs Turbot was less in awe of Sasha than the other women, and Sasha thankfully seized on her company. At least Angelina Turbot did not limit her conversation to pious platitudes, nor did she place heavy emphasis on anecdotal bodily sufferings – what was it about being a doctor's wife that made people think she must have a particular interest in boils, bilious attacks and medical remedies?

They retreated from the bevy of spinsters to sit on a bench by the wall.

Mrs Turbot believed she had something in common with Sasha, for she played the piano when required at the Chapel Teas; Mr Turbot, an auctioneer and land surveyor, was a 'professional' man like William; and, more importantly, the Turbots had two daughters who 'sang'. Sasha, in a private joke to William after an 'Evening of Song and Symphony' at the Turbots' house, had nick-named them 'the Musical Turbots'; they took a continuing delight in the fishy image. There was a Musical Society in Penbury, to which all the Turbots belonged. From time to time they asked Sasha to join them, and to contribute piano recitals at their concerts. Sasha made excuses as often as she could, vaguely uneasy that her talents should be reduced to performing with a bunch of amateurs. William was disappointed in her. It would have pleased him to see her dash off a few show-pieces, and to attend regular soirées in the Turbots' or the Wotherspoons' drawing room, so that people would say his wife had raised the tone among the bawlers and scrapers that constituted the usual musical entertainment in Penbury.

Mrs Turbot's glance moved from Lily in her dusty black mantle and grim bonnet to Aunt Georgie, dressed in a voluminous pink crinoline and girlish hat. Aunt Georgie's red curls nodded energetically; her hands twisted and untwisted, tying themselves in knots around the fastenings at her neck.

'Miss Sparrow has come to live with us now that her father has died,' explained Sasha.

'Poor thing.' Mrs Turbot decided Aunt Georgie was simple. 'What a Christian man Mr Elliman is.'

'I think she'll soon settle down. She likes children. And she and Pippa have already become firm friends.'

'Is she musical at all? I only ask, because my brother – Mr Viggers – is coming to visit us shortly. He has a fine voice, but I'm afraid my efforts on the piano don't do it justice. I told him, "I know the perfect accompanist for you . . ." Mrs Elliman, wouldn't it be splendid to repeat our little soirée of last spring? Oh, *wouldn't* it?'

Sasha murmured that they must arrange something. She saw Meredith out of the corner of her eye. He was walking the length of one of the tables, surveying the plates of cakes speculatively, selecting the most tempting. She blanched as she thought of the repercussions if Meredith were to *steal* from a Chapel tea.

'Do excuse me, Mrs Turbot.' Sasha stepped smartly sideways, reached Merry the second before he made his move, and returned with her son's hand clamped securely in hers.

'The dear boy. What were you up to?' smiled Mrs Turbot. 'Oh, such soft, pretty hair.' Meredith, with a silent look of anguish, suffered his curls to be ruffled. 'Is he musical? Are you teaching him the piano?'

'We have begun. But Meredith has very little patience and, quite frankly, I have hardly any aptitude for teaching.'

'I want to play the viola,' said Meredith.

'Ah,' nodded Mrs Turbot wisely. 'Mr Viggers plays the viola. Perhaps he could give you a few lessons.' She turned to Sasha. 'Do let me tell Mr Viggers you'll play for him one day. He *should* be heard against a decent piano.' Her expression was expectant, waiting.

'Perhaps you could bring your brother to supper—'

'A musical evening? At the doctor's house?'

Sasha, feeling trapped, heard herself turning what had begun as little more than a vague possibility into a firm commitment.

William had left the surgery in a poor mood that lunchtime. He had spent the morning dealing with a succession of malingerers. The queue of patients seemed to have been especially constituted to drive home the truth of Sasha's label, 'small-town doctor.' William could not rid himself of the phrase as he waited for Cope to harness the gig so that he could set off on his rounds. He thought of all he had hoped to achieve when he had first come to the town. Had he become like Wotherspoon and Scrope, and all the others who gave every appearance of wanting change? Men who were governed by a primary interest of maintaining their social position, of thinking of cost, thinking of profits – or, in William's own case, his fees.

He *had* achieved things, he protested as he clicked the

horse into action; he was on the Board of the Guardian and Friendly Society and a member of the Scientific Institute; thanks to his efforts Penbury had a town council; he had influenced the founding of a waterworks, a gasworks and a sewerage scheme. But a nagging voice told him that all the real improvements had benefited only the better-off families in the town. What had the council done for the cause of reform? Covered a few drains? Employed a town surveyor who shuffled papers and pretended that various projects were imminent? Penbury had a waterworks, but people still lived without running water to their homes. There was a sewerage scheme, yet the lower part of town was still reeking and filthy. Where were the water closets for all?

William drove past the town hall with its towering columns and pilasters; the large, many-paned windows looked down on the square across a balcony of marvellous proportions and from beneath a magnificent marble-faced clock that struck 'one' as he passed by.

What more could he do than he had done already? He had worked hard on the local board of health, until attendance at meetings had dwindled to one. He needed allies for fighting battles. Brewer had left the local newspaper, gone to more fertile pastures, and his successor was less committed to the need for social reform. And William had his practice to consider. He would be forty in a few years, time for a man to have established himself. Gone were the days when he might have crossed swords with greedy factory owners. What man in his right mind would make enemies among his paying patients?

William's first call was on Wotherspoon, a fact that added to his uneasy frame of mind. Perhaps Sasha's comment 'small-town doctor' was all that had unsettled him, he thought, as he waited in Wotherspoon's hallway, where he was kept waiting for almost ten minutes. Did the man do it on purpose, to remind him he was, after all, only the doctor, and that he owed all he had to Wotherspoon?

A maid appeared and showed him up to the first floor.

'Come in, Elliman. Come in.' Wotherspoon, hoarse with laryngitis, was nevertheless in an expansive frame of mind.

'The old trouble again?' William said cheerfully.

'Up to a point.' Wotherspoon unwound the scarf at his neck to reveal a large boil. 'I've been a bit out of sorts. Throat's raw inside and out. Sit down, man. How's Mrs Elliman?'

The distinctions of social position having been made on the threshold, Wotherspoon was prepared to treat William generously; he poured him a tot of whisky.

William drank it down; he examined his patient's neck and said he would lance the boil for him. 'And I'll make something up for your throat and have it sent round to you this evening.'

'I'd be much obliged. Though, I must say, I can't understand why you mix your own prescriptions. By God, Elliman, you're a scholar and a professional man, not a storekeeper. Been to a university, haven't you? Most good-class practices don't dispense these days. Their patients go to the chemist with a prescription.'

'But I'm saving you the inconvenience of sending down into town,' William said. He told himself, less amiably, that if Wotherspoon paid his damned bills regularly, he would be glad to shed the duties of mixing remedies and the extra income from selling prescriptions. He wondered briefly what Wotherspoon would have made of his father's apothecary shop. 'Gad, man! You mean to say your father was a quack? A trader?' Somewhat lower on the social scale than small-town doctor, William mused; Sasha's criticism still rankled.

'You're too obliging, Elliman. You know that? You're a sound fellow. Everyone says so. I don't know why you don't stand for the council one of these days.'

'That would be gratifying. Unfortunately, the practice and Board work takes up—'

'That water closet you recommended. Damned efficient. Mrs Wotherspoon is highly delighted.'

William opened his medicine chest. 'Good. I look

forward to the day when the whole town is similarly equipped.'

'All in good time. First things first, eh? You concentrate on dealing with this devil on my neck that's been stopping me sleeping at night.'

William placed a clean towel round Wotherspoon's shoulders and set himself to the task of lancing the boil. Wotherspoon gripped the arms of his chair. He barely flinched at the incision, though William knew the agony was intense.

'How's the family? How's your sister?' Wotherspoon continued their conversation as if nothing had happened. 'How's that boy of yours coming along?'

'To be truthful, Meredith's behaviour is causing us some concern.' William cleaned up swiftly around the wound. 'He's a lively lad. Very unruly.'

'Have you got his name down for a school yet?'

'No. I had been thinking we should . . . but Mrs Elliman would never hear of him going away.'

'Too many women in the house. That's the trouble. You'll never make a man of him with women fussing round.'

'You know how mothers are about their sons.' William gave a jocular laugh, hearing its falseness ring in his ears.

'Mrs Elliman will feel differently when a few more come along. They'll soon be grown up. Best thing in the world when they've flown the nest. All off and married. A job well done . . . You send him off to school.' Wotherspoon fell silent. Evidently more than Meredith's schooling was on his mind.

William paused. 'I'll have some opium and tincture of iodine sent up to you.' Remind him about his bill, he told himself. Do it now, before it's too late and you're outside on the drive.

But Wotherspoon still seemed preoccupied. A peculiar change came over him: he glanced round as if to be sure they were alone and lowered his voice. 'Heard a rumour, Elliman. Only a rumour, mind, that you have a particular

245

medicine in your dispensary. Supposed to . . . be efficacious in certain cases?'

William froze. How the devil had Wotherspoon heard? The pages of his father's recipes flew accusingly through his mind. He remembered doing his rounds the previous winter, arriving foot-sore, shoes filthy, drenched with rain, on people's doorsteps; in a fit of frustration he had bought a pony carriage with a hood. The cost and upkeep had been a strain, but to let it go again would have been an admission of failure; it would have meant a loss of respect. People would see him on foot and think, 'So, Elliman's over-reached himself and is going down again in the world.' And then, like a gift from heaven, a patient had come to the dispensary, in tears, desperate because his wife wanted a child. Wickham was gentry. He had inherited several thousand a year, and his stables on Batford Hill could have accommodated half a dozen carriages. 'Damn it, Elliman, you're a medical man,' he had pleaded. 'You must know of something to make John Thomas work. I don't care how much it costs.'

He had remembered his father's recipes: cures for debility, mixtures to restore the animal and vital spirits, bordering on witchcraft; powdered snail shells, feathers; herbal and homeopathic ingredients. Not all were archaic, or simply innocuous vegetable concoctions. There was Elliman's Elixir, 'For the secret infirmities and disorders of the generative organs.'

William had made up the mixture and charged the man two pounds for the bottle. He had been ashamed of himself for weeks afterwards and had vowed he would never do it again. And then, Wickham had returned; he swore the Elixir had made a new man of him, and begged for more of the magic potion . . . Two pounds a bottle had become a useful extra.

How had Wotherspoon heard? The two men were fellow trustees of one of the almshouses; they hunted together, moved in the same circles, but surely Wickham had not been boasting? A chance remark? Something said off-guard?

246

Should he deny the 'rumour'? Offer Wotherspoon something harmless?

'It isn't a medicine to be taken lightly,' William said with a composure that disguised the rapid pounding of his heart. 'It's not strictly orthodox . . . It's potent stuff. One has to be careful.'

'I'm at the end of my tether, Elliman.' Wotherspoon tried to appear casual. 'Women can be very cruel. One feels less than a man, you understand.'

William had a mental picture of Mrs Wotherspoon, unalluring but kindly and amiable. It occurred to him with a sense of shock that it was not she who had caused Wotherspoon's loss of self-esteem.

'Think of our old association, Elliman. Doesn't it count for something? The years you've enjoyed in that house? The practice? Nobody would be any the wiser about the medicine. You know how discreet I can be.'

As Wickham was? thought William. He bent his head, hesitating. 'I'll send some Elixir round with the throat linctus this evening. Under a plain wrapper.'

'My dear fellow. I can't tell you how grateful . . .'

'It's a *general* restorative, you understand. It works on the whole system. One needs to treat the whole man in cases of the failure of . . . in cases such as this.' William decided to press home his advantage. 'There's the little matter of your account.'

'Of course. Send in your bill. Send it in.'

'I wouldn't mention it, except . . .'

'I understand. It will be paid in the morning.'

The postman had delivered a letter while Sasha was out. She opened it as William came in from his afternoon rounds. 'Leah has written to say she would like to stay with us for a few days.' She scanned the letter. 'How extraordinary. She says there's something she wants to discuss. It all sounds very mysterious.'

'She'll be company for you.' William kissed her absent-mindedly.

'I should have thought I had enough company already

with your sister and your aunt.' Sasha glanced at him. 'Is anything wrong?'

'Wrong?'

'You look worried.'

'I've been to see Wotherspoon. He made me late for the rest of my round. He thinks I've all the time in the world to gossip.'

'Poor darling.'

He smiled. 'I'm glad your sister's coming. I've always liked Leah. She's so sensible somehow.'

Sasha returned to the letter. 'What would the Musical Turbots make of her, I wonder?'

'The Turbots?'

'I've asked them to an evening of musical entertainment some time in October. What a pity, Leah will have gone back to Yorkshire by then. She could have played her violin for them.'

William sat for a long time in the dispensary looking at the bottle of Elliman's Elixir on his desk. He thought of the many times he had sneered at his father's claims to being a medical man, called him a charlatan and a quack for taking his customers' money under false pretences. It was too late to go through a crisis about ethics at this stage, he told himself. It had already been too late when he had prescribed the stuff for Wickham. And was it so very terrible? Surely, the cure justified the unorthodoxy of the means.

He took a label and pasted it on thoughtfully. This was the last, he told himself. After Wotherspoon, he would confine himself to standard medicines and scientific methods.

Chapter Twelve

'You remember Father's waifs and strays?'

Leah and Sasha were picking runner beans in the garden for Mrs Ash to string. Lily slept in a garden chair. Aunt Georgie was with the children, gathering flowers for the table.

'Of course. William was one of Father's strays when we first met him,' said Sasha.

'So he was. And now Mr Elliman has taken you under *his* wing.'

There was a hint of mockery in the remark that unsettled Sasha. Increasingly these days, her rare encounters with Leah made her feel at a disadvantage. Her sister might look like a dowdy spinster in her serviceable grey skirt and old braided jacket, with her ugly boots and her hair scraped back; and yet, it was impossible to feel either superior or sorry for her.

Sasha remembered the years at home, the young men who came to visit, her dreams of fame as a musician, and her dreams about William, who had smiled up at her one day as she perched on the schoolroom window sill. Suddenly, and very vividly, Sasha was flooded with other memories: of a time when she had done as she pleased, played the piano for hours on end, when she had been free, as Leah was free now. She pretended to be very intent on reaching the beans under the leaves at the centre of the frame.

'Lavinia is expecting again,' Leah said after a while.

'She says to tell you it's your turn to produce the next grandchild.'

The challenge seemed unutterably depressing. Sasha had not forgotten her relief at the recent discovery that she was not, after all, pregnant, and said with unnecessary force, 'Is that really all Lavinia thinks we are fit for? There's more to being married than producing children, you know.'

'It's funny – that's the only thing I envy about it,' said Leah seriously.

'You had your pupil. That boy.'

'He's hardly a boy any more! He's nearly twenty-six.'

'And you've hung on to your freedom. While I'm tucked firmly *under Mr Elliman's wing*.'

'Regrets?' There was no obvious provocation in Leah's remark.

Sasha thought of summer afternoons in Avondon long ago: musicians and artists invited to the house, friends of her father and friends of Herr Lindau; croquet and bowls, tea and strawberries, witty talk. What was wrong with her? She had not revelled in all of that and could remember a time when she had wanted to escape. She straightened up, easing her back, and dropped a handful of beans into the trug at their feet.

'There's more satisfaction than you think in being in control of a household. I never had that sort of responsibility until I married.'

'So, you've decided, all in all, marriage isn't so bad.'

Sasha frowned. Leah made it sound as if she was making the best of it. She swung round as she heard Pippa shrieking; Meredith was tormenting one of the cats by trapping it under a bucket. She called to him to leave the poor creature alone. Lily looked up from her chair and shouted hoarsely that he was a 'naughty, wicked boy' who deserved to be whipped. Merry stuck out his tongue.

'Oh, leave him be,' murmured Leah, as Sasha drew in her breath to call out again. 'The old witch earned it. And the cat can fend for itself . . . You see?' The cat had arched its back and was jumping sideways; it darted over

250

the wall before Merry could catch it again.

Aunt Georgie, in a pale yellow crinoline, multi-coloured ribbons flying in the breeze, was walking slowly across the lawn towards them, arranging the flowers in her hand into a posy as she came.

'Merciful God. Whatever does she look like!' said Leah under her breath.

Sasha felt a leap of defence for Aunt Georgie. 'She's very kind. Pippa and Merry think the world of her. I know she's a bit dotty . . .' She tailed off. 'What made you think of waifs and strays?'

Leah ran her hands through the tripod of runner beans. 'Gabriel thinks he has some chance of playing with Merrill's Chamber Orchestra in Bristol. I can't bear, somehow, to imagine him in grim lodgings when he arrives. Do you suppose the parents would take him in? I wanted to ask you what you thought. Father *is* more than sixty. Mother is getting less tolerant. It's a long time since those lively days . . .'

Sasha gave a gasp of incredulity. 'You can't, Leah. You can't foist that lumpish young man on them. Is *that* why you came all this way?'

'Of course not. I wanted to see you. But Gabriel is very dear to me. He *is* like a son in a way. And he *needs* to play. I see that now. He's been studying in Paris for the past year, to improve his counterpoint and harmony and his technique in the violin. He's extremely talented. One day . . .' she paused. 'One day, he is going to be a name everyone has heard of.'

'And he's almost twenty-six? He had better hurry up.'

'He had a difficult start, Sasha. He became an engineer for a time when he left London . . .'

Leah broke off, remembering Gabriel's refusals to 'sponge off' the Hammonds any longer; her heart ached at the thought of the two years he had wasted designing bridges and railway cuttings, playing the violin in his spare time until he had earned enough to pay back some of her father's money and study in Paris.

'I simply thought – it would be so much more *congenial*

251

for him . . .' Leah knew in her heart that Gabriel was no longer any concern of hers. Then why did she feel this need to mother him? She had worried all the time he had been in Paris: that he would be disappointed, that someone – through his music, or his extraordinary vulnerability over women – would break his heart.

'If he can gain some introductions around Bath and Bristol . . . He says he has a personal introduction to Merrill; he's been carrying it around for years; and now that Merrill has become so prestigious . . . Music is where he *must* make his mark, Sasha.' She threw her a look of pleading. 'I would have thought you of all people would understand. You were so committed once.'

'I understand he might want to fiddle for a living. But haven't you done enough? Why shouldn't he manage by himself? True artists are supposed to starve in a garret.'

'*You* didn't,' Leah retorted quickly. 'And neither did I. We had the best of everything.'

Aunt Georgie by this time was listening unashamedly to their conversation while arranging and rearranging her flowers.

'Why doesn't he give lessons?' She startled them both with the interruption. 'He could charge enough to live somewhere very congenial in Bristol. Chopin charged one guinea a time.'

'He's a farm labourer, not Chopin!' said Sasha laughing. 'He plays the fiddle and talks with flat vowels!'

'He *has* resorted to taking pupils in the piano as well as the violin,' Leah said, ignoring Sasha; she was surprised by the intelligence of Aunt Georgie's suggestion: there was a thoughtfulness behind the woman's blinking eyes in spite of the silly clothes and the handful of flowers. 'But he's been working more as a general tutor recently.'

'A tutor?' Aunt Georgie looked at Sasha. 'A general tutor, Sasha.' She turned away and drifted thoughtfully towards the house.

'Oh, no,' Sasha responded to Leah's look of inquiry. 'Not here! Definitely not.'

★ ★ ★

At dinner that evening Lily complained about Meredith teasing the cat. 'He was extremely rude to me,' she told William. 'It's time you took him in hand.'

William glanced at Sasha. 'It *had* occurred to me that we might send Meredith to a reliable preparatory school. Wotherspoon knows of a good—'

'Wotherspoon!' broke in Sasha indignantly. 'What ideas has he been putting into your head now? The doctor's son must be sent away to school? Sometimes, William, you take my breath away.'

'He's right,' interrupted Lily. 'It would do the boy good to go away.'

'He's not yet seven. Still a baby!'

'Huh! You mean you and Aunt Georgie make a baby of him.'

'We can send him to the school here in Penbury,' Sasha protested.

'You can't mean that,' said William. 'He would be mixing with charity boys – and Flock is hopeless at keeping discipline.'

'Well, I shan't let you send him away. Not yet. He's too little.' Sasha was savage in her opposition.

'Meredith *is* unruly,' said Aunt Georgie thoughtfully. 'He needs a man in charge.'

'Exactly.' William smiled at her.

'So, why not get a tutor for him?'

'This is some sort of conspiracy,' said Sasha in exasperation. 'Leah and Aunt Georgie are in league together.'

Leah was looking at Sasha in eloquent silence. She turned to William. 'I do know of someone.' She told him about Gabriel, and the fact that he had been to the London University and had studied music in Paris.

'He sounds just the thing,' said Aunt Georgie. 'As you know, I have a little money saved. I would be pleased for you to use it. A young man about the place is exactly what Merry needs.'

'They have a point, you know,' William said, when he and Sasha were alone. 'A tutor could cost us little more than

253

an extra servant if he lived in. Your sister says the fellow is keen to live in the area for a while.'

'You're a small-town doctor, William. We can barely afford to keep a pony and carriage and two servants, let alone a tutor.'

There it was again, the implication that what he had achieved in Penbury was less than she had expected.

'You had a governess when you were a child.'

Sasha bit back the retort that her father had been able to afford a governess. She reminded herself that she had been proud to marry William, who had always cared more about people than wealth. Why must they quarrel about money? Money was not the issue, so much as William's inconsistency over how it should be spent. He was anxious enough to skimp if it came to a question of quality, or aesthetics, or anything to do with the refurbishment of the house – which had been done on *her* earnings and dowry, Sasha remembered. And yet, if it was to do with his social standing – a brass name-plate on the gate *and* on the surgery, the ostentatious water closet, a pony and trap – the expense was not only justifiable, it was necessary.

'Anyway, Aunt Georgie has said she will pay.' William unwittingly silenced Sasha's arguments. 'Either we employ a tutor or we send the boy away to school. I'll leave the choice to you.'

He had decided to make a stand. Sasha was becoming altogether too obstinate in situations where a wife ought to back down in deference to her husband's opinion. Sometimes he wondered whether she opposed him simply for the sake of pitting her will against his. It wasn't womanly, or wifely.

'I'll teach him myself,' said Sasha.

'No.' William's expression implied it was his last word on the subject. 'He needs a man in charge.'

'I hope he's not *old* and *strict*.' Meredith leaned on the sill of the upstairs window and peered down the road towards the new railway station.

'Oh, I'm sure he's not old,' Aunt Georgie murmured.

'As to strict . . .' She ruffled Meredith's hair. 'That probably depends on his pupil.'

'Father hasn't said for sure he'll have him. Mother says I don't need a tutor. She will teach me.' Meredith screwed his thin face into an anxious frown.

'Your father has the last word.'

'Yes, but—'

'No buts. Now look. Here comes someone. A fellow in a hurry because he's late.'

And he *was* late, Aunt Georgie reflected, looking at the clock on the wall of the upstairs sitting room that had been hastily equipped as a schoolroom. It was not a very good start.

Sasha, watching from downstairs, was thinking much the same thing as she saw Gabriel arrive at the gate. She stepped out of the light from the window and listened, hearing the scrunch of feet come at a pace up the gravel, one-two, one-two. A pause, the peal of the door bell, and then the sound of Bertha going to answer it.

Sasha walked up and down in frustration. William had elected to interview Ridgeway in the dining room. She pictured him, sitting in state with his list of questions, waiting for Bertha to show the stranger in. She hoped he would realise straight away how very unsuitable the man was. He was inefficient. He had no manners. He was *late*.

Sasha went to the door and pressed her ear to it. She could hear voices, but could not make out what was being said. Really, this was too ridiculous. She would not be kept so much in the dark. Merry was her son as much as William's and she had a right to interview his prospective tutor. She opened the door and went into the hall.

'Mr Ridgeway?' She held out her hand. 'How do you do. You are late.'

'I know.' He turned a brilliant smile on her. 'I do apologise. I got into an argument with a fellow on the train. He said Schumann's music was unintelligible, and I couldn't let it go, could I? I'm afraid the argument continued on to the platform and I lost track of time. The man was a blockhead. I had to tell him so.'

Sasha did not return the smile. She hardened her reaction to him and searched for echoes of the ill-bred youth Leah had taken a fancy to all that time ago. There was a button missing from his coat, she noted. His hair was long and not pomaded. His voice had lost its broadness, but he had said 'blockhead' with a reassuring coarseness. Whatever was William thinking of to want to employ him, another person in the house, adding to their lack of privacy? Sasha felt as if the whole question of Meredith's schooling had been taken out of her control.

'Thank you, Bertha. You may go back to the kitchen,' Sasha said, as the maid hovered still by the door; she returned her attention to Gabriel. 'I think you might have done well to interrupt your discussion on Schumann since you had an appointment.'

Gabriel's smile faded. 'I can only repeat, I apologise.'

'I hope it's not going to be an example of your time-keeping should we decide to employ you.'

William came out from the dining room and saw with a look of annoyance that Sasha had intercepted their visitor.

'This is Mr Ridgeway,' Sasha said. 'Mr Ridgeway, may I introduce you to my husband?'

Gabriel restated his apologies for being late.

Sasha followed them into the dining room. She sat beside William, ignoring his frown of disapproval. They talked about the requirements of the position. Gabriel offered his credentials; his proficiency in mathematics, in Greek and Latin, and in geography and music.

'My wife, as you know, is a talented pianist,' explained William. 'You'll be required to teach the children music only under her specific instructions. Mrs Elliman insists on being in charge of their piano tuition.'

'I shall take over myself when they have mastered the basics and made progress,' Sasha explained.

Gabriel looked at Sasha and saw that here was a potential area for conflict. He had judged her husband quickly; the man was harmless, easy to impress with his qualifications and the recommendations from former employers. But Leah's sister was a different matter. If he were to accept the post, she would be critical of his teaching, possibly obstructive. Was it worth all the trouble, simply to be close to Merrill's Orchestra? He had exaggerated when he had told Leah he had secured a personal introduction. He had, it was true, letters from the Conservatoire and from Drossel, but the rest was no more than a tattered note from a stranger who had once praised his playing in Eskton. He did not even know the man's name.

'As to discipline,' William continued, 'Meredith is a lively boy. I should like you to tell us how you see your duties in respect of his moral guidance.'

'I should teach Meredith to form his own principles and ideals and be true to them. One has to believe in principles to be able to live up to them.'

'You will not, I hope, teach him to be a rebel,' Sasha said quickly. 'Meredith has natural tendencies towards anarchy.' She realised she had allowed a faint humour to break through her armour of reserve.

'I shall base my moral instruction on situations as they arise. I trust Meredith already knows the basic values of right and wrong.'

William looked at Sasha. 'Well then, I think I can say—'

'Mr Ridgeway, would you step into the hall for a moment?' Sasha interrupted. She looked at William. 'My husband and I wish to discuss the matter.'

Gabriel left the room.

'Really, Sasha. It isn't quite the thing, you know. I thought you were going to let me talk to him.' William spoke with a sense of injury.

'Hang the "thing". I wanted to get a good look at him.'

'Well. You've looked. What do you think? He seems modest-mannered enough. He's well qualified. Your sister can vouch for his good character.' He rubbed his hands, looking pleased with himself.

'He's very scruffy.'

'He's a musician, creative – an artist.'

'I was a musician, but I retained some dress sense. My

father was creative but he never went around looking like one of the Lakeland set.' Too late, Sasha remembered that her governess had once levelled similar criticisms at William. Could it be possible, horror of horrors, that she had begun to make the same sort of judgements as Miss Holloway?

'Sasha,' William coaxed, 'do you have to be so difficult? I think you're being uncommonly hard on Ridgeway. He seems ideal to me.'

'I know his credentials are good. It's not the man I object to.'

'What then?'

'It's the principle.'

What principle? Sasha asked herself. Because I don't like to be over-ruled by my husband? Or because I remember Ridgeway as a boy, and his peculiar relationship with my sister? Because I don't quite trust the look in his eyes, half innocent, half knowing? 'We don't need a tutor,' she went on. 'If this is simply to impress Wotherspoon . . .'

'I was thinking of you – and the children.'

Sasha knew it was true; William had been willing to compromise over sending Merry away to school; and it would be hard work teaching him herself.

'Oh, what's the use of arguing with you if you're determined? And if Aunt Georgie insists on interfering. I seem to be a lone voice for common sense.'

'You'll have him?'

'If Meredith likes him.' It was a half-hearted proviso. Sasha knew she had given in.

'My wife's father has exhibited in London,' William said as they headed for the schoolroom. He pointed out the pictures in the hall and on the stairs.

'I know Mr Hammond well. He's been very kind to me. I've seen several of your father's paintings,' Gabriel said, turning to Sasha. 'But one in particular has always stayed in my mind.'

'Which?' she said in surprise.

'The one of you and your sisters in medieval dress. I saw it when I was much younger, when Leah took me to the Royal Academy Exhibition.'

'It was a good likeness of my wife, don't you think?' said William. 'Of course, she too was much younger then.'

'Yes, it was a good likeness.' Gabriel looked at Sasha as they reached the landing, comparing the image of her as a girl with the one she presented now. A shaft of multi-coloured light struck her face and shoulders, and the effect softened her features and darkened her eyes. He was about to say something more, and changed his mind.

'We have said many times how splendid *The Beautiful Hammond Girls* would look down in the hall,' said William.

'Yes. It would look very dramatic.'

'Her former agent has the painting now.' William turned to Sasha. 'Do you know, I believe that was when you and I met again? At the exhibition in London.'

'It was.' Sasha remembered he had gone there to look at Kitty. Had he forgotten? Had he forgotten that other matter? She recalled with sudden vividness a kiss, a look as if he were drowning, his hand up Kitty's skirts.

'And now we've been married seven, going on eight years, Mr Ridgeway. Oh, the boon of a good wife, oiling the wheels of the domestic machinery, attending to the works with a touch as light as a feather duster.'

Sasha saw Gabriel's uncertainty.

William laughed to show he had spoken half in fun, and Gabriel laughed too, but with less enthusiasm.

The fact was, William meant it, joking or not, Sasha thought. She was – or at least, he wanted her to be – his wifey, his goody, his little woman.

She turned and led the way to the new schoolroom. 'Come, Mr Ridgeway. Come and meet your new pupil and his sister.'

Gabriel was a natural teacher. He knew how to excite the imagination of a child. Having discovered that Meredith's high spirits were mixed with a strong sensitivity, he channelled both into the boy's schooling. The result was that Meredith was naturally 'good' during his lessons and learned quickly in general subjects.

But Merry had been slow to read fluently and his spelling was poor. William had given him the nickname 'Snail' because of it. One day, some weeks after Gabriel had been with them, William came to the schoolroom to observe how the lessons were going. In the blustering, teasing way he had with his son William now took the opportunity to criticise Meredith's writing, protesting to Gabriel that a good hand should be legible at least. 'I'd be grateful if you'd bind Meredith to doing so many pages of writing a day, Ridgeway – to perfect a hand that's small and neat.'

Gabriel sent Meredith from the room. 'I would rather we didn't denigrate Meredith in his presence. It isn't my policy,' he explained.

He went on to defend Meredith's progress. 'I myself was slow to come to learning. I believe the master almost gave me up at one time. All I thought about was the violin. I came on my own to studying seriously. And then your wife's sister, Leah, encouraged me as no one else had. We are all different, Mr Elliman.'

'All the same . . .' William insisted. He looked at the tutor doubtfully, considering whether he might have made a mistake in engaging someone with strong 'policies' to teach his child. He said nothing more, but concentrated on examining Meredith's exercise books. He looked askance at Gabriel's comments scrawled in the margins. 'Your own hand leaves much to be desired, Ridgeway. It looks as if it wants to fly off the page.'

Gabriel laughed good-naturedly. 'I believe it does want to do that sometimes.'

'It was as if I had offered him a compliment,' William complained afterwards to Sasha.

'Yes,' she mused. 'There's a disconcerting self-esteem about him.'

'He had the nerve to send Meredith out of the room when I was commenting on the boy's handwriting.'

260

Sasha made sympathetic noises. And yet, she could not agree with William that Meredith was making poor progress under the tutor. She had noticed his eagerness for his lessons; she discovered that her own games and songs with the children had been added to and incorporated in the teaching of mathematics and geography.

When asked why he liked Mr Ridgeway, Meredith answered that his lessons were fun. 'Mr Ridgeway is my very best friend,' he said one day, protesting when he was told his tutor had not been included in an invitation to a tea party at a neighbour's house.

Sasha was surprised – recalling tears and tantrums at the keyboard – to learn that both Pippa and Meredith looked forward to their piano lessons. Here lay the only room for complaint as far as she was concerned; for Gabriel's teaching of music was as unorthodox as everything else. He rejected all the mechanical studies, such as those by Czerny that Herr Lindau had once set her and which she in turn had set Meredith at the piano. Gabriel had begun making up little exercises out of the pieces Merry was working at; he would make him play them using different rhythms, to strengthen his fingers, he said. And he had put the metronome away in a cupboard.

When Sasha asked where it had gone, he said, 'I've never believed music should be mechanical. That instrument makes the boy terrified of losing count. I'd rather Meredith relaxed when he's playing.'

How could he speak with such authority? she told herself angrily, returning the metronome to the lid of the piano. She had been playing for years before Ridgeway had seen even sight or sound of a piano. She remembered he had once walked miles simply to hear her play. Geography was one thing, but what right had he to lay down the law about the way music should be taught?

She was surprised to learn that Gabriel had, in his very first week with them, joined the Penbury Musical Society; he had agreed to conduct the local orchestra, and had begun recruiting schoolmasters and tradesmen into a men's choral society; the Turbots' visitor, Mr Viggers, had joined whilst staying in Penbury. All this Sasha learned one day when she met Mrs Turbot in the High Street.

'My brother speaks very highly of your young man,' Mrs Turbot told her. 'What a pity he won't be with us much longer.'

'No?' Sasha was bewildered to learn that Gabriel had become so popular, amazed too to hear that he was giving lessons in the violin to the Turbots' daughters.

'. . . Henrietta says he has his hopes set on the Merrill Orchestra,' said Mrs Turbot.

'Yes. He did mention—'

'He told Lottie he has an appointment next week to see Merrill himself.'

'I see.'

'You didn't know?'

'It seems, Mrs Turbot, that Mr Ridgeway confides more in your daughters than he does in his employers.'

Mrs Turbot looked injured. Sasha was sorry; she had not meant to be so sharp. To compensate she found herself reviving the invitation made some months earlier.

'Mrs Turbot – Angelina – you must all come to supper as we planned – and Mr Viggers too, so that he might sing for us?' They arranged a definite date.

Mrs Turbot clasped her hands in excitement. 'We shall ask Mr Ridgeway to play! Oh, we shall. He plays so *spiritedly*. It would be the high point of the evening.'

Sasha felt oddly insulted as she and Mrs Turbot parted. I have always been the high point of any evening, she thought, a little wistfully. Was he really that good? The truth was, she had not, in the weeks he had been with them, heard him play.

William was out on his rounds the next day. Aunt Georgie and Lily had taken the children to look for hazel nuts. Sasha had been visiting a neighbour. She closed the front door behind her, and at once heard the violin. It was an overcast afternoon; the only illumination in the hall came from the oval coloured window above the stairwell. The sound of the violin poured a melancholy beauty into the jewelled half-light.

Sasha halted at the foot of the stairs, and knew at once what Leah had meant when she had said her protégé played like an angel. This music was more than heavenly. There was a depth and magnificence to it. It tore at one's senses. She leaned against the wall and let the sound go through her. The emotion in it embraced all the years of her childhood; it made her want to weep with a sense of unbearable loss. In the purity of the music she detected some quality of living, or even of loving, that she had only ever touched upon fleetingly. There was a suggestion of wasted years, of talents unfulfilled.

The music stopped abruptly. Sasha realised that she had been weeping. She dried her eyes on her sleeve and looked up.

Gabriel had come out from his room; he leaned over the banister rail on the attic landing.

'Mrs Elliman? Is that you? I'm sorry, I thought everyone had gone out.'

'Don't apologise. When you play as well as that . . .' She shook her head. 'You should *not* be apologising.'

He came down towards her, his feet thudding on each flight of stairs. 'In the old days I could simply go out to the moor and play my heart out without disturbing anyone,' he said when he reached her.

'Which is how my sister first heard you.'

'Yes, it was. I was playing – or trying to play Mozart. I doubt it was very recognisable.'

'Do you miss the moors?' She was genuinely curious, suddenly aware how very much he had changed since those days.

He had a way of seeming distant, preoccupied, when anyone asked him a question, she noticed. But then he would give his whole attention to responding to it. He lifted his eyes and engaged whoever had spoken with a directness that was both startling and flattering.

'It's a while since I lived there, but I suppose I do. And I

263

miss your sister. Somehow with Leah, letters are not the same as talking.'

Sasha remembered the peculiar affection between him and Leah. She changed the subject. 'And what do you think of Somerset?'

'Very pretty. And so is Dorset. But the South is too soft for my taste. Don't you find it too rounded, too soft?' He did not give her time to answer. 'The scenery in the North is more invigorating. It seems, I don't know, to *expand* your mind in a spiritual way. I suppose the Alps must have that effect – though I haven't travelled on the Continent further than Paris, so I can't really tell. The moors are stimulating. There's something about granite that's unnerving. But the landscape round here . . .' He paused. 'Penbury is a little bland, don't you find?'

'Perhaps. But I'm surprised to hear you say so, when you've so quickly become indispensable to the town. I've been hearing only today from Mrs Turbot about the influence you've had on the Musical Society.' And on Mrs Turbot's daughters, she might have added.

'I mean to build the players up into a good amateur band,' he said. 'There's some promising talent here. I'm surprised you haven't discovered it.'

'Will you have time?' Sasha said with a touch of sarcasm. 'I mean, once you are gone to the Merrill Orchestra, the Musical Society – not to mention Meredith – will be left high and dry.'

'Ah . . .' He hesitated, puzzled. 'Have I offended you, Mrs Elliman? It was understood the situation in your household would only be temporary. I am first and foremost a violinist.'

'And one worthy of Merrill,' Sasha said more generously. 'Mr Ridgeway, would you play for us at a musical evening? I've asked the Turbot family to supper next week. Do say you will?'

'I shall be glad to. Are you going to play the piano?'

'Oh, yes. It seems I cannot escape a few show-pieces.'

'I shall never forget the very first time I heard you.'

Sasha looked at him in surprise.

264

.

'It was a magical experience.'

She wanted to believe that he was flattering her, deliberately trying to charm; she guessed the art of winning women to his side was a habit with him. But there was a sincerity in the smile he gave her. Had her playing once touched chords of feeling in him in the way his violin had moved her?

'You should join the local musicians,' he said. 'They really need good players.'

'I don't have time for the Musical Society.' Sasha resented the inference that she had given up all claim to professional status; she felt vaguely insulted for the second time that week. 'I have the house and the children to attend to.'

'Of course. You have your children.'

Why did the tone of his voice remind her of Leah's gentle questioning – a mild disbelief that a house in Penbury and two small children could be satisfactory enough?

'Don't you miss the relationship you once had with your piano?' he continued. 'I've been wondering why you don't play any more. I couldn't believe that you'd really given up until I saw the dust settling on the piano lid.'

'There's no dust . . .' Sasha began indignantly.

'Music is so personal. It speaks so very intimately. I forget everyone when I'm playing. I always play for myself – even when there's an audience.'

'Your concern is very worthy,' Sasha said quietly. 'But I gave up my music career when I married. There are more important things than music.' The statement sounded hollow. She knew he did not believe it. His look betrayed an irritation with her. Disappointment even.

Gabriel wrote to Leah that evening:

You are right. Your sister should never have given up her piano. I can confirm that she hardly touches it. I have rarely heard her play, even for her own pleasure, except now and then to dash off scales and exercise pieces. These she knocks off one after the

265

other, as if she is unwilling to go rusty but must get it all done with as quickly as possible. Is she afraid, do you think? Is music a threat to her, like gin to an alcoholic? One must cut oneself off altogether? Just one drink! I know what it is like. Music is a drug, a solace, a joyous oblivion. Leah – if only I was with an orchestra! If I can simply get Merrill to listen to me. Meanwhile, I have my amateurs for consolation – and very willing to console they are too. I am doing my best to persuade your sister to join Penbury's Musical Society. I suspect she thinks she is too good for them. There is something of the snob about Mrs Elliman. Oh, my darling Leah, how very different you are! . . .

Leah smiled as she read parts of Gabriel's letter to Felicity. 'Poor boy. He is like a bear in a cage in that household. Much better if he had gone to Hanover Terrace. He asks after your health and hopes your throat is better.'

Even as she spoke, Felicity struggled to subdue a fit of coughing. She waved a hand at Leah's offer to fetch her some water.

'We should never have gone out in the rain!' said Leah in exasperation.

'Oh, but it was fun, wasn't it? Didn't the wind blow?' Felicity's cheeks were bright with fever.

'It all but blew us off the cliff,' Leah grumbled. 'And you knew it would make your cough worse.'

'I suppose this means no visit to the young Pickersgills tomorrow?' They looked at one another gleefully. 'No squalling babies, no stories about teething from Lavinia, none of my nephew's monologues on fishing?'

'Just you and me, and muffins by the fire, and the wind rattling the shutters like dead men's bones at the window. What a shame!'

Felicity laughed, and was convulsed by a fit of coughing. She lay back exhausted on the sofa and smiled dreamily at Leah. 'Play me something on the violin.

Remind me of Gabriel. I can't sing tonight, but it's such a joy to hear the violin. He's right. Music is a kind of drug – a beautiful comfort always.'

Leah tucked a rug round Felicity's knees. She fetched her violin from the corner. 'Poor Sasha. To have cut her piano out of her life like that. At least Gabriel has a chance of playing. It may not be long before Merrill scoops him up.'

'No mention of falling in love? He has been in Penbury more than a month and not yet fallen in love?'

Leah scanned the letter. 'Unless you can count some-one called "Lottie Turbot". She is going to Sasha's musical evening.'

Chapter Thirteen

Aunt Georgie had been looking forward to the Turbots' visit for days. It was an excuse to wear pretty things: soft lace and frills, and a huge, swaying crinoline that practically forced one to glide along a corridor like a glorious ship entering the channel of a river port.

She watched Sasha move gracefully among her guests, dressed in a bright ultramarine gown trimmed with velvet and with ribbons and a camellia in her hair. Sasha was very lovely still, Aunt Georgie reflected. Motherhood had filled out her figure and softened the edges of her sharp temperament. And yet, Aunt Georgie could not quite say that marriage suited her. There was an air of restlessness about her; Sasha was not happy. She pretended she was, she probably thought she was, even as she thought she was enjoying this party. And she had every reason to be happy; most women would have suggested she was spoiled, less than womanly, to expect more from life than was offered her. But there was something Aunt Georgie could not quite put her finger on, a disjointedness about Sasha's relationship with William.

Take the matter of the tutor. Sasha was still uneasy over it, because she considered William had made the arrangements highhandedly. They had quarrelled too about the evening party. William had displeased Sasha by inviting the Wotherspoons and other worthies in the town, and Sasha had upset William by spending too much money on the food and by decorating the dining room artistically.

The trouble with William, Sasha had said, was that he wanted the trappings of society without the expense.

In Aunt Georgie's opinion, Sasha should be pleased the Wotherspoons had come; they were obviously the most important people in the town. She admired the way Mrs Wotherspoon made prominent use of her fan and wore her jewellery with such confidence.

Aunt Georgie thought Sasha made a magnificent hostess. Everything looked very beautiful. Oh, it was so very pleasant to be a part of it all, after years of living in Norfolk with no one for company but her father. She hoped there would be lots of musical evenings, now Mr Ridgeway was here.

Her attention wandered to Mr Viggers, a tall man of fifty or more, with a high forehead, handsome features, and a chest like a rock. The impressive chest came from being a baritone, Aunt Georgie supposed: all that deep breathing from the diaphragm. When he had sung on Sunday in church, Mr Viggers' eyes had engaged hers during his solo; his glance had slid away at the end of the bar of music, but the moment had stayed in her memory.

He was coming towards her. Aunt Georgie's heart fluttered as if it were trying to escape from her breast. She stood her ground, and smiled. 'I'm looking forward to hearing you sing this evening, Mr Viggers.'

'Thank you, Miss Sparrow.'

'Are you staying long with your sister?' She was pleased to have engaged him in conversation so early in the evening.

'It's hard to say. I have recently retired from business. I'm looking for a home in the West Country, Miss Sparrow. One suitable for a confirmed bachelor.'

Aunt Georgie's spirits rose considerably. 'Never any wife?' She lowered her eyelashes; one of the more pleasant aspects about growing older was that one could flirt without harming one's reputation. She tried to picture Mr Viggers as a prospective lover, but it was a difficult exercise.

Many of those present would have been surprised to

learn that Aunt Georgie had once had a lover: a man from Norwich, who had been killed in a brawl in connection with the Reform Bill. It had been very distressing at the time, she remembered; her family had known nothing about him, and the agony of concealing her grief had been terrible. His death seemed to Aunt Georgie, thirty years on, to be a very romantic end to a short and glorious life. The pain of the reality had softened, but the myth remained sharp, a story to be enjoyed, to be re-embellished, and turned over and over in her mind. How surprised they would all have been to hear it. She would have liked to tell them: I have known what it is to be loved; you are not the only ones – you married women, with your self-satisfaction and your pitying looks.

'Alas, I have never found the occasion to marry,' Mr Viggers said very seriously. 'But I believe I have led a full and useful life, Miss Sparrow. A wife might have diverted my purpose. A family would have been a drain on capital. No. All in all, I believe I am as content with my lot as any married man could be.' His attention focused with a superior air on the married men in the room.

Aunt Georgie considered all the difficulties of converting a confirmed bachelor to a more agreeable way of thinking, and faltered a little at the task, though Mr Viggers might have made a presentable husband – if a not very exciting lover. She was tired of living on the margins of other people's lives: first as unpaid housekeeper to her father; now, however pleasantly, on the edge of her nephew's household, watching his children grow, mending their clothes and telling them stories and longing – too late – for children of her own. Aunt Georgie wanted for once to be at the centre of things. She wanted to be in charge, to be able to say, 'I am going to do so and so today,' or 'Oh, tell Cook, breakfast at seven, Bertha', or, 'I'm taking the children to Bristol. We shan't be back until late.' She longed to make decisions. Unlike Sasha, she would have told William from the start that a tutor was an excellent idea. She would have insisted on it if she had been in her place.

But she was not in Sasha's place; she was simply an accessory to her existence. Sasha was talented, charming, beautiful; she could have had the pick of any eligible man in the kingdom for a husband, while she, silly, frumpy Georgie Sparrow, had only known one real love, and he had been such a dunderhead that he got himself clubbed senseless in a brawl.

Sasha felt a mixture of relief and anticlimax now all the arrangements were made, the children in bed, and the party was underway. She knew that the table in the next room, laid out for supper after the music, was a picture of elegance and good taste. But the extra effort – always made by the servants in Avondon – had taken all her energies. William said she had gone too far; people would think the flowers on the table, the silver and candles, and the pyramids of fruit were too showy. A wise word in her ear might have convinced her that William had a point; but Sasha took her knowledge of good taste very seriously; she had been brought up to an artistic way of life.

She was already weary of the fatuous talk and dull preoccupations of her neighbours, for whom the moral laxity and drunkenness in the town, and the exploits of one's offspring were perennial topics for airing. Lily and Miss Scrope were trying to persuade Mr Viggers to join the Total Abstinence Society; he declined, but acknowledged – accepting a glass of William's sherry – that everyone should take a moral stand over incidents of drunkenness.

Sasha could hear William talking to Mr Scrope and Mr Wotherspoon about hooligans, or was it barrel organs? She felt as if she were growing heavier and very dull. The Turbot daughters were going to sing, and she must accompany them and Mr Viggers with 'Home Sweet Home', or something equally sentimental. She could see Henrietta and Lottie from the corner of her eye, pretty girls with pink and white complexions and curling lips. They were talking to the tutor by the fireplace, quizzing him about Paris with girlish laughter and rapt attention.

He had absolutely no drawing-room graces, Sasha told herself; yet, she supposed, to girls like Lottie and Henrietta, Gabriel Ridgeway seemed the perfect romantic rebel-figure with his forceful way of expressing an opinion. His free and easy manner seemed to have worked a considerable charm on Lottie Turbot in particular.

Sasha felt excluded and matronly. The room seemed to be expanding, and the sounds in it grew louder. Mrs Turbot and young Mrs Wickham were in a corner, talking very animatedly with their heads close together. Sasha was becoming too wooden to wonder what they were talking about, but Mrs Turbot's cap, wagging energetically, had become the focus of the room for her; she saw the lappets bob to and fro. The ribbons in the lace were like the frills on babies' petticoats. She remembered Lavinia's challenge that it was her turn to produce another baby. Perhaps, if she *were* to have another child, these odd, unhappy feelings she had known lately would go away . . .

The room was gradually emptying from the centre, dividing naturally into a segregation of the sexes – the men crowding together by the fireplace, the women, even Lottie and Henrietta, drawn towards Mrs Turbot and Mrs Wickham by the window. Drifts of their conversation reached Sasha, and she joined them.

Mrs Wotherspoon was telling everyone in hushed tones about an incident one evening at the lower end of the town. It seemed the wife of one of her husband's leather-workers had been set upon by a crowd of women, thrown to the ground and covered with 'pure', a mix of bran, alum and kennel dung used in the leather-dressing factories.

'Her neighbours showed their proper feelings – however distasteful the method they chose,' Miss Scrope offered as an opinion to the swelling party of women. 'At least, it shows there's some awareness of morality among the lower orders.'

The others agreed.

'But why? Whatever had she done to deserve it?' Aunt Georgie's face expressed her disgust that anyone could have been so horribly treated.

'Oh, something far more loathsome, you can be sure of it. The women were perfectly justified in behaving as they did.' Mrs Wotherspoon lowered her voice. 'The woman concerned was very indecent, very indecent indeed.'

'She's a bad person. You can be sure of that,' said Henrietta. 'I've heard about her behaviour.'

'*Filthy* ways,' said Mrs Wotherspoon.

'But what exactly had she done?' said Aunt Georgie.

Mrs Wotherspoon, warming to Aunt Georgie's credulity, was losing her squeamishness about details. 'She was caught with one of the gangers from Mr Wotherspoon's factory. They were seen!' She lowered her voice to little more than a whisper, so that her listeners had to lean forward to catch her words. 'Caught . . . you know. In an open field!'

There was a mutual intake of breath as the women's imaginations digested what they had heard.

'It's true.' Mrs Wotherspoon was pink now with tension, speaking more rapidly. 'There was a gap in the hedge. One of her neighbours *saw* them. She could see *everything* they did quite plainly.'

Sasha glanced round, hoping the men had not overheard the story. Thoughts of copulation, vague memories of pleasurable moments with William flitted through her mind.

Lily had become very excited by the story. Her voice rose to a squeak: 'They're like animals. They rut like animals!' There was a shocked pause, and Lily subsided into silence. Sasha looked anxiously at William by the fireplace – had he been diligent enough about the sherry?

'What will happen to the woman?' said Aunt Georgie in a hushed voice.

'If her husband throws her out, no one will blame him, that's for sure,' said Mrs Wotherspoon with satisfaction.

'Poor thing,' said Sasha and turned away. She did not see the combined glance the other women gave her, or know that her instinctive sympathy for the offender seemed to them more shocking than anything Mrs

Wotherspoon had revealed. They avoided looking at one another as Sasha raised her voice to address everyone. 'Ladies – and gentlemen. Shall we have some music?'

Sasha went to the piano. The men began arranging the chairs in two semi-circles across the room. 'I've persuaded Mr Ridgeway to open our evening recital by playing his violin for us all,' she said when everyone had shuffled for places. 'My sister once told me he plays like an angel – should the *Angel* Gabriel decide to take up the violin instead of a harp.' There was a ripple of laughter. Mrs Wotherspoon's story was forgotten.

Gabriel bent to unpack his violin from its case on the piano stool. 'I'd be much obliged if you'd accompany me.'

'You agreed to play an unaccompanied piece – an Irish air,' Sasha reminded him.

'I've changed my mind. You have music for violin and piano here. You must have played the pieces with your sisters.'

She nodded.

He flicked through the pile. 'How about Mendelssohn? I noticed you have the F minor sonata. The final movement only? The rest is beautiful, but too sad for a party.'

She hesitated, saw that everyone was smiling, attentive now that they were seated. 'Very well.' She sat at the piano and waited for Gabriel to tune the violin.

He had not chosen a difficult sonata, but his playing gave it a peculiar intensity, and he drew a mellow sweetness from the violin, as if he were pushing her to acknowledge the emotional content of the music.

Sasha, annoyed because he had asked her to accompany him without any preparation, resisted a total commitment to the performance. She played elegantly and with authority; she would show him she was not going to be intimidated by the years of neglect. But he played the violin solo so exquisitely that she felt compelled to moderate her own playing. Something was happening to her. The music was taking precedence as it always had done in the past. A breathless pleasure suffused her; it was a sensation she

274

had all but forgotten since she had played with her sisters in the early days: a sense of union with them and with the music. The movement ended with the wistful final notes on the violin. Reluctantly Sasha returned Gabriel's smile.

It was the turn of Mr Viggers to sing. Sasha played the accompaniment to 'Hearts of Oak' and 'The Good Ship Rover', and afterwards Mrs Turbot played for Lottie and Henrietta as they warbled 'Begone Dull Care' and 'Home Sweet Home', in unison but off-key. When they had finished, Lottie blushed and confided to Gabriel that she had been terribly nervous. Gabriel said, teasing her, that she sang better than she played the violin.

Then Gabriel played the Irish dance tunes he had promised; he set everyone's feet tapping, and the audience applauded with considerably more zest than they had applauded the Mendelssohn. 'I like that better,' Wotherspoon remarked. 'I like something with a bit of a tune to it!'

Sasha had practised Chopin's Third Ballade for a solo piece. She enjoyed the technical brilliance and the difficulties of the piece as she played, an enjoyment she had not experienced when rehearsing it, nor had felt for years.

'We're extremely fond of music, Mrs Elliman,' said Mr Wotherspoon as she walked with him in to supper. 'We like to hear the best. We're very fortunate to have you in our town, you know. It's a wonderful opportunity to hear a professional musician play. I wish you'd do more of it.'

'Your tutor is a fine violinist,' added Mrs Wotherspoon. 'No common fiddler there, though they say he can play any tune he's a mind to – Oh, I say, Mrs Elliman—' She drew in her breath with a gasp. 'What an elegant supper!'

Sasha absorbed the murmurs of appreciation as the guests walked into the dining room and saw the festoons of chrysanthemums and trailing plants, the pyramids of fruit arranged with leaves and feathers, the plates of salads and meats and pies and pickles, and the architectural jellies and blancmanges.

'How very *artistic* those pears are,' murmured Lottie Turbot, hanging on Gabriel's arm. 'I should guess she's put the whole garden on the table.'

Sasha, fortunately, heard only the compliments. Mrs Wotherspoon said Sasha must ask Mrs Ash to give her own cook the recipe for the game pie.

'It's one thing to hear good music played in a concert room,' said Mrs Turbot returning the conversation to the evening's recital. 'But quite special to listen among friends and in pleasant surroundings. The setting makes everything all the more delightful.'

'In general I prefer sacred music,' said Mr Viggers. He ate sparingly, vain enough to want to avoid a double chin. 'Or at least, music with a moral tone.'

'Oh, yes. You can't beat church music,' agreed Mr Wickham. 'Music – *all* music should speak of divine love. It should bring a man nearer to his Maker.'

'Music should be whatever the composer wanted it to be,' said Gabriel drily. 'In my experience, it more often speaks of profane love than divine inspiration.'

He was unaware of the shock waves caused by this casual remark; coming so closely upon the women's earlier conversation it seemed provocative and disagreeable. But Gabriel had been thinking about Sasha's playing.

The fact was, he felt profoundly and personally frustrated by Sasha's attitude to her music. He hated waste, and – conscious of his own struggle to become a musician – he hated a waste of talent most of all. He had disliked her almost mechanical playing of the Mendelssohn, detecting only a glimmer of true sensitivity in it; and he thought her performance of Chopin too much of a virtuoso affair, performed with a surprising brilliance, after so many years away from a concert platform, but brittle and shallow.

Gabriel tried to analyse why it mattered to him whether she should play with emotion or mere technical competence. He reminded himself that he had taken the post with the Ellimans as a matter of expediency, and because Leah had arranged it for him and he had not wanted to offend her. Perhaps the memory of the first time he had heard Sasha play had lodged too firmly in his mind. A subdued tension, an energy had seemed to come from the girl in the white dress, with ash-gold hair like shining thistledown. Why was the image so seductive? The lovely, animated girl had turned into a snob, he told himself. Any spirit she might have once had was well and truly submerged by domestic trivia.

'You've upset Mr Wickham rather.' Lottie stood by his elbow. 'He's very strong on hymns and psalms.'

'Have I? I was only speaking my mind.' Gabriel turned his full attention on her. She looked more enchanting than he had yet seen her, very pretty and dimpled, and her hair, a glossy nut-brown, was gathered up in a rich cascade of curls. He felt in a mood to let himself be charmed by her. 'If a man is hurt by someone else's opinion, it's a poor do for him. Wouldn't you say?'

'Oh, I would, a *poor do*, indeed,' mimicked Lottie, making him smile. They moved away from the table to a space where it was quieter. 'Are you still going to see Mr Merrill tomorrow?' said Lottie. 'And will you come and give me a violin lesson, and tell me all about your interview afterwards?'

'I might. If you promise to practise your scales. Will you wish me luck with Mr Merrill?'

'If *you* promise to come and see me and give me lessons when you're leader of his orchestra.'

'I promise.'

'Very well, good luck . . . Though I'm sure I don't mean it,' she added.

'Lottie,' he said with a look of injury.

She spoke in a rush, her colour heightening. 'The fact is – I don't want you to leave Penbury. I know, if you do go, you'll forget all about me. You'll marry a famous prima donna who sings in perfect tune.'

'Never. I can't stand opera singers. Too self-opinionated . . .' He lowered his voice. 'Don't look like that, or you'll make me want to kiss you.'

Lottie parted her lips with a little gasp. 'You mustn't say such things – someone might hear you.'

He smiled. 'I promise I shan't marry a prima donna.'

William and Sasha returned to the dining room when the last visitor had gone and the rest of the family had gone up to bed. William declared he had not enjoyed the evening. He surveyed the ruins of the supper and said that eating late always upset his digestion. The truth was that Wotherspoon had been pestering him for more of Elliman's Elixir and wanted to recommend it to one of his friends. William felt very much out of sorts. He was getting in deeper than he had anticipated.

Sasha walked round the table, humming to herself, nibbling at the food that was left over. 'Didn't you enjoy the playing, then?'

'Of course I enjoyed the playing. Everyone did. That's not the point. Did all the rest have to be so – elaborate?'

'I thought you expected me to put on a good show. I thought you wanted everyone to think well of us.' She was irritated by his refusal to acknowledge all the hard work she had put into the evening.

'They probably thought it slightly ridiculous, to be honest.'

'Ridiculous?' Sasha was unsure whether to laugh or be angry.

'All these fal-de-lals.' He fluffed up the petals of a chrysanthemum. 'It would have suited Hanover Terrace well enough. But this is Penbury, not Avondon. A *small town* – as you're so fond of reminding me.'

'A small town in which you are determined to make your mark, William. I have to say – you're very inconsistent about how it should be done. You'll spend the earth if you think it will boost the practice, but you're as mean as anything when I want to break out a little. I *enjoyed* arranging the evening.'

William recalled a concert long ago and a party at Hanover Terrace: silver cutlery and cut glass, Sasha's mother saying she liked to dine with the *soul* in mind as well as the stomach. Such excess. And he remembered Sasha on the arm of Herr Lindau, being congratulated by everyone, Kitty drifting among the guests, conversations from which he had felt excluded.

'What is it you want? More attention? Is that it? I wasn't appreciating you, so you had to put on a show?' He swept his hand across the table, dislodging one of the pot-plants which came crashing down from its stand on to the table. They stared at it as if they could not believe such a small gesture could have created so much mess.

'Bertha will clear it up.' Sasha brushed ineffectually at the soil, succeeding only in rubbing it into the cloth.

'If you're discontented you could find other ways of amusing yourself,' William said. 'Play your piano by all means. I don't mind inviting people round, but this—' He managed to restrain himself from aiming his arm at another pot. 'The expense is enough to cripple us.'

'*You* invited some of those people!' By now Sasha really was beginning to feel angry. 'And for *your* benefit, not mine. At least the Turbots appreciate music a little. Do you think I wanted to hear Mr Wotherspoon's opinions on what constitutes a good tune? But we must have him, because he's important in the town. And the Scropes and the Wickhams have to come, because they are on the council, and worth a bob or two.'

'Sasha, my whole career depends on these people.'

'I had a career once,' Sasha reminded him.

'Ah, so, now we're getting to the point. I was right. You wanted all this fuss tonight, simply because you had to have an audience again.'

Sasha looked at him in amazement. 'That's got nothing to do with it. You know I never minded giving up my public. I've always believed I could free you from the petty business of the household, so that you could give your life to serving people. I *have* made sacrifices. I admit, I think about that sometimes. But I don't mind – *didn't* mind, when I thought you might make great strides for sanitary reform.'

She paused, unable to say what was in her heart. That he had not kept his side of the bargain, that her own role seemed to have less and less purpose when his ambition had dwindled to a need to keep in with men

279

like Councillor Scrope. What was left if one stripped away the years of domesticity? His standing in the town? She turned away. 'I really don't know what we're quarrelling about. I'm going to bed.'

'What do you *want*!' William shouted after her.

She did not reply; perhaps there was no answer. As the door of the dining room closed behind her, Sasha's crinoline, caught by the momentum, was pushed forward, and for a moment she was forced to stop and disentangle herself.

She looked up. Gabriel was above her on the landing. Their glances met as she came upstairs towards him. He stepped aside to let her pass.

'I'm sorry. I didn't mean to . . .'

'No, of course you didn't, Mr Ridgeway. But can anyone do anything in this house without someone, somewhere, overhearing!'

William brooded for a while, then slowly followed Sasha upstairs, calling to Bertha to clear away in the dining room.

He tried to understand why they had begun to squabble. She seemed disappointed in him, he realised. But wasn't he disappointed in himself? And, if he were honest about it, wasn't he a little disappointed in Sasha? The evening *had* been ridiculous — a display of unnecessary extravagance, the artistic table, the serious music, as if to make the point that she was superior, when people like the Wotherspoons only wanted to hear familiar and jolly tunes. What had she said? That she had made sacrifices? Well, he too had made sacrifices. He let her believe domestic matters interested him, when in fact they bored him to tears. What colour the curtains should be. What the children had said. What Mrs Ash had remarked to Cope and how Sasha had smoothed over a quarrel between them. Or how she had spent her day, planning a flower bed, making jam, discussing Meredith's lessons with the tutor. He sometimes wished she was still the bright young girl he had discovered he was in love with once after a concert in London. He sometimes wished . . . His thoughts drifted to Kitty, remembering a kiss, sensations of rapture and guilt.

Sasha was already asleep by the time he got into bed.

Sasha was putting away the music in the piano stool the next day. She found a Mozart Sonata and, remembering how Herr Lindau had once loved Mozart and Beethoven, she sat at the piano. There were no words for the sense of melancholy the music drew from her. She thought of her early love for William when she was a girl; she pictured Herr Lindau, whom she still mourned.

'That's better.' Gabriel stood in the open doorway.

Sasha broke off playing. 'I didn't know you had finished Meredith's lessons.'

'May I come in?'

'Yes. Please do.'

'I wondered if you would mind if I went to Bristol, Mrs Elliman? My interview with Merrill is this afternoon. You remember – the orchestra appointment?'

'Yes. I remember.'

'It *was* the whole point of my coming south. I'm sorry if I led you to think—'

'Don't apologise, Mr Ridgeway. Though we should be sad to lose you so soon. Meredith has grown very fond of you, and his behaviour has improved enormously.'

'I should be sorry to abandon the boy. He's doing well. But I can't say . . . Perhaps I could combine an engagement with my duties here.'

'I think, if you join his orchestra, Mr Merrill might be rather more demanding on your time.' She hesitated. 'Thank you, Mr Ridgeway, for playing for our guests yesterday. They enjoyed the evening. It was a very varied programme.' She smiled, remembering 'Hearts of Oak' and 'Home Sweet Home'.

'I wish you would play more often,' he said suddenly. 'But I wish you had not chosen to play Chopin in quite that way.'

'No?'

281

'I can't help feeling there was something lacking. You must have felt it, Mrs Elliman. I remember so well . . .' He hesitated then said in a rush, 'I thought you had lost something, that it was a virtuoso performance, but without real substance. I can't help feeling your talents have gone to waste.'

'Mr Ridgeway,' she said gravely, 'are you implying I've become a purely domestic creature?'

'But you have,' he protested. 'That is exactly what you have done.'

'I can assure you, I've plenty to occupy me in the domestic sphere. I've been perfectly happy to relegate music to its proper place. And, if I might say so, it's no concern of yours how I play the piano.'

'Its proper place?' He looked at her with a passionate expression of affront. He repeated the phrase, as if trying to comprehend its meaning.

'Yes. As a diversion from the things that really matter in life.'

'What a ridiculous remark for anyone to make! And for you, a musician, to have made.'

Sasha flushed scarlet as his rebuke hit home. There was a time when she would have reacted in exactly the same way if anyone had told her that music was no more than a pleasant diversion. She sought refuge in indignation. 'Mr Ridgeway! I would rather you kept your opinions to yourself!'

'I'm sorry.'

'Chopin should be played with panache and delicacy. The point is to demonstrate a technical mastery—'

'No,' he said with a restrained anger. 'I'm sure you're wrong. The point of music is always to reach out and touch the emotions. To convey thoughts, feelings, passions. What's more,' he added with a pained expression, 'you know that to be true. You know there's more to your art than a technical display. Those final passages of the Third Ballade have such an emotive pulse when they're played with feeling. Have you never been in love? Have you never felt deep passion, or pain?'

'Mr Ridgeway!'

'I'm sorry,' he said again.

'Do you think you have a monopoly on soul? What do you know?' She sat at the piano and played from memory the final pages of the Ballade with an anger and a passion that made the blood rush to her head. When she had finished her heart was pounding violently.

'Better,' he said dismissively.

'Better! It was good! And you know it.'

Yes, it was, thought Gabriel as he caught the afternoon train for Bristol, remembering her at the piano. Don't be a fool, she's the wife of your employer, he told himself. But he could not forget the way she had played. There was a dangerous hint of disappointed passion there; it was tempting to want to do more than stir her up a little. Don't be a fool, he told himself again. He had his own genius to nurture. What did it matter if Leah's sister had let her talents slide? *What does it matter? What does it matter?* The train took up the rhythm of the words and mocked him.

Gabriel shifted restlessly. He saw his own reflection in the window of the carriage and recalled how she had looked up at him with an expression of triumph after her playing, as if to say, 'There! Find fault, if you will, with that!' Her eyes had a spark of fire in them, as if they had released a little of the potential behind them. At the same time, there was an openness about her challenge, a childishness in her face that had made her seem vulnerable. It was a combination of childlike reactions and womanly mystery that Gabriel always found intensely seductive. If he wasn't careful . . .

He remembered meeting her on the stairs the previous evening. She had been arguing with Elliman about something. Was she unhappy? Was the marriage going badly? Leah had said they were hopelessly in love, that it had been a storybook affair: she had been in love with Elliman since she was a girl. But perfect marriages were seldom the idyll they seemed – or so experience had taught him.

He shrugged off his preoccupation with Sasha as the

train neared Bristol. The sooner he left the Elliman household the better. He was getting too interested in his employers, too fond of Meredith, too involved in their lives.

Gabriel arrived at Merrill's house armed with his letters of introduction. The musical director was of the theatre impresario type: waxed moustache and heavy side-whiskers, plenty of teeth, eyes masking a mind that worked quickly, totting up figures. There was a strong scent of commercialism about him and very little of the artistic integrity Gabriel had expected when people had told him Merrill was the best.

The director read Gabriel's letters slowly, lingering a few seconds over the note written years ago at the Rose and Crown. 'I haven't seen Gessner for years. How did you meet him?'

Gabriel told him a little about his early life.

'Well, I've no vacancies at the moment. But,' he glanced at the note, 'you impressed my friend, even at so young an age. "A genius," he says. Play something for me.' The man sat easily behind his desk as Gabriel picked up his violin case.

He played some Mozart and part of the Mendelssohn Violin Concerto. Merrill listened intently.

'You're competent enough. Better than most. And you've got the touch of magic that means you could succeed as a soloist. You know that?'

'Yes. I know that.'

'Give me your address. I'll keep you in mind if I have anything.'

Gabriel wrote down the Ellimans' address for him.

He decided to call on the Hammonds, and walked away from the city and up the hill towards Avondon. He told himself he should have stayed in the North, or gone back to London, or worked on the Continent. If he had been patient, something would have turned up with Hallé in Manchester, or in Leeds or Liverpool one day. It was hopeless here in the West Country holding out faint hopes

284

of working with Merrill. He would be buried first without trace. He would never make his way as a first violin, let alone a soloist.

He reached Hanover Terrace and tried to imagine the four sisters living there. It was hard to visualise Leah as a girl, but he could picture Lavinia, who, even with three children of her own, had a girlish prettiness about her. And then there was Mrs Elliman, Sasha. The image of her as a girl was strong; it had shone out from her father's portrait. It was fixed in his mind alongside the memory of her in the Exchange Rooms in Eskton.

He could not recall the fourth sister, the most overtly beautiful of them all and the one who had gone to the bad, according to Leah. But it had been an impressive portrait. He had been impressed by the artist too, he remembered, even to the point of feeling intimidated by him long ago at a first meeting. Gabriel had not expected he would grow to like Nathaniel Hammond so wholeheartedly.

'Come in. Come in. Leah has told us all about your latest exploits,' Nathaniel said when Gabriel was shown upstairs. 'I hope you realise you're her pride and joy.'

'I know,' laughed Gabriel. 'Confidence like that puts a great responsibility on a man.'

'You mustn't let Leah frighten you, Gabriel. That's the secret.' Mrs Hammond came forward to greet him. 'Leah has always been very confident about anything she set her mind to, even when she was a little girl.'

'And she's always been very determined, for a female,' added Nathaniel.

'How did your interview go with Mr Merrill?' Mrs Hammond gestured him to a seat.

Gabriel told them, adding his opinion that he should have stayed in the North.

'Nonsense. You need a manager.' Nathaniel turned to his wife. 'Is Sasha still in touch with that fellow Ross?'

'I'm almost sure Mrs Elliman has dropped her friendships with all the people she once knew on the concert circuit,' said Gabriel. 'I've noticed she plays hardly at all.'

'She fell in love and that was that,' said Mrs Hammond.

'A woman has to give up many aspects of a single life when she marries. But tell me, how are you getting along with Merry? Isn't he a dear? Naughty – but a darling boy.'

They talked about Meredith and Pippa for a while, and about Sasha. And as they talked, Gabriel felt as though he was reaching a new understanding of Leah's youngest sister. They told him for the first time about how much Julius Lindau had meant to her, that he had been Sasha's greatest inspiration, and how much she had changed after he had died.

Gabriel thought about Sasha as he returned to Penbury early that evening. In his mind he saw her playing the Chopin again, her body alive with energy, a passion in her eyes. The more he dwelled on the picture, the more he convinced himself that it was he who had succeeded in rekindling the fire in her.

William met him in the hall. 'How did you get on? My wife tells me you've been to Bristol. There's some supper laid out for you in the dining room. The family has eaten.'

Gabriel gave him a brief impression of his interview with Merrill.

'There'll be other opportunities,' said William, but without much real regret that the interview had been a disappointment. 'I don't mind telling you, Ridgeway, we should be sorry to lose you.'

'In spite of my bad handwriting.'

William frowned, then perceived the joke. 'In spite of all your failings, Ridgeway. Your methods are sometimes unorthodox, but you *have* worked wonders on Meredith. And . . .' He hesitated. 'I have other reasons to be grateful.'

He invited Gabriel into the dining room and offered him a glass of port, as if the possibility of losing him had jogged him into trying for a firmer bond, man to man.

'The fact is, my wife has renewed her interest in her music, Mr Ridgeway. I think last night's party might have had something to do with it.' William remembered with a sense of shame the bad grace with which he had attacked Sasha's precious supper table; he recalled her good

286

humour in forgiving him that morning – in fact Sasha had been in a good humour all day. 'She has been playing the piano all afternoon.'

'She has?' said Gabriel in delight.

'All afternoon. It was a pleasure to hear her again. I think I may have you partly to thank for it. The duet? She did enjoy playing the duet.'

'The Mendelssohn sonata.'

'Mm? Yes, I believe so. I have one small criticism about the evening, Ridgeway. In the ordinary course of events I would admire a man for putting down pious garbage, but when it comes to people I've invited to my house—'

'Ah, you mean, "music should speak of divine love"?'

'Mr Wickham was my guest.'

'Yes, I'm sorry. It was perhaps uncivil of me.'

'He was offering a valid opinion.'

'He was talking rot, and he knows nothing about music, simply echoing empty ideas.'

'But one has to be circumspect, Ridgeway. What's the point in being honest if you alienate everyone? Not that I believe you've done so, but be careful. An unguarded moment can ruin a man's career – or that of his employer. Do you understand my meaning?'

'Perfectly.' Gabriel regarded him steadily. 'Though I cannot agree one should be insincere in order to survive.'

William felt uncomfortable. Had there been a note of personal criticism in the remark? He decided not. On the whole he decided he liked the tutor. Everyone in Penbury talked about him. His looks and personal attraction were always commented on. Young women followed him with their eyes whenever he appeared in the town and when he accompanied the family to church. The attention had annoyed William at first. He had thought Gabriel a flirt when people began linking his name with one of the Turbot girls. And somewhat effeminate – to William's mind – with his long hair and almost foreign features. Music was an odd profession for a young man to take up, especially for a young man who had been trained as an engineer. Now, he began to notice more endearing qualities about him.

He refilled Gabriel's wineglass, deciding he thoroughly liked the fellow. 'Are you happy with us, Ridgeway?'

'I am very happy with my pupil, sir. And you have made me more than comfortable.'

'Your reply suggests you have a reservation.'

'My life is music,' Gabriel said simply.

'I have to confess, I'm beginning to hope it takes you a while to find a position that will take you away from us. It's good to have some company in a house full of women.' What was it Aunt Georgie had said? It was a blessing the day he walked into their lives. Well, Aunt Georgie always did exaggerate, but the tutor was an asset to the household, there was no doubt about it. William leaned back in his chair and said confidentially, 'I'm glad my wife is playing the piano again. Marriage isn't always plain sailing, you know. I mean—' He laughed, to show Ridgeway he was implying no serious criticism, and to reassure himself that the disagreement with Sasha the previous evening had not been very serious either. 'Mrs Elliman can be difficult. Oh, don't misunderstand me, she's a wonderful wife, the model of the perfect housewife in her management of the household. But in other ways . . .' he hesitated, wary of becoming indiscreet. 'Women are a mystery, don't you think? I sometimes wonder what goes on in their minds? My wife . . . gets bored. She comes from an artistic family, you see. You understand artists, so you know what I'm talking about. The Hammonds are all unusual when judged against other women.'

'Perhaps your wife should not be judged at all. Wouldn't it be better to forget altogether one's preconceptions about women?'

William laughed. 'It's true. One has to accept Mrs Elliman as she is, with all her faults. But my point is, that it's not easy to keep a woman like my wife happy, Ridgeway. She needs an artistic diversion. If you could play a few more duets with her, encourage this interest of hers in playing again – in an amateur way. It would, I'm sure, do her the world of good.'

'You want me to play the violin with Mrs Elliman?'

'Yes.' William beamed. 'Exactly that. Pieces for the violin and the piano. Would it take up too much of your time?'

'No,' Gabriel said thoughtfully. 'I should be pleased to oblige you.' He smiled and swallowed some port and thought that he should have dearly liked to have punched the man.

What an oaf, he told himself later, after he had eaten the supper of cold meats and was going upstairs to the attic. Play a few duets with her! Keep her happy! What right had a man like that to marry a woman of talent if he hadn't the slightest idea himself how to satisfy her?

The light was on in the children's room and he could hear the sound of singing. The door was open. He paused as he saw the scene through the doorway: Sasha and Aunt Georgie were sitting with their skirts spread all about them on the floor and a child in a nightshirt on each of their laps. They were rocking, as if in a boat tossed in a violent storm, singing in rough harmony: 'My bonnie lies over the ocean . . .' They were laughing, and singing so loudly, and rocking so much that the song was in total confusion.

Gabriel contemplated the picture of Sasha, and his stomach lurched uncertainly: her hair had fallen loose with the violence of the game; it hung in strands over her shoulders; her face was bright and animated, and her eyes danced with laughter; he could see the whiteness of her teeth and the pink tip of her tongue. It was not the face of a 'difficult' wife, nor the one she presented to the world in general. And then, Meredith twisted in his mother's lap, caught Sasha's face between his hands, and kissed her laughing mouth.

They had not seen Gabriel in the darkness of the landing. He walked along the corridor to his room, and lay on his bed, his heart thumping in his chest. He tried to plan the rehearsal the next day with the Musical Society, sorting in his mind the sparks of talent from the indifferent fiddlers and cornet players. He filled his mind with images: of the ironmonger, who played the bass fiddle, Mr Viggers singing 'The Good Ship Rover' . . . But the thought of ships reminded him of the rowing game.

The house was quiet now. He imagined Sasha tucking her children into bed, her hair cascading to touch the pillow, catching the lamplight, her mouth . . .

If only Merrill had offered him a position that afternoon. If only Leah had not interfered by getting him a place in her sister's house. If only he had not concerned himself so much with Mrs Droman's piano playing.

He turned his face to the pillow. He was falling in love with her, he thought with a feeling of despair; and he remembered that, by going to the Hammonds, he had broken his promise to give Lottie Turbot a violin lesson. He tried to think of Lottie's pretty face and pert lips. But one picture, one face and mouth, filled his mind.

'Stop thumping. Don't play chords with your arms, as if you're swinging a cricket bat,' Gabriel told Meredith. 'Play from your wrists. Play scales with your fingers, chords with your wrists, *cricket* with your arms.'

Meredith laughed.

'I'm not joking, boy. You think I'm joking?' He put on a mock severity. 'Ha! I'll show you a joke—' He took the child by the scruff of the neck, making him scream with laughter. Gabriel turned. Sasha stood in the doorway.

'Mrs Elliman.' He straightened. 'I didn't know you were there.'

'If you had known, I suppose you would have thought twice about violently attacking my son.'

'Oh, I don't know about that. Come on, boy. On with the lesson.' Gabriel pointed to a place on the exercise sheet and, turning again to Sasha, left the piano.

'I don't want to interrupt,' she said as Meredith played. 'May I listen?'

He looked surprised, gave her a swift uncertain smile, then returned to his pupil. 'You're letting that wrist relax again. You should be able to hold an imaginary hedgehog in the palm of your hand.'

'A hedgehog!' Meredith chortled.

'Yes. Without dropping it.'

'It would hurt.'

'Music does hurt. Anything worth doing well hurts. But that hedgehog is very precious, so don't let it fall. Now. Play legato, but without using the pedal. We're aiming for a round, cantabile tone, to charm your mother who is expecting great progress.'

Sasha waited until the lesson was over, then flicked through the music on the piano. 'My husband has suggested that you and I play together. I think it's an excellent idea.' She looked up. 'It will give you an opportunity to practise your violin. The children will benefit from hearing music in the house, well played. And I should like to play a little more than I have done in recent years.' She smiled and turned to Meredith. 'You would like that, wouldn't you? To hear Mr Ridgeway play his violin and your mama play the piano?'

'Then I'm at your disposal,' said Gabriel. 'When do you want me to start?'

'This afternoon? Is that convenient?'

He nodded.

'You'll be paid, of course.'

If was as if she had struck him. He dropped his gaze quickly and pretended to be occupied with pencilling in the fingering on Meredith's sheet of music. 'That's not necessary.'

'But of course we must. We wouldn't expect you to extend your duties to us without payment.'

He managed to look unmoved. 'Thank you.'

'There's something else.'

Sasha sent Meredith from the room. She walked round the piano and fingered the keys. 'Much as games amuse Merry, my husband thinks you should moderate your manner with him a little, Mr Ridgeway. Particularly in the schoolroom. He fears you might be encouraging a frivolous attitude in the boy. He asked me to tell you.'

'Is that what you think?' Gabriel remembered the riotous singing and laughter the previous evening.

'I would dilute my husband's criticisms a little. Neither of us want to frighten you away now that we know you're going to stay with us a little longer.'

'I know I'm unconventional, Mrs Elliman. A bit of a risk. If I were your husband I wouldn't have engaged me in the first place.'

Sasha's eyes widened, caught by surprise. Then she laughed, smothering the sound with her hand.

He said, suddenly serious, 'I am so glad.'

'Glad?'

'I was afraid – until last night – that no one in this household except the children and Miss Sparrow had any sense of humour. I had to pass the children's room,' he explained. 'I couldn't help hearing your singing.'

Sasha was sober. 'As you know we forget sometimes that there are other people in the house.' She went to the door. 'I'm sorry you had no luck with Merrill yesterday.'

'Something will turn up.'

'I'm sure it will. You must be patient.'

Gabriel waited in the corridor outside the drawing room. Sasha came towards him. She always walked quickly, he noticed, purposefully, and with an unconscious swing of the hips. Her slight figure had an air of determination that was very appealing.

'I thought I would leave the choice of music to you,' she said as he opened the door for her. 'But something rather difficult and elegant to start with, I thought.'

'Which leaves no choice at all. It has to be Bach.'

'My thoughts precisely.'

They played some Bach and moved on to Mozart, saying little, finding it easy to adapt to one another at first. But as their choices became more dependent on mood, a change came over their playing. It was as if they were struggling for precedence as one instrument tried to dominate the other. They could not find a common ground.

'Do you have to be so violent?' Sasha said at last,

halting halfway through a phrase. 'Is that how you behave with the Musical Society?'

'I'm sorry. My own feeling was that the piano was far too aggressive. And no – the Penbury musicians have no ideas of their own importance. They are remarkably humble in fact.'

'We're forgetting the music. We should only consider the music,' Sasha said passionately. 'Listen!' She repeated the phrase and played on, tenderly, with a powerful impulse that carried the music through several bars.

He looked at her flushed face. Something wonderful was happening to her. She had lost the artifice that had spoiled her playing for him at the musical party. She was entirely natural and immersed totally in her playing. How gratifying it would be to see her perform like that for a public audience again. What a crime! he told himself. What a blunder! To have married and almost buried herself in the management of Elliman's household.

'Try something else,' he said abruptly. 'We'll come back to it.' He looked through his own music and chose some miniatures by Schumann. 'Can you sight read, do you think?'

She studied the manuscript for a few moments and nodded. 'I've played them before.'

Their determination to consider only the music made them immediately sensitive to the moods of the pieces. Sasha grew tense as they played; she felt each note from the violin combine with the pulse of the piano; something stronger than her own will seemed to push the music on. After a while she entirely relinquished the struggle for mastery, and felt herself become one with the piano, with the violin and the man who could draw such sensuous and bewitching notes from it. She had no control over what was happening. Exultation drummed through and through her as she felt the thrill of being locked into the music with him.

Sasha sat for several seconds without speaking when the final piece was over. Then she said, 'That was wonderful. I had forgotten . . .'

He put away his violin with a studied casualness. 'When would you like me to come again?'

She was not listening, still immersed in the excitement of their playing. 'I felt I had recaptured the essence of it – that terrifying tightrope one walks between control of the music and total abandonment. Of course, sight reading, no one can let go altogether, all the same . . . you know?'

'Yes, I know. You had allowed control to gain too much importance.'

She looked at him for a long time, an enigmatic expression in her eyes.

'Tomorrow?' He pressed. 'Shall we play again tomorrow?'

She looked away. 'Perhaps one day next week. I'll let you know.'

So, she was going to resist. He felt an overwhelming disappointment. She would rather be Elliman's perfect housewife with a little piano playing to stave off the boredom; she would relegate her music to its proper place as a diverting pastime, rather than upset the status quo.

'Very well, next week,' he said coldly and left the room, taking his violin. He went into town to the Three Bells and played there for the entertainment of the customers while he waited for Viggers and the others to arrive for a rehearsal of the Musical Society. If she could trivialise her talents, so could he.

Chapter Fourteen

Sasha sat for a long time after she had heard the front door slam. Why was he so angry? Did he know that he had stirred her? She had not felt so at one with her playing since Herr Lindau had been alive. She began to play from memory the first movement of the *Appassionata* Sonata, but she stumbled partway through, unable to recall what came next, while her fingers fumbled over what she could remember. She began to play finger exercises and chords, repeating them over and over until her hands were cramped and aching. She would have to get up the strength in her fingers again and to work at the bigger stretches. Chopin was good for that. She began on one of the studies from memory.

'Are you playing properly again?' Lily said, coming into the room.

'I've neglected the piano for *eight* years,' Sasha said over her shoulder.

Lily sniffed. 'It sounded all right to me the other night.'

Sasha stopped. 'Oh, Lily. Do you think so? Do you think I might get back to concert performance standard?'

'Your husband wouldn't like it.'

'Wouldn't he?' Sasha said in genuine surprise. 'I thought William seemed to want me to play again.'

'He'd soon change his mind if you wanted to go gallivanting off on your own again for concerts and suchlike.'

'Oh, I didn't mean that. Not touring again. But to play

well. To feel in control again.'

'In control of a piano?'

No, thought Sasha. Not that. In control of me. Of my life.

It was Sasha's idea that they should all go to a concert in Bristol and that Gabriel should go with them. They visited Hanover Terrace first, where the children were fed biscuits and petted by Mrs Hammond. They left for the concert in the afternoon.

There were people Sasha recognised in the audience; she was occupied for several minutes, greeting old friends and introducing William and the children, his sister and his aunt. As the orchestra began tuning up for the performance, she sat down and realised that in all the chatter they had forgotten about Gabriel. He stood, waiting for the family to be seated before he took his place in the row. She wondered how keenly he felt his position as tutor, remembering that, though he knew her parents well, he had stayed in the background at Hanover Terrace in the way Miss Holloway always used to do.

Sasha glanced at him secretly as the orchestra began to play. How hard it must be for him to sit there as a spectator, when he so much wanted to do more than conduct an amateur orchestra in Penbury. He was listening to the music with a look of intense concentration; now and then a frown of impatience crossed his face, or an expression of contempt, almost of physical pain, would show from time to time.

'How I hate music that is too perfectly polished,' he said afterwards as they left the theatre.

William smiled at the vigour of the remark. 'Surely you wouldn't have admired a bad performance?'

'I should if it were performed with sincerity – even though I might wince at all the wrong notes. Even the Penbury band plays with feeling.'

'I didn't detect any wrong notes,' said Lily, coming to the conversation late. 'Really, Mr Ridgeway, I should have thought you would be more grateful after my brother invited you along.'

'I'm sure Mr Ridgeway didn't mean to be ungrateful.'

'Indeed not,' said Gabriel quickly and correctly, reminded of his position. 'But surely a sense of proper gratitude doesn't prevent my having an opinion on the music.'

'Which was too perfect,' reiterated William.

'Too polished,' corrected Gabriel. 'When a thing becomes facile, then is the time to question whether it's worth doing.'

'You mean, a thing is only worth while if it's a struggle,' said Aunt Georgie.

'Mr Ridgeway requires blood and sweat,' remarked Sasha drily.

'A little sweat at any rate,' said Gabriel.

William laughed, but Sasha, walking a little ahead of the others, made no response. I like him, she realised. I respect the things he has to say. And I'm grateful to him. He's brought me back to my music.

They had reached the pavement and stood waiting for the hired carriage to draw up. William went with Lily to seek out a reason for the delay. Aunt Georgie took the children to look at the posters on the theatre walls, and Sasha and Gabriel were left briefly isolated at the side of the road. They were hemmed in by carriages in the darkness.

'Have I annoyed you?' Gabriel had interpreted her silence as vexation.

She looked at him. 'I was thinking about what you said. That music is only worth listening to if it's performed with feeling.'

'Miss Elliman misunderstood me. I know it was a favour on your part to ask me to join your party—'

'I wasn't angry.' She looked at him in surprise. 'We don't expect *gratitude*. Not for anything. Believe me, Mr Ridgeway, I have a lot to thank you for. I realise now how *empty* my life had become.' The others were already returning. She opened her mouth to say something more, and then William was by her side.

'The driver misunderstood the place. He's been waiting round the corner. He'll bring the carriage up directly.'

They spoke little on the journey back to Penbury. The children quickly fell asleep but as they drew near to home a noise outside awoke them. A crowd of men swarmed round the carriage as it progressed through the lower end of the town. They were shouting and laughing, making a crash and a rattle with an assortment of kitchen utensils, tin baths and cooking pans.

'A full orchestra,' said William.

'They have all the enthusiasm Mr Ridgeway found missing in the theatre,' said Aunt Georgie. 'But what's it all about?'

'It's a skimmington,' said Gabriel. 'I heard them talking about it at the Three Bells. One of the factory gangers has left his family and gone off to live with another fellow's wife.'

'Oh, the women treated her so badly,' said Aunt Georgie. 'You remember, Sasha. Mrs Wotherspoon told us.'

Sasha opened the window. The crash of sound flooded in, and the children pushed one another aside, trying to get closer to see what was happening.

The carriage swayed and juddered to a halt. After a moment the driver appeared at the window. 'I can't get through. They're frightening the horses.'

'We'll go the rest of the way on foot,' said William. He paid off the driver and the family clambered from the carriage, Aunt Georgie with the children, William assisting Lily.

Gabriel helped Sasha down last of all; at the same time, a trio of youths carrying a dummy hurled into him knocking them both sideways. Sasha grasped for the door handle.

'Mr Ridgeway!' She saw him stumble and go down as the crowd swirled round. Afraid that the horses would drag the carriage wheels over him, Sasha lunged and reached for Gabriel's arm, but one of the men carrying the dummy caught her by the waist; they pulled her along with them, away from the others and the carriage.

'Louts! Fools!' Sasha struggled, looking round wildly; she jabbed her elbows into ribs and kicked out at shins until the man let her go. But by then she was several yards from the spot where the carriage had halted. She could not see Gabriel, nor even William and the others, only the laughing, jeering revellers.

'Give us your bonnet,' shouted one of the youths close to her ear.

'What!'

'Your bonnet. Our lady needs a bonnet.' Sasha looked then at the dummy they carried: it was mounted on a pole, an effigy of a woman, with hugely padded breasts, dressed in a crinoline and shawl. Her face was made of a knitted stocking stuffed with straw, with a crude face painted on it. The lips were large and red. The eyes stared into space.

'Find your own bonnet,' Sasha shouted, turning away.

The man caught hold of her again. He held her firmly from behind, pulling her against him while one of his companions untied her bonnet with an almost tender civility and said, 'Much obliged, Missus,' before jabbing it on the dummy's head. They tied the ribbons under its chin affectionately, and the man who had held Sasha let her go. Laughing and shouting, they whirled away from her, raising the effigy above their shoulders, pushing on towards the point where the crowd was at its noisiest. Here a second dummy, very stout and wearing a battered cloth hat, was dancing up and down. There was a violent clashing and crashing of pans, and the two dummies were thrust together as if to kiss one another.

Sasha fought down a growing panic. What if Pippa or Meredith had been separated from the others? What if they were trampled underfoot in the crush? She saw then that several of the men in the crowd were carrying lighted torches, waving them about with drunken recklessness. Already some were shouting that they should set the dummy's skirts alight. She felt a hand grasp her arm again and she twisted away with a cry of alarm.

'Thank God!' Gabriel pulled her towards him. 'Are you all right? Have they hurt you?'

'They're going to set fire to them!' Sasha said passionately. 'It's awful! I can't see the children anywhere.'

'The children are with Miss Sparrow. And I've seen your husband and Miss Elliman. They're all quite safe. They took shelter in the factory doorway.'

By this time someone had set the dummy's crinoline alight and it blazed up with a roar. There was a tremendous shout from the onlookers. In the pause Sasha and Gabriel pushed a path through the crowd. They watched as the revellers set light to the second dummy and began tossing the burning crinoline and bits of clothing above people's heads.

'My bonnet!' Sasha gave an involuntary cry as the dummy's head was enveloped in flame.

'*Yours*?'

'Too late – ah. It's gone.'

Gabriel watched as the bonnet blazed up. There was a peculiar energy generated by the crowd, and in the flickering fires. It was primitive, exhilarating. He looked at Sasha. Her teeth were parted, her face alight with an expression that was halfway between fear and excitement. What an exquisite look. What a passionate, lovely face when it was unguarded.

She turned to him, and the moment too was gone. 'We must go to find the others. I thought you had gone under the carriage,' she said, as they walked away from the crowd. 'I was so afraid you would be hurt.'

'I tore my coat.' He looked down at his sleeve ruefully. 'And you have lost your bonnet.'

She laughed, suddenly carefree. 'It was more exciting than the concert.'

'Weren't you frustrated with the orchestra? Didn't you want to shake them all up just a little and say, doesn't this music *mean* anything to you at all?'

She was silent for a moment, then halted. 'Mr Ridgeway. You have heard me play – *encouraged* me to play. Do you think I could reach concert-performance standard again?'

He caught his breath, tense with a feeling of achievement. 'Is that what you want?'

'I don't know, to be honest. But I realise now that music is still in me. *You* have made me see that.'

'Then I'm glad. And I think you should follow your heart.'

'Oh, Mr Ridgeway, that's so much easier said than done.'

They walked round the edge of the crowd and came upon William and the others.

William hurried towards them. 'Thank you, Mr Ridgeway. I'm very much in your debt.' He took Sasha in his arms. 'My darling. Are you safe? I couldn't get to you.'

'Where's your bonnet?' said Lily.

'They took it for the dummy. I'm afraid it's gone up in flames.'

'The villains!' William exclaimed. 'We'll prosecute. We'll find out the culprits in the morning.'

'Leave it,' said Sasha. 'It doesn't matter now.'

'It was very exciting,' said Meredith as they climbed the hill and the shouts of the revellers grew fainter. 'I liked all the people and the fires.'

'I liked the dummies,' said Pippa. 'But why did they have to burn them?'

'It's a bit like on Guy Fawkes Night,' explained Aunt Georgie.

'But Guy Fawkes was a bad man,' protested Pippa.

'And those effigies tonight represent bad people,' said William. 'They are very bad indeed; they've broken their marriage vows. The townspeople were showing their disapproval.'

'I think the bad people were the ones who stole Mama's bonnet,' said Meredith seriously. 'Anyone can break a promise, but it's more wicked to steal.'

'The man they burned in effigy did steal,' said Gabriel quietly. 'He stole another man's wife.'

Sasha lay in bed and said in a practical, matter-of-fact voice, 'William, I want to go back to the concert platform.'

'You mean Ridgeway's players – the Musical Society?

Well, I see no reason why not . . .'

'No. I mean professionally.'

He did not reply as he climbed into bed beside her.

'William, I said—'

'I heard. Are you out of your mind?'

The words cut her like ice. Sasha had supposed he might oppose her a little – playing professionally was hardly the same as a few drawing-room pieces to entertain their neighbours – but she had not expected him to be so damning. She began again, calm, rational.

'No. I'm not mad, William. I've been thinking about it very hard for several days. I'm sure I could be good enough again. My public never gave me up—'

'But you have the children. You're their mother . . . you're my wife.'

'That needn't make public performances impossible.'

'It's your duty—'

'Duty? William, how can you talk like that!' Sasha was silent for a while, then added, thinking it might persuade him, 'Mr Ridgeway seems to think I should follow my inclination.'

'If I'd known playing with Ridgeway would lead to this, I never would have suggested it!'

Sasha leaped to Gabriel's defence. 'We should be grateful to him. He's made me see how wrong I was to think I could discard my art. Why should marriage cut one off from one's talents?'

'Ridgeway has a lot to answer for. Putting ideas into your head. I shall tell him.'

'But I would probably have come back to the piano anyway, sooner or later,' Sasha said passionately. 'Perhaps when the children were grown. It's always been my first love.'

'I thought I was your first love,' William said ironically. He turned over with his back to her.

'And Kitty was yours,' Sasha responded, unable to resist a counter-attack. 'Don't let's forget Kitty. You could never refuse *her* any request, however much it made you stray from your duties.'

302

She knew she had briefly defeated him. The shock waves continued to reverberate between them: they never mentioned Kitty; it was an unspoken rule.

He said nothing for a moment, then muttered, 'You'd better put out the light.'

Sasha was surprised by the force of her resentment. She turned out the lamp and fell back on the pillows, remembering the fervour with which William had kissed Kitty, remembering it as clearly as if it had happened a few days since, not years ago. Was it then, seeing him with Kitty in the library, that she had begun to question the character of the man she had married?

After a while, William said, more placatingly, 'I don't understand, Sasha. You weren't happy performing. You wanted to give it all up when I met you again. You've hardly touched the piano since then.'

'Because I wanted so much more. I thought I didn't need it. I thought marriage would be enough.'

'You mean me. You thought I would be enough.'

'Yes. I suppose that's it.'

The silence in the darkness grew more solid. Every second added weight to the damage done.

'Oh, Sasha, you know how to wound! Kitty isn't the only Hammond with a talent for cruelty,' William said at last.

Sasha wondered about the nature of cruelty. Had William been cruel when he yielded to Kitty? No, he was weak, she thought bleakly. One forgave weakness. But to say, in effect, 'I'm disappointed in you.' Yes, that was cruel. She knew she must restore a normality before more things were said, irrevocable things that would make their world crumble.

'You *were* enough,' she said after a while. 'It all seemed so simple when we married. Your career was the thing. I so much admired your dedication.'

'I'm still dedicated to my work.'

'But I'm not part of it. Oh, we're affectionate with one another still – when we're not being disagreeable – but you've shut me out. I find I'm making conversation with

Aunt Georgie, or Lily, or left with the children.'

'Women *do* that. They gossip with other women. They care for their children. Why do you always have to make things so difficult?'

'Is that being difficult?' Sasha said in genuine surprise. She did not think so.

She stayed awake after he had gone to sleep, trying to discover whether she was being unreasonable. She knew that she was not, and lay, feeling angry with him. She saw the years stretching before them, filled with similar conflicts, reproaches and bitter conclusions – and no escape from one another.

After a while Sasha moved over against him. His back was warm and firm, and she stroked his neck and ran her hand down his spine, reassured by the familiar hollow above his buttocks, curling herself into him for comfort.

'I won't do anything about it for a while. But I shall play again. You mustn't try to stop me playing.'

William reached his arm to her and, turning over, pulled her to him.

Gabriel was silent at breakfast the next day. Aunt Georgie teased: 'I think Mr Ridgeway must have fallen in love. He's keeping the lady a dark secret. But I wouldn't be surprised if her name were to begin with "L", and she had a strong connection with the sea.'

'Very fishy,' laughed William, remembering Gabriel's monopoly of Lottie Turbot at the musical party. He had recovered his good humour, and told himself Sasha had not been serious about resuming her career; she would see, in the cold light of day, that performing with the Penbury musicians was the best solution for her boredom, and that the life of a professional musician was impractical, quite out of the question.

Gabriel went along with the pretence that he was in love with Lottie Turbot. He heard Sasha play that morning from the schoolroom. Scales followed relentlessly one after another, legato and staccato. Chords crashed through the house.

After Meredith's lessons, he went for a long walk alone, his absence confirming everyone's suspicions that he was courting. On Batford Hill, he looked down on the chimneys and factories, remembering the skimmington, Sasha's bonnet in flames and her expression in the weird light from the fires.

When he returned, she was still playing the piano; he could hear her from outside, and from his room in the attic. Gabriel lay on his bed, and the sound of the piano rolled and swelled up the stairs, filling his mind until he could hear nothing but her music. He had thought he wanted to make her play again, to revive her love of her piano, but as he listened to the ferocity of her playing, he knew he wanted something altogether more selfish and urgent.

They practised together almost every afternoon after the night of the skimmington. They were formal with one another always as Gabriel unpacked the violin and Sasha went to the piano. Then, as they began to play, Gabriel forgot the difficulties of loving her. So long as they had these moments together it did not matter that he was being eaten up with desire for another man's wife. He began to believe that he could bear it, that he could sublimate his emotions in his violin, translate his frustration into his playing, and that the purity of his art would carry him through.

At mealtimes with the family Gabriel was cheerful. He threw his energies into rehearsals with the Musical Society, his lessons with Meredith and violin lessons outside the household. Everyone assumed he was making progress in his courtship of Lottie, or had transferred his attentions to the more docile Henrietta. It suited him to let them think so.

Lottie had in fact dropped him from her affections; she had said he could not be trusted to keep promises. He tried to convince himself that he found Henrietta as captivating, may even have been guilty of allowing Henrietta to believe as much. But the hours dragged when he was not with Sasha;

and he lived only for the afternoons, when she allowed him to share her music.

William confided in Gabriel that there were areas of conflict in his marriage.

'My wife wants to go back to the concert platform, Ridgeway. What am I to do? I have to say I hold you partly responsible. She seems to think you've encouraged the idea.'

'Let her do it.' Gabriel swallowed Elliman's port; the drink was the only consolation in this excruciating half-hour after dinner each evening, when Elliman detained him in the dining room and talked to him about the difficulties of being married to a woman who did not conform to his feminine ideal.

'I shall lose her if I let her go back to the concert platform.' William fixed Gabriel with a look of earnest appeal. 'Why, if she is content with the marriage, as she says she is, does my wife need her music to be a public thing again?'

'I'm sure you're taking it all too personally.' Gabriel spoke with a barely concealed irritation. 'I'm sure Mrs Elliman doesn't want to distress you. What reason could she have?'

William thought of Kitty. Did Sasha want her revenge after all this time? They said women held grudges. He considered confiding in the tutor about the business with Kitty; he felt a wild need to confess. How soothing it would be to hear Ridgeway tell him that what he had done had not been so terrible. A kiss? He would laugh at William's overactive conscience and tell him that a dozen men would have kissed Kitty if they had been in his shoes; after all, she had thrown herself into his lap.

William kept silent. He had an uneasy suspicion that Ridgeway might sympathise with Sasha; he did not know Kitty and her peculiar fascination.

The sound of the door bell clanged through the house. William acknowledged it with an inquiring tilt of his head towards the hall and continued talking.

'I feel that my wife was once properly in love with me but that now I'm only half appreciated. Why, Ridgeway? My feelings for her haven't changed. Can't a man give himself to his career without his wife feeling so slighted she has to seek out a career of her own?' William was becoming morose. He listened to the sound of Bertha going down the corridor to the front door. 'Her duties – the care of relatives, the demands of young children – have exacted sacrifices from her. I freely acknowledge that. But women accept sacrifice as part of their lot. How can she contemplate abandoning everyone for a return to the concert platform? Chaos would result. It's a wife's place to be a stable influence in the domestic sphere. It's expected.'

'I would guess that what people expect and what your wife wants are entirely different things,' Gabriel said. 'And it seems to me, since you've asked my opinion, that it isn't enough for a woman of Mrs Elliman's talents to concern herself with the welfare of her children, two dependent spinsters, myself and the servants.'

'Why not? It sounds enough to me.'

There was a knock at the dining-room door. Bertha appeared in the doorway.

'Sir, Mr Wickham's here, and he says he'll see nobody but yourself.'

A look of annoyance crossed William's face. 'You'll have to excuse me . . . a patient.'

Gabriel heard him talking in the hall; the door swung back a little on its hinges and Wickham's voice carried into the dining room. The man sounded drunk.

'You've got to help me, Elliman. Can't you make it stronger? I need—'

William silenced him. The voices became muted and moved towards the dispensary.

Gabriel glanced at the clock on the mantel shelf; it was late, well out of surgery hours. He puzzled over the incident a little. After a while he left the dining room, glad of the interruption.

A strip of soft light showed under the door of the

Ellimans' bedroom. Gabriel paused halfway up the stairs, his eyes level with the bottom of the door, and his stomach lurched as he saw a shadow darken the line of brightness. He stood, hoping the door would open, painfully alert to the fact that it separated Sasha from him by no more than a few yards; half fearful, not knowing what he would do if she appeared. Then he continued, walking quickly as he passed her room and on to the attic stair.

Sasha was decorating a bedroom screen with coloured prints: pictures of birds, flowers, and ladies dressed in costumes that were indecent, according to Lily, but artistic in her own eyes, and no more suggestive than those she and her sisters had worn to sit for her father's painting. She knelt on the bedroom floor, cutting out the pictures and pasting them with a childlike pleasure in their arrangement. The screen, in three sections, was to be a Christmas surprise for William in a few days' time.

She paused as she heard footsteps on the landing, and waited, ready to push everything under the bed if the door should open. But the footsteps did not hesitate and walked on past. She recognised a masculine rather than feminine tread and guessed that William and Mr Ridgeway had finished their amicable chat over the port and that Gabriel had gone up to his room.

She packed away the screen in case William came upstairs. Her work on the Christmas present had made her think of Lavinia as she undressed for bed. Her sister, grown plump and placid and contented with Mr Pickersgill, had filled her house in Yorkshire with similar projects.

Sasha climbed into bed and felt a shiver of apprehension. Was that how she too would become – perhaps was becoming already? And was William growing as dull as Mr Pickersgill? She heard him come upstairs, and she closed her eyes, turning her face from the light.

'Sasha? Are you awake?'

She did not answer, and if he suspected she was pretending to be asleep he did not press the matter.

★ ★ ★

Sasha had been practising all morning. She was sitting in the
window seat of the drawing room with several music sheets
spread about her, when Gabriel came into the room.

'I'm sorry,' he said. 'I assumed no one was here and
thought I might play the piano.'

'Oh, but stay, Mr Ridgeway.' Sasha felt a strong urge to
detain him, without knowing why, except that he seemed
to have been avoiding her lately. 'I should like to hear you
play.'

He sat at the piano and began a piece by Bach, but he
seemed uneasy and, she thought, sad. Sasha remembered
everyone's assumption that he had fallen in love with
Henrietta as well as Lottie Turbot. Was it true? She stole
little glances at him. Had he been in love with many
women? According to Leah, his heart had been engaged,
broken and mended several times over. Sasha felt a
strange urge to confide in him about William's hostility
over her plans to play again. She wanted to tell him about
her restlessness, that she was so afraid she no longer loved
her husband, nor even admired him.

He finished playing and put away the music without
looking at her.

'Shall we play some more duos this afternoon?' Sasha
said quickly.

'I'm afraid I've promised the Musical Society . . .'

She nodded, disappointed. 'Perhaps another day.'

He sat drumming his fingers silently on the piano lid.
After a few seconds he got up to go.

'I believe the Musical Society have been practising for a
Christmas concert,' said Sasha. 'I could play something –
if you think it's appropriate. I mean, I should like to
contribute something to the programme.'

'That would be wonderful. I shall tell them.' He hesitated, and turned again to go.

'Have you thought what you will do after Christmas? I
mean . . . will you try for another orchestra? If not, I
should like you to instruct Meredith in the viola. He's
been wanting to learn.'

309

He halted, as if impatient to be gone, and answered her with an odd note of reserve in his voice – she had noticed it more frequently lately: 'Merrill did say he might let me know if a position arose. But—' He looked at her with a directness, almost a hostility that startled her. 'Perhaps in any case I should find some other work. I wonder if it would be better, Mrs Elliman, if I were to look elsewhere after Christmas . . .' He hesitated a moment longer, and left the room.

Sasha walked restlessly to the piano, going over the past minutes in his company. What had he meant by his parting words? And that look, almost as if he disliked her? A shock ran through her as she heard him say again: 'I wonder if it would be better if I were to look else-where . . .' Did he imagine she was bored, lonely, a wife who had reached that middle point in a marriage where the limits of her world had become so narrow that she sought out another man's company – any man's company – to relieve the long hours? Did he feel himself in danger? Was that why he had been avoiding her?

Sasha felt a flush of anger, trying to remember whether she had given him cause. She recalled how she had wanted to keep him a few more seconds in the room with her after his playing, and the indignation drained from her. If he had made the supposition that she preferred his company to that of her husband – and she was sure now that he had – could it be true?

Sasha went for a walk up the hill behind the town. She had gone out without hat or gloves. A thin, squally rain blew in the air, but it was not enough to soak her and the sting of it against her cheeks and hands was invigorating. The only sound in her ears was the heavy roar of the wind through the Scots pines along the road.

It was good to be out in the open, away from the house and the people who filled it. She tried to free her mind of them, all those members of her household, and remembered the day she had walked here after she had told William that Kitty was Randolph Portland's mistress. She

310

stood above the town, looking down at the factories, and thought of all that had happened in the years since then. Despair swept through her. What was she to do? Her marriage was empty of feeling, a performance without meaning any more. She seized on the metaphor. How could she go on performing the same tune, when she recognised there was no heart in it? Gabriel had shown her the waste and futility of that.

She returned to the house where William and Cope were setting up a Christmas tree in the hall. The children were sitting on the stairs, watching with barely suppressed excitement.

'Sasha, there you are!' said William. He threw her a smile. 'We were wondering where you'd got to. My darling girl, you'll catch your death going out in this weather.'

'No, I won't. It's quite bracing.' Sasha wriggled between the children and, wrapping them in her cloak, sat with them for a while, watching the preparations. She could hear Gabriel playing the violin in his room.

'It sounds sad,' whispered Pippa, laying her head against Sasha's arm. 'Why is Mr Ridgeway so sad?'

'Perhaps he's missing his family. We all need our loved ones at Christmas.'

'Mr Ridgeway's family don't speak to him because he's a musician. He told me. And anyway, he loves Miss Turbot,' said Meredith. 'So he will see *her* at Christmas, at least.'

'Merry! What a thing to say. I'm sure Mr Ridgeway didn't tell you that as well.'

'No. Aunt Georgie told us about Miss Turbot,' confided Pippa.

'Aunt Georgie should know better,' frowned William. 'All the same, I thought we might ask a few people over during the New Year festivities. The Turbots again perhaps – since we seem to be matchmaking? Aunt Georgie seems very friendly with Mr Viggers since he came to stay.'

'Now who's spreading gossip?' murmured Sasha as Meredith giggled.

'Shall we make it another musical evening to keep your hand in? You and Ridgeway could play something again.'

His attempt to appease her about her playing aroused a mixture of guilt and irritation in Sasha. 'Oh, do you really think that's necessary?' She remembered Gabriel's embarrassment that morning in the drawing room and thought of the necessity of practising together; he would be convinced she was looking for excuses to be alone with him.

William looked at her in surprise. 'You don't want to play?'

'Oh, very well. But perhaps *you* should ask Mr Ridgeway. I'm sure it would be more proper coming from you.'

Sasha felt unsettled, and went to the bedroom to take off her cloak. She could still hear the violin. Pippa was right. He was playing the Mendelssohn sonata they had played for the Turbots; the melody was unbearably sad. She pictured him in his room and went to the door, opening it to hear more clearly. How intensely sweetly he played.

The vividness of her picture of him surprised her. She knew the shape of his head, the line of his jaw, the way his brows half shadowed his eyes, the way his hair fell, not as a general observation, but *exactly* how it was, and the fact that it was not a deep black but flecked with rusty brown.

She closed the door again and got out the screen she had been making for William, to put the final touches to it. I am becoming unhealthily interested in him, she realised. He has shown me the way back to my music, and in response, in *gratitude*, I have begun to turn to him. But it must stop. From this moment, it must stop.

A letter came for Gabriel. Aunt Georgie thrust it into his hands later that afternoon. He took it to his room and sat for a long time reading the words from Merrill: 'Come and see me . . .' There was a vacancy for a violin player in his next season of concerts. It was the answer to his prayer: a means of escape lay in his hand.

Gabriel waited for the joy, the feeling of release that

only weeks ago would have accompanied such news. He felt nothing at all, except the remembered pain of being in the same room as Sasha that morning and unable to tell her of his feelings. Had she understood when he said he thought it would be better if he looked elsewhere for a position? Had there been a momentary dismay at the thought of his leaving? He could not tell. He dared not speculate.

He folded the letter, and took out pen and writing paper from the drawer, and wrote to Merrill quickly, before he could change his mind, his pen scratching the paper, scraping his nerves. He thanked him for the offer, said he much regretted he had made other commitments, and thanked him again for his trouble. Sealing the letter, Gabriel ran downstairs and out to the Post Office in the rain.

Sasha was practising in the drawing room when he returned. Gabriel leaned against the bottom stair post with his hands pressed to his head. The only sounds were the pounding notes of the piano and the lighter ticking of a clock on the wall, out of time with the Beethoven sonata she was playing. He pictured her – small and tense over the keys, absorbed by the piano.

He had turned down a chance to play in a professional orchestra because it would mean not seeing her again! Was he going crazy? She is married, he told himself. She is absolutely forbidden to you.

'Mr Ridgeway – are you ill?' Aunt Georgie was standing at the top of the flight of stairs.

He knew now for certain that he was going mad. *He had turned down a chance to play in an orchestra . . .*

'No.' He started to climb the stairs. 'A headache. That's all. I thought the fresh air would clear it.'

'Can I get you some laudanum?'

'That would be very kind.'

He went to his room. After a few minutes there was a tap at the door. Aunt Georgie surveyed him with an anxious expression. 'You do look pale.'

'I'll be right enough.'

She smiled and handed him the glass she carried. He drank the water and laudanum quickly.

'I always find it helps,' she said as he handed the glass back to her.

'You suffer from headaches, Miss Sparrow?'

'Oh, yes. Frequently. When I'm worrying about something.'

Gabriel looked at the frivolous figure in the ridiculously wide crinoline. 'Miss Sparrow, what have you to worry about here?'

'I worry about Mrs Elliman when I hear her play like that,' Aunt Georgie said in a rush. 'So much feeling!'

Gabriel faltered. 'Mrs Elliman is very talented.'

'She has more feeling than is good for her. I'm afraid for her, Mr Ridgeway. Something is troubling her. I'm afraid for my nephew when she plays like that.'

After breakfast on Christmas Eve, the children, Gabriel and Aunt Georgie decorated the tall fir tree in the hall. Everyone watched as Gabriel, perched on a ladder, placed a star at the top. Sasha caught her breath when he leaned across holding with one hand to the staircase, and she said involuntarily, 'Do take care.' He glanced down, and for a second a look passed between them. It was charged with an odd tension, a look more dangerous than the possibility that he might fall.

William was already walking along the corridor towards the dispensary. 'Work to be done. Christmas or no Christmas. Morning lessons, Meredith.' He called over his shoulder, 'See there's no slacking, Mr Ridgeway.'

'Oh, it's a triumph, Mr Ridgeway!' said Aunt Georgie clapping her hands as the star was lodged in place. Bertha, Mrs Ash and the children joined in the applause.

Lily sniffed. 'So long as we remember what it's all about.'

'Jesus,' said Pippa. 'And the star that led the wise men. And the Angel Gabriel who spoke to Mary.'

'Mr Ridgeway is called Gabriel,' said Meredith.

'But I'm no angel.' Gabriel climbed down the ladder.

'To work! To work, lad!' He hoisted Pippa on to his shoulder and shooed Meredith up the stairs.

'Oh, to be young again! He's so full of life!' said Aunt Georgie, collecting up the unused trimmings from under the tree, and bustling upstairs with them in her arms.

'I'll swear Aunt Georgie's in love with the tutor,' muttered Lily to Sasha. 'It's ridiculous. A woman her age.'

'Oh, no, Aunt Georgie is in love with Mr Viggers, and Mr Ridgeway with Miss Turbot,' said Sasha lightly.

William put his head round the door to the dispensary corridor. 'I forgot to mention to Ridgeway about playing for the Turbots, Sasha. Perhaps you would ask him this morning?' He shut the door before she could reply.

The children had decorated a small tree for Gabriel in the schoolroom. Pippa, with her tongue between her teeth, was balancing a paper lantern on one of its branches. Merry sat at his desk, crayoning a Christmas greeting. It did not seem as if William's cry of 'no slacking' was being taken very seriously. Gabriel was sitting on the corner of Meredith's desk. The children had made little gifts of drawings and letters for him, and he was opening one and laughing heartily at the message in it.

What would he do if he knew how much, and how powerfully, she had thought about him since their conversation the previous morning? thought Sasha as she stood unnoticed in the doorway. Would he think it imperative that he look elsewhere for a position? She imagined his amusement in private; a secret satisfaction, perhaps, at making another conquest? She remembered her involuntary fear for him as he had reached out from the ladder, and the look from those dark eyes, which she had engaged for a fraction too long. There had been no cynical self-satisfaction in his expression then.

'Mrs Elliman! I didn't hear you come in.' Gabriel got up from the desk.

'Mama, I've made you something.' Meredith put a

hasty last touch to his drawing and jumped up to give it to her.

She examined the picture – a winged angel – and its message: 'To dear Mama, a Merry Christmas and a Happy New Year to you.' She kissed Meredith with a swift hug of pleasure, aware that Gabriel was watching her closely. She did not look at him as she said, 'Mr Ridgeway, my husband would like us to play a duo when the Turbots visit after Christmas. Would you oblige him?'

'Of course,' he replied, but the request seemed to throw him into confusion.

'I heard you had a letter from Bristol. Was it good news?' Sasha prompted. 'I thought it might be from Merrill.' She must make it clear that it was nothing to her if he was leaving them after all.

'Yes, it was from Merrill . . .' Gabriel hesitated. 'I'm afraid he holds out very little hope of a place for the next few seasons.'

Sasha covered her delight and became all concern. 'I'm so sorry.' The look of rueful sympathy in her smile stabbed at Gabriel's heart.

And yet, he told himself, kindness was safe. He could keep his own feelings in check, play any number of duets, if he could prevent her from knowing how he felt.

From today this must stop, Sasha told herself as the family walked to church on Christmas morning. I must be on my guard when we rehearse together. I must be careful at the town concert this afternoon. This infatuation must go no further.

Yet, though she rationalised what was happening to her, she could not take her eyes from the figure in the pew beside Meredith. Her gaze lingered on the edge of his cheek, the dark fringe of his eyelashes as he turned the page of Meredith's hymn book and pointed out the place to him. Searching for something else to occupy her, she saw that her own gloved hands were clasped tightly, suggestive of pain rather than prayer. She raised her head again to see Meredith look up and smile at his tutor; and

Gabriel smiled in return with a curve – oh, the tenderness of the curve of his mouth. Sasha drew herself up sharply. She was a married woman. The love between a husband and wife was inviolable, and it was wicked, a crime against her marriage, to think such thoughts about a man who was not her husband. She would not, *would* not behave like Kitty.

The haze of the altar candles formed mysterious patches in the gloom of the church beyond his head. As Sasha watched, the candle flames dimmed and flickered. It's a sign, a warning from God, she told herself with a leap of terror.

'Mr Ridgeway has presents for us.' Meredith tugged at Sasha's sleeve. 'He has presents for all of us.'

'Presents?' William handed his hat and cane to Bertha. 'No need for that, Ridgeway.'

'It's nothing,' Gabriel said in an offhand way. 'Simply a gesture of thanks for all your kindness towards me.'

Pippa ran across the hall. 'They're here, under the tree.'

Sasha's heart beat erratically as the children handed round the presents. 'Mr Ridgeway, it's very generous but you shouldn't . . .'

'Please,' he said with a light, dismissive smile as she unwrapped her own gift carefully.

Sasha was determined not to be moved. But as she stared at the bound volume of the Chopin Ballades, wave after wave of shock swept through her. She held it in her hands but did not trust herself to open the covers and see the familiar notation.

'It's a very beautiful present,' she said at last.

He glanced up, and a look passed between them that sent further shock waves through Sasha.

'A very handsome gift,' said William, referring not to the music, but to his own gift from Gabriel, a pair of carved book ends in the shape of owls. 'I believe this is the work of Chisholm in Penbury – am I right, Ridgeway? He's a fine craftsman.'

Gabriel tried not to betray his tension as he watched

Sasha. Would she understand the significance of his gift, the longing concealed in the music? Would her husband understand too? He reassured himself that Elliman would see only the intrinsic merit of the binding and the manuscript pages, not the music they contained. He had allowed himself this one indulgence. Hang the consequences. He did not care any more. He did not care if he lived or died. But after this – after the concert in Penbury, when he would see her play with feeling and know he had brought her back to music – after this he would leave.

There were other gifts: a scarf for Aunt Georgie, a collar for Lily, books for the children.

He knows I am falling in love with him, thought Sasha, nursing the music book. He has done this thing in front of everyone. As a cynical gesture? No, she thought fiercely: he was not cynical. But if not . . . Sasha felt as if the ground were giving way beneath her. A feeling close to panic engulfed her, a realisation that if he shared her feelings, she would have to do something about it.

Chapter Fifteen

All Christmas morning, Sasha's moods and resolutions changed by the hour. One moment she had decided to confront Gabriel; the next, she would admit her confusion to William – he would understand, he would remember Kitty. And she would tell Gabriel to leave; she would explain very rationally, how it was impossible to continue as they were . . .

Or, she would say nothing. Her sense of duty and affection for William would conquer this infatuation, for that was all it was: boredom had made her an easy prey to the good looks and appealing nature of her son's tutor. Nothing more. And nothing more would happen, as long as she did not give way to feeling; it would fade in time, and Gabriel – notorious for his impulsive romantic attachments – would confine his attentions to one or other of the Turbot girls again.

Luncheon was a festive affair of roast beef and plum pudding and wine; Sasha had succeeded until then in avoiding Gabriel, who had been boisterously occupied with Aunt Georgie and the children. Afterwards, everyone walked to the Penbury schoolrooms for the Musical Society's Christmas concert.

Sasha sat between William and Aunt Georgie. The schoolchildren had decorated the hall with wreaths and festoons of holly and ivy. Gabriel stood at the back of the hall, helping to direct the players who waited their turn in the corridor.

Sasha, confident of being unobserved, was alert to Gabriel's every move. He conducted. He played the piano, his hands producing the strains of a popular melody while Henrietta Turbot sang. The Choral Society performed a number of choruses accompanied by the small orchestra; and Mr Viggers rounded off the first part of the concert with a rousing vocal composition of his own, accompanied by his sister.

Sasha joined the other performers during the interval. The more serious items – Mr Viggers's selections from *Verdi*, her own playing of Mendelssohn, followed by Gabriel's violin solos – were reserved for the latter half of the concert. She chatted with Mr Viggers, and waved to Meredith and Pippa who sat on the edge of their seats, craning their necks and waiting for her to take her turn.

Mr Viggers was called upon to sing again and Sasha withdrew into the shadows of the corridor. The rest of the performers had taken their seats in the audience, and she found herself alone with Gabriel. They stood for a while, not speaking. Sasha could see his profile against the light from the hall. Her contemplation of it sent little tremors of sensation through her that she struggled to control. How enthralling it was to be alone with him, hidden from view and at a safe distance from the bellow of Mr Viggers's strong baritone. She longed to reach out and touch the line of his jaw, to trace her fingers over his mouth . . .

Sasha felt a wave of terror engulf her. What was happening to her? Was she completely out of her senses!

Gabriel too seemed agitated. After a while he paced up and down.

'I hope you weren't offended,' Sasha whispered when he came close again. 'I said hardly a word about the copy of the Ballades. It's a very fine gift and one I shall treasure.'

He fell back against the wall. 'Mrs Elliman – I am going mad. I have to talk to you.'

Sasha's senses jerked into a response.

After a moment in which he seemed to gather all his

strength, he reached to his pocket and pushed a letter into her hand. 'Don't open it here. Please – later, when you're alone.' Before she could speak he had turned away.

She stood for a moment in indecision. Mr Viggers was taking his bow and it was her turn to play. Casting a last glance at Gabriel, she put the letter in the pocket of her dress.

Sasha played Mendelssohn's 'Spring Song', and the other miniatures she had chosen, automatically and too quickly. He had written to her. What did it mean? She could not see him when she had finished her solos. She made a curtsey and went to sit next to William, her heart beating quickly. Gabriel was next. The audience waited, and then Gabriel walked on to the platform, raised his violin to his shoulder and announced he was going to play an arrangement of Hungarian dances. Sasha felt she must have dreamed the incident in the corridor. *Had* she dreamed it? He seemed lighthearted and relaxed as he spoke to the audience. She put her hand in her pocket and felt for the letter he had given her. It was cold under her fingers. After two violin pieces she whispered to William, in a voice that did not seem to be her own, 'I feel a little faint. I think I shall take a breath of air. I may even walk home.'

'Let me come with you,' William said, full of concern.

'No, no. I shall be well enough once I'm outside. Stay and enjoy the playing.'

No one questioned her sudden need for air as she left her seat and went to the door. Gabriel put his bow to the violin, and began again with a fresh melody, a haunting, passionate little tune. Sasha went outside and along the street with the sound of it in her ears. Only when she was out of sight of the schoolrooms did she take the letter from her pocket and unfold it with trembling hands.

My dearest Mrs Elliman,

I can no longer conceal the fact that I am in love with you. I am sensible enough about what society would make of my predicament to be sure that there

321

is no hope for me, and I would die rather than cause you harm. And so, I have decided to go away – far away from here. I shall tell your husband I have been offered a position with an orchestra in London.

I thought, I hoped I might stay without declaring my love for you. I see now it is impossible. I cannot go on living in close proximity to one who has become so very dear to me. Every time you speak, every note you play, every breath is exquisite and like a knife turning in my heart. You must not think that I am going with any sense of ingratitude for your courtesy towards me or for the very happy time I have spent with Meredith. I shall miss the children more than I can say.

Your friend, G.R.

Sasha stared at the letter. A clamminess crept over her, and she pressed the sheet of paper into her ribs as if trying to push away the sick pain in the pit of her stomach. Then she thrust the letter back into her pocket.

She walked quickly, blindly, not minding the rain, as if a demon were following behind her. She saw again his profile in the darkness of the corridor, heard him say again, 'I am going mad . . .' She pictured the light on his hair as he played the violin. She saw his long supple fingers on the strings, and gave a sob. 'Stop it! Stop it!' What was she going to do? How could she bear to carry on alone if he went away. With no one to think of except her husband and her children and all the other worthy, decent members of her household . . .

She did not hear the sound of a horse and carriage until it was almost upon her, startling her, making her jump aside on to the edge of the road. But instead of continuing on its way, the carriage slowed alongside her. Sasha saw that it held Mr Scrope and his sister.

Mr Scrope called out to her. 'May we take you anywhere, Mrs Elliman?'

Sasha looked at them and saw their expressions of consternation. What a strange thing she had done. To leave the concert like that! She imagined the Scropes telling people afterwards: 'Christmas Day, walking as if the devil himself was after her, and her cloak flying in the wind.' People would talk about her leaving the concert: the Wotherspoons and the Turbots would discuss her among themselves. They would wonder if she and William had quarrelled? They might even remember that she had left in the middle of Mr Ridgeway's solo, and reflecting on the fact that she and he had been alone together between the concert items, ask themselves if it was significant. Was William wondering about her sudden departure? And Lily and Aunt Georgie?

Sasha forced herself to smile at Mr Scrope and his sister. 'Thank you. I was at the Musical Society's concert. You weren't there? You missed a very pleasant afternoon.' She knew she was gabbling. 'It was so very hot in the hall, and since the performance was all but over, I thought I would walk with a message to the seamstress for Miss Sparrow. It was quite unnecessary, today, Christmas day, of all days, but—' She pulled the corner of Gabriel's letter from her pocket as proof. 'Since I had it on me.'

'Climb in,' said Miss Scrope. 'We are going past the very cottage.'

Sasha's heart sank. 'I'm afraid I shall make the seat wet.'

'That doesn't matter.' Mr Scrope opened the carriage door.

Reluctantly Sasha climbed in. She insisted they need not drive her home again afterwards. 'No. No, I shan't mind walking back at all.'

And so, the lying and deceit have already begun, Sasha thought. She listened to their chatter and responded. Yes, she had played the piano for everyone. She agreed it was wet and mild for the time of year, though unusually stormy. And yes – upon Miss Scrope's eager inquiry – Mr Ridgeway had played his violin at the concert.

'We have been visiting relatives, Mrs Elliman,' said Miss Scrope. 'An ailing cousin. Otherwise we should have been there.'

'Such a shame about Mr Wickham.' Scrope shook his head with an air of deep concern.

'Mr Wickham? Was he going to play this afternoon?'

'He was going to sing, I believe. But he's been too poorly.'

'He was once such a strapping fellow,' said Miss Scrope. 'Now he looks as if a breath of wind could carry him off. He's more than poorly. Very ill, I believe.' She lowered her voice. 'They say he's taken to drink. Oh, it's very bad. And him such a keen church-goer. Has Mr Elliman not told you?'

'Mr Elliman doesn't discuss his patients. Doctors don't tell their wives everything . . .' said Sasha.

They had reached the seamstress's cottage. Sasha stood at the side of the road, willing them to drive away and not watch for her to take her non-existent message up to the door. She waved encouragingly from the gate, Mr Scrope raised his hat and the carriage moved off. Sasha waited until the rattle and rumble of wheels had grown fainter before she turned back along the road – the way she had come.

The house seemed oddly empty as Bertha came to meet her in the hall; she said the others had returned some minutes since from the concert, and that William had been called out almost immediately to a patient in the next village.

The afternoon light was fading. The Christmas tree in the hall with its decorations looked tawdry. 'Light the lamps, Bertha,' said Sasha. 'And tell Mrs Ash to put back some supper later, for Mr Elliman when he comes in from his visit.'

She could not face going into the drawing room, where she could hear the children talking. Was Gabriel there with Aunt Georgie and Lily? She looked up the stairwell and saw a glow of light from the attic landing. Drawn to it, like a moth to a lamp, Sasha climbed the stairs.

She paused on the first landing and looked over the banister. Bertha passed below her, lighting the lamps in the hall before knocking on the drawing-room door; the sound of voices overflowed as she entered. Sasha looked up at the light above and moved along the landing to the attic stair.

She halted outside Gabriel's door, hugging her arms about her. She had no idea what she was going to say. Her hand was raised, poised against the panel when, with an abruptness that drew a gasp of terror from her, the door flew open. A flood of light burst from the room with Gabriel, dark and alarming at its centre.

'Mrs Elliman!'

The anguish on his face was shocking. Sasha's heart beat rapidly and her mouth was dry. She thrust his letter at him. 'Mr Ridgeway. I will have no more talk of your leaving us. How would you live? I know you have no orchestra position yet. And how would Meredith progress without you? He has been looking forward to lessons on his new viola. He would be heartbroken, poor child.'

'I thought—'

'You thought I would react to your declaration with sickly, feminine outrage – or in panic. But you will see, we can ignore this incident – we shall pretend it never happened. Please, take back the letter and tear it up.'

Gabriel took the letter from her. His heart felt like lead. She cared nothing at all for his feelings! She thought he was a poor love-lorn idiot who must be chivvied out of his sickness.

'But you must never again speaking of feelings,' Sasha said firmly. 'If you do, we could not keep a normality about the matter. I should find it impossible to let you stay.' A tremor in her voice betrayed her; she turned quickly, afraid that the flaring of hope in his eyes would make her give way entirely to those feelings she had only that moment declared to him were forbidden.

She turned from him, went to her room and sat on the bed, her heart beating against her ribs as if it would burst its way through. What was she going to do? She had discovered that she no longer loved William. She had admitted to herself that her marriage had been a mistake, that she was attracted to another man. And now she had ridden roughshod over Gabriel's attempt to take a decent and honourable course of action.

The screen she had decorated for William stood in the corner accusingly; he had been amused by it, she remembered. He had said he could imagine the long, pleasant hours she had spent in secrecy pasting her pictures. 'What a charming deceiver you are.'

I can control this, Sasha told herself fiercely. If I don't give way we shall stay friends. He will see there's no point in loving me. And I shall soon get over this temporary fascination – for that is *all* it is.

In a torment of indecision Gabriel wrote to Leah:

What am I to do? I have fallen desperately in love with your sister. If I stay, the agony is going to tear me apart, but how can I go, knowing I must never see her again? My only solace is music, but I have betrayed even that – I have turned down the very first offer to play in an orchestra that came my way. Tell me, dearest Leah, before I go mad, what I am to do . . .?

Leah wrote by return: You must leave the house at once. For your own sanity and for the sake of Sasha's reputation, I repeat, you must leave. I will not have another scandal in our family. And I will not have you, whom I love dearly, at the centre of such a scandal. For that is how it will end. Believe me. There can be nothing but unhappiness for you in following this foolishness. *Sasha loves her husband.* William is a good man. You must leave . . .

'You should never have sent him down there,' said Felicity, reading over her shoulder.

'You're right, of course. As always.' Leah reached up and caressed her friend's arm.

'Will you go? Will you do anything more positive to interfere?'

'And leave you? I don't know.'

Leah, usually decisive, found herself irresolute. It was strange, how she invariably followed Felicity's judgement. Felicity – so soft and fragile and vulnerable to physical sickness – was so much stronger about rights and wrongs than she was. 'Do *you* think I should go to him?'

'I think Gabriel, in his inimitable way, will rush quickly to his own doom if you don't do something to stop him.'

Leah read Gabriel's letter again. 'Sasha clearly has no idea how the poor boy feels. Do you think I should warn her?'

Felicity was thoughtful. 'That could make things worse.'

Leah clucked her teeth. 'Why doesn't he simply find a nice girl and settle down like most young men? Why does he have to be so complicated?'

Felicity laughed. 'You wouldn't love him so much if he was like most young men. Why don't you ask him to come to us for a while – until he gets over his infatuation?'

'You wouldn't mind? Remember how ill you've been.' Felicity's cough and fever had made her frail, and the cough still plagued her.

'My darling Leah, of course I don't mind. I love him almost as much as you do. And I've been so much better this winter. The dear boy can stay for a while to ease his wounds and he will be right as rain again before you know it.'

Gabriel tore up Leah's letter when it came. He had forgotten how rigid her reactions could be. He told himself it was the predictable response of an old maid. Then he remembered how much he owed to Leah; how he relied on her even now. He wrote again, thanking her for her advice and the offer of a refuge. He had appealed to her too hastily, he said. The situation was under control.

'Don't forget the Turbots are coming this afternoon,' said William a week later as he went to the dispensary.

'Shouldn't you and Ridgeway have been rehearsing something?' He laughed. 'Or is he so good you don't need to practise?'

'All musicians need to practise,' Sasha said drily. 'But to tell the truth, I'd forgotten you wanted us to play.' How easy it was to lie, she reflected. It was becoming a habit.

'Why don't you ask Ridgeway this morning, get up a programme together?'

A flutter of fear and anticipation ran through Sasha at the possibility of delicious hours of music in Gabriel's company – hours that had been sanctioned by her husband. She feigned a casual irritation. 'Oh, very well. I'll ask him after Meredith's lessons.'

Gabriel had set Sasha a secret test.

If she chose Schumann or Beethoven it was a sign; it meant she shared his feelings after all. He remembered her voice when she had said she would find it impossible for him to stay, the tremble of her mouth as she had turned from him; Schumann would mean she had lied when she said they could pretend nothing had happened.

If, on the other hand, she chose the Mendelssohn sonata, she was contemptuous of the depth of his feeling; she cared nothing for his peace of mind.

'What do you suggest we play?' He unpacked his violin.

She was slow to answer, and when she did her words were like a douche of cold water. 'Perhaps the Heller I once arranged for violin with Leah?'

'Yes,' he said flatly. 'It sounds very suitable.'

Heller. Light-weight, drawing-room pieces arranged for a performance with Leah – whose advice was to leave the house immediately. So, she was insensitive to his feelings, he thought, as he placed the music on a stand. And he had an over-ripe imagination that fed unhealthily on such small hopes as 'I should find it impossible . . .' and the looks they had exchanged, and all the other little signs.

They practised without enthusiasm for almost half an hour, repeating passages until suddenly Sasha broke off. 'This was an appalling choice.'

'Yes.'

'I arranged it when I was young. I knew nothing at all about the way a violin could speak.'

'I couldn't agree more.'

'Do you mind if we try something else? We've already played parts of the "Kreutzer" Sonata together. We could do the slow movement?'

He nodded, feeling miserable and sullen. But after only a few bars, the lyrical strength of Beethoven's music dispelled their unease with one another. Gabriel forgot to pull a long face, forgot difficulties, responsibilities, hopelessness and despair. The combination of violin and piano took him, and Sasha with him, into a world of mind and feeling. If only they could play like that – a musical partnership – in public. If only she were not married to Elliman! He knew he had never felt so complete with anyone before.

He played the final violin notes and leaned across the piano towards her. 'We play so instinctively together. One day, we shall play it all – the first movement, it's so invigorating.'

'And the Finale!' said Sasha. 'We shall make the whole house shake!'

He has fallen in love with me, and I am in love with him, she thought. And while we have music there is no such thing as sin.

Reality came flooding back. Gabriel said gravely, 'How lovely you are when you're lost in your playing.'

Sasha bent her head to the keys and ran her fingers through an arpeggio. 'We agreed . . .'

'No. I agreed to nothing. And anyway, I'm not speaking of feelings. I'm stating fact. You are never lovelier than when you're at the piano. Your face becomes a beautiful mirror of your thoughts.'

Sasha was silent for a moment. She looked up and said briskly, 'Well then . . . Shall we play the slow movement for the party, do you think? And you shall play a solo. Do you need to practise?'

He shook his head. 'Let's play something else. For

ourselves. We still have some time.'

She hesitated, wanting very much the pleasure of playing for longer with him. He was right, they played so well together. She felt she had beaten the malevolent forces that had made her attraction to him seem problematic and wicked. 'You choose.' She smiled.

'Mendelssohn. The F minor sonata,' he said quickly.

The pleasure drained from Sasha's expression. 'No. It's too sad.'

'It's beautiful,' he insisted. 'So simple and poignant.'

'I know. We played it before.'

'Mrs Elliman, let me prove to you I've taken your words to heart. I'll forget the letter. I won't talk of love any more.'

But what about me? thought Sasha. What if I can't forget?

They began to play. Haunting, wistful, the opening notes of the violin carried them into a territory they should not have entered. The melancholy mood of the sonata cast a spell over them.

'It's too sad,' Sasha said after the first movement. 'No more.' She sat looking down at her hands.

'Please.'

They played on, united by the emotional outpouring first from one instrument, then the other. Sasha could not look at him. Confidence drained from her. How could she hide her feelings from him? She had fooled herself for a few days, but what sort of substitute was it, to play duets for a few hours when she wanted so much more? It seemed as if he knew that she was weakening; as if he wanted to push her to the edge. The music swelled to a crescendo of emotion.

Sasha broke off playing, jumped up from the piano and ran to the door.

Gabriel's heart leaped. He threw down his violin and caught her before she could grasp the door handle.

'What is it?' He held her, his fingers circling her arm and holding it fast. 'Don't stop. We must finish it.'

'I can't. I can't play with you. Not any more.' Sasha's

heart beat with terror and a wonderful sense of release. She looked up at him and her eyes were brilliant with tears. 'Don't you see? I asked you to stay because I couldn't *bear* to lose you.' She kept her eyes on his, and saw the pain in his expression change to hope and then to joy.

There were footsteps in the hall; they went past the door and up the stairs.

'What are we going to do?' Sasha whispered. They stood, his hand still gripping her arm, as if he could not or would not release it.

'I don't know. Nothing. Everything. We could go away.'

'You know that's impossible!'

There were footsteps again, this time they halted outside the door. Slowly Gabriel released his fingers from her arm. Sasha moved quickly, away from him and back to the piano. By the time Aunt Georgie entered, Sasha was packing up the music and Gabriel had retrieved his violin.

'Mrs Ash is asking where you want the meringues.'

'Meringues?'

'For this afternoon. She says the damp is getting to them in the pantry. She wants to put them in the dining room.'

Meringues! thought Sasha. Had the world gone mad?

She turned to Gabriel and said with as much composure as she could summon, 'Thank you for the rehearsal, Mr Ridgeway. I'm sure we shall be note perfect this afternoon.'

The Turbots sat at various points in the room, listening to Lily loudly debate the rules of bezique with William. Family and guests, Sasha surveyed them all. Mr Turbot was in a wing chair, his hand cupped to one ear to listen to the various conversations. His daughters sat in a huddle on the seat in the window. Gabriel stood by the piano. Henrietta and Lottie pretended to ignore him, but betrayed by their looks and whispered comments that they were very conscious of his presence.

She could not go through with it, Sasha thought. She would faint, or weep and give them both away. She went to join the children on the floor; they were pasty-faced from a surfeit of rich food and excitement over Christmas, engrossed in arranging a cardboard cut-out theatre. She pretended to be engrossed with them, at the same time talking to Mrs Turbot about a recipe for syllabub.

Aunt Georgie was fluttering and flirting with Mr Viggers, making the Turbot girls giggle. But Aunt Georgie knew that she was making progress; Mr Viggers had begun to call her 'Miss Georgie' instead of the drab 'Miss Sparrow'. He pronounced it with a soft lisp: 'Jh-eor-jh-ee', as she imagined a French lover might say her name. She was both agitated and amused by the idea: she could not pretend for long that Mr Viggers was anything but a stolid Englishman.

He was talking about church music and mourning the decline of oratorio in concert performances. Aunt Georgie said that she had heard the first performance of *The Fall of Babylon* in Norwich, and had signed a petition for the composer to be allowed to come all the way from Germany to conduct the work himself.

The Turbot girls began talking in hushed tones about Mr Wickham, who it was said was worse since Christmas. William suggested games. 'Let's have some riddles.' But the atmosphere had become lethargic and Lily was falling asleep.

'I do hope you will play for us this afternoon, Mrs Elliman,' Mrs Turbot said to Sasha. 'Mr Elliman tells us that you and Mr Ridgeway are going to play something by Beethoven.'

Gabriel threw her a glance and their eyes met with a mutual uncertainty.

'Play for us now, Sasha,' William said. 'I heard you from the surgery when you were practising this morning.'

Sasha felt her throat constrict as she crossed the room to the piano. Her hands trembled when she placed the music on the music rest and her heart was beating furiously. She could not go through with it. How could they avoid revealing their feelings for one another in the music?

Gabriel bent his head. He began to tune his violin.

Sasha waited. In her heart she felt a chill of despair. Feigning a smiling serenity, she told herself over and over that she must not, by an unintentional glance or a signal, betray him.

She began the slow measured opening bars of the Andante of the 'Kreutzer' Sonata. Gabriel's playing was sweet and intense, and Sasha bowed her head over the keys. She played through two pages of music and, hearing the violin throw in little echoes to the piano part, knew she would not be able to play to the end.

Suddenly, as they embarked on the second variation and the violin part became more vigorous, a string broke. There was a gasp of alarm from the listeners.

Sasha stopped playing, exhausted by the effort of performing under tight control, feeling as if she too had snapped under the strain. She sat unmoving as Gabriel examined the violin. He expressed annoyance, and she watched him, her heart thumping violently as he turned to their audience. Had it been a fortuitous accident or had he manufactured the break?

'Oh, you've been hurt!' said Henrietta in alarm. Only then did Sasha see the blood and the graze on his cheek.

'It's nothing.' Gabriel raised a hand to his face. 'Please – excuse me.' He hurried from the room.

'What a shame,' said Mrs Turbot. 'You played it so beautifully.'

Sasha closed the piano lid softly. 'Another day.'

'Let's have some riddles.' Mr Turbot rubbed his hands. 'Your husband suggested riddles, and I like a game of wits. This is a *musical* one. Tell me, why is a fashionable young miss like a nightingale?'

There were various half-hearted guesses at the riddle until Henrietta and Lottie begged him to tell them the answer.

'Because both a fashionable young miss and a nightingale will reject all suitors who come with only a *cheep* ring to their proposal.'

333

The Misses Turbot groaned loudly. 'Father!' said Henrietta. 'Your riddles are always so terrible!'

'And not quite proper,' frowned Mrs Turbot, uneasy about allusions to mating calls.

'I have one. I have one. What is the best way to keep a man's love?' Henrietta glanced involuntarily towards the door as if hoping for Gabriel to appear and hear the answer to her riddle.

'*Not* to return it,' said Lottie sharply. 'We all know that one.'

'Why is marriage like an umbrella?' volunteered Mr Viggers, warming to the notion of riddles and pressing his fingers together.

They all pondered the riddle. Sasha sat with her arm round Pippa, holding on to the warmth of her daughter for salvation. It was hopeless. They could not go on living in the same house. He would have to leave and she would not see him again: never again share his love of music, never relive the joyful passion of playing together.

She heard the clang of the front door bell only distantly. Like the riddles, it hardly punctuated her thoughts. She glanced up and wondered why Bertha stood in the doorway. William jumped from his seat and hurried across the room. Coming to her senses, Sasha went to join him.

Something had happened to Gabriel. She remembered the blood on his cheek. Why hadn't he come back to the drawing room?

'Oh, Mrs Elliman, a terrible thing!' said Bertha, and she began to weep.

Something had happened! 'Where is Mr Ridgeway?' Sasha said in a whisper.

'Ridgeway? What's this to do with the tutor? It's Wickham,' said William.

Sasha looked from William to the weeping Bertha. 'Mr Wickham? What do you mean?'

William lowered his voice and steered her into the hall. He was very much agitated. 'It seems I'm needed. The poor fellow is dying. I must go straight away. Can you look after our guests?'

334

'Mr Wickham,' Sasha repeated, stupid with relief, staring at William's ashen face. 'Of course. You must go. I'll explain.'

'We think we should not stay,' said Mr Turbot gruffly when the situation had been explained. 'It isn't seemly in the circumstances. It's hardly right people should be enjoying themselves when poor Wickham . . .'

They took their leave with more expressions of regret and long faces.

Sasha leaned against the wall with a sigh as the door closed behind them.

'Poor *Mrs* Wickham,' said Aunt Georgie.

'Yes. Poor woman.' Sasha felt a twinge of remorse. She remembered the concern on William's face. He always felt so strongly for all his patients. But she could not stay long in the shadow that had fallen on the afternoon. What did she care about Wickham? Her emotions were too much concerned with the living.

The children and Aunt Georgie were not solemn for long; the three of them returned to the drawing room to play at cards. Lily disapproved. 'We should be attending to the Bible on such an occasion,' she protested, but nobody was listening.

'Come along, Mama.' Meredith waited for Sasha in the doorway.

She put a finger to her lips. 'You go along. Play without me. I want to see whether Mr Ridgeway was much hurt by the snapping of his violin string.' She waited until he had closed the door and the hall was empty.

Sasha ran up the stairs. With a swift action, scarcely pausing to knock, she stepped inside Gabriel's room and closed the door behind her. She leaned against it breathing quickly.

Gabriel started to his feet.

'I am so happy, so happy.' She threw back her head. 'I thought I would *faint* down there.'

He crossed the room to her in one step and took her in his arms. She kissed him feverishly.

335

'My husband has been called out to a patient. The visitors have gone.' His arms folded her closer to him. She felt herself dissolve into him, passion deepening as their mouths and bodies met.

'Sasha!' He kissed her. 'So soft . . . such a beautiful name. If only I had the right to call you by it. *Sasha*. My own Sasha. I want you to be with me, not him. I can't stand the way he talks about you, the way he treats you. With no sensitivity at all. His wife. His *wife*.'

'All the same, it's a fact. There's nothing we can do.' She kissed him again and they clung to one another. 'Oh, but we shall be punished for this.'

They sat on the bed close together, holding hands, becoming sober.

'If we channel our feelings into our playing,' said Sasha. 'If we try to ignore . . .'

'It doesn't work. You know it doesn't. How can you go on talking that way?'

'Because it's the only solution.'

Gabriel let go of her hands. 'It will drive us to desperation. I don't simply want to play duets with you. And I *know* you now. I know your nature. If I stay, you and I will be driven to more, far more than stolen kisses. I thought I could go on pretending I didn't want you. But I do. I want you for my own, to hold and love. I want you – all of you, until I'm sick with wanting and can't sleep at night. But if I had thought before Christmas that your peace of mind could be one bit spoiled by me . . .'

'My peace of mind. Oh, Gabriel, if you only knew—' She stopped his mouth with kisses. And then, as if in the same moment cold reality had intruded, they parted again.

'What are we going to do?' said Sasha, looking at him bleakly.

'I lied before Christmas. Merrill had a place for me with his orchestra. I think he might still let me join them.'

'You turned down a place in an orchestra?'

'I thought I could hide how I felt from you. I thought, as

336

you put it – so rationally – that I could keep a normality about the matter.' He kissed her again. 'So. You see there's nothing to prevent my going. You'll soon find another tutor for Meredith.'

'You mustn't. You shan't leave me.'

He looked at her in despair. 'Then what are we to do? Run away somewhere? Or stay together and let what *must* happen sooner or later take its course? And soon everyone finds out: Miss Elliman and Miss Sparrow, your husband and your children – Sasha, your children! Is that what you want?'

She shook her head.

'I *shall* . . . go away tomorrow.' He put his hand over her lips as she protested. 'If you care anything about me at all, you won't try to stop me. It will be terrible. And yet, today you've made me the most happy as well as the most unhappy man in the world.'

She touched his cheek tenderly, and kissed the graze made by the broken string.

'Dear Gabriel, dear, dear Gabriel—' She began to cry. Drawing herself to her feet, she moved away from him as he tried to comfort her. 'No, it's true. We mustn't think of one another after this.'

She began to plan quickly. She walked about the room, hugging her arms tightly, making decisions as she spoke. 'I shall make an excuse not to be here when you leave. Lily or Aunt Georgie would suspect something's wrong – I couldn't hide it. The thought of watching you go . . . No. I shall take the children away. Into town. They will be upset too. Oh, Meredith's viola lessons, the games, his schooling—' She fell back against the door and pressed her knuckles against her teeth to prevent herself from crying out. 'What have we done? Why did we have to spoil everything?'

'May I talk to Merry? I can't simply disappear,' Gabriel pleaded softly, brokenly. She nodded and opened the door to go.

'Sasha, this is agony.'

★ ★ ★

337

Gabriel waited for William to return. It was late when he heard the carriage. He listened, heard the bang of the front door and voices in the hall, then footsteps go into the dining room. The women had long since gone to bed.

Gabriel went downstairs quietly. The dining-room door was ajar and he could see William seated at the table with his head in his hands. 'May I talk to you?'

William looked up. 'Come on in.' He reached for the decanter of port and pushed away the plate of cold meats in front of him. He looked very tired and his hand trembled as he poured a glass of wine, offering to pour one for Gabriel. Gabriel refused. He wanted the interview over and done with quickly.

'The fact is, I've heard from an orchestra in London, and they want me right away. I need to leave tomorrow.'

William laughed in disbelief. 'What? You know how to strike a man when he's down, Ridgeway.'

Gabriel did not pause to wonder about his meaning. 'Yes. I'm sorry it's such short notice. I didn't tell you over Christmas. I thought you'd hardly look for a replacement anyway during all the festivities. And . . . I wasn't certain. I spoke to Meredith earlier this evening. It's best I don't drag out a parting from the boy. I spoke to your wife. She was very kind. She says . . .' His voice was hoarse. 'She says she will release me.'

William did not notice Gabriel's agitation. He had troubles enough of his own after his appalling visit to the Wickhams and was too exhausted to make a fuss. 'Well, I suppose if you've accepted a position we have no choice in the matter.'

'It was always understood . . . my music would come first.'

'Of course. It was only a temporary position. Everyone knew that. Meredith will soon get over it.'

'You said – something about striking you when you're down,' said Gabriel remembering. 'I'm sorry, is Mr Wickham—'

'Dead, Ridgeway. Stone, cold dead.' William drank down the port in one gulp; he shook his head with a weary bewilderment. 'The fool! If he'd been more moderate.'

'You mean he drank.'

'What?'

'I thought . . .' Gabriel remembered the night the man had come to the house. He had looked pale and attenuated.

'Yes, yes. The fellow drank,' William said testily and then repeated, 'He drank too much. That's right.' He looked up thoughtfully. 'So, you're leaving us. Well, I'm sorry. You've been good company, Ridgeway, and I shall miss you. I shall miss our little talks together.'

Sasha pleaded a sick headache and stayed in bed the next morning.

Aunt Georgie tiptoed into the room after breakfast. 'How are you feeling now?'

'Aunt Georgie, would you take the children into Penbury for me before Mr Ridgeway leaves?'

Aunt Georgie nodded. 'That's a good idea. It will be less upsetting for them.'

'Thank you.' Sasha sank back on to the pillow.

'Oh, we shall miss him so dreadfully.' Tears filled Aunt Georgie's eyes. 'And all so sudden. If only he had warned us.'

'I expect he thought it best this way.' Sasha closed her eyes. 'Say goodbye to him for me. Apologise. But don't say I'm unwell. You know what it's like when you're leaving somewhere. You don't want to hear about someone else's sick headache.'

Aunt Georgie sat on the bed and took Sasha's hand, rubbing it between her own. 'Shall I fetch you some laudanum?'

'No. It will go. I'll sleep for a while.'

Sasha listened to the sounds of the house, identifying the servants, the children and Aunt Georgie leaving for town. Finally she heard Cope carrying Gabriel's luggage downstairs.

She stood by the curtain and watched as Gabriel left the house, almost hoping he would look up. She felt a strong impulse to open the window and shout out to him, wilfully to bring disaster down on their heads. Her hand reached towards the window catch. Then she turned away and threw herself across the bed. Misery beat through her forehead – she had not lied about the headache. With her face pressed to the counterpane, she heard the sound of carriage wheels on the road, and arching her back in despair, she gave way to a dry hopeless sobbing.

Sasha's head ached more intensely when, later, she went out to the silent landing. She could hear Bertha and Mrs Ash talking to Lily downstairs. William would be in his surgery. Bertha had been told not to disturb her before lunch, and had left all the upstairs rooms untouched. Sasha climbed the attic stairs to Gabriel's room and stood in the doorway. The bedcovers lay in untidy confusion, as if the occupant had slept badly. The emptiness of the room was poignant; it felt as if he had died.

Sasha went to the bed. The depression made by his head was still in the pillow. There seemed an exquisite tenderness in the shape of the hollow; she touched the place where he had been, and lay and pressed her face against it.

A footstep on the landing made her leap up from the bed. Pippa stood in the doorway.

'Darling – you're back. But creeping about so mouse-like!'

Pippa put her finger to her lips and whispered. 'Aunt Georgie said we mustn't disturb you.'

'Well, you may disturb me now. I'm quite well again.' Sasha picked her up and untied the ribbons of her bonnet.

Aunt Georgie appeared in the doorway.

Sasha put the child down. 'Run along and take off your things.' She turned her face away from Aunt Georgie. 'I was wondering what we should do with the room.'

'You'll think of something.'

Sasha met her glance. Aunt Georgie too had been

crying; her face was pinched and red. Sasha saw something else, an intelligence, a look of awareness in the other woman's eyes. She turned for a last glance at the bed before closing the door.

'I suppose we shall have to advertise for another tutor.'

Chapter Sixteen

Leah stood at the foot of the stairs with a cup of broth in her hands. She listened to the dry, frightening sound of Felicity's cough. It had been worse since Christmas; and she had brought up more blood than usual that morning. They both knew what it meant; but still they pretended nothing was wrong, continuing with their painting, with their brief walks along the shore when Felicity was well enough; and their music, of course. Leah could face the truth when she took up her violin.

She went to the bedroom and helped Felicity to sit up, tucking the pillows behind her.

'I think I shall not get up this afternoon.'

'Won't you even come down to lie on the day couch for a while?' Leah coaxed with a casualness that hid her fear. 'You could look out of the window.'

A wistfulness flickered in Felicity's expression and faded quickly. She pushed the cup of broth away.

Leah took Felicity's hand and pressed it to her mouth. 'Don't give up, Fliss. You mustn't give up now.'

'I don't want to. But it's such an effort.'

'Well then, there's nothing for it. I shall carry you.' Leah peeled back the bedcovers and wrapped the shawl more securely round Felicity's shoulders.

She was as light as a child, and she cried with a mixture of relief and shame as Leah carried her down the steep staircase. 'What have we come to?' she whispered, laying her head against Leah's shoulder.

Leah wanted to weep too, remembering so many things: Felicity's rounded prettiness when she first knew her, and her lovely singing voice that would never fill the cottage again. She set her down on the day couch and placed cushions behind her and a travelling rug over her knees. The couch had been pushed into the window overlooking the harbour. Leah sat on a chair beside it and held Felicity's hand.

From that day Leah carried her everywhere: to the commode as she grew weaker; downstairs to the sitting room each afternoon; or into the garden when the weather was mild enough, to view the snowdrops and daffodil spikes pushing through the grass. She was sitting in the bedroom window one morning while Leah changed the bed-linen.

'There's someone outside. He's been standing there for ages. He keeps looking at the house.'

Leah glanced out of the window. 'A beggar.'

'No.' Felicity looked up at her. 'There's something familiar . . .'

Leah turned again to the window and looked more intently at the figure in the street, a young man, tall, unshaven and dishevelled. A sense of shock stole through her as she saw the violin case at his feet. 'It's Gabriel.'

'Yes. I was afraid it was.'

'I must go to him.' Leah carried Felicity to the bed; she put her down very gently, kissed her and hurried from the room.

Gabriel crossed the street as soon as he saw Leah. He was filthy and exhausted, and looked as if he had been on the road for weeks. He had nothing with him but his violin.

'My darling boy—' She held out her arms. 'Whatever has happened to you?'

'Sasha—' he said faintly. 'I'm so cold. Leah, it's Sasha.'

'Merciful God! Her husband hasn't found out!'

'She loves me, Leah,' he said when he was in the kitchen and sitting against the stove. 'She loves me – and it's all totally hopeless.'

343

Leah ran a hand through her hair. 'You're a fool, Gabriel. You're your own worst enemy. Do you know that?'

'I had to leave.'

'To wallow in self-pity and let yourself go to the dogs?' She placed a pan of soup to warm over the fire.

'I thought there might still be something for me with Merrill's orchestra, but he'd filled the place. I tried a few things. Then my money ran out . . . I didn't know where else to go. You mustn't tell her. Don't let her know I've turned up like this.'

He was very white under the dirt and growth of beard. Leah took pity on him. 'Where else should you go? I told you to come, remember? You know I'll always be here for you.' She poured him some soup and watched him drink it – greedily, without regard for table manners.

'Sasha doesn't love you,' she said after a while. 'You're fooling yourself if you think she does. I don't know what's happened – and I shan't ask – but Sasha and William are very happy together. She's been unkind if she's let you think anything different.'

'She is not unkind. And I lived with them long enough to see the truth.'

Leah remained unconvinced.

He looked round the kitchen. 'Where's Miss Ferrers? Will she mind my being here?'

Leah hesitated. 'No. Miss Ferrers won't mind. You can sleep on the sofa. Gabriel, I have to tell you something.'

She was surprised how easy it was to talk, and to tell him that Felicity was dying.

'Does she know what's happening to her?' Gabriel said when Leah had finished.

'Oh, yes. I'm sure she does. But we don't talk about it.' Leah's resilience faltered. 'I don't think she has long. Gabriel – I don't know what I shall do without her.'

'You have me – for what that's worth.'

Leah reached out her hand. 'It's worth a lot. I probably need you this time, as much as you need me.'

Felicity's slow death shook Gabriel out of his self-pity.

The disintegration of her body and spirit, and Leah's anguish over losing her, drove out his absorption with Sasha. He and Leah played the violin together and made one another laugh again. He read to Felicity and took over the task of carrying her up and down the stairs.

When the end came, it was sudden and peaceful. She died in Gabriel's arms: he had carried her to the door one morning to look at the first buds breaking on the apple tree.

'She's gone,' he said quietly, not moving from the doorway, sensing the change in her, a deeper stillness, after she had acknowledged the bursting of new life outside.

Leah came swiftly to his side, bent and kissed Felicity's cheek, and closed her eyelids. She gave a shudder, as if some part of the other woman's spirit had gone from her too. 'Thank God, it's over.'

'Will you stay?' Leah asked.

'That depends on you.'

'I should like you to stay for a while. Do you mind?' She seemed drained of all energy. The black mourning clothes made her skin look sallow. Her eyes were large and the look in them was distant with pain.

'Of course I don't mind, but there are people who will say I shouldn't be taking up space on your sofa, now that you're alone.'

'People can say or think what they want. I've long since stopped worrying about other people's opinions.' She linked her arm in his as they walked along the quayside. 'So, now that's settled, I have to tell you something. I've been talking to someone about you. I think he can get you a place – second violin – in Scarborough. What do you think?'

Gabriel was surprised. He had thought Leah too much taken up with her sorrow to be concerned about his problems. And where was the comparison? What had he lost – except a snatch at happiness? Sasha wasn't cold in her grave; she still had her vigour and beauty; she had her piano and her children. 'I don't deserve you,' he said.

'I know you don't. And you've a long way to go if you're going to be a musician. You aren't practising enough. Tonight. Three hours at least. I shall help you.'

They played violin duets that evening. After a while Leah stopped playing and laid her violin in her lap. She sat as if she were listening to something and stared into the fire.

Gabriel went to the piano. He played a song tune from memory that he remembered Felicity singing.

'Thank you,' Leah said when it was ended. 'I miss her vitality, you know.' She picked up her violin again. 'We were very happy together. But it's a part of my life that's ended. Let's play something else – choose something with a bit of life in it.'

Secrets had made Sasha and William turn in on themselves. Sasha was mourning the loss of Gabriel, but William too had a secret – more terrible, more guilt-ridden than the near violation of his marriage vows. William had the death of a patient on his conscience.

Not that anyone was likely to accuse him of having a hand in Wickham's death. No one, except William, knew that the man had become an arsenic-eater as well as a heavy drinker during the last months of his life. The symptoms, as Wickham lay on his deathbed – the delirium, the cramps and vomiting, could easily have been caused by alcohol poisoning; the empty brandy bottles spoke for themselves. William had almost convinced himself. But the other, more dreadful possibility nagged at the back of his mind.

The fool, William told himself. The medicine was perfectly harmless taken in moderate amounts. The arsenicum content of the Elixir was slight; if it was absorbed gradually, in small, regular doses, the body gained a tolerance. He had warned him. He *had* warned him, the same as he had warned him about the drinking. But William had been busy around Christmas; was it his fault if he had lost track of the number of times he had supplied the fellow? Towards the end, Wickham himself had been unable to remember exactly how much he had been taking. Even then he had begged him for more. 'It makes me feel well,' he had whined, grasping William's hand.

'I'm sorry to have to record the death as delirium tremens,' William had told the confused and grieving widow. He had suggested she throw out all the brandy bottles, had asked for the return of the medicine bottles for the dispensary, prescribed tincture of opium to help her sleep. She had said he was 'very kind' and that Wickham had thought him the 'salt of the earth'.

The salt of the earth. A poisoner. The irony of it was not lost on William. Here he was, trained in all the modern methods for healing – and he had allowed a patient to pickle his innards with one of his father's quack cures.

'You're very glum,' said Lily one morning. 'In fact you're both very glum these days. What's the matter with you? It's spring. You're still young. What is there to be so miserable about?'

William glanced at Sasha across the breakfast table. Was she brooding about something too?

'Sasha needs a holiday,' said Aunt Georgie. 'It's been hard on her since she took on Meredith's schooling all by herself.'

It was true, Sasha was very pale. William realised he had not paid much attention to her since Christmas. He had been so obsessed by his own worries, and by work – January and February were bad months for any doctor, and Wickham's had not been the only death. He should have insisted they employ another tutor, *would* have insisted in different circumstances, but it had been so much less trouble to let Sasha do it; she had seemed to get a satisfaction from taking over the schoolroom.

'A holiday.' All at once the idea of Sasha going away for a while seemed very pleasant. He needed a breathing space; life would be easier without the constant fear of her discovering what was troubling his conscience. 'Why don't you visit your parents?' he suggested. 'You could take the children with you.'

'No, no. Don't take the children.' Aunt Georgie put her arm round Pippa as if to prevent her being snatched away that minute from the breakfast table. 'I should miss my little cherubs dreadfully. Lily and I can look after them.'

Sasha's spirits lifted at the prospect of going away. She looked at William; their glances met and shifted uneasily. Sasha saw how grey and careworn he was becoming but felt unmoved by the thought that he was overworking. Had she ceased feeling altogether since Gabriel had gone? Would she never recover from falling in love? It occurred to her that she needed to go far away from William, and from this house with all its associations, even from the children.

'Why don't you go to visit your sisters?' said Aunt Georgie. 'You were saying only yesterday that you haven't heard from Leah since her friend died. She must be feeling very lonely.'

Sasha considered the idea. Leah had sent such a brief, restrained note to say that Miss Ferrers had died. She felt a stab of guilt, she should have done more to console her than reply with a conventional letter. She remembered Herr Lindau. Death was so final and uncompromising; even its promise of eternal life shut one out in a chilly isolation.

'I shall do it,' she said. 'I shall visit Leah, and Lavinia and Mr Pickersgill.'

'At Easter?' suggested William, warming to the plan.

Sasha nodded. 'But I shan't tell them I'm going. Lavinia would only create a great deal of fuss and make Mr Pickersgill's life miserable with spring-cleaning. I'll simply arrive.'

'Oh, what a splendid idea!' Aunt Georgie clapped her hands with excitement. 'On their doorsteps! Like a surprise parcel sent in the post.'

Sasha was aware of a growing optimism as she travelled to Yorkshire. Was it the sense of having escaped or simply because it was spring? A mist of green buds veiled the hedgerows; lambs ran about in the fields, and wild daffodils grew on the railway embankments. She felt as if she were alive for the first time in months – since Gabriel had held her in his arms. She would forget him, she promised herself. She would get over the madness and her preoccupation with what might have been.

But as the train travelled north Sasha let her mind drift among memories. She remembered when he had first come to them, late, because he had got into an argument over Schumann. How fierce she had been with him, how determined not to like him. What would she have done then, if she had known she might grow to love him? Would she have sent him away, denied herself even the little happiness she had known?

Sasha tried to imagine where he was now – she had discovered he was not with Merrill in Bristol. She supposed she must be thankful; but it would have been less bleak to have heard something about him from time to time; or to have seen him – a chance encounter perhaps. Gripping her hands tightly in her lap, she tried to think of other things. But her mind returned, as it always did, to that last fateful day.

It was late when Sasha reached Runsby, too late, she decided, to arrive unannounced on anyone's doorstep. She went instead to an hotel near the station and booked herself into a room.

She awoke early the next morning, and went to the window. The fishermen had brought in their catch and the harbour was full of activity. The boats reminded her of the quayside in Bristol, except here the cargoes were almost exclusively of fish and the North Country voices sounded rough and foreign. She dressed, and ate breakfast alone in the dining room, fending off polite inquiries from the hotel-keeper about her business in Runsby, enjoying the bacon and black pudding and the notion of being a woman travelling alone for the first time in years.

Outside, the fishermen's catches were laid out on the wooden boards of the fish quay; men and women sat on

349

boxes and fish barrels, shouting and gossiping with one another. The women had coarse shawls over their hair and shoulders. They looked tough and hard, and their loud talk was invigorating. Sasha bought two herrings from a fishwife, and the woman tied them together for her to carry them. She and Leah would have the herrings for their dinner, thought Sasha, as she walked along the quay.

The sun glittered on the sea; the air smelled strongly of fish, and was dense with the cries of gulls and the noise from the harbour. She walked along by the water, seeing Leah and Miss Ferrers's cottage across the estuary. Would she tell Leah about Gabriel? But perhaps Gabriel had already told her what had happened – she remembered how close they had once been. Would Leah be hostile? Would she feel she had corrupted her boy, her beloved pupil?

Sasha crossed the swing bridge over the harbour, reluctant, now she was here, to spring herself on Leah too soon. As she reached the steps to the cottage, she pictured Miss Ferrers, who had sung so beautifully . . . How unfair God was, she reflected. Why did he always take the people one needed most?

Leah opened the door.

'Come in, I . . .' The smile of welcome died on her lips.

Sasha held out the fish. 'I've come bearing gifts.'

Leah glanced along the street. 'Are you alone?'

'Quite solitary. I've left them all behind. Husband, children . . . Aren't you going to ask me in?'

'Yes. Of course.' Leah hesitated, then opened the door wider so that Sasha might walk past her into the tiny entrance hall.

She seemed odd, Sasha thought, as Leah took the fish from her and disappeared into the kitchen with them; her hair was tied back loosely from her shoulders and she was still in her nightgown. But it was Leah's manner that was strange. Almost furtive – a strange adjective to apply to her – but the more Sasha thought about it, the more she was certain it was the only word to describe her sister's behaviour.

350

Leah returned quickly, wiping her hands on her night-gown. She glanced at Sasha and lowered her eyes. 'You'd better go through.'

Sasha's attention was distracted at once by a framed portrait on the sitting-room wall. 'You know how sorry I was about Miss Ferrers. I thought— well, I thought you'd want some company. But perhaps I shouldn't have come without telling you.'

'Darling, it's I who should be sorry.' Leah went to the window. 'It's lovely to see you. Of course it is. You simply took me by surprise.'

'Why? What are you hiding? You're behaving very peculiarly.' Sasha took off her gloves, slowly pulling the fingers free. At the same time, she heard the front door slam.

Leah's expression took on a vague air of desperation. 'Sasha – I'll explain.' She ran to the sitting-room door. 'Promise me . . . Look, simply stay there and don't move!'

Sasha waited, feeling profoundly unsettled. As she walked about the room, she tried to distinguish individual voices and words from the conversation in the hall. She was sure she could hear a man's voice, and Leah, talking urgently, her voice rising from time to time. Sasha remembered the joyous smile with which her sister had greeted her, and the nightgown . . . Did Leah have a lover? No wonder she was embarrassed. Why would she answer the door looking as if she had only that moment got out of bed, unless she had been expecting someone? Or someone's return?

Sasha went to the window and looked out at the grey, choppy sea. It was so out of character. Leah could hardly conceal anyone now. She might as well introduce him and be done with it. Did she think she was too narrow-minded to understand? Sasha looked round the room, searching for tell-tale signs. If the man *had* spent the night there, it was obvious he had not slept on the sofa. And the cottage had only one bedroom. She scanned the books scattered on the table. Aha! *two* empty coffee cups from the previous evening; a music manuscript, as if they had been studying it together. Her glance fell on the piano and on Leah's violin case. A second case leaned against the wall behind the piano . . .

The shock of recognition hit Sasha in the pit of her stomach. She would have known his violin case anywhere: the battered corners, the handle mended with string. She gave an involuntary cry of protest, remembering, years ago, Gabriel's infatuation with Leah. She pictured again Leah's air of abandon, the welcome in her expression when she had greeted her . . . Sasha was gripped by waves of revulsion as she went to the sitting-room door.

Leah was standing in the shadows by the stair. She had her arm round Gabriel as if trying to shake him into action. They turned to look at her, the sunlight from the sitting room illuminating the guilt on their faces – though Gabriel had an air less of guilt, than of having been struck by a blow that had all but felled him. Sasha tried to say something; but no words would come and she sank back against the wall.

Leah abandoned Gabriel. She ran to Sasha, shutting the door firmly on the hall and standing with her back against it as if to bar the way. 'Sasha, where else was he to go? He's told me all about his infatuation for you. He told me why he had to leave Penbury.'

'Oh? What did he say? That I made a complete fool of myself over him?' Sasha lifted her head with a bitter laugh. 'It's Kitty all over again. It seems all the men I've ever loved are bound to betray me with one or other of my sisters.'

'It isn't as bad as you think. He and I are . . . a comfort to one another. Oh, if you could only be less rigid! Do you have to see things in terms of morality or immorality?'

'Are you saying it isn't immoral for Gabriel to share your bed, when only last Christmas he was telling me he was in love with me?'

'He knew there was no hope. You had let him go.'

'What else could I do?' cried Sasha. 'Should I have left William and the children and run off with him?'

'No. Of course not,' Leah said more soberly.

'Why not? That's the way Kitty would have done it!'

They paused. In the silence they heard the front door open and close again quietly. Sasha felt hysteria rise in her. She folded her arms to stop herself shaking.

Leah went to the window and stood watching the street for several seconds. 'I asked him to stay here. I needed him very much while Felicity was so ill. And he has needed me. It hit him badly when he fell in love with you.'

'So I can see!'

'It's true.' Leah twisted her hair distractedly. 'Oh, why on earth did you have to encourage the poor boy in the first place? You knew what he was like. I told you how hopeless he always is.'

'I couldn't help myself. I was in love with him.' Sasha gave a cry of despair. 'I loved him, Leah. I did love him. I still love him dreadfully. I can't sleep at night for thinking about him. I dream of leaving William, of William dying . . . dreadful, dreadful things.'

'Oh, Sasha. My poor Sasha.'

Leah made a move towards her, but Sasha backed away shaking her head. 'I don't want your sympathy.' She put on her gloves. 'And you clearly don't need mine. I'm sorry. This is all my fault. I should of course have let you know I was coming.'

'Don't go. Not like this.'

'Yes. I really think I should.'

Sasha did not look about her as she left the house. She prayed she would not meet Gabriel at the quayside, and went straight to her hotel where she arranged for her trunk and boxes to be taken to Eskton. She caught the train, and did not begin weeping until it pulled out of the station, and then she could not stop. People stared at her. Her travelling companions looked the other way, embarrassed by the sight of a beautiful well-dressed woman behaving with such a loss of dignity in a railway carriage.

As Gabriel walked along the shore, he knew that he would never forget Sasha's expression. In that split instant he had seen that she still loved him. And then, such a look of loathing as her eyes had met his! What did it matter to her that before Leah took him in he had given up all hope of her, or of ever knowing happiness again? He saw in her eyes that he had betrayed her. He kicked out at a piece of driftwood, and it bounced along the sand.

He walked to the edge of the water, and for an instant seriously contemplated walking on into the waves. He imagined the sea lapping over his boots, over his knees – and on, deeper, until it swelled and broke over his head. In time the waves would deposit him, a piece of flotsam, on the shore.

He turned away. He knew his own nature well: his life was too precious to him. He knew too that he would recover from this latest blow.

Hours later, he returned to Leah's cottage and waited outside for a long time to be sure that Sasha had gone. Leah came out to him in the end.

'You foolish boy. You'll make yourself ill.'

Gabriel crouched by the sitting-room fire, his body hunched and brooding. 'I can't stay after this. It wouldn't be the same. And you don't need me – I do know that you don't really need me in the way I've needed you. It's best if I leave.'

'I was afraid of that.' Leah curled her legs under her on the sofa. 'So – where will you go?'

'I don't know, and to tell the truth I don't really care.'

'Oh, that will do,' Leah said impatiently. 'Haven't we had enough of that sort of talk?'

'You don't understand.' He went to the piano and played a few fitful notes. 'You don't know how it was between me and her.'

'You've only got yourself to blame. Falling in love with a married woman! Tell me, would it have been so desperate if she had not been married to William? You didn't even *like* one another when you were younger.'

He turned on her savagely. 'Have you any idea at all what it is to love someone and not be able to do anything about it – to feel as if you're being torn apart?'

'Yes,' Leah said simply. 'You don't stop loving someone when they're dead.'

Gabriel went to her, at once contrite, and knelt beside her. 'Leah, I'm so sorry. What a selfish pig . . .' He buried his head in her lap.

'No, no.' She stroked his hair. 'We mustn't quarrel. You and I have been friends too long for that. But now, I think you're right. You have to go. I've been wondering. Why don't you try again for the Hallé?'

'Don't tell anyone I'm here,' Sasha said when she had stopped crying and was sitting by Lavinia's fireside.

Lavinia handed her a glass of brandy and water, and waited for her to drink it. Mr Pickersgill, after a shocked conference with his wife, had left the two women alone. But Lavinia, faced with a white and shaking Sasha, would have been glad of his solid support.

'Especially, don't tell Leah I've come here,' Sasha warned her. 'I don't want *anyone* to find me.'

Lavinia threw up her hands in submission. 'Not if you say so. But you have to tell me what has happened.'

Sasha told her about falling in love with Gabriel and about Gabriel leaving Penbury. She described the shock of finding him at Leah's cottage. She told her everything except that Gabriel was Leah's lover.

'Of course, it was impossible for me to stay there knowing that Gabriel is lodging with her.'

'Impossible!' Lavinia echoed. 'Oh – but you did the right thing, Sasha. You were right to send Gabriel away once he had declared himself.'

'Not that William guessed anything . . .'

'Nevertheless, it happened. And if you love your husband—'

'Oh, I don't think I love William any more.' Sasha finished the glass of brandy.

'But that's terrible!' said Lavinia in a whisper. 'How can you *not* love the man you married?'

Sasha looked at her curiously. 'Don't you ever doubt

your feelings for Mr Pickersgill? Aren't you ever a little bit disappointed with him?'

Lavinia shook her head vehemently.

'The thing is,' Sasha said. 'I don't think I want to live any more as William's wife. I think I *could* leave him. Not for Gabriel. Not now. But simply to abandon the notion of marriage.'

'Leave him!' Lavinia's voice rose to a squeak. 'Sasha you can't leave your *husband*! You would have nothing. No reputation. Your life would be in ruins!'

'Your own life can't be that idyllic surely? Haven't you ever wanted to leave it all and run away?'

Lavinia paced the floor with her arms folded tightly. Taking the empty brandy glass from Sasha, she twisted it in her hands and then sat down suddenly on the opposite side of the fire. She glanced at the door as if there might be someone hiding behind it.

'Yes. Of course I've felt like escaping sometimes,' she said in a harsh whisper. 'When Mr Pickersgill makes me angry. And yes, I've been disappointed – irritated and frustrated. I know Martin has his faults, that he's slow and pompous, that he'll never set the world alight. But he has so many good points too. He's kind and affectionate and good with the children. And I make him very happy. What more can I ask from my marriage?'

'What more? Is making a man happy all we are to expect from our lives?'

'It's more than some women achieve. And there's very little a woman *can* achieve without the support of a husband. Am I so special that I should expect to accomplish things without him?'

'Yes! Why not? Why not demand a deeper fulfilment?'

If the catastrophe of loving Gabriel had done nothing else, it had made her discover her real needs again, Sasha realised: her need for music, for the things that mattered. 'William won't consider my returning to the concert platform. But Gabriel understood passionately about my music. He made me realise I'm only half alive without it.'

'Do you really think you could have found happiness

356

with Gabriel?' Lavinia said with an uncharacteristic look of scepticism. 'He's notoriously fond of being passionate about things. He's very engaging, very easy to love, but he's fickle, Sasha. He would have been head-over-heels in love with someone else after six months. Gabriel is a young man who falls in love at the wink of an eye.'

Sasha fell silent. How could she hope to make Lavinia understand the wonderful release, the joy and energy and feeling of relevance she had known with Gabriel? How could she understand it herself? He was living with her sister. He was sharing Leah's bed!

She leaned forward to warm her hands at the fire. 'May I stay here for a few days until I've decided what to do?'

'Isn't William going to wonder where you are?'

'He knows I'm here. He thinks I came to cheer Leah up after Miss Ferrers died.' Her mouth twisted in a bitter smile.

'Then, of course, you must stay as long as you like.'

'Don't tell Mr Pickersgill about Gabriel,' Sasha said as Lavinia showed her upstairs to one of the bedrooms. 'We'll make something up to explain why I was upset. Tell him something happened on the train . . .'

Lavinia promised not to tell her husband the true story. But of course she told Mr Pickersgill everything; they had few secrets from one another. Martin comforted her, saying she was not to worry about Sasha – who would come to her senses after a few days and go back to her husband. He told Lavinia how fortunate he was to be married to such a sweet, uncomplicated and faithful wife.

Sasha tortured herself that night with thoughts of Gabriel in Leah's arms, at one moment racked with spasms of jealousy, the next prostrate with self-pity. She tried to analyse why she had fallen in love with him, when he was so patently unworthy. Had she merely been tempted by the sinful nature of the friendship? One thing was clear. She could not go home again. How could she go on, year after year, married to William? How could she ever be happy again?

After a few days the torment lessened. Sasha began to

think of her children: Pippa would be missing her; and Meredith's lessons would have to resume after Easter. She thought of Lavinia's arguments that without a home or husband she would be deprived of all respect and dignity; and it occurred to her that it was not so terrible living in Penbury; she had her children; she had Aunt Georgie; she had her piano and her music . . .

'I've made a decision,' she told Lavinia one morning. They were walking through Eskton after visiting a sick neighbour with Lavinia's children; the girls had run ahead for a few yards.

'Sasha, I'm so relieved.' Lavinia hugged her. 'You're going home? It's been such a worry to us—'

Sasha halted. 'I'm going home. But I'm going to return to the concert platform as well. I shall do it with or without William's approval.'

'But you can't . . .' Lavinia's mouth widened in dismay.

'He'll come round. William's not used to my defying him. But once he sees I'm determined . . .' Sasha continued walking. She could hear the children's voices ahead of them, and the spring call of starlings, thrushes and blackbirds in every tree and bush along the way; they seemed to be heralding a new beginning.

Lavinia was quiet for a while. 'You know, William's a good man—'

'Yes, he is,' Sasha broke in quickly, as if reluctant to acknowledge the fact, but with a certainty that it was true. 'And being a good and decent man, William will see that our future together depends on my doing this, no matter what.'

William no longer feared the consequences of Wickham's death; nor did he dwell on what had caused it. Everyone seemed eager to attribute the sad affair to the evils of drink. William too began to accept that there could be no other explanation. What was more, he had decided there was no point in dissuading Wotherspoon from taking the restorative. Elliman's Elixir was harmless. To change the

358

medicine simply because Wickham had died would arouse unwarranted suspicions. Wotherspoon wasn't a medical man, he might get the wrong idea.

By the time Sasha returned, William had almost forgotten the Wickham incident and was looking forward to having his wife back where she belonged. She looked better, he thought, glancing at her from time to time, as he drove her home from the station. She did not have much to say, and seemed lost in a world of her own as she looked about her. But the trip to see her sisters had obviously done her a world of good.

'The Yorkshire air has put some colour in your cheeks again,' he told her, squeezing her waist as he helped her down from the carriage.

She looked at him with a bemused, distracted air.

They left Cope to put away the carriage and walked through the house to the garden. The children saw her from the lawn and came running towards her with whoops of joy.

'It's nothing to do with the air,' Sasha said. 'I feel well because I'm excited about the decisions I've been making.' She threw him a smile and hugged the children.

They approached Lily and Aunt Georgie sitting under the apple tree, Pippa and Meredith hung on to Sasha's arms.

'Decisions? Am I going to like them?' William murmured.

'What aren't you going to like?' asked Lily.

'My wife has been making decisions.' William bit his lower lip, watching as Sasha kissed Lily and Aunt Georgie, and sank into a garden chair.

'You look better, Sasha. You needed a holiday.' Aunt Georgie searched Sasha's face and seemed relieved at what she saw.

'What sort of decisions?' pestered Lily.

'It's an old one really. I'm going to play the piano professionally again.' Sasha smiled at them all. 'Why does sitting in a railway carriage always make one so very tired?'

Meredith caught hold of the apple tree and swung round the trunk. 'Mama is going to be a famous pianist

359

again. Mama is going to be a pianist again.'

Pippa took up the chant.

'Be quiet!' thundered their father. 'Sasha. We've talked about this before—'

'And I said at the time that I wouldn't do anything about it immediately. I wasn't so sure as I am now. I see now that it's *absolutely* what I have to do.'

'Ever since Ridgeway—'

'That man has nothing to do with any of this any more,' Sasha said coldly. 'It's my decision. Nobody has influenced me.'

William glanced at the others uneasily. Pippa was droning a protesting wail into Aunt Georgie's lap.

'We seem to have stalemate.' There was a malicious enjoyment in Lily's voice.

'I've written to Algie Ross.' Sasha took up the argument again when they were alone that evening. 'And I shall need to take a few lessons.'

'No. Categorically no, Sasha. I forbid you to contact your manager.' William climbed into bed.

'You can't *forbid* me!' Sasha turned on the dressing stool with her hairbrush poised in her hand.

'You will see that I can. I'm perfectly within my rights to prevent you from neglecting your family.'

'But you know very well the children wouldn't suffer! Your sister and your aunt are only too willing to play disciplinarian and nursemaid. Pippa already runs to Aunt Georgie rather than to me . . .'

'Ha! Exactly! I rest my case of neglect.'

'I shall do it anyway.' Sasha went on brushing her hair with elaborate serenity. 'I shall make a fuss and tell everyone what a horrible monster you've become.'

'Sasha, please. Be reasonable.'

'I *have* been reasonable. For years I've been reasonable, and dutiful. I've been the model doctor's wife. Now I want to do something that's important to *me*.'

'I'd forgotten how wilful you can be. You're not a child—'

360

'And this isn't a childish request. I *need* to play again. It would make me less . . . *discontented* with my life.'

'What about me?'

'You're not a child,' Sasha echoed.

He took comfort in bluster. 'You have responsibilities and duties.'

'Don't be so pompous!' Sasha flung down her hair-brush. 'Oh, William! What's happened to us? I don't seem to know you any more!'

The battle continued for days. The sound of raised voices carried up and down the stairs. Doors were slammed. Long silences lay heavily at mealtimes.

'Sasha seems very determined.' Aunt Georgie listened at the foot of the stairs to the rise and fall of an argument. She turned to Lily. 'I hope she wins. I think she's right. She *should* go back to being a pianist.'

'Her place is here.'

'And she still would be here most of the time. Are you and I such pathetic old souls that we can't run things without her from time to time? I shall talk to William.' Aunt Georgie folded her arms to reinforce her air of conviction. 'I refuse to be treated as an incubus! I have a place in this household. And so have you! It's time we got off our skinny old-maid backsides and did something useful for our keep!'

William gave way suddenly in the end. He stood in the doorway of the drawing room one afternoon as Sasha was playing part of the *Appassionata* Sonata. She heard him come in but ignored him.

'It's the first thing I ever heard you play,' he said.

'Yes. I remember.' She was surprised though that he too should have remembered it.

'Aunt Georgie seems to think this is important. She says that for you it's more than a battle of wills. She has offered to instruct Pippa, and suggests the Penbury curate might take on Meredith's schooling. He's a sound enough fellow.'

'I've always said Aunt Georgie talks more sense than people give her credit for.'

He cleared his throat a little. 'I've decided to be more reasonable . . . I mean, perhaps it wouldn't be so much of a sacrifice to let you do this thing. You could take a few lessons to polish up if that's what you think you need. See how you get along.'

Sasha stopped playing. She sat with her hands in her lap. 'You won't regret it,' she said at last. 'You'll see. It will make a great difference.' She looked up. 'I mean . . . if you had continued to treat me with such contempt, William, I think it would have been the end for us.'

He was uneasy with the word 'contempt' and puzzled as to what she could mean by 'the end'. But Sasha always did exaggerate. 'Yes, well, time will tell.'

Sasha did not hear him close the door. She began playing again. The music, turbulent, insistent, filled her head and body with exultation.

Chapter Seventeen

For hours every morning and afternoon Sasha practised scales and Herr Lindau's favourite exercise pieces; she studied new works to expand her repertoire; she took weekly lessons from a tutor in Bath. By the summer she knew she was ready.

'I'm sure you never played better. When āre you going to let it be known you're available?' said Aunt Georgie one afternoon, shielding her eyes from the sun as Sasha came towards her in the garden.

Sasha, exhausted by the hours at the piano, flopped on the grass beside Pippa, who was making daisy chains. She avoided looking at Aunt Georgie. 'It's not that easy.'

'I thought you had a manager.'

'Yes. Algie keeps writing to me. He's getting impatient and wants me to agree to a firm engagement.'

'Then perhaps you should.'

Sasha lay back on the grass and closed her eyes. She thought of the years of neglect, the piano gathering dust, the interruption to her career; waves of fright swept through her when she imagined how it would be to face a critical audience again. A shadow fell across her and she felt the brush of Pippa's fingers on her neck and the tickle of a daisy chain as she placed it over her hair. Sasha reached up, pulled Pippa down and kissed her, then released her as she wriggled away. She felt for the knots of flowers in her hair.

'I'm scared, Aunt Georgie. How can I bear to play in

front of a hall full of people? My hands will go rigid. My mind will go blank.'

'You've done it before.'

'I was only a girl, full of the arrogance of youth. I had a natural inclination to perform. What if it's all gone?'

Aunt Georgie was thoughtful as Sasha twisted the daisy heads between her fingers. 'Mr Viggers is singing in the chorus at a concert in Bath next month.'

'You think I could play there?'

'You know most of the people involved, and I don't think the programme is too rigidly fixed. It would be a good way to start.'

Sasha was silent. 'You're right, of course. You're always right. I'll talk to Mr Viggers.'

'Good.' Aunt Georgie caught at Pippa as she passed and pulled her on to her knee. 'Your Mama has made a great leap forward, my precious.'

Pippa laughed. 'No she hasn't. She's lying down.'

Sasha sat up and regarded Aunt Georgie with a quizzical smile. 'Mr Viggers' stay with the Turbots has become rather a permanent arrangement, wouldn't you say?'

Aunt Georgie blushed. 'He likes the area – and he's very popular here because of his singing.'

'Of course. His singing,' said Sasha gravely.

Mr Viggers was becoming well known in Bath and Bristol where he had frequently sung in oratorio. Sasha found herself placed low on the programme in the Bath concert. She took comfort from the fact, thinking people would have forgotten the early days of her career; they would not expect too much.

But the applause was loud and persistent as she walked to the piano; it was very clear that she was remembered in the town where she had made her début, and that expectations were high. Sasha grew cold with terror: she would disappoint them; they would sit in uneasy silence, applaud politely afterwards and say to one another that she had gone off.

As soon as she sat at the piano, self-possession took

hold of her. The music came to her rescue as it always had in the past. She played some of the *Songs without Words* and some Chopin. The applause was deafening as she took her bow.

When it was known that Sasha was playing in public again, the invitations began to arrive – from Bristol, Exeter and Bournemouth, and the smaller towns in the area. By the end of the summer, she had played in more than a dozen concerts, and her fear of audiences had faded.

William went to very few of her concerts. At first she assumed he was too busy: there were the matinées, when he was out on his rounds; there were days when Sasha had to travel some distance to afternoon rehearsals and it was impractical for him to travel separately to an evening performance. Lily made a point of staying behind to 'look after' William. But Aunt Georgie came to matinées with the children, and sometimes with Meredith's new tutor, Mr Duff, the Penbury curate.

The children sat in wonder through Donizetti and Berlioz, Mendelssohn and Schubert, and applauded vigorously after their mother's solo pieces.

Afterwards they would stroll together through whichever town Sasha was playing in. On the quay by the river in Exeter, they laughed at the memory of a lady soprano in a hat with a feather that had jiggled all through an aria. And they sang on the journey home, rounds – in silly voices, and at unconventional speeds – songs with actions to them, and melodies from the concerts they had heard.

There were many performances when Sasha travelled alone, stayed overnight in hotel rooms, and wondered why it was so impossible for William to get away from Penbury.

After a concert in Salisbury she returned home early the next morning, invigorated by the walk from the station, and met William in the hall.

'I caught the early train so as to get back sooner.' She seized his arm and kissed him affectionately. 'You should have come with me. The railway could easily have

365

returned you to your patients in time. You *must* come next time, William. It would be so satisfactory for me to know you were in the audience.'

He watched her as she removed the pins from her hat. 'Does it never occur to you, Sasha, that you expect everyone else to fit in with your plans, while accommodating yourself very little in return?'

She swung round in surprise. 'I don't mean I want to take you from your work. Only sometimes . . .'

'*Sometimes* it would be satisfactory for *me* if my wife thought her proper place was with her husband and family.' He turned and went through the door to the dispensary with an air of peevish dignity.

'He's jealous.' Aunt Georgie came out from the dining room.

Sasha ignored the remark. 'Where is everyone?'

'Lily is in her room. The children aren't up yet.'

Sasha followed Aunt Georgie into the drawing room and sat on the piano stool. As she leant her arms on the piano, she became aware of the draining effect of the previous night's concert. She had forgotten how physically exhausting performances were. William, she was sure, had no idea of the demands on her. 'I wish he would try to understand how important this is for me, Aunt Georgie.'

'My nephew is jealous,' repeated Aunt Georgie. 'He's angry because you've a vocation stronger than his own.'

Sasha looked up with a dry laugh of surprise at the idea that William was not wholly absorbed by his medical career.

Aunt Georgie set her mouth in an expression of confirmation and nodded her head.

She was right, thought Sasha. William's youthful idealism was gone, eroded by more worldly concerns. The realisation lessened him a little more in her eyes and she felt depressed. 'We've grown so distant with one another, Aunt Georgie, and I don't know who has been at fault. William would say it's because I'm no longer being a *proper* wife . . .'

'Not a proper wife?' Aunt Georgie frightened by her

own question, pretended to be interested in something outside the window. The phrase implied the kind of intimacy between a husband and wife that was not a subject for discussion.

Sasha exchanged a glance with her. She thought of her recent sexual encounters with William, which had become a mere contractual habit: a man had the right to enjoy his wife; a woman was bound by duty . . . Sasha sometimes wondered whether William found any enjoyment at all in the act, so perfunctory had it become for him. For herself, only a shadow of her former tenderness remained; there was rarely any pleasure.

'We don't share anything any more, Aunt Georgie. No confidences or jokes or talk about the children. I've got so used to coming home after a performance, you telling me stories about what the children have been doing, and me telling you anecdotes about the concert and the players. If I'm honest about it, I would *rather* share them with you. You don't judge and censure and make me feel as if I'm being selfish. *Am* I? I *do* feel guilty when I'm away. But what am I to do? I can't turn down opportunities to play. Not at this stage. Is it self-indulgent of me to want to play again?'

'Perhaps. A little.'

'But aren't *men* selfish too? Don't they pursue *exactly* what they want and demand their wives want the same, as a matter of course? Life according to rules laid down by the master of the house. Have I to be a slave to all that simply because I'm a married woman?'

'Don't most women marry for selfish reasons? Because they want a home and respect and children, and marriage is the only way of achieving those things.'

'Is that what you would have wanted?' said Sasha gently.

'If the chance had come I would have taken it, the same as everybody else. I might have pretended to be in love. But it didn't happen. No man ever considered me a good enough catch.'

'There's Mr Viggers.'

'He hasn't asked me,' Aunt Georgie said quickly. 'Nor likely to, I dare say.'

And what a mercy that was, thought Sasha to herself. How could she leave her children at home if Aunt Georgie were to desert her?

Sasha's performances were being talked about. It was said in musical circles that she had returned to the concert platform with an added dimension to her playing. Her total absorption, her fire when playing virtuoso passages and an air of pathos in the lyrical ones, aroused an emotional response in her audience. They said she played without affectation; that it was as if she understood the music intimately, as if at one moment she was deeply moved by some remembered joy, in the next weighted by sadness.

'You can't hide away in the West for ever,' Algie wrote to her that autumn. 'People have long memories and they want to hear you again. I'm planning a winter series of concerts in the Midlands. Can you say yes?'

Sasha folded the letter carefully. 'Algie Ross wants me to do a tour. It would mean being away for longer than usual.' She shared a glance of suppressed excitement with Aunt Georgie across the breakfast table. William was eating grilled kidneys. He did not look up, nor did he comment.

Lily spoke first. 'You knew it would come to this sooner or later.'

'Yes. I suppose I did.'

'You ought to say no.'

'Why ought Mama to say no to a tour?' said Meredith. 'I think she should play everywhere – Bristol, Edinburgh, Africa, America. All over the world.'

'Be quiet, Merry!' said William. 'You don't know what you're talking about.'

Sasha said nothing. Aunt Georgie opened her mouth to speak in her defence and Sasha silenced her with a shake of the head.

'Come along.' Aunt Georgie scooped the children from

their chairs with a sweep of each arm. 'Your tutor will be here in half an hour. Up those stairs. We have to be ready for him.' She glowered at Lily and waited until she took the hint and left the room as well.

'Very diplomatic,' said William when they had gone. 'I'm beginning to wonder whose side Aunt Georgie is on.'

'There aren't any sides,' Sasha said. 'And she means well. If it wasn't for Aunt Georgie . . .'

'You know what is meant by a tour. How long does Ross propose to keep you away?'

Sasha looked again at the letter. 'Three weeks. Perhaps four. But it will be over before Christmas. We shall have a family Christmas. And I could probably get home in between some of the engagements—'

'This is only the beginning,' William said miserably. 'You're going to do more and more concerts that will take you away from us. What are you trying to do, Sasha?'

'To be *myself*. I'm a musician. I can't live the rest of my life denying it.'

'You managed very well before.'

'Because I was fooling myself. Because there was no choice while I had to take care of the children. Now we have Aunt Georgie.'

'You are so irresponsible! Do you really think Aunt Georgie is a substitute for the children's real mother?'

'They love her. And they have me all to themselves when I'm here. You heard Merry. He *wants* me to do it.'

William wiped his mouth with his napkin and stood with an exaggerated air of resignation. 'I long since discovered there's no use arguing with you when you've set your mind against me, Sasha. You did it over not sending Meredith away to school. You do it constantly over domestic affairs. You'll have your way no matter what.'

'So, I have your blessing?' she said eagerly. 'Oh, William. We don't have to be bitter with one another about it. We could make this work so well. We *will* make it work—'

'No, Sasha, *you* will make it work. You will convince yourself that your performances bring colour to people's

369

lives, and you'll go on closing your eyes to the fact that you're neglecting your home and children. You'll win Aunt Georgie to your side. You'll try to manipulate the situation to make it seem as if I've become a cruel, tyrannical husband. But I shall not give you that pleasure. You may go on this tour. You have my permission, but you don't have my blessing. In fact, you can go to the devil for all I care. I wash my hands of the whole business.'

Sasha sat, stunned by his parting shot. Did he hate her so much? And in such a short time had they come to this? She wanted to run after him, to shake him and make him see how obstinate and stupid he was being. She made an involuntary move . . . and checked it. William *expected* her to run after him! He wanted her to beg his forgiveness and say that she wouldn't go, like any normal, docile wife. Simply because he had told her to go to the devil.

Sasha reached out and took a piece of cold toast from the stand; she buttered it slowly and deliberately and smeared marmalade on it. She ate the thin, chewy wafer as if relishing it, though she was not hungry. Yes, she would go to the devil, she vowed; she would embrace the devil with all the vigour and passion of her art.

Algie Ross had his own theatre in London where he had become both trainer and conductor to a small orchestra. In Sasha's nine-year absence he had brought Ross's Orchestra up to almost fifty players, and the names of Ross's Theatre and Ross's Popular Concerts were becoming as famous as those of Hallé in Manchester and Merrill in Bristol. He had invited Sasha to play in a series of solo, chamber and orchestral engagements, touring the country with his orchestra; he had already booked the theatres and halls and engaged other solo players.

'You and I were bound to work together again,' he told her when they met in London. 'It was the worst mistake you ever made when you gave it up.'

'And the best thing you ever did was to start your own orchestra,' said Sasha. '*Director* Ross! If only Herr Lindau could have lived to see it.'

'It's tempting to become a tyrant,' he admitted. 'The public almost expect it. And the orchestra would tolerate an ego-maniac so long as he paid them. But I've seen too many orchestras run on fear – they don't give of their best.'

If the orchestra gave of their best for Algie, he gave in return. At the end of a performance he seemed half dead from exhaustion. 'A conductor only has to wave his arms, and he's in possession of the most wonderful sound!' he told Sasha one day. 'It's ten times better than playing a single instrument!'

'I shall stay with my piano,' Sasha laughed.

'You've matured,' he reflected. 'I remember you as all light and passion. Now, you seem to have found the darker side of music.'

'You have to have taken a few knocks in life to discover it,' said Sasha, half joking.

He nodded, taking her seriously. But there was still something missing, Algie thought. Sasha played with an almost fearsome passion, but the fire in her playing had little comforting warmth or joy.

The tour of concerts took in Leicester and Birmingham, and other towns in the Midlands. Ross's Orchestra was received with ever larger audiences. Sasha wrote to the children, and she wrote to William, filling page after page with cheerful, unrepentant accounts of her performances. She received stilted letters from William in return.

'I want you to play with the orchestra in London, Sasha,' Algie told her towards the end of the tour. 'I'm planning a series of concerts early in January. You've got to say you'll do it.'

'So soon?'

He smiled, waiting for her reply. Sasha had confided in him a little, and he knew of her difficulties.

'The *Musical World* has been printing glowing notices after your triumph in Birmingham; you'll have them all in the palm of your hand, Sasha.'

'Oh, Algie . . . Let's get Christmas over first?'

'You'll agree. You know you can't resist the idea. It's

time that husband of yours recognised how much more valuable you are to him as a pianist than you are as a domestic drudge.'

'Would you say the same if it were your wife?'

'My wife's talents are more naturally inclined to feminine preoccupations,' Algie said complacently. 'Her greatest pleasure is in making my life comfortable.'

Sasha could not deny that the role of public performer and domestic comforter were totally incompatible. Over Christmas, she formed an uneasy truce with William. She had missed the children, and was thrown into a more mellow mood. After all, she *had* deprived them all of her presence for three weeks; she *had* neglected her role as wife and mother.

'I don't know how you do it, Mrs Elliman. Everything runs so smoothly, even though we never see you in Penbury these days,' said Mrs Wotherspoon with a hint of spite when they met outside church on Christmas morning. 'You must bless the day you took on dependent relatives.'

'But it's only right we poor relations should earn our keep.' Aunt Georgie had overheard. 'My nephew might feel inclined to consign us to the workhouse if we didn't, Mrs Wotherspoon.'

'Don't be silly, Aunt,' William said evenly. He smiled and tipped his hat at the Wotherspoons, and taking Aunt Georgie by the elbow steered her down the church path towards their carriage. 'But I might consider the workhouse, if you don't mind your tongue,' he hissed. 'We can't afford to upset people like the Wotherspoons.'

'We soon shall though,' said Lily, with an enigmatic glance at Sasha. 'If Sasha goes on as she is doing – concerts here, concerts there. You'll soon be a rich man, William.'

It was a side to things that William had not overlooked. If he was truthful, it was the one thing about Sasha's venture that had contributed towards his letting her have her own way. He remembered only too well the money she had brought to the marriage from her earlier career;

and it was tempting to look forward to such riches again. Financial security would cushion the stresses of being a doctor. There would be no need to worry about the cost of keeping up a carriage – nor all the other essential ingredients for maintaining a lifestyle appropriate to his position in the town. He would feel at one with people like the Wotherspoons; he would be able to wave an airy hand about unpaid fees. And he would tell Wotherspoon he refused absolutely to supply him with any more bottles of Elliman's Elixir and warn him to give up his immoral ways.

At the same time, the money from Sasha's playing made William uneasy. Was it moral to pocket his wife's income while professing disapproval over the way it was earned? *Professing* disapproval? No, dammit. He did disapprove. He wanted the old Sasha back, the one who had told him when she married him that she was weary of the concert circuit, that nothing mattered to her except being his wife, helping him in his career and making him happy. Since coming home from her tour she had been loving and affectionate towards Aunt Georgie and the children, but her manner with him was . . . polite. What a cold, ugly little word, and yet it exactly described her. His wife was polite towards him. He glanced at her opposite him in the carriage, and with a profound shock he felt a sob rise to his throat. She seemed more lovely than ever since she had been playing again – alive and vivacious; and yet she was cut off from him; he had no idea what she was thinking, no means of getting beyond that barrier of indifferent courtesy.

Sasha was remembering another Christmas. Was it really a year since Gabriel had held her in his arms? She had thought she loved him – *could* have loved him, she knew, more than any man she had ever met. Was it her destiny, always to be cheated of deep happiness? She glanced at William. If only they could get back to the relationship they had once had, before the fading of his ideals and her loss of commitment to them had spoiled it all.

She thought of London, troubled by a conflict of

loyalties. That morning, she had put the notion of another tour to William. He had said with a pained look that she must do as she pleased from now on, and then he had given her a Christmas present, a silver bangle inscribed with both their names. She would not give in, Sasha told herself fiercely. Not to moral blackmail, nor to her own mistaken sense of moral conscience. She *would* acknowledge that devil or angel that was her spiritual driving force.

Meredith crept closer beside her, and she put her arm round him. He had always been her favourite. For all his pretence at self-reliance, he needed her more than Pippa did. She squeezed his arm. 'I love Christmas. Don't you? I'm glad it's cold and frosty and there's a lovely fire waiting when we get home.' She threw back her head and let the wind sting her face.

There had been a time, she recalled, when she had held out against William buying a pony and carriage, and had given in only because of the children, though she could not now remember what the children had to do with it; the carriage had only made Pippa and Merry demand they ride short distances, where previously they would have walked. Even she had been seduced in the end by the convenience.

Meredith was too full of the moment to speak; he loved the pleasure of bowling along on a level with the hedgerows, the pungent smell of the pony on the sharp air, the rumble of carriage wheels and the clop of hooves on the road. When he was a man, he would have a dozen carriages; he would drive his mother about and take her to concerts and parties. He would not resent her concerts the way his father did. He hated him for making his mother unhappy about wanting to play the piano for people. Meredith remembered the duets Sasha had played with Gabriel, and he felt an acute longing for those days to return. He could never tell anyone how much he missed his tutor; it was a secret disappointment at the bottom of his heart, which caught him unawares sometimes and made him want to cry. His present tutor was dull and strict and did not understand when he made mistakes in his spelling. Mr Duff did not play the piano, and had no idea at all how to play the viola.

The Penbury Musical Society had asked Sasha to play in a concert on Christmas afternoon. Afterwards, she went upstairs to the bedroom and sat on the bed with Algie's contract on her knee. Sounds drifted up to her; Aunt Georgie calling to the children, and the clatter of crockery and cutlery as dinner was being prepared. She was aware that they could all manage without her, even on Christmas Day.

'So – why hesitate?' she asked herself. Why did it seem such an irrevocable step to commit herself to the London concerts? Sasha looked at the document in her lap and took it over to her writing desk. She sat for a long time before taking up her pen to sign her name.

The first engagement was to be a concert at the Crystal Palace. The building glittered in the January sunshine, a vast, almost mystical edifice. Sasha had travelled by train from her hotel, and even from outside she could hear the players already tuning up for the morning's rehearsal.

Algie hurried along the gravelled walk to meet her. 'Sasha! A happy New Year to you. Wonderful! Wonderful!' He talked excitedly as he hurried her towards the concert room. 'It's going to be a splendid season. We'll discuss the programmes later.' He paused outside the door. 'Sasha, I've arranged for another soloist to join us.'

She raised her eyebrows. 'Playing safe, Algie?'

'I didn't know whether you would agree to come. I had to have some kind of insurance. I heard this fellow play a few weeks ago with Arabella Goddard. He only arrived, like you, this morning. But my instinct was right. He's a genius, Sasha. He's exhilarating, hypnotic. The public will love him.'

'Another pianist?' Sasha felt slightly aggrieved.

'No, no. Not a pianist . . .'

Sasha came to an abrupt halt as they entered the hall.

She was at an advantage, in that she saw Gabriel a few seconds before he saw her; she was thankful for those seconds as her stomach somersaulted violently.

He was talking to a couple of viola players, laughing in the relaxed, easy way she remembered. He had changed not at all since the days when she had fallen in love with him – and a great deal since the morning at Leah's cottage when his face had been white with guilt.

Sasha found her voice. 'Mr Ridgeway and I already know one another. We've played together before.'

'You have? But then you'll understand why I'm so excited about him.'

In that instant Gabriel turned and saw them. He looked from Algie to Sasha, then recovered quickly as they walked towards him.

'You're surprised, Mr Ridgeway?' said Algie. 'I understand that you and Mrs Elliman are already old friends.'

'Yes,' said Gabriel doubtfully. Then with more conviction, 'Yes, I'm surprised. I thought Mrs Elliman was never going to return to the concert platform.'

'Algie can be very persuasive,' said Sasha in a low voice. She held out her hand. 'Mr Ridgeway. How do you do?'

'I'm very glad you're playing again.' Gabriel shook her hand and released it quickly as if he had been stung. 'And I'm well enough. Thank you.'

Sasha turned to Algie. 'I should like to talk with you in private for a moment.' She moved away, not daring to look back at where Gabriel was standing.

'I can't play with that man,' she said. 'You should have told me about him sooner.'

'But I've heard him play. He has the same compelling quality as you have, Sasha. Together—'

'I know him,' Sasha hissed. 'He once tutored my son. He's . . . not to be trusted.'

'I don't understand.'

'He's a notorious flirt, Algie. He had to leave our employ. The man is quite without principles where women are concerned.'

376

'You mean – he chased your servants?'

'No—' Sasha protested, picturing poor Bertha. She thought of Lottie and Henrietta Turbot. 'But there were young women. He had to go.'

'You can't let your objections to a man's morals get in the way of a concert performance. I would have to dismiss half the orchestra!'

'Algie,' she said desperately. 'Please . . . It's all very embarrassing.'

'I don't care what Ridgeway's done, you'll simply have to put your moral scruples aside.'

'This is important – a matter of honour. Either he goes – or I do.'

Ross's patience snapped. 'Do I have to remind you that you signed a contract at Christmas, Sasha? I want you to discuss the programme for the series with Ridgeway, and play the "Kreutzer" with him at this evening's concert. And you'd better be pleasant to him. I've told him you'll rehearse together for a couple of hours after the main rehearsal.' He beckoned Gabriel over to them. 'I'll leave you to sort the matter out.'

'I can't go through with this,' Sasha said, shaking her head as Gabriel came towards her.

'But we must. Everyone will guess. Sasha, you'll be compromised.' He glanced over his shoulder. Already they were attracting attention from the other orchestra players.

'I can't! And that's an end to it.'

'I'll try to keep out of your way.'

'Keep out of the way? How can you, when Algie wants us to play the "Kreutzer" this evening. Oh! This is impossible!'

'No,' he said under his breath. 'You'll get through it. And so shall I – as I've got through everything else until now. We must both know the "Kreutzer" well enough to play it blindfold. That's how we shall rehearse it and how we shall perform it. Blind and deaf to everything except the music.'

Sasha watched Gabriel return to the ranks of violinists.

Her mind felt numb. She would not be able to play. He had ruined everything. Why? Why him, Algie? she asked silently as she walked to the piano. She took off her hat and gloves with trembling hands.

'Mrs Elliman won't be late for your rehearsal together. She's reliable – as far as that sort of thing goes.'

Algie waited with Gabriel in the cold shadows outside the concert hall. Sasha had made an excuse not to eat lunch with the other players, who were taking a break before the evening performance.

Algie began to pace up and down and to look more frequently at his watch. 'I don't understand.' He cast a doleful look at Gabriel. 'I must say, if this is your fault, it's something I didn't bargain for. You'd better tell me about it.'

'There's nothing to tell. I tutored the Ellimans' son for almost six months . . . We didn't get on and I had to leave.'

'Mrs Elliman says there was some trouble. That you left the town under a cloud.'

Gabriel's composure wavered. He struggled to understand what Sasha might have told him.

'Come – we're both men of the world, Mr Ridgeway,' Algie laughed. 'I'm not going to hold it against you if you sowed a few wild oats in Penbury. But you know how word gets around. You must have been careless for Sasha to have taken moral umbrage. Am I going to have outraged fathers coming after you with shotguns if we do any concerts together in the West Country?'

'I think not. It was all a misunderstanding,' Gabriel said. 'I'll explain properly to Mrs Elliman.'

'Good man. I simply need to know you won't let me down. We have thirteen concerts to get through and a number of musical parties at my house.' Algie paused. 'Thank God! Here she comes. Talk to her. Charm her a little.'

Gabriel caught his breath as Sasha came towards them. The sun lit her hair from behind, giving it the effect of a wiry halo. He was struck as always by her energy and the air of determination she carried with her. Where had she been? Had she eaten alone because she could not bear to be near him?

'Mr Ridgeway and I have been clearing the air,' said Algie. 'And I want you to be reasonable, Sasha.'

'I've never been *un*reasonable,' Sasha said with a chill little smile. 'We've known one another a long time, Algie. Have I ever given you cause to complain?'

'Sasha, please . . . For me. Make an effort.' Algie gave them a tight smile and walked away.

'You seem to have given Ross the impression I despoiled half the women in Penbury,' Gabriel said as they walked back towards the concert hall.

'No,' Sasha protested. 'No. But he assumed that was it . . . How could I have explained?'

They walked on in silence. Sasha opened the paper Algie had given her, listing the proposed programmes for the concerts. To her relief he had concentrated on light-weight, popular pieces, nothing too demanding on the emotions, little except the 'Kreutzer' to remind her . . . She thought of that moment over a year ago when her longing for Gabriel had overwhelmed her. She had loved him. She had believed him when he said he loved her.

'There wasn't a day went by when I didn't long to see you,' Gabriel said quietly, intercepting her thoughts.

'All I can say to that is, you didn't lose much time in finding consolation.'

'I'd given up all hope of you. What was I to do? Leah has always been my sanctuary when I was in trouble . . . Besides, she needed someone there after Miss Ferrers died.'

They entered the empty concert room and Sasha closed the door firmly behind them. 'Do you love her?' she said leaning against it.

Gabriel turned away impatiently and, walking to the violin stands, unpacked his violin from its case. 'Of course I love her. I've always loved her. But not in the way I loved you.'

'How many ways are there? You shared her bed!'

'And you wanted *me* all the time you made love to your husband. Bedding someone doesn't make it the real thing. You know it doesn't.' He flung her a look almost of hatred, challenging her to deny it.

Sasha was shocked by the speed with which they had reached this point. She had set herself such reasoned conditions for the rehearsal: there would be no questions, no recriminations, no looking back. They were thrown together by chance as colleagues, and they would find a rational basis on which they could work together: music would be the common ground.

She went to the piano. 'This isn't what we're here to talk about,' she said, but she could feel the heat of the blood in her cheeks, and her heart beat erratically.

'I agree. It's irrelevant now. We must forget it.' He began tuning the violin. 'What has Ross planned for the rest of the series?'

She read out the few violin and piano duos.

'It sounds straightforward enough. We needn't spend too much time rehearsing together. Shall we begin on the Beethoven?'

They began to play.

The warmth and passion of the sonata worked its familiar magic on Sasha, and she began with a fierce energy, fuelled by anger and memories of her journey to Yorkshire. She sensed a violent energy in Gabriel's playing too. But after a while the vitality of the music took possession of her; she felt the rapport she had always known when playing with him; their partnership became selfless and unselfconscious. They worked at it in the way Gabriel had said, the only way possible – blind and deaf to everything except the music.

When Algie entered the hall they had perfected the Finale. He looked from one to the other. There were tears in his eyes when it was over. 'Thank you. I knew, you see . . . Thank you.'

Sasha looked at Gabriel. Their glances met and Sasha realised with a shock that she still wanted him. Worse, there was no mistaking the expression in Gabriel's eyes. He was still in love with her, she thought, with a leap of her heart.

She packed up her music briskly. This was not why she had defied William and almost forsaken her marriage. She had not practised for months and months on end to come back to this. She had escaped because of her music, to be herself, to discover the truth about what she wanted and what was fulfilling.

Algie waylaid her as she got up to go. 'Do you think you could both manage a soirée tomorrow evening? I've promised some old friends. Very informal. You need only play the finale to the "Kreutzer" – and some fill-in pieces perhaps. There will be one or two critics . . .'

'Yes,' said Sasha. 'Of course.'

'At my house. Come in the morning for a brief rehearsal and stay for lunch. Mrs Ross will be delighted to see you again.'

'I have to go,' Gabriel said. 'I have to find lodgings still.' He went to the door. 'Until the concert tonight.'

'And tomorrow's soirée?' Algie prompted. 'A rehearsal – and you'll stay to lunch too, Mr Ridgeway?'

'Yes,' called Gabriel. 'Yes. I'll be there.'

Algie Ross lived at Holland Park in a mansion surrounded by elm trees. The trees offered a backdrop beyond the windows of the music room where the Ross family often held private soirées, and entertained artists and musicians.

On the morning after the Crystal Palace concert, a fire burned in the hearth in anticipation of Gabriel and Sasha's arrival. The room was empty except for a lone figure; Algie sat at the piano and fingered the keys in a wistful way that would have surprised many who knew him.

Algie Ross had a reputation for being short on sentiment, and was known as a man who lived by music rather than for it. He would have been the first to acknowledge that he was a failed musician; his career as a pianist had ended many years ago with a painful rheumatic condition

in his hands. But Algie could recognise genius in others –
and not simply for its commercial potential. In Gabriel's
playing he heard a sublimity that he would not easily
forget. Sasha was good, very good, now she had matured;
and there were times when her playing could make the
hair stand up on the back of his neck. His mind buzzed
with the excitement of his discovery. A partnership of the
kind impresarios dreamed about. But, on a practical level,
if he had to choose between them, Ridgeway was a man
and dependable; women had a tendency to let you down.

He considered Sasha's reaction to playing in concerts
with Ridgeway. She had always been so professional
about her playing before. If there was any discord still, if
he had to choose . . .

The sound of the door bell interrupted his thoughts.

Gabriel handed his coat and hat to the maid and walked
into the music room.

'Mr Ridgeway, come and warm yourself by the fire.'

'Mrs Elliman isn't here yet?' Gabriel laid his violin case
on the piano and went to the fire, spreading his hands and
flexing the fingers. He glanced at the painting on the wall
over the mantelpiece; he had known that *The Beautiful
Hammond Girls* was in Ross's possession; but it seemed
strange to see Leah looking down at him, dressed in a
clinging green robe. The painting transported him immediately to the days when he had been a raw youth, visiting
London for the very first time, eager for the experience of
university, of falling in love, of grasping life and all it had
to offer. He could not look at the image of Sasha for more
than an instant, seeing a figure in warm red velvet, small
neat curves, a fiery vitality. She was not one of those
women who offered serenity and an air of feminine calm.
There was a restlessness in everything about her.

'I'm glad you sorted out your differences,' Algie was
saying. 'You'll learn to ignore small unpleasantnesses
after a while. They happen all the time in an orchestra.
Disagreements. People get on your nerves on tour. It all
disappears in the performance.'

'Yes . . . I'm sure.' Gabriel had stopped listening; he

heard only the clang of the outside bell. He had thought he was calm. After the previous night's concert he had convinced himself he was in control of his feelings. He listened to the sound of voices in the hall and his heart pounded harder and faster as he counted the unbearable seconds. He turned to the door, hands behind his back, digging his nails into his knuckles until it felt as if they would touch the bone.

In a burst of glory Sasha came into the room. He had thought about her all night; the way she moved, the way she looked, the way she spoke. Her energy seemed bound in tightly: a sense of so much passion reined in. She wore a close-fitting dark red dress with very tight sleeves and a richly embroidered collar, over it a fitted black velvet coat which she was unbuttoning as she came, and a little hat with an upturned brim and a feather; these last she handed to the waiting maid. Gabriel took in every detail of her. He noticed the way she avoided his eyes as Ross took her hand and kissed it, the uncertain flick of her eyelashes, the firm dark curve of her eyebrows, the small lines of tension between them and at the edges of her mouth – had she spent a sleepless night too? He saw the curve of her breast rise and fall in agitation and the shimmer of light on her ash-coloured hair. She raised her eyes only briefly as she stepped towards him and their hands touched in a brief gesture of greeting.

Algie went to the door. He wagged a finger, like a schoolmaster admonishing his pupils. 'I'll leave you to run through the music.'

Gabriel stood by the fire with his hands still thrust behind his back. He wanted to run away from the situation. How could they play duets together, eat lunch at Ross's table, behave as if they were indifferent to one another? He felt rooted to the hearth. The heat from the fire burned his hands and the back of his neck, and he felt faint with indecision. He knew if he moved, he would go to her this time and crush her in his arms.

Sasha hesitated. She looked at the painting on the wall because she could not bear to look at Gabriel. *The*

Beautiful Hammond Girls. How they had all changed. How naive she had been then, with her imaginings about love. She had known nothing at all. Herr Lindau's words came back to her and would not go away: 'You have other needs, Sasha. Everyone needs more than their art . . .' She wanted Gabriel. Nothing had changed. And she did not know what to do today, any more than she had when he had handed her a letter saying his love for her was destroying him.

She went to the piano. 'Do you want to play the "Kreutzer" again at this evening's party – or something less intense?' She spoke in a tight, cold voice that seemed disconnected from her, and played a phrase from the sonata.

Gabriel gave a frantic, reckless cry. 'How can you go on behaving as if we mean nothing at all to one another?'

She did not look up. 'We've been apart for a year. You shared a bed with my sister. We have to.'

'No. We don't. For a whole year . . . It's been like losing my senses.'

'This is very wrong of you to stir it all up again. I'm a married woman, Gabriel,' she said in a low, insistent tone. She tried to continue playing, and banged out chords. 'I have children and a husband – a good husband, who needs me.'

'But you don't love him!'

Sasha picked up Gabriel's violin case. She concentrated on opening it and taking out the violin. The sheen on the polished wood, the details of the instrument's contours and the knowledge that he had held it close sent an unbearable longing through her. She handed it to him with the bow, without looking at him. 'Take it! Tune it!'

He took the violin from her reluctantly and tuned it with a restrained, almost violent negligence.

Suddenly, as she hesitated, Gabriel put the violin to his chin. He began the opening phrase of the Mendelssohn F minor sonata, playing with a haunting and passionate intensity, as he had played that afternoon in Sasha's drawing room when she could no longer hide her feelings from him.

'Don't—' Sasha begged. 'You mustn't. It isn't fair of you.'

But he did not stop, and the violin notes rose and twisted and filled the room with sound. 'Help me,' Gabriel said. 'For God's sake, have pity on me.'

Sasha began the simple melody and the piano and violin mingled in a sweeter sadness than she had ever known. She could not look at Gabriel; she knew that if she did she would weep. They found a solace in the music; but as the notes became more impassioned and despairing, the hopelessness of their situation entered Sasha's playing.

She began the second movement, and the violin tore at her heart. She tried to go on, and could not. 'So sad! So sad!' She broke off, looked up, and saw that Gabriel was weeping. 'No. My love . . .' She sprang from the piano and went to him, taking the violin from his hands. She kissed the salt from his cheeks, felt his mouth against her hair. They could stay apart no longer and pressed each other close, hands clutching hands, his mouth to hers.

'My love. My own,' Sasha breathed.

'When you saw me with Leah . . .'

'Hush! It doesn't matter. None of it matters.'

'I wanted to die. I want to die now – I couldn't believe it yesterday – meeting again, playing together again. It was like a dream. It was agony. If I lose you now . . .'

'We have to decide what we are going to do,' Sasha whispered. She touched his face, hardly daring to believe that she held him, that his arms were around her and she could feel his heart beating against hers. 'Algie will be back. We have to eat *lunch* with Mrs Ross.'

'I can't let you go. Not now. We can pretend. We'll fool everyone.'

'You haven't met Mrs Ross. She's that rare combination – inquisitive *and* intelligent. Oh, Gabriel. This is lunacy.'

But a recklessness had entered Sasha. Her resolve had evaporated when he held her, and she knew that this time she was not going to let him go. She was tired of forever doing the right thing, of the emptiness and sterility of a marriage without love. They would find a way to fool everyone – William, Lily, the whole of Penbury, and Algie and his perceptive, hawk-eyed wife. A tide of exuberance welled up inside her; she put a hand to her mouth and smothered a burst of laughter.

'It isn't *funny*,' Gabriel protested.

'No. It's not.' She was sober again. 'We're going to have to be careful . . . and sensible.'

'Devious and underhand.' He had caught her wildness. His eyes reflected her excitement.

She looked at him in wonder. 'Are we mad, do you think? What are we doing?'

When Algie came in, they were practising the 'Kreutzer' with glorious bravura. Their flushed faces caused Algie no more thought than that the heat from the fire and the vigour of the music had contributed a healthy radiance to the Finale of the sonata.

They sneaked little glances at one another during lunch and congratulated themselves that they had beaten the observant eye of Mrs Ross.

'If we've not already lost our senses, I soon shall be in that pitiful condition,' Sasha whispered later when they toured the garden, and she was able to brush against him.

'I love you.' He caught her hand in his.

But Sasha had not entirely lost her senses. A cold voice of reason told her that her happiness was only temporary; any woman who entirely disregarded her marriage, who even considered the wrecking of her home and family, deserved whatever punishment society could inflict on her. Before very long, shame and guilt would join with reason. Already she had drawn involuntary comparisons with Kitty, and told herself fiercely that she would not compare the way she felt for Gabriel with Kitty's self-indulgent and odious affairs. But would others recognise the difference? Would Mrs Ross, or William, or concert audiences and the gossip-hungry public? Sasha closed her mind to the prospect of disaster. She told herself she did not care.

And she did not, an hour later, when they got into the carriage Algie had hired to take them to their separate lodgings. The leave-taking went on interminably, with thanks and smiles and instructions to the driver, and Algie cautioning them to be back at nine in time for the soirée. They sat far apart, as if barely tolerating one another's company and the convenience of sharing a carriage.

The luxury of being alone with him again! The driver pulled away, the carriage moved out of sight of the house, and they fell into one another's arms. She sought his mouth with her lips in the semi-darkness and felt the back of his head under her hand. Was this what love was like? This desperate tenderness, and the need to touch and constantly touch again with a sense of wonder? Was this what she had once felt for William? She could not remember, did not want to remember anything about William. She had not understood anything at all about love until now . . .

'We have to be more careful.' She tore herself from him. 'We *must* be careful.'

He fell back against the seat, and she leaned against the crook of his shoulder to look out of the window. They held hands, caressing fingers.

'I want nothing else to happen, *ever*, that might take away this feeling,' said Sasha. 'I want to pretend I shan't ever have to go back. To that house, the dead silences, Aunt Georgie's prattle, Lily's sneer.' She refused to think of the children. She thought instead of William, the patients coming and going in that grey little dispensary. 'Oh, let's walk! We have all afternoon. I can't bear the thought of my hotel room. Five hours until I see you again!'

'Time for regrets and second thoughts?'

'No. Never.' She pressed his fingers to her lips. As they approached Hyde Park, she moved away from him. Gabriel banged on the roof and the driver pulled the cab to a halt.

He helped her down, and they crossed the streams of

traffic and entered Hyde Park. They walked in silence, content to be with one another, not needing to talk, not wanting to complicate things by making plans.

'I don't *feel* wicked,' Sasha said at last. 'I want to stay with you for ever – and it doesn't feel wicked at all.'

'It's as if you and I have always belonged to one another. I think I knew as soon as I heard you play. You wore a white dress. And your hair was on your shoulders. You thought I was a pauper.'

'I fell in love with you when I first heard you play your violin. You thought you were alone in the house. In your little attic room. But I don't think I realised until one evening – do you remember? You were so impatient with the players after the Bath concert and we were caught up in the skimmington.'

'You lost your bonnet to that mob.'

'I was so afraid you'd been trampled or dragged under the carriage wheels. And then you found me, and nothing else mattered when we watched them burn the dummies.'

He recalled the flaming crinoline, the figures consigned to a symbolic hell. 'Society hasn't much pity for lovers who don't keep to the rules.'

A melancholy mood was already settling on them. The light was fading and a mist was rising under the trees; the Park had become a grey shadow world; lights were coming on in the nearby houses.

'We haven't long before it's dark,' Gabriel said as they turned in the direction of Marble Arch and Sasha's hotel. He told her about his lodgings, that he had found rooms off Russell Square.

'I should like to see,' said Sasha. 'I want to picture you there.'

'You shall.' He nodded. 'Yes, you shall.'

'I mean . . .' Her glance met his and, shocked by the violence with which she wanted him, Sasha lowered her eyes. 'I mean, I want to see them now. It will be dark by the time we get there. No one will know me.'

★　★　★

They sat apart in the cab, each sharply aware of the step they had taken.

Gabriel spoke once. 'Are you sure?'

'Yes,' said Sasha quickly. 'I've never been more sure of anything in my life.'

He let his head fall back against the carriage seat. 'Was it only yesterday? I thought the world had come to an end! I thought Fate couldn't have dealt me a crueller blow than you being there for the Crystal Palace concert – except for that day in Runsby, of course. Nothing could beat that. The look in your eyes when you knew about Leah . . . If you had only known as well what a wreck I was when I went to her, what leaving you had done to me.'

'Hush.' She put out a hand, and he caught and held it. 'I want to be with you, Gabriel. I don't want us to part again. I love you. I *love you*. I never stopped loving you – even when I saw you with Leah.'

They reached his lodgings. Sasha waited as Gabriel paid off the driver. Her teeth chattered with the tension and frustration of negotiating the pavement, the entrance, and then the stairs and the landing outside his door. No one saw them as they ran the last few yards.

Gabriel unlocked the door with trembling hands; he slammed it behind them and fell against it, pulling her to him. They kissed in the darkness as she unfastened her hat; he trapped her hands and tenderly removed the pins for her, letting them drop to the floor.

'My darling, darling.' Sasha wrapped her arms round his neck, as he picked her up and carried her across the room in the darkness.

Sasha felt the coldness of the counterpane against her neck, and his mouth on hers. She gave a little cry of protest as he left the bed, and she heard him moving about, the sound of a match being struck; an oil lamp flared and brightened, throwing long shadows across the ceiling.

He took off his coat and came to her. 'I don't want darkness. I don't want shame and secrecy and wishing afterwards we hadn't done this.' He spoke with a desperate edge of anxiety, offering her a chance to rescue herself from damnation, candidly scared she might take it.

'Is that what you think?'

'It's too much like my dreams. Last night, after the concert, I imagined you here in this room . . . in this bed. In my dreams you come to my bed, and – still in my dreams – when I wake you're always gone.'

'No, no. You mustn't believe that!' She reached for him and pulled him down to her in a loving embrace. 'I'm here. This is where I want to be. Always.'

He unfastened the buttons at her neck. His hands, practised as they were at physical demonstrations of love, shook with anticipation.

Sasha pulled at the folds of his shirt and felt warm flesh. They struggled briefly for a sense of calm, then abandoned all hope of lingering over small pleasures and undressed with frantic haste, fighting petticoats and sleeves, fastenings and seams. With a cry of wonder Sasha took Gabriel into her body. They lay very still, and when they moved it was with a sense of savouring each second, each fraction of a moment of sensation.

They played all three movements of the Beethoven sonata at Algie's soirée with a brilliance and a fire that left their listeners breathless.

'Gabriel! What can I say! And Sasha! You played as if a herd of angels and demons were driving you,' said Algie.

'You played together as if you were one instrument,' said someone, pressing Gabriel's hand.

Gabriel's glance met hers, and Sasha felt desire for him flood through her again. They must all know, she thought. How could they not know that we are lovers? It could not be clearer if it were emblazoned on our foreheads in blood-red letters.

And yet, it seemed no one suspected; Algie assumed that Gabriel had acted as a catalyst to Sasha's playing, that the antagonism between them had added a spark of fire. A rumour had escaped among the company that, though their playing was wonderfully compatible, their temperaments were not. Sasha and Gabriel encouraged an impression of mutual sufferance in the cause of their art and avoided contact during the soirée, except to frown and discuss the music when they were asked to play again.

They spent that night together and the next, emboldened after fooling Algie and everyone else. Then, sobered by a fear of their luck breaking, their minds turned to the future and reality.

'What are you thinking?' Sasha traced the lines of his mouth as they lay together in his room one evening.

He turned to her. 'That I've never loved anyone as I've loved you, and love you now. That I can't bear the thought of it ending. But I know it will have to end one day, because you have to go back to your husband. You'll always be his.'

'Stop it.' She pressed her fingers against his lips. 'We have to promise one another we won't talk like that, and anyway, it isn't true. I'm only William's because I married him.' She sat up and looked at Gabriel tenderly, marvelling at the pleasure his body gave her, reluctant to think of the need to dress. 'We could find a hideaway where no one knows us, a place where we could be together sometimes.'

'In London?'

'In the country. We could be . . . Mr and Mrs Gladstone or Mr and Mrs Palmerston, or Smith or Baker.' Sasha began to dress, talking excitedly as she saw that the idea was possible. 'William would think I was on tour. Algie would assume I'm at home. And you . . . can make up whatever story you please.'

Gabriel leaned on one elbow watching her. 'You mean it, don't you?'

'Of course I mean it. It's the only point of sanity I can imagine.'

'It's full of risks.'

'We'll go somewhere where no one knows anything about us. We'll be careful.'

'Elliman might find out you're not where you're supposed to be. Someone living near Mr and Mrs Gladstone, or Smith, or Baker in their hideaway in the country might come to a concert; they would recognise us and say that Mr and Mrs Smith are not the respectable couple they seem. Catastrophe!'

'Mr and Mrs *Love*.'

He laughed.

She went to him with shining eyes. 'Oh, yes, Mr Love – Gabriel. My love. We have to do this, or I shall die!'

They placed an advertisement with an agency: 'WANTED, by a gentleman and his wife, furnished apartments with piano and without attendance . . .'

They waited for a day when there were no concerts or rehearsals, and took a train out of London, feeling like escapees, children on a spree, believing they would soon be found out and dragged back to the reformatory.

They had decided only to look at replies that lay within easy reach of Bristol and London, on the premise that Sasha might need to leave, or return home at short notice. The first on their list was a house in a village on the chalk uplands between Swindon and Bath.

Lavender House was 'genteel and congenial' and a two-minute walk from the railway station. They fell in love at once with the large airy rooms, the sitting room with its upright piano, and the walled garden beyond the french doors; they adored the bedrooms under the eaves with their broad oak floorboards and panelled walls, and the snow on the hills through the windows.

'My wife plays the piano a little,' Gabriel explained, as the owner – Mrs Mynott, a 'respectable widow much reduced by circumstances' – explained that she was moving into a smaller house down the lane. Round-eyed, she watched Sasha run scale after scale up and down the piano.

'Horribly out of tune. It will have to be seen to. But not bad for an upright.' Sasha turned to Gabriel with a smile that made his heart turn over.

Lavender House was ideal: secluded without being isolated, away from prying eyes and ears. They said at once that they would take it and moved in at the end of the concert tour.

Sasha sent William a telegram from London. 'Regret, tour extended another week.'

Sasha sat on the hearthrug with her head against Gabriel's knee as he played the violin. The touch of his leg sent a pleasant sexual heat through her; the flames from the crackling logs warmed her face; the coffee in the cup in her hand heated her fingers. 'I ought to feel sad because we can never marry, but I don't. I ought . . .'

'You ought to be practising the Schumann for the Bristol concert series.' Gabriel stopped playing and put down his violin; he bent and kissed her soft, flame-warmed mouth and wanted to make love to her, as he had made love to her that morning and again earlier that evening. She glowed with an all-over radiance, and Gabriel knew he had never seen her more beautiful.

'I don't want to think about it. I want to spend the rest of my life here with you by the fender, drinking coffee and smoking, and playing the piano for you and me – Mr and Mrs Love and nobody else.'

'Mr and Mrs Love will cease to exist if we don't attend to the concerts that are to finance them. Music is our reality, Sasha.'

Sasha stretched and threw out her arms. 'And so is this.' She flexed her fingers languidly before stroking them along his thigh, pleased by the immediacy with which she felt the sexual surge in him, like a chord that responded without coaxing.

He pulled her on to his knee. 'You and I are going to be the musical sensation of the world,' he said as he pushed up her petticoats.

'I'm perfectly happy being a private sensation here with you.' Sasha bent her head and kissed his mouth, spreading her crinoline skirts like a foaming whirlpool.

'Sasha, Sasha,' he whispered, closing his eyes as he

wrapped his hands round her waist and helped her judge the rhythm, slow, lyrical, mounting to small crescendos which they held, tense with delight. The firelight flickered; the clock ticked on the mantelshelf with a soft counter-rhythm and, as they waited, sustaining the breathless sensation of crisis, it struck the hour of midnight.

Each day merged into the next. Music and love had become the focus of their existence. The house reverberated with passionate scales and chords on the violin, and to the sound of piano scales following swiftly, leading from one key to another. Each morning they studied apart for three hours, Sasha downstairs at the piano, Gabriel in the room above; the sound of the violin drifted down to her, enticed her, beguiled her, and frequently lured her to him.

They shared music study together; there were hours of oblivion when they were drunk on music, conscious only of sound.

I can't bear the necessity of leaving him, Sasha thought. Was it possible to preserve their love once she had gone back to Penbury? Yet she could not imagine defying the world and throwing herself entirely on Gabriel's protection. Much as she loved him, she had missed Pippa and Meredith during the tour. Could she abandon her children?

'We can never be together properly, never make our happiness permanent,' Gabriel said, echoing her mood as they walked on the hills on their last day before she had to return home.

'Need it matter?'

'No.' But Gabriel knew he was lying as he kissed her gloved hands. He wanted her for his own. He wanted to force her to abandon the straitjacket of her marriage.

She turned to him, and her lips were cold against his. 'Even if I didn't care about my own future, we have to think of yours. A mistress would drag you down – a *married* mistress, who had deserted her husband and children! What would the world say? You have barely set out on your career.'

'I don't care about my career.'

'Yes, you do. You know you do,' she scolded. 'You have a brilliant future ahead of you. You're the best violinist after Joachim.'

'*We* are the best,' he said. 'Audiences will fall in love with us – because you are the most angelic creature that ever set hands to keyboard, and because I am privileged to play beside you.'

'You ask a lot from people if you expect them to fall in love with us simply because we're in love with one another.'

They turned back to the house and, as they reached the last stretch of the hill, began to run. People seeing them in the lane, hand in hand, believed them to be newly-weds.

'There's nothing more wholesome than seeing a young couple so wholeheartedly taken with one another,' said Mrs Mynott after they had gone.

Chapter Eighteen

Sasha could no longer think of Penbury as home. She climbed down from the carriage and looked around. Home was Lavender House and Gabriel, the duets they had played in the sitting room with its crackling fire, and the snow on the hills beyond their bedroom window.

The snow in Penbury had turned to slush in the drive. Aunt Georgie came to meet Sasha as she banged off her boots at the door; taking the boots from her, she stood with her head crooked on one side, curious, like a small yellow bird.

'You look different.'

Sasha threw up her head in alarm. 'Different?'

'Healthier. Fitter.'

'Oh, Aunt Georgie, I am!' Sasha, unable to hold in her happiness, seized Aunt Georgie and kissed her. 'I am! I've never been so healthy.' She wanted to confess that she was in love with Gabriel and with her music – that she had found fulfilment at last. 'It must be because I'm playing again.' She looked around. 'Where is everyone?'

'Pippa's helping Mrs Ash in the kitchen. Lily's at a Chapel meeting. William is upstairs. Sasha . . . Meredith's been ill. He's had a fever.'

The happiness drained from Sasha. Guilt burst upon her with the full force of a flood tide. Meredith was lying sick? Her child had needed her? She hurried to take off her hat and coat. 'How ill is he? Where is he? I must go to him at once.'

'We wrote to the address you gave us in London, but you can't have heard.'

'The letter must have gone astray—'

'He's over the crisis. And William hasn't been too alarmed. He only sent for you as a precaution.'

'He thought there was a possibility . . .? Oh, my child. Merry. My poor Merry.'

'Is that you, Sasha?' William leaned over the landing rail, his head and shoulders silhouetted against the coloured window. Sasha had a fleeting and bizarre impression that God – or at the very least one of his emissaries – was looking down on her, waiting to pass judgement.

He met her on the stairs. 'Not to panic. The boy is over the worst.'

'Are you sure?'

'He'll soon be running about again.' He kissed her on the forehead, his lips cold and formal. He turned for her to follow him. 'There's really no cause for alarm.'

'I should have been here.'

'You couldn't,' he said, with a chilly self-righteousness in his voice and in the stiff set of his shoulders. 'You had your concert engagements, remember?'

Meredith was sitting up in bed. A book lay open on his lap. He was pale and his eyes looked out from dark hollows, but his face broke into a smile when he saw her.

Sasha ran to the bed and hugged him. 'My darling. Are you really better? Oh, my poor Merry.'

'Take care, Sasha,' said William tetchily. 'The boy's still very weak even though the fever's gone.'

Sasha released her fierce hold. She sat on the bed and held Merry's hand, searching his face for signs of the illness, deliberately punishing herself. 'What a cruel mama to leave you all alone.'

William sighed with ill-disguised impatience.

Sasha stroked Merry's hand. 'What else has been happening while I've been gone?'

Meredith wriggled down among his pillows, his face creasing into lines of concentration. 'Nothing much. Oh – except that Aunt Georgie is going to marry Mr Viggers.'

'Surely not?' Sasha turned to William for confirmation.

'It's in the air. He's been very much more attentive since Christmas.'

'But is that what she wants?' Sasha said in dismay. Aunt Georgie could not, must not marry. She was the one person who had to be there for her or everything was lost.

'Aunt Georgie's entitled to fall in love,' said William in a sardonic tone.

'But with Mr Viggers?'

Meredith giggled, and William frowned. 'Sasha! Not in front of the boy.'

'But Mr Viggers – he's so . . .'

Sasha kissed Meredith and followed William on to the landing. She lowered her voice. 'He's so *stuffy*. And he's patently not in love with her. He simply wants a cheap housekeeper.'

'He has an independent income and he's well liked in Penbury. He's thinking of buying a house here. She could do a lot worse – and at her age . . .' He did not finish the sentence.

'At her age, a woman should think herself lucky to get anyone at all?'

'Well, if you want to put it like that.'

'Oh, that's typical! We women should count ourselves lucky to get a husband, however self-centred, however pompous, however disappointing he may be!'

William stiffened as he realised where her anger was directed. 'Are you sure your objection to Aunt Georgie's happiness doesn't have a purely selfish motive? After all, everyone knows who's been looking after your children for you while you pursue your musical career.' He turned from her and went downstairs.

'Is it true?' Sasha said to Aunt Georgie, finding her alone in the drawing room. 'Are you going to marry Mr Viggers?'

'He hasn't asked me.' There was a twist of self-mockery to Aunt Georgie's smile. 'It's all rumour. And I have to say, it's getting very annoying, knowing everyone is discussing one's future behind one's back.'

'Do you . . . *care* for him?'

'No.' Aunt Georgie regarded Sasha thoughtfully. 'But that isn't necessarily the first consideration.' And she would say no more on the subject.

'It's good to have you back,' William said that night, before he turned over in bed and went to sleep. He had not tried to bridge the distance between them, and Sasha was glad. She could not have endured it if he had laid claim to his rights as a husband. Was her distaste for intimacy shared? The thought that William might no longer want her struck her with a little shock of surprise.

Sasha lay awake for a long time, feeling empty, wanting Gabriel's arms about her and the pulse of his body against hers. Memories drifted in and out of her thoughts; they were spoiled by a small fear that had been nagging recently at her mind. She counted the days; but however many times she made the calculation, she came to the same conclusion. As she stared at the ceiling, waves of panic swept through her and settled in the pit of her stomach. Why had they not been more careful? There were ways – she and William had employed them . . . She fell into a fitful sleep.

The following day brought deliverance. Sasha greeted the menstrual flow with a fervent promise to the gods that she would be more careful in future. The future! She thought of the next concert tour and of seeing Gabriel again, and her heart skipped a beat.

'Where are you playing next?' said Lily. Meredith had been allowed downstairs for tea and the family were seated in the dining room.

'In Bristol. But not for a week or two. So, I shall be at home for some time, to spoil the children horribly and undo all the good work Aunt Georgie and Mr Duff have done.'

'A West Country tour?' said William.

'Bristol and Bath. Then a tour in the Midlands.' She hesitated. 'You remember Mr Ridgeway? Well, it seems Algie has taken quite a shine to him. He may be playing in one or two concerts with me.'

'Good gracious. So, he achieved his ambition to become a soloist?'

'Algie believes he has "discovered" him. He wants him to play duos with me.' She paused and added casually, 'We shared several concerts in the London series.'

William shook his head. 'Well, well. Who would have thought? Mind you, I always said he had the manner to be a musician. The long hair. Something not quite—'

Aunt Georgie threw Sasha an odd look, and Sasha was glad of Meredith's interruption. 'Papa, can we go to a concert? Oh, please say we can go to hear Mr Ridgeway and Mama play in a concert?'

'Mr Ridgeway was very good,' conceded Lily. 'I'm not surprised he's doing well.' She added knowledgeably, 'People are always drawn to a pretty face.'

Meredith chortled with his old enthusiasm, 'Mr Ridgeway hasn't got a *pretty* face. He's a man.'

William cleared his throat. 'Well now, I don't see why we shouldn't attend one of Mama's concerts. It would be pleasant to renew our acquaintance with Mr Ridgeway.' He reflected on the prospect, remembering the amiable conversations with his son's tutor over a glass of port. 'I'm pleased. Yes. I'm pleased he's met with some success.'

Oh, but Gabriel *was* beautiful, thought Sasha as she walked into the Victoria Rooms. He had not seen her. He was deep in conversation with one of the cellists, his violin slung from one hand, tapping the edge of it idly with the bow. Sasha followed each small gesture with greedy adoration.

'Mr Ridgeway . . .'

He turned at the sound of her voice, and the space between them was at once charged with a heady delirium. She wanted to run to his arms, to kiss his face and lips, and his smile – it sent little shocks of happiness through her.

'Mrs Elliman . . . you're here. I'm so glad. We can start the rehearsal.' He spoke as if irritated by the delay; he consulted his watch. But he could not keep the desire from his voice, nor could Sasha hide it in her eyes. They talked about the concert, about the music they were to play, about the order of the programme, and all the time the tone of his voice told her: I love you, I want you; and the expression in her eyes answered: I'm yours.

They played a Schumann violin sonata and again some of the 'Kreutzer', and Sasha went through her solo pieces quickly, with a consummate brilliance. She sat at the back of the hall while Gabriel rehearsed with the orchestra. He had been given the central work in the programme; Algie was promoting him above her, she realised, and could not prevent a creeping jealousy. She reminded herself of his genius, her own impatience for his recognition; but the thought of being supplanted was not welcome, even if the usurper was the man she loved best in the world.

He was playing Mendelssohn's E minor concerto; he played with a poignant tenderness, and Sasha knew he was playing it for her. A sadness overwhelmed her. She went outside, afraid that someone would notice her mood, and walked up and down in the cold under the colonnade, watching the cabs and horses rumble about in the dirt beyond the railings. She could still hear the strains of music from the orchestra. A light snow was falling; tiny white specks drifted through the grey air, disappearing as soon as they landed, melting into the puddles and ridges of slush.

After a while the music stopped. Some of the orchestra players came outside to smoke and walk about. Gabriel came towards her and they moved away from the entrance.

'Two whole weeks! I've been going crazy. When can we escape again?' His expression was urbane for the benefit of any onlookers, but his voice was low and urgent.

'I'll let you know,' she whispered. 'Listen, William wants to bring the family to a concert. I don't think I can bear it. What if he suspects something?'

'I almost want him to. Great God, I hate all this secrecy. I want to kiss you. I want to plunge my hands through that wonderful hair and bring it down – and us down with it. I want to defy them all, Sasha. I *love* you.'

'Gabriel, no . . .' She moved further away from the other players, who stood with their backs to the street, laughing and joking; the smell of cigars and cigarette smoke drifted under the colonnade.

He followed her. 'I want to kiss your white shoulders, your skin . . . Sasha! The taste of your skin!'

She leaned against the wall for support and closed her eyes. 'I've told William about the Midlands tour. I shall say it's four weeks long instead of three. We could spend a few days at Lavender House.'

'The spring!' He spun away from her in ecstasy. 'Sasha – think of the spring on those hills!'

'I want you,' Sasha whispered. 'I want you so much I think I shall die of it.'

They were all there: her parents, William, his sister and his aunt, Mr Viggers, even the Turbots and the Wotherspoons had come.

Aunt Georgie knew, Sasha realised, watching her shepherd the children to their seats with little distracted flapping movements of her arms. Would she warn William? Would she do anything at all to interfere? Sasha remembered Gabriel's bravado about wanting to defy the world and knew it was impossible – even if it were not for the children, it would be impossible. The world would destroy them, burn them up with its condemnation. Gabriel's impatience frightened her. How long would he stand the guilt and secrecy? What if the situation should become so intolerable that it soured his feelings for her? She remembered her fright when she had thought she was pregnant. What if they *were* found out, and he abandoned her? What then – if she were left entirely alone, with no income, no reputation, no means of support?

It was time for them to make their entrance. A hush fell over the audience. She glanced at Gabriel in the shadows and saw that his expression was tense. 'I love you,' she whispered.

He turned to her with a look of anguish and then they

stepped into the pool of light, trapped for everyone to observe every gesture, every lyrical phrase shared between violin and piano, in the brilliant and airless space of the concert platform.

'A capital performance!' pronounced William, who knew nothing about music but could appreciate the fiery rhythms of a tarantella, and was flattered by the spectacle of his wife being admired and to hear her called 'the best female player in all of England'.

'Sasha! Wonderful!' Her father embraced her.

The Turbots and the Wotherspoons came up to add their congratulations, and people too from Sasha's childhood, friends of her parents who had forgiven – though certainly would not have forgotten – Kitty's disgrace. They crowded round, and said that Gabriel and Sasha had seemed inspired, and that they had always known Sasha was destined for a life of music.

They had noticed nothing. Not one of them suspected that Sasha's whole heart had been with the violinist as much as with the music. A rumour had spread with their reputation in the London concerts. Algie Ross had dropped hints; the orchestra – and even audiences – had taken up the idea of two different and conflicting personalities, united only by their love of music.

Sasha looked round for Gabriel and saw that he had moved to the edge of her circle of admirers. He had more admirers of his own, orchestra players and members of the audience, and young women who clamoured for him to pencil his signature on their concert programmes. Stories of a turbid past added considerable glamour to his appeal. A shiver of apprehension ran through Sasha. What if he should tire of the pretence and leave her for someone less troublesome? She was trapped. Her only path to happiness lay through Gabriel – but he would always have an escape route; she could make no demands of loyalty on him. He turned and caught her glance, and Sasha's anxiety faded.

'William and Sasha, you must come back to Hanover

Terrace,' said Nathaniel. 'Yes, yes. You must come for supper. It's already arranged.'

Sasha began to protest that William had ordered a carriage home; that it was late for the children.

'Then all the family must stay the night,' said her father. 'I'll not take a refusal. It's a Sunday tomorrow, so, William, you can't pretend you have patients to see.'

'Nor would I want to,' laughed William, tempted by the comfortable prospect of a stay at Hanover Terrace.

'Then, that's settled. You must come to supper. Oh, this is like the old days!'

Mrs Hammond had fallen into conversation with Gabriel, drawing him away from the other players. 'Come with us,' she said. 'It's such a long time since we saw you. Nathaniel talks about you very often, and we're so glad you're playing in concerts with Sasha. We like to hear about your success.'

Gabriel threw a glance at Sasha. He murmured something about it being a family party, but William had overheard and intervened. 'Nonsense, Ridgeway. You were always one of the family.'

So much for her smoke screen about Gabriel being dismissed from them in disgrace, thought Sasha. She looked round for Algie, praying he would not see her husband with his arm round the scourge of Penbury's female virtue. She breathed a sigh of relief; none of the orchestra seemed to have noticed that Gabriel was being coaxed into the Hammonds' carriage.

Sasha avoided Gabriel at first. But the children repeatedly drew her back to him; they could not keep from under his feet, incoherent with excitement and clamouring for his attention, competing to tell him all they had been doing. Sasha watched him waltz about her parents' drawing room with Pippa on his back.

'They've missed him – and so have I,' said Aunt Georgie. After a while she added casually, 'I expect you missed him too.'

'Yes,' Sasha said noncommittally.

404

'One wouldn't blame any woman for falling in love with him.'

'Did Mr Viggers enjoy the evening?' Sasha asked, changing the subject quickly.

'Oh – how is one to tell?' Aunt Georgie gave an irritable little flick to her lace collar. 'He hardly spoke a word to me except to worry about getting back to Penbury so as not to be late for a choir practice.'

'Poor Aunt Georgie.'

'Am I? I don't know. There are so many things to think about.' Could she bear to give up Pippa and Merry, for instance?

'Aunt Georgie, if you want him you must have him.' Sasha pressed the other woman's hand and gave her a hard straight look. 'You must *not* sacrifice one ounce of your own happiness because of a mistaken sense of duty.'

Aunt Georgie gave her a tremulous smile. She seemed peculiarly close to tears. 'I envy you, Sasha,' she said softly. 'Whatever I feel about Mr Viggers, it's not the same as being in love.'

No. Nothing could be the same as that, thought Sasha. She turned away and saw Gabriel standing chatting to her father and William – her father, solid and patrician; William, sleek and colourless; and Gabriel . . . beautiful, brilliant, turning her insides to water. They were the three men, apart from Herr Lindau, who had so far moulded her life. The image was powerful; it produced a profound effect on her; she felt stifled and afraid. Was her destiny always to be guided by her relationship with a man – her father, husband, lover . . .?

Her mother was complaining to Aunt Georgie about the 'tag-rag' of Bristol who now frequented Avondon. Sasha wanted to shake her, to ask her what had happened to her in forty or more years of marriage to change her from a woman of talent and with opinions into a social hostess who echoed everyone else's prejudices. She moved towards the trio of menfolk.

'What's this I've been hearing about you two not getting on?' said Nathaniel, looking from Sasha to Gabriel.

'It's true,' said Sasha quickly, before Gabriel could reply. 'We never can agree on what to play or how to play it in rehearsals. And yet – in the performance, it always comes out right.'

'Algie is a showman,' laughed Gabriel easily. 'He likes to build up little myths about his players, so that everyone will sit there hoping for fisticuffs in the middle of a bravura passage. Needless to say, we disappoint them every time.'

The others laughed. 'I wish I could understand music better,' Nathaniel said. 'I suppose I was destined to express myself through paint. I can feel music when I hear it, but I can't always understand what it's about.'

'Musicians can only be true to themselves if they play what they *feel*. One has to have suffered,' said Sasha, echoing Gabriel's early opinions when he had first brought her back to her music. Did he remember?

William laughed. 'My dear girl. When have you ever had to suffer in the real world? Surely, a musician – and in particular a female musician – is expected to pretend a little, especially when playing a tragic piece.'

'Are you saying you would sanction dishonesty?' said Gabriel.

'Ridgeway, you always were a stickler for principles. Are we still talking about art and music?'

'More generally if you prefer.'

Nathaniel laughed. 'I'm sure a doctor must pretend frequently when he puts on a grave and knowledgeable face.'

'Indeed. It's true,' said William. 'A doctor often has to conceal his true feelings and doubts – pretend a little.'

'But how much more satisfactory it would be, if everyone were to show their true nature,' said Gabriel. He was looking at Sasha. Oh, for a more noble morality than that imposed by society. Oh, for a chance at real honesty, so that for Sasha to have fallen out of love with her husband would not be a crime against her marriage.

'Should we all wear our hearts on our sleeves?' said Mrs Hammond. 'I'm afraid that would never do.'

'It *is* very hard to know a person at face value,' Sasha acknowledged, remembering how she had once misjudged Gabriel.

'Indeed. The sweetest face may hide all manner of falsehoods,' said William suddenly, and with a peculiar edge of bitterness to his voice.

Gabriel asked himself why Elliman had used such an emotive word as 'falsehoods'. He had no doubt that the man was talking about Sasha – though Sasha did not have a 'sweet' face. Her expression in repose was gentle, but anyone looking into those eyes might have seen the passion haunting them, the longing for release. Did Elliman suspect Sasha of a particular kind of falsehood? Was that why he had pressed him to come back with them to Hanover Terrace? A confrontation? Accusations made? Humiliating denials?

But no, Elliman was talking of something else of course, blaming Sasha for her need for music, meaning only that she had not turned out to be the sweet, self-sacrificing creature he once thought he had married.

'I disagree that a sweet expression could hide deceitful thoughts,' said Nathaniel. 'If you have the perception to see beyond the superficial, people cannot hide much from you.'

'But what about Kitty?' murmured Mrs Hammond, so that only Sasha heard. 'Kitty fooled us all.'

Sasha looked round the drawing room. It had been here, in this house, that she had found the two of them together. Did William remember? Did thoughts of Kitty ever haunt him?

'Come, let's have some more entertainment,' said Nathaniel, tiring of the direction the conversation had taken. 'Sasha, Gabriel. Are you too exhausted to play some more for us?'

Gabriel gave them one of his party pieces. Sasha had heard him perform it before, improvising on the piano in the style of Liszt, with exaggerated arm movements and a violent expression. She laughed with the others and saw that William too was laughing. So, she thought, he thinks

407

Gabriel is a dilettante, and no threat, but he is nevertheless charmed by him. Everyone was charmed by him.

'Mr Ridgeway, you told me I shouldn't swing my arms as if I was waving a bat, but you were swinging them like windmills,' said Meredith afterwards, when Sasha prepared to take Pippa and Meredith away to bed.

'And I hope you still reserve that technique for the cricket pitch,' laughed Gabriel. 'Unless we are talking about *vampire* bats, who flap their arms like this.' He whirled around, swooped on Meredith and sent both children shrieking from the room.

'Mr Ridgeway!' said Lily in alarm.

'You always did excite them too near to bedtime,' laughed Aunt Georgie.

Sasha turned on Gabriel, half crossly, but with a sense of nostalgia. 'Now, I suppose I shall have to calm Pippa down!'

She had settled the children down to sleep, and given them a nightlight. The corridor was empty except for Gabriel coming towards her.

'I'm sorry. Did I frighten them?'

'Not really. I don't think you ever frightened the children. Not like William does when he's cold and stern with them . . . I admit, you frightened me though with all that talk of honesty.'

He pulled her towards him and kissed her, pressing her against the wall. 'Oh, Sasha, Sasha! I don't think I can take any more.'

'Think of Lavender House.'

'I am, but we have to go back in there first.' He jerked his head towards the drawing room. The doors formed a fragile barrier between them and the raised voices and laughter of the party. 'Great God! I wish you weren't married to Elliman. I hate him more than ever for his moronic opinions and the way he takes you for granted. I hate you for marrying him. I think I would rather you were dead. Oh God, the misery of thinking about you married to Elliman and not to me. Why not to me?'

'Gabriel . . .' she said tenderly.

He released her. 'Why must a husband and wife stay together when they no longer love each other? It's a crime. And society is rotten through and through for upholding all that hypocrisy.'

'If it's getting too much for you,' Sasha said without looking at him.

'Oh, yes! Yes, it's getting too much. This last fortnight, I've been half crazed – it's no exaggeration. I've thought, I must give you up. Like a bad habit. Like drink or opium. I think of all the unhappiness we're laying up for ourselves, and I know it would be better to put an end to it right now.'

Sasha could not speak. Fingers of fear clutched at her heart. So, she had not been so very far wrong when she had been afraid it was not going to last. How long did they have? A year? A few months? A few snatched nights only at Lavender House? She smoothed her skirts and stepped away from him. 'It's been a long day . . .'

'Sasha!' He caught hold of her wrist. 'Don't you know I didn't mean it? Listen! I've been thinking. Planning. I want us to tour properly together instead of working all the time as separate soloists. We'll always share the same platform. What do you think? I'm inviting you to become my permanent accompanist.'

'You're inviting me,' she repeated slowly.

'We would belong together – through our music.'

'You said, you're *inviting* me. You want me to be your accompanist.'

'Yes!' He ran a hand through his hair. Still hot with anger at the frustrations that kept them apart, he did not see that he had said anything to hurt her.

'I'm a *pianist*!' Sasha said. 'I'm not a lady accompanist. I'm a soloist in my own right.'

A burst of sound came from the drawing room and she moved away.

'Sasha – I'm sorry. I meant partners. Call it what you want.'

'An accompanist! In any case, you know it's impossible.

409

To be so closely linked . . . It's too dangerous. People would guess the truth of it, if we were *always* seen together. It's wonderful as a dream, Gabriel, but our names can never be permanently linked in that way.' Sasha hesitated. 'If you're already tiring of the way things are . . .'

'Of course I'm not. I didn't mean it. Let's stop – before we say anything we regret.'

'Does Algie know about this idea of yours? Does he think I should become your *lady accompanist*?'

'Algie thinks you have too many family obligations to join every single tour. He thinks it wouldn't work.' He did not add that Algie was planning a long autumn season of mainly orchestral works with Gabriel as his principal soloist.

Sasha digested the phrase 'family obligations'. She had used it herself often enough when Algie had asked her to take part in concerts, and she could not blame him for looking after his own interests. She felt tired and dejected. Too many realities were intruding on the idyll.

They left the winter behind after the Midlands tour. The garden at Lavender House burst into life with spring flowers. In the mornings they lay in bed until noon, making love as the scent of narcissi and the sound of birdsong drifted in at the open window. In the afternoons they walked on the hills or practised for hours on the piano and violin, working at unfamiliar pieces, arguing sometimes, rarely still. When they were tranquil with one another it was with the drowsy calm of sleeping cats after an hour or two on the prowl. They did not mention parting, but it was never far from their minds. Nor did they discuss the future again, for fear that by talking of an end, they might make it happen.

They played in several concerts that spring and summer, separately and together. There were points of conflict between them – real, as well as contrived to sustain the myth about their incompatibility.

Gabriel loved the excitement of an audience; he never seemed to tire of the applause.

'One gets very sick of it,' said Sasha, feeling older and wiser, remembering how it had palled early in her career. She still felt she was the more experienced player. She coached Gabriel a little when they were rehearsing; complaining that his rhythm was too free.

'It comes, I suppose, from being self-taught.'

'It comes with playing from the heart,' he replied.

She reminded him that he had once hidden her metronome when he was teaching Meredith. It was a subject on which they would never agree.

They took a delight in the arguments; everything for them was heightened: their music, love-making, partings, reunions.

Later in the year the orchestra toured the East of England and Sasha went with them. The players travelled together by train. They played games, and sang songs to pass the journey in different moods and voices – tragic, jolly, basso and falsetto, legato and staccato, conducting with their arms and led by Algie, sitting with his feet up on the carriage seats. Sasha and Gabriel stole nights in hotel rooms and escaped to Lavender House again between concerts.

But it became more rare for Sasha to be invited to undertake the longer tours with the other players; Algie told her he understood, that tours of more than a few weeks were a problem for her, and that she did not always want to share the platform with Gabriel.

Gabriel was becoming more and more in demand.

Sasha thought he was trivialising his talents with showpieces. 'What happened to your talk of honesty? I dislike the idea of you becoming another virtuoso like Paganini. I wish audiences didn't need flourishes and excitement. They are all the time waiting for something spectacular to happen.'

'I agree. Audiences are painfully ignorant.'

'But it's our task to educate them and make them care about your music – *our* music.'

'And I shall. I shall play Schumann and Beethoven at the next concert,' he promised.

'Without me.' Was it really the music she cared about? she wondered. Or was she resentful because she knew that audiences would rather hear Paganini's *Witches' Dance* as a solo, than a violin sonata played with her?

'Sasha—'

'Oh – it's all right. I know audiences want you, Gabriel. Algie wants you. I'm not a beautiful Hammond any more. I'm a woman who will soon be thirty, with two children. The public can't see any glamour in that.'

'They want you too. They love you, Sasha.'

'*You* love me,' she corrected, kissing him.

On her thirtieth birthday Gabriel bought her a Broadwood grand piano. It was in the sitting room when she arrived at Lavender House one January weekend; the old upright had been moved out.

Gabriel had covered the top of the piano with orange and white hot-house lilies; and there was a metronome – a private joke – with a note attached: 'To my love – we are two beats of the one note, two halves of the one soul.' He had added a postscript: 'To my love who has perfect timing. I am wretched! Because I shall be late. Blame Algie.'

Algie must have booked him for an impromptu engagement. It was another reminder that his popularity with audiences was rising, and that Sasha was taking second place.

He arrived at midnight, and she cast aside her resentment. They made love with indecent haste, on the piano among the lilies.

'I'm going to Europe next autumn,' Gabriel said one evening in early spring, after he had returned to her from London. She was playing the piano and did not look up. Gabriel threw his hat on the piano, kissed her and fell into a chair with his feet on the fender. He smiled at her. 'Algie thinks I'm ready to face the French and Germans.'

Sasha stopped playing and said very calmly, 'He didn't suggest that I . . .'

'He wants this to be a solo tour.' He shifted his gaze away from the look of hurt in her eyes. 'He thinks we shouldn't become too closely linked in the public's mind.'

'He didn't always say so. Didn't you contradict him?'

'What could I say? It's you who didn't want that to happen, remember? You once said it would be too dangerous.'

'You could at least have *suggested* he include me. You know I told you how good it is to work in a country where they really understand music. We could have travelled together . . . Gabriel, weeks and weeks with one another!'

'And Algie. With Algie there as well. We'd be sure to be found out sooner or later. Or at the very least we would arouse his suspicions. Not to mention your husband's. Look how risky it is on a tour. We start getting careless . . .'

They were her own arguments used against her. 'You don't want me to go,' said Sasha in disbelief.

He looked ashamed; he could not deny there was an element of vanity in being asked to go alone. And Gabriel too was becoming frustrated by the commercialism of English concerts. On the Continent they appreciated a musician for his music. At home, everyone talked of how much money was being made; even Algie talked of money and appealing to popular taste. In any case, Algie had made up his mind; he had said their dislike of one another was becoming a barrier to planning tours and concerts. They had convinced everyone too well.

'Sasha,' Gabriel said lazily, trying to humour her, 'why do you always have to over-react?'

'Stop it!' She put her hands over her ears. 'Stop it. You sound like William. I won't have you sounding like my husband!'

They lay apart that night, and for the first time after a separation they did not make love. In the morning Sasha rose early and made a great show of being occupied with

413

practising at the piano. Gabriel came into the room half-dressed, in shirt and trousers, fastening his cufflinks. He propped himself against the fireplace, willing her to look at him.

'You're right,' Sasha said at last. 'It would have been very risky. So. How long will you be gone?'

'Three months. From early October until after Christmas.'

Sasha did not want him to go where she could not follow. She remembered how they had once talked of a musical partnership; now she would give anything to have swallowed her pride and to go with him as an accompanist. She forced herself to say, 'Shall we meet again when you come back?'

He jerked his head up in alarm. 'Sasha – of course . . .'

'I simply ask, because I see all this leading nowhere.' Her voice broke a little as she banged down the piano keys in a chord. 'I can see us becoming bitter with one another. Me resenting every time you do a concert or tour without me. You getting tired of me. You'll meet someone else. In fact, sometimes, I think it would be better if you were to meet someone else.'

'Don't be so *stupid*.'

'Am I? What sort of life is this for you? You could marry. You could live a normal life – with children.'

He did not answer. She had hit upon the most bitter aspect of the situation for him.

'We both know there's no future for us.' She began the piece again.

'You're playing badly,' he said miserably, watching her hands move with a random, distracted rhythm.

'I think it would be better if we ended the whole affair now.'

'Very well. If that's what you want. Do you want to close the lease on the house?'

Sasha stopped playing. 'No!'

They looked at one another, terrified by what was happening to them. He crossed the room and took her in his arms. 'I didn't mean it.'

414

'We've been so happy here.'

'I didn't mean it,' he repeated, kissing her eyes, her lips, her hair, and her palms and fingers. He carried her upstairs and they made love with a passion and tenderness that held an edge of fear.

This is what it would be like without him, Sasha told herself when she returned to Penbury and he had gone back to London. She pictured him playing at Ross's Theatre. The public would be happy for him to do nothing but stand there and play them scales. People went to his concerts simply to say they had seen him. And of course Algie needed a charismatic figure on the concert platform.

They did not talk about his tour the next time they met. By avoiding it, they thought they could preserve the enchanted world they had created at Lavender House. After all, they had the whole of the summer before his tour began. They walked for hours on the chalk-white hills, lay side by side under the blue and white dome of the sky, and picked strawberries from the garden. They played their music until the early hours of the morning, and kept at bay the thoughts of parting.

Sometimes Sasha wondered how she had kept the two separate existences so successfully apart. For almost eighteen months they had planned their meetings at Lavender House with the cunning of a military undercover campaign. At Penbury everyone believed she hardly ever saw Gabriel any more; they had played in fewer and fewer concerts together. Soon, there would be nothing except her life with William.

'I'll write to you,' Gabriel had promised. 'You can collect the letters from the house. I'll address them to Mr and Mrs Love.'

And she had pretended to herself that letters would be enough.

She lay in the shade of the apple tree in the garden at Penbury one September afternoon, remembering scenes at Lavender House, feeling melancholy. Everyone was out – William on a call to the Wotherspoons, Lily and Aunt Georgie with the children. Solitude. It was the greatest of luxuries, when you were confident of someone's love, but a curse when it brought the threat of isolation.

Sasha felt restless and uneasy. She began to weep again, and knew that weeping was not in her nature. Hearing the children return from their outing, she quickly dried her eyes, and as she stood, nausea swept through her. It was momentary, but familiar enough for her to be certain what it meant. A cold fear wrapped itself round Sasha's heart. She compared her recent moods, the restlessness and the nausea, with symptoms of her former pregnancies.

Sasha's fears bound tighter with each day that passed. She went for vigorous walks, ran up and down stairs, played the piano violently and counted the days, hopeful each morning of salvation. She had been rescued before, why not again?

She was engaged to play in the West Country during the weeks leading up to Gabriel's foreign tour; but they had arranged to spend one last day together at Lavender House before he left. Sasha travelled there with a determination to live every moment together to the full. But too many changes had begun; she could no longer live on a tide of happiness. She gathered Michaelmas daisies from the garden and put them in a glass vase in the bedroom window; the autumn light made patterns of shade among the mauve flowers.

They made love in the long afternoon. But there were silences between them filled with private terrors. When Gabriel asked her what they meant, she could not tell him. How *could* she tell him she thought she was expecting his child?

'I think you should treat this tour as a trial,' Sasha said as they got ready to leave. 'When you come back, I want you to feel no obligations towards me. I mean, I'm giving you your freedom.'

'That's very noble of you. But you don't mean it. And I don't want it.'

'All the same. Think about it. You may change your mind.'

The leaves along the lane to the railway station lay in muddied drifts at the sides of the road. The wind, with a touch of winter in it, rustled and whispered through them, shifting them around their feet. Sasha kicked out with her boot; she wanted to fling her arms round Gabriel and tell him she thought she was pregnant; she wanted to confess she was afraid and beg him not to go. Her train for Bath was already in the station, and they hurried as they saw the lights and heard the hiss of the steam.

'You'll write to me?' Gabriel was frightened by the strangeness of her mood. 'I'll send you a poste restante address as soon as I can.'

'I shan't write often. I shan't . . . pester you.'

He halted. 'For God's sake, Sasha. Self-martyrdom doesn't suit you.'

'I mean it.' She touched his mouth tenderly. 'I'm so afraid. But I think this might be goodbye.'

Gabriel swung her case into the carriage at the last moment as the guard came along the platform slamming the doors. She climbed in after it and kissed him fiercely as he leaned towards the window.

'You're being foolish.' He stood on the platform, feeling helpless as her train moved out of the station.

He wrote from Paris, and again later from Berne. He wrote of the weariness of long rail journeys and about the difficulties of language and communicating with musical directors, and rehearsals with unfamiliar orchestras. He poured out his loneliness and the heartache of being parted from her.

In Berne, there were letters from Sasha. He sensed a constraint in them; she talked of 'responsibilities', the difficulties of their love and the impossibility of looking to the future; and he was fearful again about the change in her. Was she jealous because he had gone abroad without her – or was she falling out of love?

Gabriel rented rooms in Interlaken, overlooking the

417

mountains; he walked in the snow and watched the sunrise each morning before his hours of practice on the violin. Switzerland seemed too tame, with its pretty little villages nestling in the valley bottoms and the picturesque white peaks against a blue sky. He remembered a conversation with Sasha long ago, when he had said he thought the mountains would have a grandeur comparable with that of the Yorkshire granite moors. He was wrong. The Alps did not extend one's spiritual horizons. They were claustrophobic. He remembered when he was a boy, roaming on the rocks and heather and over streams, perched on a rock playing the violin his Great-uncle Jacob had given him, letting his mind soar with the music. He had felt himself in tune with the wildness of the landscape. It was then that music had first stirred in his soul.

Leah had first heard him on the moor, he remembered. Memories of those early days made him realise how shamefully he had neglected her since he had been in love with Sasha. He had written hardly at all, and he had not been back to Yorkshire. He wrote to her now, telling her about meeting Sasha again, how he could not live without her, and that he was terrified their love might be over.

Leah wrote back at once:

Forget her. You are exposing yourself to too much pain again – and for what purpose? She is married, and will have to give you up because of William and the children sooner or later. Ask yourself, hasn't this already occurred to Sasha? Won't she have said to herself that it is better to deny yourselves a little happiness now, than to let this dreadful business drag on for years? Sasha has chosen the honourable course by giving you your freedom. You must let her go. Find someone else . . .

Sasha did not know what she was going to do. Her mind flew into a tangle of fright and panic whenever she thought of the future; she was incapable of making plans, except to disguise, with crinoline skirts and tight corseting, the fact that her body was thickening. She stopped

418

going to Lavender House to collect Gabriel's letters. She stopped writing.

Concerts in London and the West Country allowed her to forget her pregnancy for a few days or hours at a time, but music offered small consolation; whenever she performed something she had once played for Gabriel, she fell afterwards into a melancholy hopelessness; and when she was alone she wore herself out with weeping.

Then, one icy morning in December, Sasha was woken by a stronger nausea than usual. She climbed out of bed while William was still sleeping, and ran downstairs. She prayed that no one would hear her as she retched into the outside closet. After a while she went indoors and crossed the kitchen towards the hall.

It was Sunday, still barely light; Mrs Ash and Bertha had not yet begun work. The house was very silent. Sasha could not go back upstairs. The thought of lying beside William filled her with terror. She stood in the hall, shivering in her nightdress. What was she going to do when she could no longer hide Gabriel's child? When they all found out . . . her sisters, her parents. She remembered the scandal Kitty had caused, the hurt to the family. Kitty's sins were nothing compared to the disgust everyone would feel when the truth was out. She pictured her mother's face, the pain in her father's eyes, the condemnation of everyone she knew. She saw the end of her playing, and the betrayal of Gabriel's career.

The door to the dispensary corridor was open, and she went to close it. She paused, her hand on the edge of the door. A terrible idea came to her, a desperate, unthinkable solution. A moment later, she had entered the dispensary. She lit the gas and surveyed the tidy desk, the trays of papers, bowls and boxes and medical instruments. Sasha's resolve hardened. She crossed the room to the medical books on the shelves, the rows of medicines and powders in jars and bottles; she read the labels feverishly, searching for what she needed, though she had no idea what would be effective – a purge, something . . . anything.

419

Calomel, Linseed, Rhubarb . . . She took down a bottle of calomel and a jar of castor oil. Behind them stood more jars and bottles; she could read *Antimony*, and *Arsenicum*. A brown paper parcel rested beside them, and a notebook was pushed carelessly between the bottles.

She recognised the mould-stained cover. Surprise distracted her from her purpose. Had William been using the old recipes from his father's apothecary? She tipped her head to read the label on the parcel: 'For J. Wotherspoon, Esq. The Elixir. To be taken only as directed and with care.' The last words were underlined.

The door opened, and Sasha swung round, fearing William; but Aunt Georgie stood there in her nightdress and shawl and with her hair in papers. Her glance rested on the jar and the bottle in Sasha's hands.

'I was looking for something—' said Sasha.

'I heard you being sick outside.'

'It was nothing . . . probably something I ate last night.'

'Then you won't be needing that.' Aunt Georgie came towards her and took the calomel and castor oil from her. She put them back on the shelf; the parcel for Wotherspoon was lost to view.

Aunt Georgie turned to face her. 'I may be a spinster but I wasn't born yesterday, Sasha. You're going to have to make some plans. And if castor oil is all you can think of, it's a bad state you've got yourself into.'

Sasha sat down heavily at the desk. 'How did you know?'

'I guessed days ago. Is there no chance it's William's?'

Sasha shook her head. 'It's Gabriel's. I'm expecting Gabriel's child.' She pressed her knuckles against her mouth. 'Oh, Aunt Georgie – what am I going to do?'

Aunt Georgie seized her by the shoulders and made Sasha look at her. 'I'll help you. Whatever happens – do you hear? – I'm going to help you. Could you go to him? I mean, would Mr Ridgeway take you in?'

'How could I tell him? If I were to go to him and leave William everyone would know. Everyone *will* know! Aunt Georgie – help me. I can't think what to do!'

★ ★ ★

Hope burned in Sasha's mind for the first time in weeks as she walked to Lavender House from the railway station. Could she go there in the last months of the pregnancy as Aunt Georgie had suggested, pretend Algie had booked her for a longer tour than usual, and stay until after the baby was born? Amazed by Aunt Georgie's composure, she had told her about the house, and about Gabriel being abroad.

'You must write and tell him,' Aunt Georgie had said. 'You don't have to work this out alone . . . You're not alone.'

Was it possible, with Aunt Georgie's collusion, that she might keep the child a secret? Mrs Love and her baby. She began to plan with a frantic, desperate kind of rationality. They would hire a nurse to live in at Lavender House. They would decide together how to bring up the child. She would write to Gabriel at once; she would tell him that everything would be arranged by the time he came back from the Continent. There would be no scandal. No one would know except Aunt Georgie. Excitement seized her as she hurried up the path and unlocked the door.

The house was very cold. A pile of letters lay on the mat, all from Gabriel. She picked them up and tormented herself by leaving them on the piano unopened; she would not read them until she had lit a fire in the sitting room and got the stove going in the kitchen. But she touched them every time she passed the piano. Ripples of happiness ran through her, as she imagined herself sitting by the fireside. At last, wrapping herself in a shawl, she curled her feet under her in the armchair with the pile of letters in her lap.

My Darling Sasha,

Your last letter was so strained and formal. Have I hurt you by boasting about the welcome I received here in Interlaken? Write soon. Put my mind at rest that it could never be over between us. If I had thought I would be so affected by the separation, or

that it might do us so much harm, I would never have
left England. I picture you going to Lavender House,
sitting by our fireside with this letter in your hand,
perhaps playing the piano a little afterwards. I try to
remember how happy we have been, but the memory
of your strangeness before we parted fills me with
fear and torment. Believe me, Sasha, the acclaim of
audiences means nothing to me without you.

I think of you – your wonderful passionate way of
playing, and I long for you with all my body and soul.
I am here in Interlaken for another two weeks. If you
do not write soon I shall die.

Gabriel.

The next letter was dated two weeks later.

Darling Sasha,

The truth is, it is hard to think straight, or plan
anything, or envisage a future where I could ever be
happy again if you were not beside me. Write soon,
my darling.

I wish you could share the beauty of the mountains
with me. I wish you could see how pretty the little
houses look against the hillside, and hear the sound
of the cow-bells that carries for miles on the pure air.
I want you for my own. For years and years together.
For the whole of eternity.

Why do you not write? I have been to collect my
letters every day this week and there are none –
except a message from Algie extending the tour
beyond Christmas, and pious messages from Leah
telling me I should give you up. Never. Never. Have I
hurt you still? Or is it harder now for you to escape to
Lavender House? Does your husband keep you in
Penbury? Are all your concerts near to home? Are
you angry with me? You see how my mind goes in
circles? I cannot tell which is the worse torture – the
prospect of spending Christmas alone here abroad, or
the thought of you in the bosom of your family, with

Elliman demanding you play Chopin, or Mendelssohn! for the Turbots and Mayor Wotherspoon.

You talk of impossibility with regard to the future. Do you remember – when we first knew that we loved one another – how impossible it seemed then? And yet, it was all so very simple in the end. We love one another. There is nothing that can keep us apart.

If you read this letter soon and are in a position to write to me, then direct your mail from now on to Wiesbaden at the address below. I love you more than life itself, Sasha, more than anything in heaven and earth. I remain, your

Gabriel . . .

The next was a brief note – the handwriting scrawled and desperate.

Darling Sasha,

It was the stupidest thing I ever did to come away on tour. I am distracted with longing for you. Write, write, write, write.

Sasha held the letter to her cheek. How could she have believed it was over? She tucked it into her bodice and opened the next . . .

My Darling Sasha,

Has our correspondence gone astray? Perhaps your letters have been misdirected? I shall go on writing, and hope to hear from you here in Wiesbaden. I have been playing with a German orchestra, very talented, they come regularly to play at the municipal theatre. And here I have a piece of amazing news for you. I will tell you how it was, as closely as I remember it.

The orchestra had put up at the same hotel in the town. I had been watching them from the hotel lounge; the players milling about in the vestibule, arguing over the instruments being unloaded from the carriages outside. Their confusion made me smile, recalling tours with Algie's orchestra, thankful almost to be travelling alone.

There was a woman amongst the players. She was very graceful and beautiful, with fair hair, like yours, under a little blue hat. She was very much at ease with her fellow musicians. There was something else about her, more than the remarkable colour of her hair, that made my attention return to her again as I read my newspaper. It was almost as if I had seen her before. Something about her made me think of you, as all beautiful women make me think of you, as other things – a perfume, a sound, the strains of a piano – remind me.

The musicians came into the lounge before dinner, and I introduced myself in my execrable German. The woman held out her hand and said, 'Mr Ridgeway. We have heard all about you.' She paid the usual compliments with regard to Vieuxtemps, Joachim, etc – though I have heard them too often now to be flattered. 'You are English,' I said in surprise. 'Very much so,' she replied. 'Though I have lived abroad for some years.' She said she knew I was from Yorkshire, and that she had family living in Yorkshire.

'What a coincidence,' I said at first. Not guessing – as I am sure by now you have guessed, my clever Sasha – who she was. 'My sister has written from Yorkshire,' she continued. 'She told me you were going to be in Germany, and I asked our Director to make a special point of meeting you.' She regarded me steadily, and at last I understood. She said, 'I am Kitty Hammond. I am very much looking forward to playing with you.'

It seems that Leah employed an inquiry agent several months ago. The man eventually located your sister Kitty playing with an orchestra here in Germany, where she has carved out a musical life for herself. She does not in any way resemble the wicked creature I remember Leah once telling me about.

Leah has written to her on several occasions urging her to get in touch, sending news about your parents, and the nieces and nephews, and all the Runsby gossip about people Kitty says she does not know from Adam. She says she is afraid to get in touch with Leah, or indeed with anyone in the family, she is so ashamed of ill feeling in the past. I did not know, Sasha. You never told me how badly your husband used your sister soon after you were married. How painful that must have been for you, and no wonder you find it difficult to forgive – though she wishes your forgiveness and asks me to tell you so. She says she may have been as much to blame as Elliman ever was. She has been very frank and open. It makes me detest Elliman all the more, when I remember that first Christmas when we fell in love and you stayed true to your marriage vows.

Leah has told Kitty all about your playing; she told her too about sending me to the university, about my career, and, last of all, about this European tour. Kitty has been very pleasant and helpful, and wants to know even more about what you are doing. I find it hard to satisfy her curiosity without revealing how much you mean to me. Talking about you brings on a terrible heartsickness for you and for Lavender House.

I really think your sister means to make amends. How satisfying it would be, if one day you could be reunited, now that your husband need not be a point of discord between you? She plays the cello with wonderful proficiency. There is a peculiar fascination in her style, less fire than in your playing, but a dreamy absorption . . .

Sasha let the letter fall to her lap. Was he really such a fool? There was no point in reading further. Like a long-limbed, elegant spider, Kitty would draw him into her web. She looked out into the gathering dark of the garden with her arms folded tightly to prevent herself from crying out. She remembered the times they had made love there in that room, and upstairs in the tiny bedroom. Kitty would corrupt the memories. Nothing would survive except the child growing inside her.

She looked at the unopened letters and was tempted to put them on the fire unread. Then she tore one open and scanned it feverishly.

Darling Sasha!

What is wrong? All these weeks, and I have heard nothing at all. If you do not write I shall lose my mind. Kitty has been a good friend while we have been in Wiesbaden. She has stayed on here and may play some more concerts with me. It is so obvious that you are sisters. In some lights the likeness is quite strong. And, in a poor way, that is a small comfort to me. I do not know now why I did not recognise her from the first. And yet – there was something familiar about her. I remember the portrait your father painted – the one that now belongs to Algie . . .

Sasha tore open another letter, scanning the lines for mention of Kitty, and then the next and the next . . .

. . . She has introduced me to the music of Brahms – I think you will soon become an enthusiast – as I am. She has persuaded me to join her and some of her fellow players in a chamber ensemble, and we have had a successful impromptu set of performances all around about . . .

Darling Sasha,

. . . It is such a comfort to me, to be in Kitty's company. You must forgive her for old wrongs. She has plans to come back to England . . .

Dearest Sasha,

Am I really to believe that you meant what you said? Algie writes from England and tells me you have played in concerts in London and in Salisbury, so I know you have been able to escape from Penbury – and that you might have gone to Lavender House. What conclusions am I to draw, except that you were in deadly earnest when you said you had given me my freedom and have decided to give me up for the sake of your husband and children?

I have eight weeks more of touring Germany and then expect to return to England. I hope you will see me, and at least give our love a second chance. Kitty has asked if she might travel back to England with me. Algie says he can get her a billing – also the pianist who travels with her. Algie has suggested occasional trio performances, about which I am only too willing. Kitty, and Kurt the pianist, have asked me to lead them. She has a good feeling for our kind of music, Sasha. And I have a fanciful dream about the three of us one day playing together. But I shall wait until I see you. Kitty says she looks forward . . .

Blinded by tears Sasha tore up the letter in her lap and threw the pieces on the fire. Systematically she began to shred the others. She flung them into the flames and, leaning forward, pushed them into the coals with the poker.

'You stupid idiot! You stupid, stupid idiot!'

Chapter Nineteen

Sasha returned to Penbury that evening and arrived after the children had gone to bed.

'Sasha, you look terrible! Why have you come home so soon?' Aunt Georgie's hands flew to her mouth. 'You haven't done anything silly? Oh, you haven't—'

'I've come to my senses. It's no use running away, Aunt Georgie. It's no use trying to hide from him.' She unfastened her cloak, and Aunt Georgie took it from her shoulders.

William had come out from the dining room. He stared at Sasha in surprise. 'Hide from whom? I thought you were supposed to be with Ross.'

'There is no tour.' Sasha glanced at Aunt Georgie, who ducked her head and scuttled away with Sasha's cloak. Sasha went towards William, seeing his expression alter, become baffled, then guarded. 'There never was a tour. I lied. And soon there'll be no more concerts. I'm going to give up playing. Can we go into the dining room? I have to tell you something.'

William frowned, then turned back into the room; he walked to the mantelshelf and reached for his cigars. 'Well—' He tried to make a joke of it. 'This is a bit of a mystery. But I'm not sorry if you mean it about giving up the concerts.'

Sasha shut the door behind her and leaned against it. She closed her eyes, fighting for air and for snatches of courage. 'There's no mystery. And there's no respectable way of saying this, William. I'm pregnant.'

He hesitated with his hand above the open box of cigars, tried to continue the movement and take one, then changed his mind and sat down on the nearest chair. For a long time he struggled to remain calm, selecting a sentence from the thoughts churning in his mind. At last he managed, 'Whose is it?'

'It doesn't matter.'

'Doesn't matter – when sure as damnation it isn't mine? You stand there, cool as . . . as . . . You say it doesn't matter!'

'It happened on tour.'

'The blackguard. Who was it – Ross?'

'No. Of course it wasn't Algie.' She sat down at the end of the table and traced her hand along the polished top, feeling for the grain under her finger tips. She had a strong and inappropriate desire to laugh. 'And he isn't a blackguard, as you so quaintly put it. It was always my fault, not his.'

He seemed truly bewildered. 'Yours! Women are above that sort of temptation. It's men who are at the mercy of their natures.'

'How can you say such a thing after Kitty! And when we've shared a bed for ten years? When you *know* how my nature responds.'

'But not to me, Sasha. Not to me any more.' His expression was bitter. His humiliation gave a direction to his thoughts. He stood and went again to the mantelshelf. With trembling hands he selected a cigar, and this time trimmed and lit it. 'I suppose you're wondering what I'm going to do about this charming piece of news?'

'I can honestly say I don't know what to expect. I mean – for once, William, I can't predict how you'll react.'

'I dare say you can't. Throw you out, eh? Throw you and your child on the street? Is that what you think?'

'It had crossed my mind.'

'You think I'm a monster?'

'No, I don't. You may not believe me – but I'm truly

429

sorry to hurt you in this way.'

He jabbed the cigar at her. 'Don't you pretend to have a conscience. Not after this. You bitch! You trollop!' Sasha flinched.

William sat down, shocked by the explosive force of words he had never before used in his life. 'You were my guiding light,' he said brokenly. 'After that business with Kitty I thought no woman could ever be as blameless and forgiving as you. I've been tempted since. Oh, I have been tempted . . .'

He remembered the offers of payment in kind for a bottle of cough or purging mixture, the soft white bodies of women who had revealed more than their ailments in his consulting room. 'But I've never again gone down that path. I was always prevented by the image of your sweetness and your goodness. You were my *wife*. Who are Meredith and Pippa to look to, except to you for their moral guidance? My wife. Their mother. The spiritual light of the family.'

'William! I'm not a guiding light! I am neither *sweet* nor *good*. We were drifting apart and I fell in love.'

'Who is he? I'd like to kill him. Does he know about the child?'

'No.' Sasha felt her tight control of her emotions begin to slip. 'And this is getting us nowhere. I need you to say what you want me to do. There's the practice to consider . . . I realise you won't want a scandal.'

'It's a bit late to think of that.'

'I can go away somewhere. I'll do whatever you want.'

He leaned forward. 'At this very moment I want you out of my sight. Oh, yes, you'd like that! Go off with your lover and leave me to face all the disgrace of a runaway wife!'

'I don't want you to suffer – I don't want anyone else to suffer. I'm truly sorry it's come to this.' She remembered the hopes they had once had, the happy times in that house when the children were tiny.

Her regret seemed to sober him. He drew on his cigar. 'It's getting late. I'll sleep in the attic room tonight. We'll talk about this in the morning.' He went out without closing the door.

Sasha heard him go along the corridor and climb the stairs. The fire was burning low; the light from the lamp hurt her eyes. She rested her face on her arms and wept silent, hopeless tears at the thought of William sleeping in Gabriel's old room.

'I've decided, for the sake of the practice and the children, I must try to live with the fact of your infidelity.' William walked to the window and stared down at the road, as if to avoid looking at the bed where Sasha sat, one arm resting on the brass rail at its foot. 'I shall allow your baby to bear my name after it's born. I realise this means your concert days are over and – since there'll be no income from that source – I see it as my Christian duty to support you and your child.'

'That's very generous—'

'To all intents and purposes the child will seem to be mine until such a time as it is old enough to inherit – but then, you can be sure it won't receive a penny in my will. Now to the domestic arrangements.' He moved away from the window uneasily. 'From now on our marriage is over in all but name. I no longer think of you as my wife. And you're no longer a fit mother for my children. However, we shall have to go on sharing this room; the servants must suspect nothing – I've explained my move to the attic last night as insomnia. I shall take Lily and Aunt Georgie into my confidence. It will be painful, but I've decided it's necessary.'

'Aunt Georgie already knows.'

He stared. 'You told my aunt?'

'She guessed. She wasn't so very shocked.'

'I've always thought Aunt Georgie was peculiar!'

'She's human. Is that a rarity among maiden aunts? William – do we have to be so formal about all this?'

'I am trying very hard, Sasha, to see the situation in rational terms, to be civilised about it – I mean, of course, about the fact that my wife has had criminal intercourse with another man.'

431

'I can't explain it. I can't excuse it. I wish you would shout at me again or something. Throw me out if that's what you want.'

'Oh, I might yet do that. You offend me, Sasha. I don't think I can bear to look at you, knowing what you've done.' William's hands trembled as he gripped the bed-rail near her hand. 'You'll give him up, of course.'

'I already have.'

'Do you . . . care for me at all?'

Sasha hesitated. 'I'm very fond of you. I'm sorry to have hurt you.'

It wasn't the answer he wanted, but it would have to do. He did not want to lose her. He could not envisage a situation where he would 'throw her out'. Not Sasha. Turn her out for being an adulteress? He still could not believe it was true, that those vile, tainted words could be associated with her. His stomach revolted.

'We haven't talked about the children,' Sasha said. 'They'll have to know about the baby.'

He frowned. Something was on his mind and he clearly felt uncomfortable about it – yet he was not so uneasy that he was going to duck the issue. 'They needn't know anything until it's happened.' He cleared his throat. 'When do you think the baby is due?'

'I don't know. April, perhaps.'

'Well then. After Christmas, when your condition becomes . . . obvious, you must arrange to go away to the coast – we'll say you've been ill and need to convalesce. I don't want to see you. I don't want to watch your body swell. I couldn't bear . . .' His voice broke and he recovered himself. 'I don't want the child to be born in this house.'

Sasha agreed, feeling cold and numb.

'My aunt and sister will take full charge of Pippa,' he continued. 'I've decided that Meredith will go away to school as soon as it can be arranged.'

'No!' she gasped. 'I won't allow it.'

'You don't have any say in the matter. They are my children. You've forfeited all rights to them as a mother. In Meredith's holidays—'

432

'No!' Sasha repeated, white with anger.

'In the holidays you will again arrange to be away. I can allow you to live here with your baby for the sake of decency, but I will not allow you to corrupt my children. From now on, Pippa and Meredith will be in the chief care of Lily and Aunt Georgie—'

'It's too cruel! To send Merry away – it would break his heart – and mine.'

'You've already shown you haven't got one. And Meredith is no longer a baby. If you remember, I always wanted him to go away to school.'

Sasha shook her head distractedly. 'You can't do it. I won't let you.'

'I think you'll find I can do anything I like. I'm their father. I have the power of law on my side.'

'People will think it strange if Meredith never sees his mother.'

'They'll simply think you're too self-absorbed to bother with him. You never bothered when a concert tour took you away from home.'

Sasha sat like stone when he had gone, gripping the rail of the bed, wanting to escape the trap she had walked into the previous evening. She wanted Gabriel; and she remembered Gabriel was with Kitty. Kitty was coming with him to England. Once Kitty had what she wanted, she did not let go.

Leah sat in the window of her cottage overlooking the quayside and read Kitty's letter from Wiesbaden:

> Well, sister dear, I am sure you needed the smelling salts when you saw a letter from me after all this time . . .

Leah sighed. She had been fooling herself if she thought Kitty might have changed over the years, or that there would be some comfort in healing old rifts. Since Felicity's death she had felt increasingly responsible about her wayward sister. She remembered the affair with Werner

Backhaus, and wondered whether she might have prevented disaster if she had been more vigilant; whether if she had exerted more influence as the eldest sister, she could even have prevented the Porky Portland affair.

Leah was lonely. The others, Lavinia and Sasha, had their husbands and children, but she was thrown very much on memories, now she had reached forty. She had the cottage; there was the garden to tend in the summer, her painting and the gallery to occupy her. From time to time she visited Lavinia, and travelled to Bristol to see her parents; she played her violin with the local musical society, and had several friends in Runsby. But since Felicity's death, and now that Gabriel no longer needed her, she was very much aware of being alone.

Gabriel rarely wrote except, more recently, to pour out his hopeless love for Sasha in the style of a doomed hero in some turgid Germanic plot.

Had it been a mistake to write to Kitty? Leah felt uneasy. Her sister's letter now it had come was a poor cure for feeling lonely. She read on:

> . . .You may be wondering why I have ignored all your efforts to seek me out until now. I have often debated with myself whether to reply to your letters, and wondered why you were so persistent. Could it be I am at last forgiven? Sasha wants to kiss and make up? Did you think I might have repented sufficiently to be brought back into the fold? I cannot tell you how often I have sat at the writing table in my room with one of your letters in front of me, my hand almost reaching for a pen. Well, curiosity has won over my better judgement. And may God have mercy on me for this moment of weakness – among my many others. You might be surprised at how little I regret most of those weaknesses, how much fun they have often been. Even more so, to learn how much I pity Lavinia and Sasha their narrow domestic worlds.
>
> I have strangely little pity for you, Leah – an 'old maid'. You see how we share that honour? And how

very glad I am, not to have fallen into the matrimonial trap. I sincerely hope you are too.

I am, in a way, reformed. I have met someone new – someone so much more promising than all the rest. And this, my dear, if I am honest, may well be the reason I have written. I have a wicked desire to shake you up a little, to knock you off that pedestal, where you have always been so pleased to plant your maidenly boots. Do you remember, you told me your pet musician was touring Germany with his violin? I thought how amusing it would be to meet this student of yours. I was curious to discover what was so extraordinary about him. You see, it sounded from your lavish praise – forgive me for being blunt – it sounded as if you were a little in love with the man.

I had no difficulty in persuading our Director to invite Gabriel Ridgeway to play in Wiesbaden. I have heard him since in several concerts. He is magnificent, Leah. No, truly. I have to confess, I admire the results of your efforts. I have persuaded him to play in a musical trio. Do you remember our trios and quartets with Sasha? He tells me he has played in concerts with Sasha, but he is curiously reluctant to talk about her. I smell an intrigue – one of a romantic nature. (And he is very romantic. The German women all swoon wherever he appears.) But, back to Sasha. Is there something to tell? . . .

Leah wrote at once. She said she was glad they were in contact again.

May I tell the parents I have found you, Kitty? Please soften that cruel heart of yours a little. It would mean so much to them to know you are safe . . .

She paused, then wrote very determinedly:

I have no gossip for you about Sasha. And quite frankly, I wish you had not implied any such thing.

435

Sasha is a devoted mother and extremely happily married to William. Give my love to Gabriel and tell him not to lose his heart to a German Fräulein. Say that I hope to see him when he comes home. I hope to see you both. It is time old wounds were mended.

'I have heard again from your mentor . . . My sister Leah.'

Gabriel looked up from his coffee. He and Kitty sat with the other musicians in a restaurant in Mainz, where they had played in an afternoon concert. It was that melancholy time in the early evening when lights illuminated all the restaurants though they still remained half empty. The darkness outside revealed shadowy figures, hurrying home from work rather than strolling out to enjoy themselves. It was a time of day that always reminded him how far away he was from home.

'Leah asks you to go to see her when you get back to England. She wants me to go with you.'

'I shall. I'm tired of touring.'

'Would you like me to come with you?'

'To England?'

'To see Leah.'

'As you like. You may not be ready to leave Germany.'

'Why don't you stay until the winter is over?' she coaxed. 'January and February are so invigorating here. And anyway, why are you in such a hurry? Are English audiences so tempting?'

'I don't suppose they are.'

'I know your lady-friend hasn't written.'

He flicked a glance at her. 'And how do you know that?'

'I see you going to the post office nearly every day. You come back with a face as long as a fiddle.'

He did not answer.

Kitty leaned back in her chair and smiled at him. 'I have friends in France. I've written to tell them about you. They want to hear you play. Will you do some concerts with us – in January?'

'Perhaps. If Algie hasn't booked anything at home.'

'It would be such fun. The French don't take it all so *seriously* as they do here in Germany. And you're a very exciting player. I was surprised, even though Leah had told me all about you. Your playing is very physical as well as cerebral. I like that in a musician. It's important, don't you think? Sasha's playing was always so internal. She was very controlled and intense at the piano. Strong, though. It always amazed me that someone so small should have all that energy and endurance for some of the more difficult Chopin and Beethoven. But of course, you know. You played in concerts together.'

She waited, watching him, smiling in that teasing way she had, inviting him to confide in her.

'The violin seems to me a much more satisfactory instrument than the piano.' Gabriel poured himself more coffee, hoping to distract her from talking about Sasha. He knew she was probing. He must be careful. 'The sound is right there under one's fingers; it throbs almost before you draw the bow, as if in expectation of coming to life. It's the same with the cello.'

'Of course. But the creature is almost as monstrous as a piano. So unwieldy. And there are the practical problems – the transportation, how to look graceful still in a crinoline, how to anchor the spike to a polished floor!' Kitty rested her chin in her hand, looking at him intently. 'I really think you *should* come with us to France. I have a feeling that you and I could get along so well.'

There was no news from Sasha at Christmas, and Algie did not mention her in his letters. Gabriel did not ask, afraid he would learn she had again been playing away from home, that she had been able to collect his letters from Lavender House and had ignored his pleas to write.

He left Germany with Kitty and the pianist Kurt. In Paris, the gossip papers were full of stories about the trio: they speculated on whether Kitty was romantically linked with the fair and handsome Kurt, or with the more enigmatic Gabriel. Kitty fed the speculations with hints

437

here and there and behaved flirtatiously, first on one arm, then another, at soirées and parties.

Gabriel had fallen under the spell of too many women in the past not to respond to her allure. Kitty was sparkling and sophisticated and at ease in any company; he was beguiled by her pale elegance and self-confidence; and her playing was dark and fascinating. She hardly ever seemed to practise as far as he could tell, and yet she rarely played badly. They were invited to private parties, to the houses of professors at the Conservatoire who remembered Gabriel from his student days. They travelled through France and were asked to play in concerts and at musical evenings at the homes of concert artists.

Kitty hung more frequently on Gabriel's arm. One evening she kissed him in the darkness of a cab as he drove with her to their hotel. Kitty was soft and scented and she pulsed with an animal sensuality. He wound his arm about her as they walked along the corridor to her rooms and they kissed again as they reached her door. Her body moulded itself sinuously to his.

'Come to my room,' she whispered.

'It's late. And we're tipsy. You'll have changed your mind by the morning, and we'll wonder what I'm doing in your bed.'

'I don't think there would be much doubt about what you'd been doing.'

'All the same.' He eased himself away from her.

She put a hand to her hair; he thought that she was going to unfasten it. The movement of her arm emphasised the line of her bodice; it barely skimmed her shoulders and revealed the fullness of her breasts.

He stroked her neck, rubbing his thumb against the pulse of her throat.

Kitty yawned luxuriously, and lifted her arms behind her head. She laughed. 'I'm not like my sisters, as you'll have guessed.'

'You've told me your history.'

'Not all of it.'

'I know about Elliman.'

438

'I didn't tell you that Sasha stole him from me in the first place. She made sure he jilted me by telling him a story about my having a love affair with a married man.'

'Only a story?' He let his hand fall from her shoulder.

'Well, perhaps there was a *little* bit of truth in it. But Sasha always was a Goody-Two-Shoes . . .' She paused. 'Wouldn't you say that describes her?'

'I wouldn't know,' he said restlessly. 'But – I'm sure you don't remember her very well. You haven't seen any of your sisters for several years.'

'And you have.'

'Yes . . . I have.'

She searched for her key in a beaded purse that hung from her wrist and turned to unlock the door. 'Algie says he's very disappointed in Sasha. He had been relying on her while you were away and she's simply given up *all* her concerts for the next year.'

Gabriel stared, taking in what she had said, seeing the curve of her neck and spine, the whiteness stretched over the small bones – like Sasha, like Leah, like so many women he had known. He gripped the smooth bump of her shoulder and forced her round to face him. 'What do you mean – she's given them up?'

'Didn't you know?'

'When did he tell you that?'

'Ages ago. Don't look so surprised. I asked Algie what Sasha was doing after Christmas. I wanted his programme for the next season. If Kurt and I are going to play in England—'

'What *exactly* did he say?'

'That he thought we might like to play in some of the northern concerts—'

'I mean, what did he say about Sasha?'

'Something about her not wanting to play any more— Would you mind not being quite so uncouth. You're hurting.' He let go of her, and she rubbed at her shoulder.

He saw the red marks made by his fingers, and murmured an apology.

'Algie says Sasha hasn't been seen anywhere in public

since Christmas. And she's told him she won't play again. She says the concert circuit was getting too much for her and she's going to devote herself to husband and family.'

'Thank you.'

'Does it matter?' She stood in the open doorway. Her expression invited him into the darkness of the room.

'I wish you'd told me sooner,' Gabriel said as he walked away.

Algie could tell him nothing more when they got back to England. He said that 'for personal reasons' Sasha had decided to give up playing. He had not seen her since her last concert.

Gabriel left Kitty and Kurt in London and went straight to Lavender House.

Snow lay frozen in drifts across the garden. There were no footprints on the front path, no signs of life except for the arrowhead tracks of birds. He let himself into the house with a deep sense of unease, not knowing what he would find. A message? An explanation of some kind?

The air smelled sooty and damp. A heap of his letters lay behind the door; he picked them up and climbed the stairs, tidying the pile like playing cards in his hand.

He went into the bedroom and stared at the bed. The room looked dreary and impersonal. A glass vase on the window sill held dead flowers: the heads were brown and crisp, the leaves clinging to the stems in blackened curls, and a greenish scum lined the inside of the vase. So she had not even been there. Nothing had been touched.

He returned to the ground floor and wandered from room to room. What did it mean? He leaned on the piano, and remembered how he had covered it with lilies on her birthday; they had made love, crushing the flowers into their clothes, leaving rusty pollen smears.

The view from the window was flat and grey; a mist lay low on the hills. He was frightened by the emptiness in him, relieved only by a craving for Sasha; he pictured her at the piano, imagined her hands touching the keys. Had she really thought he might forget her – wanted him to?

Because it had all become too much for her? Because of her children? Or because of a cracked idea about giving him his freedom?

His glance fell on the grate and he felt a pulse of excitement as he saw the charred paper. Then the implications hit him. He knelt by the hearth and searched through the ashes, blackening his fingers as he picked out scraps of paper. She had burned his early letters. So she really had decided it was over between them.

Putting the rest of the letters on the piano in case she should return for them, Gabriel went outside and down the lane to the landlady's cottage. He paid up the rent for the whole year, determined not to accept that anything had ended.

'We were wondering where you'd got to, Mr Love,' Mrs Mynott said. 'It's such a long time since we saw either of you here.'

'We've been very busy – abroad.'

'It hardly seems worth your while to keep the house on. It gets so damp,' she prompted, 'with no heat through the winter.'

'Yes, I see. Well then – we must decide whether to keep it on after another winter.' He forced an affability into his voice and raised his hat. 'We'll let you know.'

Gabriel made his way to the railway station. He had to see her. Had she given up her playing because she was afraid of meeting him again? He *knew* she still loved him. He knew it had not been a passing affair. Not for either of them.

On an impulse he caught the train to Bath instead of London; he travelled to Bristol and went to the Hammonds at Hanover Terrace.

'Gabriel!' exclaimed Nathaniel in delight. 'Oh, it's been too long, too long, dear boy. We haven't seen you since – let me see – that concert. Two years ago? What a night that was. You must tell us all you've been doing.'

Gabriel told them about his foreign tour, and was forced into telling them he had met Kitty.

'Kitty's in England?' gasped Mrs Hammond, her hand

to her breast, spots of colour flushing her cheeks. 'Oh, Gabriel! What a shock to spring on us! But if she's come home, why isn't she with you?'

It was hard to explain to them why he had come all the way from London and had not brought the prodigal with him. Gabriel made up a story about going to Bristol to see the orchestra director Merrill, and Kitty needing to play for Algie Ross in London. He told them about Kurt, and the plan to promote a trio in England with himself as leader. And all the time he wanted to ask them about Sasha.

He needed some proof that she had cut him out of her life and had resigned herself to her marriage and children. Frustrated, he talked about music, until he came at last to a point where he could say: 'They tell me Mrs Elliman has recently given up her playing.'

'Didn't you know?'

He reminded them that he had been abroad for several months. 'Ross told me she was finding the playing too much. If she's ill—'

'Bless you, not ill.' Mrs Hammond smiled at her husband. 'Sasha and William are going to have another child. She's been looking peaky, but one does in the early months . . . and a spell of sea air will soon put her right.' She went on without mercy, as if to add the final kindling to the funeral pyre. 'William is very pleased. I believe they're hoping for another boy.'

Gabriel could not speak. Sasha, Sasha, he cried silently. So you chose the safety of home and family and were too ashamed to write. But to go back to Elliman so unequivocally by bearing him a child!

He heard himself stumble out good wishes, and said he must leave for his appointment with Merrill. He promised to make Kitty go to see them when she could get away from London, and escaped as soon as he could.

Gabriel remembered he had once looked forward to seeing Kitty reunited with her sisters. Now he was less certain as he travelled with her to Yorkshire. He had

442

begun to understand Kitty a little better. And besides, since learning the truth about Sasha, nothing was a pleasure to him.

'You're so gloomy these days,' Kitty complained.

'You always manage to cheer me up,' he told her automatically.

She laughed. 'You're a bad liar.'

'So, the two of you are playing in Leeds?' said Leah when they arrived.

'Kurt's our pianist. He's arranged to follow us in a few days,' Gabriel explained. He sat in the familiar window seat and turned to look out at the choppy water of the harbour.

'Algie has planned a series of engagements for the trio, to fit in with Gabriel's northern concerts.' Kitty leaned on the piano and looked round the tiny cottage critically. Did Leah really live here all alone, with nothing to divert her except tribes of smelly fishermen and a little maidenly watercolour painting? 'Kurt and Gabriel are much better players, but I manage to keep my end up. We mostly do private parties.'

'Kitty's very good,' said Gabriel. 'She's being modest.'

'That's strange. I don't remember modesty being one of Kitty's strong points.'

Leah watched them closely, wondering about them. Kitty had a way of looking at Gabriel as if she knew him intimately; and yet, there was a coldness in his familiarity, as if he would have liked to distance himself but could not quite make the effort.

'I told you in my letters . . . I've changed.' Kitty played with the fringes on the piano cover. 'So, let's have all the news, Leah. How many little Pickersgills has Lavinia now produced? Has she forgiven me for nearly wrecking her wedding day? And will the Pickersgills let me in if we go there tomorrow?'

'Which shall I answer first?' Leah said drily. 'There are six little Pickersgills. And yes, Lavinia is almost looking forward to seeing you after all this time . . . You know about Sasha? She and William are expecting another child.' There was a noticeable pause. Leah glanced at Gabriel in the window; she sensed a tension in him and saw him tighten his jaw.

'Great heavens,' laughed Kitty. 'Will my sisters never stop producing? Do you think I should go to see them?'

'Not if you value your life,' smiled Leah wryly.

Gabriel hated them briefly for their indifference to his pain. A glance at Leah showed him that she understood, but that she would do nothing to help him. Her expression of concern seemed to mask a cruel pragmatism. She would say, if she could speak openly: Sasha's lost to you; she's another man's wife.

He felt a strong need to escape their company. 'I thought I might go to see my family.' He stood. 'I've decided to try to patch up hostilities a little. Would you be hurt, Leah, if I went this afternoon?'

'Will you stay there overnight?'

He nodded, and turned to Kitty. 'I'll be back to travel to Leeds with you in a couple of days.' Leah followed him out of the room.

Kitty listened to the murmur of voices in the hall. She could not hear the individual words, but the gist of the conversation was clear; Leah's voice consoling, Gabriel's abrupt, anxious to get away.

So, she had been right all along. Gabriel had been in love with Sasha, and Leah knew about it. He was shaken about Sasha's baby – anyone could see. Kitty went to the window and watched him leave the house, following him with her eyes, and conscious of a familiar pain, like a knife, in the gut. It was always the same. Why did love have to hurt so? She watched him until Leah came back into the room, and then said with an air of wry amusement, 'Well, now. I wonder what's upset him?'

Leah regarded her sister thoughtfully. 'Kitty – what's going on? Is there something between you two?'

Kitty shrugged. 'He's good company when he's not being gloomy. He treats me better than a lot of men I've known . . .'

'Exactly how fond of him are you?'

'Rather taken, if you want the truth.' Kitty hesitated, and said casually, 'I've been thinking I might marry him.'

'Over my dead body! If you dare to hurt him, so help me . . .'

Kitty laughed. 'That's not very sisterly of you.'

'No. It was said with every sympathetic bone in my body for Gabriel. Has he made love to you?'

'Not yet.'

'But he will,' Leah said bitterly. 'You'll make sure of that.'

'You act as if you're his mother.'

'I want him to be happy. He's made a lot of mistakes in love.'

Kitty looked out of the window. She could see Gabriel in the distance, crossing the swing bridge over the harbour, not hurrying, walking moodily. 'If you mean Sasha . . . I thought you said there was nothing to tell.'

Gabriel went back to London with Kitty and Kurt. 'You have to forget,' Leah had told him. 'For your own sake as much as Sasha's.'

Kurt was good company, a good fellow – *ein guter Kerl* among his fellow musicians. Gabriel introduced him to the players in Algie's entourage. They spent nights in coffee and chop houses and in bars together, taught the English players German drinking songs, and talked for hours about music, life, books and art, lying on couches in one or another's rooms, or on the floor, drinking, smoking. And usually Kitty was there.

Had he really once been taken in by her promises of being 'reformed' and wanting to repair the damage she had done in the past? She was totally amoral. Fascinating and shallow. She smoked cheroots like a man. She joined in the talk and said things were 'bloody' when they were, and laughed a lot and drank a lot of burgundy; and he knew that sooner or later he would want to make love to her.

Gabriel remembered drinking burgundy with Sasha,

lying in the sun side by side on the carpet, hands touching, the mere pressure of her fingers stirring him to want her. He tried to forget, as Leah had said he must, for his own peace of mind. He laughed more with Kitty, and let her sensuality work its effect on him.

Chapter Twenty

Sasha had a strong sense of being trapped as William walked towards her across the lawn. He looked harassed.

'I have to see Wotherspoon. I'm afraid it means we must cancel our arrangement to visit your parents this afternoon.'

She nodded. 'I'm sorry.'

For the sake of appearances they had adopted this pretence at mutual consideration. It was understood they did not talk about the difficulties of their situation, unless they were pushed into it by a need to discuss practicalities. Sometimes, when his glance fell on her in an unguarded moment Sasha would see William's face contract with pain, but it was a pain of humiliation more than grief.

'Have you any objections to my going without you?' said Sasha. 'This first visit with the baby would perhaps be easier anyway if I go alone.'

'You'll take the train? You'll leave Pippa here.'

'I shan't do anything that isn't *permitted*. And Pippa would far rather not be made to dress up and sit in her grandmother's drawing room.'

'She is becoming as unruly as her brother used to be. I shall have to talk to Aunt Georgie about her.'

He made such remarks deliberately. To remind her she had transgressed, she was no longer a fit mother. To hurt. William turned back to the house, then remembered the formalities. 'Give your parents my apologies and my regards.'

Sasha took the train for Bristol with a profound sense of release. She had been reluctant to return to Penbury after the baby was born, but the story of her ill health and a 'need for sea air' could not be sustained indefinitely; the doctor's wife must be back at William's side. The escape to Devon had been good for her. There, she had nursed a sense of independence, while at the same time acknowledging that it was an illusion: William had paid the rent and for the attendance of a midwife, and dictated the terms on which she existed. The story that she had gone away because of a failure of strength during her pregnancy had not altogether been a fiction; but the simple lifestyle away from Penbury had eased the incapacitating heartache, the regrets and memories about Gabriel, and thoughts of Meredith being sent away to school. There had been walks along the shore, evenings alone with her piano – the one condition on which she had agreed to her exile: 'I *must* have my piano with me if I'm to keep my spirit intact.' She had sent to Exeter for a tuner, and had played every afternoon and evening to the point of exhaustion.

'You've brought the baby!' exclaimed Mrs Hammond. Her face fell. 'But no Pippa.'

'And no husband,' Sasha said cheerfully. 'William sends his apologies.' She explained about the call to Wotherspoon.

'We heard Wotherspoon was asked to stand down as mayor this year,' said Mrs Hammond.

'I've been away,' Sasha reminded them. 'I don't know *all* the gossip.'

Aunt Georgie had told her though about an 'indiscretion'; Wotherspoon had shown a young lady over the council rooms and had apparently been 'discovered' by the Town Clerk. It had all been a fuss about nothing, said Aunt Georgie, but the dishonour of losing office had affected Wotherspoon deeply. Sasha had been shocked to see the change in him when she returned from Devon: the shambling walk and wasted physique.

Nathaniel stepped back to regard Sasha critically. 'You look much better for all that sea air. Such a long spell away though. So nervous and ill. Your mother and I have been worried about you.'

Mrs Hammond nodded. 'Come and sit down. Let me see my grandchild.' She took the baby from Sasha. 'Ah – she's beautiful. Like her mother. But dark! Is there dark hair in William's family?'

'I – believe so.' Sasha sat beside her.

Her mother kissed the baby's cheek. 'Now. I don't want you to be angry, Sasha . . . but, guess who has been coming to visit us . . .' She looked up. 'Kitty! Your sister Kitty.'

'I knew she was in England.' Sasha struggled to maintain an air of unconcern.

'She and Gabriel have played in Bath and Bristol. If you had been at home you might have come to their concerts.'

'They were very good,' said Nathaniel. 'Kitty is playing better than she ever did. They came to see us afterwards – all of them. Gabriel, and the German pianist. They played us some Brahms.'

'Was Gabriel well?' Sasha tried to keep the longing for him from her voice. The thought that he had been in the room only recently resonated in her mind. She heard echoes of the violin, saw him standing by the piano, the way he held the bow and the energy of his playing.

'He was on fine form. Of course, everyone knows him chiefly as a soloist still, but he says he likes playing chamber music. He's willing to share the lime-light, do you see. He's a generous fellow. There aren't many soloists like that. Kitty is clearly very fond of him. Your mother has been hearing wedding bells again.'

'I think marriage is a distinct possibility,' Mrs Hammond acknowledged. 'They seem to have such a jolly time playing together. And they travel all over the place.'

Sasha felt the blood rush to her head. So all her fears had been founded. Kitty already had him parcelled up and in her spell. How could she bear it if they married – the family visits, the news of children, nieces and nephews?

'Mother, have you entirely forgotten how much Kitty injured us all?' She spoke with a barely suppressed violence.

'But darling – it was all so long ago.'

'I remember it well enough.'

'If we can't forgive one another, what would be the point of the human race?' Mrs Hammond bent and again kissed the baby.

Sasha turned to her father, eager to change the subject. 'Are you painting these days?'

'On and off. I'm exhibiting at the Academy here and in London this summer. But these new bloods are getting all the attention. I've been working on a few landscapes. Country scenes round about. Come and see.'

Sasha followed him to the studio and looked at his paintings. She remembered coming here as a child, to the same smell of paint and turpentine; she remembered the cold clear light. The studio was always so sharp in her memory.

'What are you thinking about?' said her father.

'I'm remembering when we all sat for the painting.'

'Ah – I have something to tell you about that portrait. Gabriel has bought it. He tells me he saw it years ago. He always vowed that if he was ever wealthy enough, he would have it.'

'But Algie has *The Beautiful Hammond Girls*.'

'Gabriel has persuaded Ross to part with it. I expect Kitty had something to do with it. Kitty can wind anyone round her little finger. It was a very good likeness of Kitty. If he marries her, at least the portrait will stay in the family.'

Sasha, too full of emotion to trust herself to speak, pretended an interest in more of her father's paintings. 'I shall never be reconciled with Kitty,' she said after a while. 'If he marries her . . . I shall never communicate with him again.'

'But you and he played so well together.'

'Never,' she repeated.

'Kitty's our daughter, Sasha. Your sister. Your mother

and I have to forgive. You would too – if Merry, or Pippa, or that dear little creature downstairs ever did anything to hurt you.' He placed one of the paintings on his easel for her to view properly and said briskly, 'How is Meredith settling into his school?'

Sasha thought of Aunt Georgie's accounts and Meredith's letters. 'He is very unhappy.'

'He's a sensitive child. I'm not sure it will suit him. The best thing was for him to have a tutor. But Gabriel was bound to move on. It would have been criminal for all that talent to go to waste on reading and writing.'

'Yes,' Sasha said dully.

'Meredith will survive. William has ambitions for him. That's not a bad thing in a man who has had to work his way up from poor beginnings. He wants the best for his son, Sasha. You ought to be proud of him.'

Meredith did not understand why his mother never came to see him, though she sent him letters with her love and to say she hoped he would try to be happy. He did not understand why he was not allowed to write to her, nor to let his father know that she wrote to him, or why, at Easter, when he had gone home for the holidays, she had stayed in Devon all alone. 'Practising the piano,' according to his father. Did she like being alone with her piano so very much? More than she loved him and Pippa?

At least they had kept Pippa in Penbury; his father had not sent her away to a horrible place where nobody liked you. He did not hate his mother for going away; he half understood about her playing the piano; he felt the same about the viola. But he hated his father for sending him here. His father said he was not to write and tell them when he was unhappy; he said it showed ingratitude, and that he was giving him a fine education. Meredith wrote instead to Aunt Georgie, who had told him he might say whatever he pleased – even the horrible things about his school-fellows and how he had to cry himself to sleep without anyone hearing. She said she would read out only the cheerful bits to his father and his Aunt Lily, and she

451

would let his mother know all the rest.

But if his mother cared when he was unhappy, why did she never come to see him . . .?

'Elliman. Look lively, boy. Stop day-dreaming! . . .'

Meredith's attention flicked from the sunshine outside the window and he bent his head to his prep book. It was afternoon. Hours to go before tea-time. His heart sank as he heard the master's voice again, calling him out to the front of the classroom.

'Your great-aunt has come to see you, Elliman. She has asked if she might take you for an outing.' The master shut the classroom door behind them and walked with him to the stairs. 'You are very fortunate, boy. Are you not grateful for the privilege?'

Meredith murmured a dutiful appreciation.

Aunt Georgie was below in the school entrance. She looked very pink and excited and Meredith felt acutely embarrassed; he hoped none of the boys would see her fussy clothes and silly bonnet and think she was his mother.

The thought of his mother made a lump come to Meredith's throat as he went to his peg to fetch his outdoor clothes.

'Quickly! Quickly!'

'Why? Where are we going?' Meredith caught some of Aunt Georgie's excitement. He had barely had time to put on his hat, before she whisked him out of the school.

They halted. She straightened his collar and brushed his shoulders and turned him to stand facing away from her. A second later and Meredith saw at the end of the road, dressed in a dark red coat and hat . . . His heart missed a beat. He ran, joy singing in his ears, and flung himself into his mother's arms.

'Why didn't you come to see me before?' he demanded. 'Why didn't you come home in the Easter holidays?'

Sasha hugged him to her fiercely and looked at Aunt Georgie over his head.

'I told you – your mother and father have quarrelled,' Aunt Georgie said crossly; she fussed around them and seemed very agitated. She had told him the same story several times. His mother and father did not 'get on'; that was why his mother was not allowed to come to see him. It was one of those family quarrels. They must not talk about it outside the family circle.

They walked through the Abbey gardens and went to a tea-shop, and afterwards they bought barley sugar and sat in the gardens of the park.

Sasha held Meredith against her side, his head resting against her arm. She spoke very gently and in a measured tone. 'Merry, I have something to tell you. I want you to hear it from me, because I think it's important that you should – though I'm sure your father will tell you soon. You have a baby sister. That is why I had to go away for a long time, and why I have not been to see you. I've been unwell.'

'So you haven't quarrelled?' Meredith felt a sense of relief. The nightmare of the past weeks and months slipped away and everything fell into place. Fellows at school had talked of baby brothers and sisters. The whole process was shrouded in hints at female infirmities. He sucked at a barley sugar stick and felt the warmth of his mother's arm around him; he absorbed the remembered smell of her. Now his mother was here, surely she would let him go home. 'When can I see the baby?'

Sasha was close to tears. She had known the reunion with Meredith would be difficult; but she had not known how much it would tear at her heart. 'Merry, the quarrel with your father isn't over. I may have to go away again from time to time – to clear the air. You know how it is with squabbles. But I shall come to see you and—' She glanced at Aunt Georgie, praying for her co-operation. 'Perhaps, one day soon, I shall bring the baby for you to see.'

Meredith closed his mind to her talk of quarrels. He tried to resign himself to the disappointment of staying at school. 'So I can't come home.'

'Not until the holidays.'

He concentrated on the barley sugar, sweet and comforting. 'What is the baby called?'

'Felicia . . . She is named after Felix Mendelssohn. And she is very nice and good. You'll like her.' Sasha hesitated. 'When your father tells you about her, I want you to know that – however dear the baby is to me – you are still my first-born. I will always love you best.' She kissed him. 'Now. Have you been practising on the viola?'

'I am doing the exercises Mr Ridgeway once showed me. And I'm getting better. But the teachers at school are not so patient.' Meredith thought of Gabriel and the fun they had once had, and wished they could all be together again. He had never felt he was slow and stupid when Mr Ridgeway had been his teacher.

Aunt Georgie walked back to school with him. She held the boy close when she said goodbye. 'When you write to your father, you mustn't say anything at all about today. It's our secret. Yours and mine and your mama's.'

Meredith promised; but the knot of resentment inside him tightened as he entered the school building.

Sasha too had thought of Gabriel when they talked about music. An awareness of her own unhappiness struck her with renewed force on the journey home. How terrible it was to live this lie; to hear everyone congratulate William on the bonny nature of her child; to hear from her parents, or from Leah's letters, that Gabriel was touring the country with his trio and becoming a huge success. In those moments her bitterness was almost incapacitating; she longed to fling herself down and give herself up entirely to her misery. Instead she had adopted the crippling discipline of resignation as she continued from day to day.

She and Aunt Georgie reached Penbury station, and Sasha's stoicism temporarily deserted her. Perhaps she could leave altogether. She would fetch the baby, go back to the station with Felicia in her arms and step on a train for Wales, or London, or the North. They would survive somehow; she had her gifts as a pianist; if it came to the worst she could give lessons. She would run away where nobody would find her.

Sasha told herself that she only stayed with William because of Pippa; he could not cut her off from her daughter as he had from Merry. But she knew there were other reasons. Not least, because she was afraid of total independence. It had been one thing travelling from town to town on concert tours, waiting to meet Gabriel at Lavender House. Quite another when the isolation would go on and on, month after month, year after year, cut off from Pippa and Meredith altogether, a source of speculation among everyone who knew her and of bewildered heartache to her parents. Besides – and she liked to think it was a more noble reason – how could she bring herself to do William so much harm? Was it his fault she had married him and then fallen in love with another man? Penbury would revel in the scandal. Even those who shouted the loudest against a runaway wife would shun a doctor touched by scurrilous gossip.

She went upstairs when she and Aunt Georgie reached the house. The baby was fretting to be fed. Pippa was helping Mrs Ash in the kitchen; William and Lily were in the garden, discussing some horticultural matter or other. They had barely acknowledged that she was home, and did not ask her where she had been.

Sasha's energy filled the room: the portrait brought back memories of holding her in his arms. Gabriel's mind ached with images that were too vivid; he could hear the music they had played together too sharply; but he welcomed the pain. He felt a strong need to make himself suffer.

Kitty came to stand beside him. She wound her arms round his waist and rested her chin against his arm. He remembered the previous night. She had been very much at ease in his bed. Kitty had a shockingly casual way of acknowledging the number of beds she had been in. Gabriel wondered if it would have made any difference to her if she had known, when they made love, that he had been thinking of Sasha.

'It looks very splendid there.' She thought he had bought the portrait to please her, and did not believe him when he said he had for years wanted to own the painting – or if she did, she assumed it was the prestige of having one of her father's pictures that had moved him. She did not know that *The Beautiful Hammond Girls* was for Gabriel at once the most bitter and the most lovely thing – the nearest he could ever come to touching Sasha again.

'These are very pleasant apartments.' Kitty walked about the room stroking the furniture with a proprietary air. She went to the window and looked down at the traffic in the street. 'Who would have thought it? A farmer's boy. And now – "The Incomparable".'

'That was what they said about Paganini.'

'The critics are saying it about you too.'

'Paganini was a charlatan. Is that the way you want them to think of me?'

'To be honest, I don't care, so long as people pay to listen to you. You're very scratchy today. Is anything the matter? You don't wish we hadn't . . .? You're not regretting last night?'

'No.'

'Good. I don't think I could bear it if you started protesting about sin and feeling guilty. I could be good for you, Gabriel. I do care about you. I think . . .' She tried to laugh. 'To use an old cliché, I think I'm in love with you.'

He saw that she meant it. For a moment he recognised the vulnerability in her, the need to be loved, concealed so well under an act of being cold-hearted.

'You've been in love before,' he reminded her gently. 'And so have I.'

'Many times. We're two of a kind. But perhaps we've found our match at last.'

'Perhaps.'

She sat down at the piano. 'I'm tired of men who pretend to love me and then drop me. I'm tired of the ones who go back to their wives. I want to stop. I want to call a halt, here with you.' She looked up and her eyes

456

glinted with tears. 'I know about Sasha.'

His heart lurched.

'I guessed. And Leah more or less confirmed what I thought.'

'We were very happy,' he said quietly. He turned to the picture, but there was no consolation for him there.

Kitty closed her eyes. So they *had* been together. It had not simply been a flirtation. 'I know you still want her,' she said carefully. 'But you can't have Sasha, Gabriel. She's William's. For pity's sake, she went back to him!'

He moved to the door. 'I have a concert this evening. I need to practise.'

'Don't run away!' she said savagely. 'You can't have Sasha. But you *can* have me.'

He paused in the doorway. 'I'm sorry, Kitty – this isn't the right time.'

'Coward!' she called after him. And then to herself as he closed the door, 'Marry me. Let's forget the past. Let's live happily ever after.'

'How is Mr Wotherspoon?' said Sasha one evening when William came up to bed. He always waited downstairs for half an hour after she had gone to bed, and then undressed in a heavy silence punctuated by grunts and rustling.

'Rather seedy. He eats and drinks too much.' William had temporarily forgotten his self-imposed rule of non-communication after the closing of the bedroom door.

'He's going the same way as Mr Wickham.'

William turned to stare at her. His shirt was unbuttoned and his neckcloth hung loosely, giving him a rakish look that she might once – a long time ago – have found appealing. His face seemed to lose its colour.

'What do you mean – the same way as Wickham?'

'Oh, you know what everyone in Penbury is saying.'

'What are they saying about Wickham?'

'Nothing. It was I who said—'

'But what did you *mean* by it?'

Sasha was puzzled by his distress. 'What should I mean?

457

Only that it's common knowledge Mr Wotherspoon has taken to drink since he was asked to step down as Mayor.'

Sasha did not want to discuss either Wotherspoon or Wickham at such length, and she wished she had not begun it. She was remembering Aunt Georgie and Pippa at bedtime, Pippa sitting on Aunt Georgie's knee and listening to stories about Norfolk, winding her fingers in Aunt Georgie's curls. Pippa was already lost to her, Sasha realised. And in time she would lose Meredith as well. She thought of his puzzlement over the quarrel between his parents.

'William, lift your ban on my seeing Merry,' she said when he had put out the lamp and lay, brooding still about Wotherspoon. 'He may have accepted the pregnancy keeping me away, but he must wonder why I don't go to see him now I'm home.'

'I worry about the boy's lack of self-control,' William said seriously. 'He's ten. He should be able to contain his emotions.'

'It's a hard enough task for adults,' Sasha said quietly.

He did not answer.

'William, punish me as much as it pleases you to take your revenge – but don't do this to Meredith. He's a sensitive child. You can't make him like the place.'

'He may not like his school, but he'll get used to it.'

'He will think I've abandoned him. He'll think I've turned against him. Or is that it? Do you want him to hate me?'

William did not answer. He lay on his back, silent in the darkness. For a moment she thought she had moved him a little.

Aunt Georgie had hatched a plot to fetch Meredith from school one Saturday and take him to the zoo.

'I don't think I could survive without you, Aunt Georgie,' Sasha said as they watched Meredith run along the pathways towards the elephant house. 'The secret outings with Pippa. Your support when William is being difficult.'

'Yes, you could. But thank goodness you don't have to. We women must stick together.'

Aunt Georgie had enjoyed the planning and the subterfuge. She liked the thrill of intrigue, and the hint of wickedness about the arrangements they made. But, above all, her heart felt a sympathy with Sasha.

The afternoon went too quickly and, though he tried not to, Meredith cried when it was time for his mother to leave and for Aunt Georgie to take him back on the train to school.

'I'll come again,' Sasha promised, drying his eyes carefully with her own handkerchief.

'I don't know why I can't come home. Is it my fault? Have I done something to make you all angry?'

She explained that it was she who had angered his father.

Suspicion clouded Meredith's eyes. He became sullen and shrugged away from her. 'It's not fair. You're not being fair. Why don't you make up your silly quarrel? Why won't you bring the baby to see me? I've asked Papa over and over to let me see her and to let you write to me.'

'I'll write secretly with Aunt Georgie's letters. And I'll come to see you again soon.'

'With the baby?'

'It's a promise.'

'How do I know you'll keep it?'

She had lost his trust, Sasha thought as she watched him walk away from her with Aunt Georgie. She imagined him with his classmates; his answers would be self-protective when the other boys asked where he had been. He would soon learn to be as William wanted him to be and hide his true feelings.

Sasha took the train for Penbury while Aunt Georgie returned her son to his school; she felt drained by the emotion of the afternoon as she walked up the hill from the station. Life was bitter. What had she done to offend the gods except fall in love at an inappropriate time and with the wrong person? She realised that she was weeping and did nothing to halt the tears. Gabriel, Gabriel. She

459

wanted to go to him and throw herself on his protection. But it was all far too late. Gabriel was with Kitty. They were playing in concerts together, people were beginning to wonder and to hear wedding bells. He had bought *The Beautiful Hammond Girls*, and Kitty was 'very fond' of him and could wind him round her little finger.

Sasha wept into her pillow that night and, detecting that she had woken William, stifled her sobs with a sudden intake of breath. She lay, rigid with control, until she thought he slept again. His hand touched her shoulder and she shrank from his mute attempt to comfort her. She would sooner they learned to hate one another.

It would soon be Meredith's school holidays. William was already talking about her going away for the summer.

'How long can you keep this up?' Sasha said. 'Every holiday? At Christmas? Meredith might come to accept it, but people in Penbury will begin to talk.'

William said that if people talked they would see whose side to take; but he was wavering; no decision had been made about where she would go for the summer. Sasha saw that he would not be able to insist on it; he was too afraid that a hint of scandal might drive away his patients.

An invitation arrived a few days later. Mr Viggers had been spending a small fortune on doing up a large house between Penbury and Bath. They were all invited to a party to celebrate his new address.

The party was held in Mr Viggers' garden with champagne and speeches, games and dancing. Mr Viggers danced with Aunt Georgie, who looked bright and pretty in a pink and white checked crinoline. Expectation among the guests was high that there must surely be a marriage proposal before long. Mr Turbot danced with Sasha and Lily, and Mrs Turbot with William. The Wotherspoons, Mr Scrope and his sister, and several other Penbury people were there. Everyone walked about in the sunshine, and sat about under the trees, and said what a splendid job the builders had made of Mr Viggers' plans, and how modern and congenial the renovations were.

People made a fuss of Sasha's baby, and Mrs Wotherspoon complimented her on the speed with which she had regained her strength; she said she knew what it was to suffer, her own experiences of lying-in had been fraught with tribulation.

Mr Wotherspoon looked ill, thought Sasha. She said as much to William.

William glanced anxiously at Wotherspoon. It was true the man looked broken-down; his flesh was wasted, his eyes bulged in his head, and he walked with dragging steps. William had warned him recently about taking the Elixir so often and had threatened to withdraw the medicine; but the man had become violently complaining, had said he would denounce him as a quack and to hell with his own reputation. There had been enough doubt in William's mind for him to send up more of the Elixir.

Almost worse than being denounced as a quack, William dreaded the town might learn of his wife's shame. The fear was always there, that somehow people would find out and the whole story would be bandied about. His mind dwelled on the fun the local people had over such things – skimmingtons, and similar vulgarities.

And yet, as William looked round Mr Viggers' garden it was clear that no one suspected anything. None of the gossip fell quiet when he approached; no sly or knowing looks were exchanged. He glanced at Sasha and suppressed the bitterness that rose to his throat when he saw her looking so lovely. She had picked up the baby from its crib under the trees and her hair caught the sunlight. Her colour was high and so was the child's – a pretty thing with black hair and blue eyes. Could life really continue as before, as if no great tragedy had taken place? Could he accept the congratulations of their neighbours and chat about the baby as if it were his own? Had he loved Sasha so very little that he could now maintain the daily round with no outward show of grief?

Perhaps then it was not a tragedy to have one's own wife fall in love with another man. There were consolations: he was freed of any mental burden of responsibility

461

towards her and her child; it need not matter to him whether the infant lived or died. And Sasha maintained his household still. True, he had denied himself some pleasures; he could never bring himself to demand sexual favours from her – though he would be within his rights.

He thought of the future, the years of living side by side. Such an arid existence, devoid of trust or joy. He might at some time take a mistress, he supposed. An act of tit for tat. He might feel himself morally justified, provided no one found out about it. William began to consider how it might be done. Trips to Exeter, or Bath. He remembered the business with Kitty, and a cold perspiration swept over him. What was he thinking of! Did he want to make himself as morally reprehensible as Sasha?

'It's unaccountable that William has taken in the child,' grumbled Lily in a low voice to Aunt Georgie, as the musicians started up again. 'Even more so that you should have taken Sasha's side in the affair.'

'Felicia's a very good baby. Nobody with any heart could hate her. And William has plenty of heart, in spite of the way he's been behaving lately. He'll forgive Sasha when he gets over his hurt. They'll resolve their problems.'

Lily looked sideways at Sasha rocking the baby in time to the music. 'It's so shaming to have to pretend. How could she . . .!'

'She was in love.'

'She's supposed to love her husband!'

'What a woman is supposed to do, and how a feeling takes her are sometimes two entirely different things.'

Lily narrowed her eyes. 'Sometimes, I think you know who the father is.'

Aunt Georgie's fingers trembled as she looked away and made a pretence of adjusting her lace cap. One of her combs had freed itself from her nest of hair. She was rescued by Mr Viggers, who helped her search for it in the grass.

'Shall we dance again, Miss Georgie?' He took her arm

and they danced, swinging round on the grass close to Lily.

The music had led to talk of violins. Lily continued to watch Aunt Georgie as people reminisced about Gabriel, talking of his influence over the Musical Society. Aunt Georgie seemed agitated by the subject of Mr Ridgeway; she glanced repeatedly over Mr Viggers' shoulder, as if to see how Sasha was taking it. Lily grew more curious. She watched Sasha's expression when Gabriel's name was mentioned; she searched for the flicker of an eyelid, saw the tension in the mouth, and began to put two and two together, wondering why she had not done so before. How *slow* she had been! And William – poor William. What a fool he was!

'Will you resume your concert performances in a year or two, Mrs Elliman?' Mrs Turbot was asking.

'I do miss playing,' admitted Sasha.

'Perhaps when you, my precious, are a little older.' Mrs Turbot patted the baby's hand. 'Your mama is going to play in concerts again one day; she will make them all take notice of her like they did before.'

'How is your son faring?' asked Wotherspoon.

William tensed at the question, afraid Sasha would say something damning about never seeing Meredith. She was in a peculiar mood this afternoon. 'He is not going to be an intellectual giant,' he said quickly, remembering a letter from William's housemaster. The fact was, William worried about Meredith's mediocre reports. 'I thought some lessons from the curate this summer might be advantageous.'

'He'll do well enough . . .' Wotherspoon drank down a glass of wine. 'Extra tuition. That's a capital idea.'

He drank copiously, Sasha noticed; he downed glass after glass, as if needing to quench a large thirst. She watched a servant refill his glass, saw Wotherspoon's hand tremble as he raised it to his lips and heard a harsh, ugly sound as he choked in mid-swallow. She did not believe at first that anything was wrong, until she saw his face redden and swell.

Others around began to stare at the sight of Wotherspoon fighting for breath. William went to him and helped him to a chair. People turned away with distaste as the man vomited on to the grass.

There was a shocked silence. Mr Viggers could be heard calling to his servant for water. The party conversed in whispers while Mrs Wotherspoon, red with fright and embarrassment, tried to shield her husband from prying eyes.

The water was brought and Wotherspoon seemed to recover a little.

Mrs Wotherspoon said they would go home. There was a fuss about getting her husband to their carriage. He clung to William's arm for support. The party resumed, and people talked in low voices, aware that Wotherspoon drank more than was good for him.

'I get such pains, Elliman,' Wotherspoon said hoarsely. 'They seem to burn so. Like red-hot coals. They seem to want to crush me from the inside.'

'You should eat and drink less,' William said sternly. 'Try increasing your cigar smoking a little. It's good for the digestion, therapeutic for certain states of the stomach . . .'

Wotherspoon grasped William's hand more tightly, and only Sasha heard him say, 'You know what I need. It's the only thing that makes me feel well.'

'Not now,' William said hurriedly. 'Come. I'll help you out to your carriage. I'll be up to see you this evening and give you a series of blisters to the stomach.'

The incident had spoiled the atmosphere of the party. After the Wotherspoons' departure other guests began to leave, even though it was not yet evening.

On the way home Aunt Georgie thought of the pleasures of running a household such as Mr Viggers': the ordering of menus, the arranging of summer parties and winter musical evenings, being addressed as 'ma'am' by Mr Viggers' servants, and '*Mrs Viggers*' by her neighbours. It could all be so very pleasant. She would live close enough to visit William and Sasha and still be able to see her darling Pippa – Meredith, too, in his holidays. She looked at William. He would come round to loving his wife again. She was sure his heart was softening a little towards Sasha. If women could forgive erring husbands, why shouldn't husbands forgive erring wives?

Except that, after all the fuss over Mr Wotherspoon's illness, Mr Viggers seemed to have forgotten about a proposal, or else he had lost his nerve. Aunt Georgie looked out of the carriage window at the nice houses with lace curtains and gardens, and drives for carriages; she sighed, feeling cheated.

William was silent and jittery on the journey home. What if Wotherspoon were to go the same way as Wickham? Even Sasha had seen a connection, would be starting to wonder . . . He silenced his thoughts. It was the alcohol, he told himself – as he had told himself so many times since Wotherspoon had begun to look the worse for wear. Alcohol had killed Wickham. And if Wotherspoon was drinking himself into his grave as well, there was nothing anyone could do about it.

Pippa had fallen asleep against Aunt Georgie's arm as the carriage entered Penbury. They passed a figure on the road. Aunt Georgie, peering from the window, said absentmindedly, 'Oh, look. It's that poor woman they burned in effigy on the night of the skimmington. They say her lover's gone back to his wife and now she's on the street and resorted to begging.'

Sasha watched from the window, seeing a figure at the roadside and something in the woman's arms that looked like a bundle of rags. A child? Had there been a child?

Lily stirred in her corner. 'That's what happens to women who forget all sense of decency. Serve them right too. What do they expect?'

'Where's your pity, Lily?' said Sasha. 'Does nobody these days have any compassion any more?' William's glance met hers, and he looked away.

But Lily was looking at Sasha with a glint of anger in her eyes. 'Shame on you! Sitting there as if butter wouldn't melt! Have you forgotten?'

'Lily!' said Aunt Georgie mildly.

'All that time! Right under my brother's nose! And you—' She turned on Aunt Georgie. 'I'll say it again. How could you take their side against your own nephew!'

'Are you saying you know who the father was?' William looked from his aunt to his sister.

'And so would you if you put your mind to it,' said Lily. He shook his head.

'Think of the skimmington. Think of who went off together when we thought them lost in the crowd.'

William stared at Sasha and saw how pale she was. 'Surely not Ridgeway?' He remembered the night they had returned from a concert in Bath when Sasha had lost her bonnet to the mob. Was that when it had begun?

Sasha looked at him without flinching.

William thought of the way he had taken the man into his confidence, made him welcome at his table, discussed his wife with him . . . even asked him to play duets with her. His mind revolted at the memories. Ridgeway had made a cuckold of him!

No one spoke as the carriage reached the hill and began the upward climb. William sat with his head in his hands, and Lily stared steadfastly at a point beyond Sasha's shoulder. There was no sound, except for the steady grinding of the wheels. Aunt Georgie held Pippa more closely. She threw a look of anguish at Sasha, but Sasha hardly noticed. What difference would it make now he knew? Would he tell anyone? Would he become even more bitter towards her and take it out on the children?

They reached home, and William went out immediately to visit Wotherspoon without speaking to anyone. Sasha went upstairs and propped herself on the bed pillows to feed the baby who was beginning to fret. She tried not to think about the journey home and the fact that her secret was out. When Felicia was full of milk, she dozed a little and when she woke, the baby was still sleeping.

She heard William return in the carriage and looked at her dress-watch. He had been gone more than two hours.

★ ★ ★

William went straight to the dining room and closed the door behind him.

'Something has happened,' said Aunt Georgie, going to Sasha in the bedroom. Her hands twisted and untwisted the buttons on her bodice. 'I don't know what's wrong. But I really think you should go to him.'

'Keep Pippa and Lily out of the way,' said Sasha and hurried downstairs to the dining room.

William stood by the fireplace with his head bowed on his arm. His hand rested on the brandy decanter, but he had not taken out the stopper.

'What is it?' Sasha closed the door behind her.

He shook his head and said nothing. He let her take the decanter from his hand, and she poured a measure into a glass and handed it to him. He drank it down in one gulp.

'Wotherspoon's dead.'

Sasha thought of Mrs Wotherspoon, remembered how she had tried to shield the spectacle of her husband from the guests at Mr Viggers' party. 'I'm so sorry, William. I'm sorry for *them*, for his wife . . . but I know how you hate to lose a patient.' This was different, she thought. There was something odd about him. He seemed extremely shocked, as if he hardly knew she was there.

'Mr Wotherspoon *was* very ill,' Sasha went on. 'It was only to be expected really. The man ate and drank far more than was good for him.'

'No. No.' He turned wild eyes on her and gave a groan of despair. 'It was the Elixir.'

Sasha looked at him, not comprehending at first. Then a memory came into her mind. A row of poison bottles. His father's old recipes. And a parcel . . . 'J. Wotherspoon. The Elixir . . . with care.'

Her voice sank to a whisper. 'What in God's name have you been doing?'

'We were short of money. It was before you went back to your playing.'

'But that was ages ago.'

'I know. They got addicted to it. I had to keep supplying them.'

'*They*?' Sasha echoed. 'All that time ago? Who else have you been treating with your father's quack remedies?'

He stared at her, and looked down at the glass in his hand. Then he straightened and seemed to recover. He poured himself another glass of brandy and drank it quickly. 'No one.'

Sasha thought of all the possibilities. 'Mr Wickham.' She remembered William's reaction to Wickham's death, the late night visits, the man's attenuated appearance before the end. 'When he died he looked as bad as Mr Wotherspoon!'

'Wickham drank. It was well known.'

'But you *had* supplied him with the Elixir? You'd been treating him?'

'It's no more than an unhappy coincidence.' He could not look at her. 'Wotherspoon was dosing himself with all sorts – purges and emetics. He could have died for any one of a number of reasons, Sasha.'

'But you know he didn't. You *know* what killed him – it killed them both.'

He looked at her and his mouth trembled. He wiped it with the back of his hand.

'William – you're a doctor! You heal people. Have you forgotten how principled you once were? You were going to make so many changes in Penbury. You had hopes of achieving so much.'

He began to cry.

Sasha turned away and went to the window. She opened it and leaned on the sill, trying to shut out his sobs. A blackbird was singing and the scent of roses drifted towards the house; the evening air and the sound of birdsong seemed intensely sweet. Sasha thought of the handsome man who had once stood on the pavement at Hanover Terrace and smiled up at her in the window. Could William really be that same person – and she that naive, silly girl?

'Are you going to do anything?' he said brokenly, fearing exposure, revenge perhaps, for all her pent-up grievances. He blew his nose, and wiped his eyes with his handkerchief.

She turned to face him, and felt as if she had entered a space where she and William were absolute strangers; she knew their marriage must crumble now, whatever either of them did to shore it up again. There would not even be a shell to present to the outside world.

'What will you do?' he repeated.

'Do?' She closed the window again. 'I'm going to leave you.'

There was an inquest this time. William's evidence – that Wotherspoon was addicted to purges and emetics after bouts of drinking and overeating – was substantiated by others who knew him. It was known too that Wotherspoon had suffered from abscesses for which he regularly took opium against medical advice. As for the drinking, alcohol was the scourge of Penbury in every class of society.

It was decided no blame could be attached to William. He rode out the scandal with his reputation intact.

Sasha stayed in Penbury until the inquest was over and waited out the last days of her marriage, packing in secret, planning. The process of disintegration was not without pain; there were the memories, the children, thoughts of Meredith's homecoming when she would be gone, moments of panic. But she was aware, most of all, of a sense of freedom.

William recovered swiftly from self-reproach and remorse once the inquest had cleared him of blame. He had been exonerated. Sasha's adultery with Gabriel came back more strongly to hurt him. 'You behave as if I'm the one who should be forgiven,' he said one evening when they were alone; he had caught her looking at him with a mixture of pity and disappointment. 'Have you forgotten what you did – how you conducted a criminal affair and betrayed my trust?'

'No. I've not forgotten. After all, I had you and Kitty in my father's library as a shining example! Though a fling with my sister hardly bears comparison with this latest business over Wotherspoon. I feel sorry for you, William.

You will have to live with that terrible guilt for the rest of your days.'

'I did what I thought was best. I didn't know Wotherspoon was going to die.'

'You knew Wickham had died! You went on selling a quack cure that wasn't trustworthy – to keep in with the gentry, because you couldn't lose face, because the *money* was tempting.'

'Only at first. The money meant nothing later—'

'Then why didn't you call a halt?'

'I have spent all my life trying to do the right thing,' he protested. 'And for what – to have my wife vilify me? I *won't* have it. I won't put up with moral lectures from a woman who has herself behaved without any shame.'

'You won't have to put up with anything for much longer.'

William stared at her. He had assumed her dramatic declaration about leaving had been an empty threat. Women of their class did not walk out from the family home. Women in her position, knowing what she had risked on a brief, guilty excitement, did not risk their reputation further by going off and abandoning their husbands. 'You can't leave. Where will you go? If you think Ridgeway will have you . . .'

'I'm sure he thinks the baby is yours,' she said. 'I told you I'd given him up and it's the truth. No. I shall go back to playing eventually. But I shall leave you. That's the first thing.'

'Fine talk. You'll see in the morning.'

'I've written to a place I once rented when I was touring.'

'You would live in rooms!'

'It's a house. I've heard that it's to let. I was very contented there once. I think I could be again.'

Sasha remembered her correspondence with Mrs Mynott, the careful phrasing to discover whether Lavender House was vacant.

'Alone? You'll live alone?'

'I'll be with Felicia.'

470

'But what will everyone say?'

Sasha began to laugh.

'Are you out of your senses? This isn't funny.'

'Yes, it is. It's like that game we used to play. A meets B. He says. She says. They do – something unexpected, amusing, or *shocking*. And the world gives its verdict . . . usually sanctimonious, or profound, or enlightening. Do you know, I really can't trouble myself any more to wonder what the world will say.'

Chapter Twenty-One

Sasha opened the door to Lavender House and was met by the stale, faintly vegetable smell of a building that had been closed up for too long. She had brought very little luggage from Penbury. Leaving the bags and boxes where the driver had stacked them in the hall, she went from room to room opening windows.

She knew Gabriel had been there – she had discovered in her correspondence with the landlady that he had paid the rent – but the stack of letters on the piano was unexpected, and Sasha saw them with a shock of pain.

Putting down the baby in an armchair, she took off her coat and hat and hung them in the hall. The gesture was very satisfying, an act of ownership. She hesitated before going back into the sitting room, bracing herself for the ordeal of his letters.

It was chilly for July. She went to the fireplace and knelt by the log basket. Felicia burbled at her from the armchair. The charred remains of Gabriel's earlier letters lay in the grate, and Sasha's heart leaped back to the last time she had been here; she remembered the despair of reading that Kitty had found him. She remembered the phrases he had used: *Kitty has been a good friend . . . a peculiar fascination in her style . . . she is such a comfort to me . . . such a comfort to me.*

Sasha invented new ones: *I'm in love with your sister . . . Kitty and I . . . Kitty and I . . .* Taking wood from the basket, she lit a fire with newspaper and sticks, then watched the flames lick round the logs.

Sobs broke from her, dry and painful, rising one after another, as she picked up his letters and dropped them one by one on to the fire.

The landlady came to the house soon after she had arrived. 'So, you're back, Mrs Love . . . and is *Mr* Love with you?'

Sasha stood at the door with Felicia in her arms. She said her husband had gone abroad again, perhaps for several months. She saw the beginnings of suspicion in the woman's eyes as her glance took in Felicia.

'What a shame, to leave you and baby all alone.'

Sasha said that if Mrs Mynott would excuse her she had the house to air, beds to make up, the baby . . . so many things, and closed the door. She saw that even here, where she had supposed she would find sanctuary, she would sooner or later become the subject of gossip. What husband would go off indefinitely and leave his wife and baby alone?

Aunt Georgie came to see her a few days after she had left Penbury; she looked the house over with approval. 'Well – you've done it. And a fine storm you've left behind you. Lily is thinking of sending for a lynch mob.'

Sasha searched for condemnation in the other woman's eyes and saw only a look of eager excitement. Aunt Georgie had been buoyed up all morning by a feeling of exhilaration. She was pleased the situation had become so much more complicated; there were things for her to do, plans to make, so that Sasha might still see her children; she was already working out an elaborate programme of subterfuges. It was all thoroughly satisfying for a woman who had discovered she had a talent for organisation.

Sasha begged her for news of Pippa.

'She thinks you've gone on a concert tour.'

'I'll have to tell her the truth, though I don't know how. You'll help me to sneak visits? You will help me, Aunt Georgie?'

'Of course I will, my poppet. But first things first. How are you going to pay the rent?'

Sasha told her about Gabriel paying the lease until the following Christmas.

Aunt Georgie looked at her with a sharpened interest. 'Do you know why he would do that?'

'I suppose he did it a long time ago and didn't believe it was over.'

'And is it? She's his child. He has a right to know.'

'I don't need anyone, Aunt Georgie. Except you, of course, and Felicia. And the children. And my piano. What salvation there is in music!'

'You're going back to the concert platform,' Aunt Georgie said with an air of satisfaction.

'How did you know?'

'I can't see you being satisfied with giving piano lessons to the local farmers' children.'

'I shall need a nurse for Felicia, and – oh, Aunt Georgie, I feel alive again!' Sasha believed it. She saw a future that was full of possibilities. What did she care if people talked? The musical world would welcome her. Her music and her independence were all that mattered. She had surrendered the respect of society in order to preserve her self-respect. It was a small sacrifice, she decided. She could live without society's approval.

But it was hard to adjust to being a single woman again; and it was harder to have lost all rights to Pippa and Meredith. She worried about Pippa learning to hate her, and about Meredith coming home for the summer holiday and discovering she had gone. She told herself she had behaved with honour at last, by scorning convention and the tyranny of respectability.

She was free – but without a protector. Vulnerable in many eyes, cut off from decent society. And people talked in the way she had feared. Her neighbours watched her when she ventured out from the house. They nodded, and said, 'Good day,' and then put their heads together after she had gone by. She was asked, when did she expect Mr Love to join her? with less and less innocence in the question.

474

The grand piano had gone badly out of tune. Sasha had it seen to and began practising again. She wrote to various agents about taking up her career; but she did not write to Algie. She could not risk working with Gabriel again.

Music came to her rescue as it always had in the past. When she played, she felt whole and happy. But when the piano was silent and Felicia was asleep, a deeper silence fell on the house, one filled with resonances of the past. There were moments of anger against Gabriel and Kitty, anger against herself – and more diffused feelings of guilt. Guilt about abandoning a union sanctioned by God, an irrational, persistent guilt about leaving William. *Had* he spent his life – as he had protested – trying to do the right thing? And what was right? To apply oneself to society's standards, or to do what seemed moral according to one's inner conscience? There was guilt too about marrying William in the first place – a man she had never loved except in a foolish, romantic way. She was ashamed to have let it happen; she asked herself whether she had done the noble or the cowardly thing by staying with him all that time. She had supposed there was no alternative. But she knew now that only a lack of courage had prevented her from leaving him before.

None of this was as overwhelming as the guilt Sasha felt over abandoning her children. She was in danger of letting go of all her notions of independence and freedom as she wallowed in self-condemnation. She drank too much wine, stayed up playing the piano half the night, and stayed in bed until late in the mornings, weeping for Pippa and Meredith. And, even now, she wept for Gabriel when she remembered how happy, how very *right* they had been together. She supposed she had, in her heart, hoped he might come back and find her there with Felicia. She half imagined scenes where he would say that at last he understood everything, that Kitty meant nothing to him; he would take her in his arms and say he had come for her. But the weeks went by. And, if Gabriel had heard she was living alone, or wondered why she had left William, he did not come like a rescuing knight, to seek her out at Lavender House.

One morning, Mrs Mynott knocked at the door again. 'Mrs Love—' she began. 'I'd be obliged if you would tell me *exactly* when Mr Love is coming home.'

'I really can't say,' said Sasha defensively. 'Was there some reason . . .?'

'It's a delicate matter, Mrs Love. The fact is, my neighbours don't like the idea of a *single* lady . . . a lady, that is, all alone with her child . . .' The woman coloured but hurried on. 'There have been complaints. Lights showing at unseemly hours. Music—'

'I'm a musician . . . Mr Love and I are *both* musicians. You must have heard music before.'

'But now there's only *one* of you. And the baby. And all paid for, if I may say, by the gentleman.'

'Mr Love,' Sasha reminded her.

'By a *gentleman*,' Mrs Mynott repeated with rugged insistence.

Sasha's colour rose to her cheeks. 'Well then, I see no problems, Mrs Mynott – since we are "paid for".'

She closed the door and fell against it, weeping with shock and fury, the humiliation of Gabriel being called a 'gentleman', and she – in all but name – a creature of the demi-monde.

Aunt Georgie brought Pippa and Meredith to see her. A swift inspection of the house revealed the unwashed crockery and glasses, the empty wine bottles and the music sheets littering the piano. Aunt Georgie decided to take Sasha in hand.

'You must start playing in public again. And, from the look of you, the sooner the better.'

'I'm scared, Aunt Georgie. What if *everyone* out there knows? What if audiences are hostile?'

'What if you do nothing but feel sorry for yourself?' responded Aunt Georgie, busily collecting up cups and glasses from around the sitting room; she took them into

476

the kitchen and put a pan of water on to boil.

Pippa was looking at Sasha intently. 'Why is your hair like that?'

Sasha put a hand quickly to the coils of hair that hung from their moorings, aware that she had fastened it too loosely. She took out pins and re-inserted them haphazardly. 'It might have been better not to come today,' she murmured as Aunt Georgie made her next sweep of crockery from the room.

'Indeed it might,' Aunt Georgie said grimly.

Meredith walked about the room looking at pictures and the view from the window. 'It's not as clean as the house at home.'

Sasha tried to take comfort in the children, but they had grown distant; and she had invested too much of her energies in Felicia to bridge the gap. Meredith was learning to be self-sufficient, to do without affection and not complain; boys who complained at his school, he said, got bullied. He said he 'quite liked' her new home, but he wished she looked as pretty as she used to when she came to visit him at school.

'Have you heard anything of Mr Ridgeway?' Aunt Georgie said when Sasha had left the children minding the baby and joined her in the kitchen.

'I've heard of concerts here and there. I shan't tell him about Felicia, Aunt Georgie. It's no use looking at me like that.'

'What about your parents?'

Sasha avoided her eyes. 'What about them?'

'They keep writing to you. William answers their letters, but they must be beginning to wonder. They're going to turn up in Penbury one day and discover the truth. You've got to tell them you've left him, Sasha. Before William does.'

Sasha shook her head. 'You don't understand.' She remembered too well the pain caused by Kitty. How could she go to her parents and say she had abandoned her husband and children – and that Felicia was Gabriel's child?

The children knew they must not tell anyone they had been to Lavender House. They accepted that Sasha had left William in the way that children received such news, by shutting it out. They fussed around the baby and ignored their mother. Pippa seemed hardly to have missed her, so used to her absences and Aunt Georgie had she become; but she had missed the novelty of the baby, and grumbled because Sasha had taken Felicia away.

Sasha watched them go down the lane, one on either side of Aunt Georgie; she knew, as she took comfort from Gabriel's child in her arms, that she had betrayed them far more profoundly than she had betrayed William. Meredith had said before he left that Sasha might go less often to see him when he went back to his school. Without emotion, he told her that he had thought about her at first, and now he thought of her hardly at all. He said it with a sense of triumph, as if he wanted to wound.

William could not understand why Sasha had left him. He would never forgive her. His own sin, the mistake with the Elixir, had arisen because of the moral frailty of men like Wickham and Wotherspoon. It was excusable, and in any case his guilt was debatable. But Sasha had shown a loss of all restraint, had deeply attacked the institutions of marriage and family; she had soured for ever his faith in the virtue and discretion of women.

William grew morose as the weeks went by and vague hopes that Sasha would return repentant came to nothing. He told no one his wife had left him, explaining to people outside the household that she was 'away'. When the Hammonds wrote asking Sasha to visit them, he made excuses.

But gossip had leaked out in Penbury. Neighbours had begun to consider whether Sasha had left her husband for good this time and taken her youngest child with her. They witnessed William's scowling, hunched figure as he rode on his rounds, noted his near violent responses, when he was asked when his wife was coming home. They even began to wonder whether there might have been

478

some justification for Mrs Elliman going: women like that did not abandon home and family without good reason. No one had heard of any impropriety – there was no man involved as far as they knew, so she had not 'run off' in the usual sense.

But if there was a reason, nobody in the Elliman household was telling. Not Mrs Ash, nor Bertha – whose loyalty resisted wild speculations. Nor Lily, who hinted darkly to her friend Miss Scrope that Sasha had not always been all she seemed, but would reveal nothing specific to anyone. Aunt Georgie upheld a glowing public image of Sasha as a model wife and mother, and demolished every shred of gossip; but she would say nothing either against her nephew. Sasha's departure remained a mystery.

Nevertheless, Sasha's desertion was an embarrassment. William had the sympathy of many of his patients. The Scropes became staunch allies. Miss Scrope and Lily took tea together and discussed the failings of the married women they knew, enjoying stories about wronged husbands and spoiled, wicked, or otherwise defective wives. The scandal William had once feared became a brief reality, and then died quickly for want of material to feed on. His medical practice did not, as he had feared, lose patients by the score – although it may well have lost a few to William's ill humour – but it remained that 'small-town practice' William had once despised. He continued, if not to flourish exactly, then to maintain a steady income, to cure a few ills among the Penbury residents, and perhaps – despite good intentions and the burning of his father's recipes – to hasten the deaths of a few others.

One day, when William was in Bristol with Lily – avoiding the neighbourhood of Avondon and Hanover Terrace – he saw a poster for a concert in Bath.

'She is playing again,' he said gloomily. 'She's not going to come home.'

Lily read the poster without comment; but she made a mental note of the date of the concert.

Nathaniel Hammond had seen the poster too. He was becoming concerned about Sasha. His wife worried about

479

not seeing her grandchildren. Lavinia was too far away to visit often, but Sasha . . . they had not seen her for months. In the past, even on tour she had usually sent the occasional letter.

The Hammonds chewed over the puzzle together. Why had she not told them she was playing in Bath? Nathaniel decided to go and visit. He arrived unannounced in Penbury one afternoon and met William coming home from visiting his patients. The two men faced one another in the drive.

Nathaniel was shocked by the dishevelled appearance of his son-in-law. William too was shaken by the encounter. He remembered a time when he had admired Hammond more than anyone – more than his one-time hero and reformer, Edwin Chadwick. He looked into the kindly, concerned face that had once been so interested, so well disposed towards him, and smothered a desire to fall on his shoulder as he might on a father's; he longed to reveal the collapse of all his aspirations, and the terrible burden of Sasha's betrayal with Ridgeway.

Common sense urged caution. Sasha's father had once championed Ridgeway. The Hammonds were now in the enemy camp and would support Sasha no matter what he told them. He must keep his dignity. It was all he had left.

William held out his hand. 'Father-in-law. I had been meaning to come and see you.'

Sasha drove to a rehearsal at the Pump Rooms in Bath. Aunt Georgie had asked her recently if she was happy. Sasha knew that since she had gone back to performing, she felt strong and alive, and it was true she did not need anyone or anything except her art. But she did not know if she was happy. 'I am not *unhappy*,' she had answered. 'I've chosen to be solitary. I cannot now go hankering after the benefits of living with William when I threw them over voluntarily.'

Would her parents have approved? Her father had once believed in liberty, and her mother in female assertiveness. But she could not ask their opinion. She did not even know if they had heard she was playing again.

She caught her breath as she reached the Pump Rooms.
Her father was walking up and down outside the entrance,
and he came towards her as she left the cab.

'Why, Sasha?' Nathaniel's voice broke with emotion.
'Why didn't you tell us you had left your husband?' Sasha
fell into his arms.

'Who told you?' she said after a while.

'William. He cannot comprehend why you would do
something so peculiar, Sasha. To go off and leave your
husband! We've been very worried about you since he
told us.'

So – that's how it is to be, thought Sasha. William had
decided she was to be cast as a lunatic. Perhaps it sounded
better than an adulteress. 'Do something so peculiar,' she
repeated with heavy sarcasm.

'William talks of long periods of instability. We didn't
realise when you went to the coast—'

'Father, stop this.' She tucked her hand in his arm. 'I
fell out of love. That's all. I'm as sane as William – in fact,
I'm sure I'm much more so. I fell out of love. Does that
make me deranged?'

He looked at her with incomprehension at first. 'You
left him because you don't love him?'

'Would you have been prouder of me for staying?'

'I don't know . . . You made your vows, Sasha.'

'But I made them to a different man. The William I fell
in love with, the man I married . . . wasn't that disappointed doctor who now lives in Penbury.'

He shook his head. 'I don't know what you mean.'

'Perhaps it's I who have changed. I only know I have
lost all respect for him. I can't explain – but it wasn't all
William's fault.'

'And that's as much as you'll tell me?'

'That's all I'm going to say.'

He nodded. 'Come then. Give your father a kiss, and I
promise we'll not talk about it any more.'

Nathaniel walked into the Pump Rooms with her and
sat at the back during the rehearsal. He insisted she

481

returned with him to Bristol to see her mother. True to his word, he did not question her on the journey, except to ask where she was living. They talked of practical things. Her mother did not ask questions either; she looked at Nathaniel and at Sasha and pretended nothing had changed. They talked about the Bath concert, and about the nursemaid Sasha had engaged to look after Felicia.

Mrs Hammond said that Kitty was playing in Ross's Orchestra in London, and that Gabriel would soon be touring Scotland. He and Kitty still played in chamber ensembles together and it was only a matter of time before they would marry.

Sasha was very conscious of having exchanged roles with Kitty as the black sheep of the family. 'Don't tell Gabriel anything about my playing, will you?' she said as her mother chattered on about wedding plans.

'Why ever not?' said Mrs Hammond.

'I don't want him to know I'm playing again . . . and especially not that I'm alone.'

They looked at her with puzzlement at first, then a slow dawning of understanding; a wary unhappiness clouded their expressions as they reached an approximate version of the truth. There was more to tell, Nathaniel realised. A lot more. But he had given his word that he would not ask.

That evening at the performance, Sasha stood with her hand on the piano top, dressed in rose-coloured silk and black lace. She thought of the number of times she had faced an audience here . . . in virginal white when she was a girl. The applause was generous. The audience remembered her début; she would always be welcome in the town that had mourned Julius Lindau's passing. Her parents sat in the audience. Sasha scanned the rows of faces, and saw with a shock of pleasure that Aunt Georgie and Mr Viggers had come to hear her.

The applause died, and a softer, more sinister sound rose near the back of the hall. A hissing, almost imperceptible at first; but soon it grew louder.

Sasha waited. She told herself she would not be moved

by it; she had nothing to be ashamed of, nothing for which to apologise. The hissing grew even louder, and heads turned to see who was causing it.

A figure got up from the audience. It was Aunt Georgie.

'This is disgraceful. What has Mrs Elliman ever done to you – except to play the most beautiful music?' A light applause greeted her protest, then faltered as the hissing grew more strident. Aunt Georgie, looking like a true 'British heroine' in bombazine, blushed to the roots of her henna-coloured hair and addressed the unruly element again. 'Don't think I don't know who you are and who has put you up to this.'

Sasha saw then where the hissing came from, and that Councillor Scrope, his sister, and a number of their friends had come in a gang to disrupt the concert.

Sasha grew calm; she had no fear of the Scropes. She walked past the ranks of seats. Heads twisted to follow her progress until she reached the councillor. She halted, and said loudly, 'Mr Scrope, your bad manners and those of your friends are disturbing the rest of the audience. I must ask you to leave.'

People who had heard her applauded. Those who had not heard wanted to know what Sasha had said, and word was relayed from row to row of the audience. The applause was taken up; feet stamped with approval on the floor.

Nathaniel and Aunt Georgie arrived to stand beside Sasha, along with the orchestra director and a few of the players. The musicians repeated Sasha's request – in more threatening terms.

Miss Scrope muttered a protest about having paid for tickets and wanting their money back. Then, as the players closed in, her brother quickly complied with the order to leave, and the rest of his party followed.

'Who could have put them up to it?' Sasha turned to Aunt Georgie and lowered her voice. 'Surely not William?' Had he been reduced to sheer spite?

'It was Lily.' Aunt Georgie was certain of it. 'She's very

thick with Miss Scrope. Huh! She hadn't the nerve to come herself.'

Sasha returned to the piano and everyone else took their places again. She put her hands to the keys, and began, not the Chopin nocturne on the programme, but the A flat polonaise. She played it with fire and brilliance. The audience cheered when it was over, and Sasha knew that the first public battle was won.

Algie, hearing that Sasha was playing again, was wounded that she had not come to him to promote her. He went to see Gabriel, hoping for a sympathetic ear, and found Kitty alone at his apartment.

Kitty sat in the drawing room with her feet on a foot-stool. She felt a twinge of unease as she heard Algie's grievance. 'You mean Sasha's coming back to the concert circuit?'

'She's already played in Bristol and Bath. I thought you would have heard. I feel so hurt,' Algie murmured. 'Why didn't she come to me?'

'Don't you know?'

He looked at her. 'Could it have something to do with Gabriel? They never really got on.'

'She's scared of meeting him again. Take my word for it.'

All the same, thought Kitty, she must make sure Gabriel didn't hear that her sister was playing again in concerts. Sasha wasn't the only one afraid they might meet again.

'Scared?' said Algie. 'Don't you know your sister? She's not scared of any musician.'

'It's different with this one. They had a *love affair*, Algie. Don't tell me you didn't realise.'

Algie stared. Little things about Gabriel and Sasha began to click into place: the strong musical rapport between them, the mood swings, the avoidance of social contact . . . Oh, but they had been discreet. To have hidden that sort of thing from the orchestra was no mean accomplishment.

'Gabriel was in love with her for ages,' Kitty went on. 'I'm almost sure that's why Sasha stopped playing when she did. She took the easy way out before Gabriel came back from Germany. She thought too much of her reputation as a good *Hausfrau* to risk playing with him again.'

'And yet she's come back to playing again now,' Algie said.

'She probably thinks she's safe, so long as she avoids Gabriel.'

Algie wanted to believe her. But there were other rumours he had heard. A good *Hausfrau*? A woman who had abandoned her husband to take up an eccentric existence living alone except for one of her children? He had heard she had been hissed at a concert in Bath, and had routed the opposition. It did not sound like the behaviour of a woman who was careful of her reputation. He looked at Kitty. Her own past was intriguing enough to draw audiences, but nothing to attract hecklers. Should he tell her the rumours about Sasha? What if he let slip to Kitty that Sasha had left her husband?

'And what about you, Kitty?' he said. 'Is it true you and Gabriel are likely to marry? Everyone is speculating. It would be a good move for you both. A husband and wife partnership is quite an attraction.'

'And of commercial interest, Algie.'

'Of course.'

He decided not to tell her. He wanted no complications, nothing to spoil his next season of concerts. Gabriel was going on tour in a few days. With a bit of luck, he would not hear any of the gossip.

Gabriel was booked to tour Scotland and the North of England for several weeks. He went to see Leah while he was travelling through Yorkshire, and read in one of the musical papers lying about Leah's sitting room that Sasha was back on the concert circuit. 'She's playing again!' he exclaimed.

'Yes,' said Leah drily, wishing she had had the presence

of mind to hide the newspaper. Did he know Sasha was alone?

He read the article, and Leah noted his absorption with alarm. She would not have it all begin again. Sasha had left her husband, was marked by scandal. Any link between them could ruin him. Even marriage to Kitty, whose sins everyone had forgotten, would be better for him than a publicly adulterous affair.

He read aloud: ' "It is thought Mrs Elliman is playing more exquisitely than ever; audiences talk of her beautiful air of pathos, her intensity, her impassioned brilliance . . ." I'm glad she's playing again.'

'Gabriel – forget her,' Leah pleaded, 'she's obviously forgotten you.'

He did not answer. In her playing at least she had not forgotten.

'And are you going to marry Kitty?' asked Leah brightly. 'Everyone else seems to think you will.'

'Yes. I'm sure it will happen. I should like to settle down. I should like a family.'

'Do you love her?'

'I'm fond of her. We have our music in common.'

Perhaps it was enough, thought Leah her heart aching for him. Besides it was none of her concern any more. She reflected on the little influence most women in her position were granted. What had she or Felicity ever done that would make a lasting impression? And what was her art gallery, her girlhood ambition, except a browsing ground for tourists? She had once supposed, with a sense of superiority, that women who married had their sphere of influence curtailed; their lives were monopolised by their husbands. Now she saw that a married woman with children might at least manage her husband and household a little. Leah thought of Lavinia and Mr Pickersgill. She had rarely seen a woman with greater influence than Lavinia over her domestic empire.

Work kept one's soul intact, Sasha told Felicia's nursemaid. She had chosen the girl with care and had been honest about her personal circumstances; but it had taken several interviews before she found a girl who would do, one who did not throw up her hands in panic when she learned that Felicia was illegitimate. Ruth was plainspoken and sympathetic, and she believed in the Protestant work ethic without any accompanying sanctimony.

The hint of scandal that had broken in Bath had affected Sasha's concert engagements. There were directors who hesitated about including her in their programmes; few agents except Algie were likely to take her on – and she would not go to Algie. Sasha had begun to organise her own engagements, letting it be known she was playing again and relying largely on invitations. She was reducing her musical circle to people tolerant of a less conventional lifestyle: theatre managers who were not hide-bound by tradition; musicians to whom she had entrusted some of her story and who respected her request for discretion; a few strong-minded friends from the early days of her career who did not worry about society's attitudes. They were the kind of people who accepted that women had ambitions outside the domestic sphere, who scorned the ideal of the sweet and submissive female. They behaved without any pious reserve.

Sasha felt as if she were establishing a powerful new territory for herself, with new friends and new rules. Lavender House was becoming a centre where like minds could meet together, read poetry and play music, discuss the world in general, and give one another advice.

Sasha's days were taken up with her music: with practice and correspondence about concerts, with travel arrangements and rehearsals and performances. A single life had so many advantages, she realised. What freedom! To discard the obligation of being polite to people simply to please her husband. Free from entertaining guests not of her choosing. Free of all those dubious social pleasures that went with wifeliness, as she pottered about the garden, conversed with Ruth, looked after Felicia and travelled to concerts.

She had accepted a number of invitations to play in concerts in Leeds and Manchester that autumn. It was the first time she had gone on tour with Felicia. She hesitated about visiting Leah and Lavinia, knowing her parents would have told them about her circumstances by now and that her sisters would expect explanations. In the end she did not go to see them, but stayed in the hotel with Ruth and the baby, went to rehearsals, and thought about nothing except her performances.

Rumour had spread that Sasha was becoming 'difficult' – 'picky' about pianos – she knew for a fact that nothing could compare with the Broadwood at Lavender House. She was fussy too about the music she played, preferring Schumann and Brahms nowadays, and always Beethoven and the classics. Her distaste for empty, virtuoso performance led to her turning down concerts where showmanship was required. Impresarios were learning to treat her warily; since managing her performances alone she had developed a waspish tongue.

There was some consternation among the organisers of a concert in Leeds about the piano they had found for her. Relief flowed at rehearsals as she tried it out and gave her approval. She played Schumann's Piano Concerto that evening. After the performance she was approached by a member of the audience, an industrial magnate and music-lover, who said he was a devotee of Schumann and Brahms, and would be honoured if she would play at a soirée at his house with other musicians from the concert.

Sasha hesitated, reluctant to commit herself to a long and socially tedious evening; but she was tempted by the choice of programme and agreed.

She left Leeds the following evening, sharing a coach with members of the concert orchestra; they set out for an area of stately and solid houses on the outskirts of the city, chatting about past concerts, exchanging anecdotes about directors and other musicians. Sasha prayed no one would notice the violence of her agitation when the man beside her said he had recently played in a concert where Gabriel had been the soloist.

'Did you ever hear anyone play as well?' someone asked.

'Yes, frequently,' the man replied. 'They say Ridgeway has deteriorated as a soloist after playing little else but chamber music. There's a woman behind it all, of course – a charming cellist. She seems to have weakened his appetite for solo performances.'

The others laughed. Someone else turned to Sasha. 'Didn't you once share concert platforms with Ridgeway?'

'We played occasionally together.'

'And what's your opinion of him?'

There was a pause; they were all waiting for her answer. Sasha felt trapped in the closeness of the carriage, threatened by the darkness, the crowd of men, and the overpowering smell of cigars.

'If he's deteriorated I wouldn't know. I haven't heard him play for more than a year.' She was thankful for a diversion as the carriage drew to a halt.

The musicians climbed out and unloaded their instruments from the roof. 'You'll be able to judge for yourself tonight,' said the man who had raised the subject of Gabriel's playing, as he handed Sasha down from the coach.

'Judge what?' she queried, seeing their host appear in the lighted doorway with his wife and daughters gathered round him. They walked together towards the house.

'Whether Ridgeway is past it . . . Didn't I say? He's expected here tonight.'

Sasha shook her head. Too late to turn and run. Too late for escape as their host came towards her.

'Ridgeway is their prize performer this evening,' the man murmured. 'He and his ensemble generally include some Schumann and Brahms in their programmes.'

Sasha felt her hands turn to ice in the welcoming grip of the industrialist. She gave up her outdoor cloak to the servants, accepted a glass of barley water – and saw Gabriel across the room. She had lived in fear of this moment, of one day bumping into him or Kitty. He was alone, she noticed, with a bitter and passing sense of

489

comfort. At least Kitty was not with him. She forced herself to walk on to the point where he turned and saw her, then she could not go another step.

His face seemed pale, though it could have been a trick of the light. 'Mrs Elliman. They have only this minute told me you planned to be here.'

'I didn't know,' she said in a low voice. 'I assure you – I wouldn't have come if I had known. I heard you were in Scotland.'

'Yes, I was.' He spoke formally, hesitating only a little. 'And then on my way south I called on friends in Leeds and was persuaded . . . Well. You understand how one is persuaded to do these things.'

She nodded.

'I saw your sisters on my way north a few weeks ago.'

'How are Leah and Lavinia?' They would have told him about her, she thought. He must know she had left William.

'They are very sad not to hear from you for so long. I think they were surprised to hear you're playing again – as I was when I read about it.'

'Surprised?'

Sasha's voice trembled. How could they talk like this? Having once meant so much to one another, did it now not matter to him that she had cut him out of her life without a word of explanation, that she had left her husband and was all alone? Was he not even curious about her circumstances – except in this terribly remote, polite way?

'I was surprised you should return to playing so soon after the birth of your child.' He looked at her coldly, and Sasha's spirit shrivelled.

'Not so very soon,' she said faintly.

'Your husband doesn't mind?'

'My husband . . .' She lifted her eyes to his and saw from his expression that no one had told him. But of course, Leah's instinct always had been to protect him – and Lavinia had always copied Leah. 'My husband . . .' she repeated. 'My husband has no objection.'

The guests were anxious for some music. The other players were tuning their instruments and Sasha and Gabriel parted, but Sasha's heart was beating frantically. He did not know she had left William and was living at Lavender House. She had thought he was indifferent to the fact that she was alone, but he had not heard. If he had, he would have come to her; he could not have looked at her in that chilling, disenchanted way.

She sat among the guests during the individual solo items. And when she joined the ensembles, then played her piano solos, it was with a heightened nervousness, aware that Gabriel would be searching for signs of changes in her playing.

Gabriel played as superbly as ever, with a haunting depth of feeling, and a purity in every note he drew from the violin. If he had deteriorated, Sasha heard no sign of it. She watched him with a pleasure mixed with anguish, her mind racing. He struck a final passionate chord and met her eyes; his coldness had become a look of pain; and she ached to undo all the misery of the past year.

'You play better than ever,' he said to her, when the musicians took a break for refreshment.

'Thank you. I'm not sure that's true. But at least I play what I want to play these days.'

She was tense with anxiety, not knowing how or when she would tell him. *I was expecting your child. I was confused. What could I do when you were going away? You had your career . . .*

'Is the child well?' he said, as if determined to spare neither himself nor Sasha any punishment. 'She must be – what, three or four months old?'

'No. A little older,' she said breathlessly. She half hoped that some instinct on his part would help her. She tried to frame the right words. *Felicia is not William's child. I let you go without knowing because I loved you so much and didn't want to harm you.* Would he hate her for keeping the truth from him?

'Gabriel . . . How are you?' she said earnestly. 'I mean, are you happy?'

491

He looked at her with a pained irritation, as if she had asked something very stupid. 'Yes, Sasha. I suppose I'm happy enough. I'm engaged to be married. Kitty and I have set the date – after Christmas.'

Sasha's spirits fell. Her hopes . . . of what? A reunion? Happy revelations? Whatever she had hoped for dissolved to nothing. 'So it's true.'

'You must have known.'

'Mother has been planning weddings, but I thought . . .' She forced a brightness into her voice. 'Oh, you know my mother, she tends to jump to conclusions.'

'Kitty and I—'

Sasha turned away. 'Don't tell me anything about Kitty. I know all about Kitty. I hope you'll be happy, Gabriel, but – I fear for you if you marry her.'

'I'm sure we shall be happy. We have our music in common.'

'After you are married, there must never be any communication between you and me,' Sasha said bitterly. 'None. Not even of a professional nature. If we meet again – like this, by chance – I shall ignore you. And if you have any vestige of respect left for me, you'll ignore me as well.'

He was puzzled by the contradictions in her. He had to keep reminding himself that it was *she* who had broken it off, *she* who had said she gave him his freedom and had ignored all his letters. He felt a flicker of hope for an instant, and stifled it as quickly as it had come. She would have answered his letters if she cared for him at all. But she had stopped loving him and had chosen to preserve her marriage. He looked at the floor, searching for a 'safe' topic of conversation. 'How is Miss Sparrow?'

'She's well,' Sasha said miserably. 'It's rumoured she will soon be married too . . . to Mr Viggers.'

'Ah – that's very suitable. They have things in common.'

'No, Gabriel. I should say it's very *unsuitable*. Something "in common" is not enough.'

She had almost told him about Felicia, Sasha realised. A moment ago she might easily have forced him to return

492

to her out of a sense of duty, might have hurt his reputation – though Sasha was beginning to see that damaged reputations were not so terrible as she had once imagined – but now, she knew she never would tell him about his child.

She moved away and avoided talking to him again, and when someone, remembering their partnership, asked them to play a duet together, she refused, saying she no longer had anything in her repertoire that would suit. Afterwards she did not remember how she got through the rest of the soirée.

Gabriel interpreted her distance as a lack of feeling. She had reinforced his belief that their love no longer meant anything to her.

Chapter Twenty-Two

It would soon be Christmas. Aunt Georgie had persuaded Mr Viggers to go with her to a concert in Bristol.

'Oh, I am so looking forward to an evening out,' she breathed, smiling up at him in the carriage. Aunt Georgie was aware that it was not quite moral to be alone in a carriage with a man. A closed cab was supposed to incite men's passions. But she had decided to take events into her own hands at last. She was tired of sitting aside and letting things happen.

'You look very charming tonight,' Mr Viggers said, stroking his moustache. 'Very charming indeed, Miss Georgie.'

Aunt Georgie watched him in the half darkness of the carriage. How ignorant he was of the purpose of her mission. How unsuspecting. She hugged her scheme to herself as he helped her down outside the theatre, aware that she did indeed look charming. She dressed well, and looked as fine as any of the ladies being escorted on a gentleman's arm into the lighted foyer.

Aunt Georgie sat forward in her seat waiting for the musicians to be seated; they moved to their places and began to tune the various instruments. Aunt Georgie loved this moment before a performance. The discordant sounds made her nerves tingle in anticipation. She strained to hear a familiar musical phrase, to imagine how those sounds might possibly, in a matter of minutes, combine to create a concerto. But tonight, Aunt Georgie felt a particular tension in the air. She caught her breath as the conductor appeared . . .

Gabriel followed the conductor to the front of the orchestra and bowed. Mr Viggers applauded loudly, hoping people would suspect from his enthusiasm that he had once been acquainted with the soloist, or might even recognise that he, Henry Viggers, had sung on the same platform as Ridgeway. A hush fell upon the audience as the conductor raised his baton.

Aunt Georgie felt her heart lift with courage at the sound of the violin. How wonderfully he played. It was no wonder Sasha had fallen in love with him when he could create such beautiful sound. She did not speak a word to Mr Viggers during the performance, but sat with rapt attention through every item. At the end of the concert she stayed in her seat until the audience had almost dispersed. She turned to Mr Viggers, who was repeating something about fetching a carriage. 'Yes – you fetch a cab,' she said quickly. 'Wait for me outside.' She hurried towards the orchestra without looking to see if he had obeyed her.

The musicians were packing up their instruments. Tension made Aunt Georgie's head spin. Her whole body trembled. She hoped Mr Viggers had gone outside and would not decide to join her. How terrible if he were to appear beside her and begin some sentimental conversation about the good old days at the Musical Society.

'Mr Ridgeway!'

He turned to her in surprise. 'Miss Sparrow! I had no idea you were in the audience.'

'I'm with Mr Viggers. He's gone for a carriage . . . It was so moving, Mr Ridgeway, to hear you play again.'

He smiled. 'I'm flattered, Miss Sparrow. I'm pleased you enjoyed it.'

Aunt Georgie took hold of his arm, partly to emphasise her urgency, but also because she was in need of some physical support.

'Mr Ridgeway, you must forgive me if I'm speaking out of turn, but I have made up my mind that I *must* speak anyway – I have something very important to say to you in the light of your forthcoming marriage. I want you to listen carefully, because every word I'm going to tell you is the truth.'

Gabriel felt a flicker of uncertainty. The musicians around him were leaving. One or two threw him a look of sympathy, supposing he had been trapped by a too ardent admirer. He took hold of her small, claw-like hand. 'Miss Sparrow, what is it? You're trembling.'

'I'm frightened. I don't know what might happen when I've said what I'm going to tell you, but for Sasha's sake – I have to say it.'

He moved her away from the other players and sat her down on one of the orchestra chairs, pulling up a chair close beside her. 'Tell me. If it's about Sasha . . . you must tell me at once.'

'She doesn't know I'm here,' Aunt Georgie assured him earnestly. 'She would be furious with me if she knew.'

'For pity's sake!'

Aunt Georgie gripped his sleeve as if she would tear it from his arm, and her voice sank to a whisper. 'The child was yours, Mr Ridgeway. The baby . . . it's not William's.'

The colour drained from Gabriel and he did not move. 'But she went back to him.'

'To protect you – and for the sake of the child. When you went to Germany she thought she must give you up. She thought the scandal of a child might break you. Instead . . . it broke her. She knew you'd formed a friendship with her sister. She saw then how it would turn out. Miss Kitty Hammond is very winning, I believe—'

'What in God's name has this to do with Kitty?' he said wildly.

'Sasha believed it would be all over between you. She threw herself on her husband's mercy, and William agreed to keep the baby as his own . . .'

'No—' He threw her a look of agony. 'She couldn't do that to me!'

Aunt Georgie began to cry. 'She truly thought it was for

496

the best. But she was wrong. William has cut her off from her other children. Everyone has been terribly unhappy. And now Sasha has left her husband and you are going to marry her sister, exactly as she expected.' Her voice tailed off. 'I think that is the bitterest blow to her of all.'

'She has left him?'

'Several months ago. She's been living alone with the child. Your child.' She dried her eyes and stood up. 'A darling little girl. She called her Felicia – after Mendelssohn.' She turned away. 'I thought you ought to know.'

He did not answer. She left him in the empty auditorium, and went out to the foyer where Mr Viggers was pacing up and down.

Mr Viggers hurried towards her. 'I thought I should remain here when I saw you with Mr Ridgeway. It seemed to be a private conversation.'

Aunt Georgie looked at him with new respect. 'Thank you, Mr Viggers. That was very . . . discerning of you.'

He hesitated. 'You seemed upset, Miss Georgie. If I can help in any way . . .'

'No. I think not. I think I have said all that is necessary. But . . .' She turned to him with shining eyes. 'Mr Viggers – I think I may just now have done the most splendid thing of my entire life.'

They climbed into the waiting carriage and drove some way in silence. Aunt Georgie turned the conversation with Gabriel over and over in her mind, speculating on the outcome. Then, as they neared Penbury, Mr Viggers became restless. He shifted in his seat, said 'Ahem!' several times, and finally addressed her.

'Miss Georgie, I've been meaning to broach a delicate subject for some time. You and I have been friends for a long time, I think you will agree. We have interests in common, and I have a fair income from my investments and a respectable address . . . I have recently come to the conclusion that there is a void in my life – a vacancy that only a wife could fill. It is of no consequence to me that you have neither property nor a large income to your

497

name. I have formed a great respect for you, Miss Georgie. I have come to the opinion that you would fill the vacancy well. Would you do me the honour of becoming my wife?'

Aunt Georgie did not answer at once. She pictured how it would be as she had pictured it so often. A house of her own to manage, servants, the status that matrimony gave to a woman. It was true she could no longer expect children of her own, but she might make a child of Mr Viggers; her life would revolve around his needs. Everything a woman most desired in life would be hers.

Mr Viggers was waiting. The smell of hair oil in the cab was stifling; she hoped he would not attempt to kiss her. She said as gently as she could, 'I am very honoured that you have asked me, but I cannot possibly accept your proposal, Mr Viggers.'

She saw the restrictions that marriage would impose on her life: the rules of decorum, expectations of wifely support, the surrender of her will to that of Mr Viggers. She would not have Pippa to lighten her days, and would be powerless to prevent William from making of Pippa what he had made of Meredith. And, without her influence in that household, Sasha would never see either of the children again.

'You must see how it is?' Aunt Georgie continued. 'My nephew opened his house to me when I was friendless and alone after the death of my father. In gratitude, if for no other reason, I must continue to care for his motherless children. It's my duty . . . Lily has no heart for children, Mr Viggers.'

'Oh – Miss Georgie,' he said brokenly. 'Don't continue. Clearly you have a great deal of heart.'

'Please. You mustn't be hurt.'

He shook his head and blew his nose. After a while he said gruffly, 'I would be grateful if you would overlook my earlier remarks.'

'We may still be friends? I shall still visit you – take tea, go to concerts or the theatre from time to time?'

He nodded and clasped her hand. 'You are a woman with

498

a remarkable capacity for self-sacrifice, Miss Georgie.'

Aunt Georgie sat back in her seat and folded her hands with a sense of satisfaction. Self-sacrifice? To have been asked, and turned the offer down in favour of her independence? Perhaps. Though, on the whole – she thought not.

Kitty leaned on Leah's window sill and looked out at the sea. 'How long may I stay here?'

'Who said you are staying?' said Leah drily.

'Oh – Leah. Until she gets over this, surely?' said Lavinia. 'She has been *jilted*. I've said she might come to our house, but Mr Pickersgill is so *strict* about . . . things. He knows Kitty's story—'

'I remember the last visit. No thank you,' said Kitty.

'Martin doesn't mean to be rude, Kitty, but he remembers how you almost spoiled our wedding. And so do I,' Lavinia added with a hint of pique.

'I suppose you may stay here until we fall out,' Leah said with a sigh of resignation.

'That might not be too long if you're bent on defending Gabriel.'

'I think he's behaved very badly,' said Lavinia. 'It seems to me he led you on, Kitty. And you were not the first.' Lavinia thought of all Gabriel's other affairs of the heart, remembering that even Sasha had at one time succumbed to his charm.

'It seems to me he never promised Kitty anything,' contradicted Leah. 'So where is he now – still in London?' Had he simply taken fright at the idea of marriage, as Kitty supposed? Or had he . . . could he have gone to Sasha? Leah thought of the scandal the public would make of it, and longed to protect him.

'I don't know where he is, and quite honestly I don't care . . . He left me with the painting,' Kitty said, remembering. 'He said, he didn't know what to do with it. He wants someone in the family to have it. Perhaps Father?'

She turned away from the window and looked at her sisters, Lavinia's face so knotted with concern, Leah defensive because he was her precious boy, hers first before any of them.

'What painting?' Lavinia asked.

'*The Beautiful Hammond Girls.*'

'I had forgotten. I didn't know Gabriel owned it.'

'I should like to have it,' said Leah remembering the Royal Academy Exhibition and going to London with Gabriel and Felicity. 'To remind me how things once were.'

Lavinia glanced round the tiny sitting room, secretly doubting whether the portrait would look appropriate in the already overcrowded cottage. 'Do you remember when Father painted it? Those hours and hours, freezing in the studio. Could we have guessed then, do you think? That you, Kitty, would become a respectable musician—?'

'*Semi*-respectable,' protested Kitty. She left the window and sat between her sisters. 'I think I might have guessed you would become a mother of seven.' She patted Lavinia's comfortably pregnant figure.

'And I an old maid?' said Leah.

'And Sasha . . .' Kitty said thoughtfully.

'Poor Sasha.' Lavinia remembered the day Sasha had come to her and threatened to leave her husband because she was 'disappointed in him'. Her eyes filled with pity over Sasha's self-imposed fate. 'Oh, it's too awful. To be all alone! She can never marry while she has a husband living. She has no dignity, no purpose – no good name – nothing left except her music.'

Sasha had invited some friends for the weekend. The house resounded with music and laughter. They had begun playing a word game – inventing maxims for one another.

'It's a proven fact,' said Sasha, in the voice of a lecturer and standing on the piano stool, 'that if women are going to dedicate themselves properly to anything – their art or their work – they must remain single.'

'And if they fall in love?' said one of the men.

'They are made to forfeit their talents. Or at the very best, make compromises.'

'That's too long-winded to be a maxim,' someone said.

'And I object,' cried one of the women. 'I refuse to cut love out of my life altogether.'

'You wouldn't say a *man* had to remain single,' someone else protested.

'That's because a man can dedicate himself to his work quite easily,' said Sasha. 'His *wife* makes all the sacrifices.'

'We all know men never make sacrifices – though they may compromise a few females occasionally,' laughed one of the women.

Sasha went to the hearth and bent to pour coffee. The firelight warmed her face. She was contented at last, she thought, surveying the company around her. No more sacrifices and compromises. She had discovered a life that suited her and, if sometimes it was lonely, she had Felicia – and she had her piano. She could look forward to another year with cheerful confidence.

When Gabriel let himself into the house, she was playing Mendelssohn. His heart flew into his mouth at the sound of the piano. He stood in the lighted hall and listened. It was one of the *Songs without Words*. He sat on the stairs, frightened by the fact that she had company, afraid to go into the room, and afraid to leave.

The hall was decorated with holly sprigs and festoons of ivy around the pictures and along the picture rails. A large mirror reflected the blank panels of the sitting room door. Above his head he could hear movement, and a low voice – not Sasha's – singing to a child. She had named her Felicia, Aunt Georgie had said. Oh, blithe and happy Felicia, he prayed; may you never know what torment your parents have inflicted on one another.

The piano music ended. The sounds in the sitting room altered. Gabriel heard a chorus of song, and then laughter. He should not have come. He pressed his hands to his head. At any moment the song might end and the hall mirror reveal the shocked image of Sasha, or one of the

501

company. Or else the woman in the bedroom would come down and discover him there at the foot of the stairs. But no one came. Nothing altered. He could leave as quietly as he had arrived.

After a while he opened the sitting room door.

Sasha was sitting on the top of the grand piano. She was dressed in a blue and white striped frock, her hair tied loosely behind her ears. She was conducting boisterously with her arms. A number of men and women stood and sat round the piano singing 'Polly Put the Kettle on' – it was a game the orchestra had often played on tour with Algie; the conductor led the singing in various comic times: fast and slow, in march or waltz time, legato or staccato.

As the door opened, the singing staggered to a close. People turned to look at him. Sasha stopped with her hands frozen in mid-movement. She put a hand to her head in an odd gesture as if to steady herself and said, 'Who let you in?'

'I kept my key.'

'You might have frightened the nursemaid. She doesn't know who you are . . .'

Gabriel saw the interested faces of her friends; some amused, some simply curious. 'I'll go. I'm sorry. You have company. I shouldn't have walked in like that.'

'No – why don't you join us? We're playing a game you'll remember.' She hesitated, then jumped down from the piano stool and came towards him, but she did not come close enough to take his hand as she introduced him to her friends, nor did she look at him as she said, 'This is . . . an old friend, Gabriel Ridgeway . . . the violinist.'

He sat down, took the coffee someone offered him and looked at the fireside, *his* fireside; he saw the piano he had bought her and emotion filled his throat. 'I'm not sure I am in a mood for games.'

'You don't have to join in. There's no obligation. Stay, or not, as you please.'

Faces smiled at him. Everyone seemed very much at home.

She came to sit beside him after a while. 'You paid the rent. It was almost as if you knew I would come back.'

'I hoped. I once hoped we would both come here again.'

She stared into the fire. 'I'm trying to be very calm about this, but I don't understand what's happened. Last time we met you were very cold with me. You said you were going to marry Kitty.'

'Are you angry that I came?'

'No. It's wonderful. Like a dream. I don't think I can really believe it.'

'Miss Sparrow has told me everything. I know why you didn't write to me in Germany. Sasha – I know about our child.'

'I see.'

Someone began to play on an accordion. Gabriel bent closer. 'Why didn't you trust me to care for you?'

'You had your career.'

'And you had yours. You had to risk everything you'd worked for because of my child. Why did you suppose you must suffer alone?'

'We couldn't have been together. The world can be so very unkind . . . And there was Kitty. You had written to say you had met Kitty.' She looked down at her hands in her lap. How could she tell him that Kitty had stolen everything from her in the past?

'I don't love Kitty. I love you,' he said in anguish. 'How could you have thought that? How could you be so unsure of me?'

She was silent, absorbing his words for several seconds. Then she began to breathe more freely. It wasn't a fantasy. He was here. He had come back.

'Sasha, say you still love me. Say we can put this ghastly misunderstanding behind us.'

'Things can never be as they were. More than a year has passed . . .'

'That's not a bad thing. We move on. We can change. But we belong together. You know we do.'

'I don't know anything any more,' she said seriously.

503

'Liberty has become an important feature of my life. I have my friends—' She looked at the company gathered around her: people who had an instinct for music and literature, leisure and freedom, people with the Hammonds' old definition of *soul*. 'I need my independence.' Sasha thought of her earlier attempt at a maxim. If she let herself love him again, she would have to make compromises. It was inevitable.

'Play us something, both of you,' someone asked.

'I don't have any instrument,' Gabriel protested.

A violin was handed to him.

He looked at Sasha and she held his gaze, neither granting nor denying a performance. He went to the piano and tuned the violin briskly. 'Well then, what shall we play?'

She was too full of hope and happiness to dare to choose something.

'The "Kreutzer"?' someone suggested. 'The Andante.'

Sasha joined him and sat at the piano. She shook her head. 'No. The Finale.'

'You feel optimistic?' said Gabriel.

'Oh yes. I think I do.'

They played the final movement, with a sense of harmony that erased every difficulty, as it always had in the past. Sasha saw the sensual glide of his arm, the sound of the violin awakened memories, stirred longings in her soul. And it occurred to her, as she looked at Gabriel and the rhythm of the tarantella beat through her, that one's 'soul' was less a lofty, airy phenomenon than a physical reality.